IRA TABANKIN

THE SHELTER
BOOK 1: THE BEGINNING

Dedication

This book, as all of mine are, is dedicated to the love of my life, my wife Patricia.

Thanks to everyone who's provided feedback and support for my writing. A special thanks to Michael and "ConradCa" for proofreading and editing my words into something readable.

Cover design by Logotecture"

Prologue

The world's economies collapsed one year ago this week. The collapse made the Depression of 1929 look like a mild recession. Like the '29 crash, this one covered every developed country like a cold, wet blanket. The economic meltdown started small, as most disasters do, but quickly spread like a firestorm that engulfed the industrial world. Six months before the worldwide economic meltdown we won a Powerball lottery. Winning the lottery gave us the ability to survive and record the collapse of the old and the birth of the new world. A world that emerged from the ashes of the industrialized world. Edmund Burke said, "Those who don't know history are doomed to repeat it." Mankind refused to learn history's lessons. Every generation thought they knew more than any other generation. Nations voted for their leaders based on emotion versus logic. People went to the polls and voted for more freebies. They voted for socialism forgetting what Margret Thatcher said about socialism's core problem, she said, "Sooner or later you run out of other people's money." She was correct. History will record the number of workers and wealthy the governments' taxed; to pay for the benefits of those who didn't work shrank as the amount of taxes increased. Many governments discovered too late, when they increase taxes, collected tax revenues decreased. Governments continued to spend even as their revenues decreased which yielded higher debt. Governments learned that their debts became unpayable, they had to increase borrowing so they could make the interest payments on their existing debt. National debt quickly equaled and in some cases surpassed their net GNP, technically making the countries bankrupt.

When borrowers refused to continue to buy bonds and extend additional credit, country's learned they had to reduce benefits payments in order to keep their countries afloat. Citizens of these countries voted out the governments which cut their benefits. Citizens voted into office anyone who promised to restore their benefits. History records that one of the reasons for the fall of the Roman Empire was Roman citizens realized they could vote themselves increased benefit. It was then only a matter of time before Rome ran out of money and the Roman Empire fell. Europe in the second decade of the twenty-first century was about to relive the errors of the Roman Empire.

Economists had long warned the world's governments that all of their economies are interconnected. An example of how interconnected the world's economies are, think of a placid lake where a single stone strikes the calm waters, the surface of the lake ripples from the single rock displacing the water. A second rock striking the water adds its waves to those of the first rock. The third rock striking the water adds to the waves of the first two, each additional rock increases the waves and turbulence in the lake until the waves have multiplied turning the placid lake into a rough sea. The lake is the world's economy. There have been many debates about the first rock which started the waves in the world's economies. Most people think the economies had been bubbling just under the surface of the calm lake. The surface tension of the lake kept the pressure which was building just under the surface from exploding. The economic pressure had been building for more than a quarter of a century, The pressure was waiting for the first rock to break the surface tension which violently released the built up pressure. The first rock to break the smooth surface releasing the pent up pressure was a vote for a new government in Greece.

The first rock that broke the placid economic lake occurred on January 26, 2015. "Yesterday the people of Greece elected the far left Syriza party and their young, charismatic leader Alexis Tsipras. Tsipras is forty years old. He ran on the promise to write off Greece's 300 billion Euro debts. Greece's current budget is 150% of their GNP. Tsipras promised the Greeks to return their pensions, increase their pay and bring good times back to the country. Greece has survived on a 240 billion-euro ($270 billion) bailout, which has kept the debt-ridden country afloat since mid-2010. To qualify for the bailout, Greece has had to impose deep and bitterly resented cuts in public spending, wages, and pensions, along with public sector layoffs and repeated tax increases. The lenders who loaned Greece the $270 billion are very concerned about Tsipras winning. One of the German bond managers told the consortium that it wasn't possible for Greece to write off the debt, nor did he think Greece would default."

Other countries stood on the lake's shoreline watching the waves ripple in the world's economy. Thinking they had a lifeline, other countries threw their own rocks into the financial lake. The additional rocks increased the turbulence until nothing could stop the financial waves which had built into tidal waves of destruction spread around the globe.

This is the story of a small group of surviving families whom 'Lady Luck' brought together shortly before the world's economies collapsed. The group built and took refuge in a shelter when their homes were overrun by swarms of hungry, angry people. Exiting their shelter, they discovered the world was much different than the one they'd left behind when they locked the shelter door behind them.

Chapter 1

Irony is a cold hearted bitch. Its karma's way of getting even with us. It's buying lottery tickets for forty years and finally winning the big prize on the eve of the world's economic implosion without getting a chance to spend the millions on foolish toys. Irony is going from living from pay check to pay check to becoming mega rich while the world collapses before you can be foolish and waste the winnings by indulging your daydreams. Everyone has daydreams. Dreams keep us going.

Do you believe in lady luck? Do you gamble? Do you ever daydream of hitting the 'Big-One'? Do you ever daydream how your life would be different if you didn't *have to* work? Almost everyone gambles on something, sporting events, on the outcome of elections, small bets between friends, a weekly poker game or a friendly golf match. Most people gamble on something, millions spend their hard earned money every week on the dream of winning the lottery. Billboards along highways display the large prizes for the Powerball and the Mega Millions lottery. The billboards encourage you daydream what it would be like to win. It's natural, everyone driving past the billboards daydreams what their life would be like after winning. The lottery counts on us having the daydreams, their advertising plays to our daydreams. When the lottery prize breaks $100 million, people wait in lines for their chance to pick six numbers which will change their lives. When the lottery prize exceeds $200 million, people stand in lines for hours to buy a ticket, even though, the odds of being struck by lightning is higher than winning the lottery.

I admit I daydreamed what I would do if I won. It wasn't just the $200 million plus lotteries that got me daydreaming, my mind drifted with thoughts how I would spend even the base lottery prize of $12 million. I was hooked on the dream. My wife, Lacy, used to laugh at me, she told me I'd never win as long as I was married to her because she was bad luck. I laughed, telling her that I was lucky because she was my wife. I purchased lottery tickets every week. I figured I couldn't win if I didn't play. $15 a week was a small amount of money to risk for the chance of winning millions. I knew I had no chance of winning if I didn't get into the game. I know I'm the typical sucker the lottery targets their advertising to. I was the average 'Joe' who dreams of winning the big one. I knew and ignored the odds which said I had a better chance of being struck by lightning than I did of winning the lottery.

The lottery is an addiction. I typically won small prizes every couple of weeks, the more $5.00 and $10.00 prizes I won, the more I was driven to buy more lottery tickets. I always thought, I won something, so there's a chance I can win the big one. Every ticket I purchased was a potential dream waiting to come true. I typically purchased my lottery tickets when I finished food shopping. I went from the cashier to the customer service desk with the money burning a hole in my wallet, my dreams ready to kick into high gear. I passed my lottery tickets to the clerk and I held my breath when the clerk straightened my tickets before sliding them into the lottery machine. I didn't even know I was holding my breath as I waited for the bells to ring which meant I won. Today was no different from any other late January day in Northern Virginia.

Wednesday, January 27th was a cold clear winter day. In a way, it was a funny day. It was the day after the massive blizzard that didn't happen. For three days, the weather people screamed the blizzard of the century was bearing down on the Mid-Atlantic and North East states. Food stores were swamped with people buying enough food to hold them over until the many feet of snow we were supposed to get melted. Looking at people's overflowing shopping carts, one would have assumed they didn't think the snow would melt until May. January 27th was the day after the Mayor of New York City closed the city. I wondered if a mayor could close a city before a disaster. The storm never materialized. The weather people actually apologized for blowing the forecast. News reports placed the loss to New York City alone at over $700 million because of the Mayor's closure. Central Park received only 5 inches of snow. I tried to explain to my friends this was a perfect example of how the government isn't prepared to handle a real emergency. If they weren't prepared for a January snowstorm in the North East when it always snows in January, how can they handle a real emergency? This was a perfect example of how the government gets things wrong. I tried to explain to my friends they had to be prepared to take care of their own families because the government wasn't going to be there when we'd need them the most. I reminded my friends of Katrina and Sandy, how so many families are still waiting for help to arrive years after the hurricanes. Our typical liberal government worker looked for someone to blame for their error versus taking responsibility. The Mayor never explained how he could order the city closed, he ordered people arrested for walking on the streets. Another example of the mess we'd voted into office occurred in New Jersey, where two teenagers decided to earn some extra money. They went to their neighbor's homes offering to shovel the snow from their driveways. Their town has laws on the books mandating snow removable within 48 hours, the teens were stopped by the police for being outside in an emergency. The emergency being, it snowed. The teens were ordered to go home, leaving many elderly unable to clear their sidewalks within 48 hours. Like many government rules, the left and right hands didn't talk to each other. Perfect examples of why, when the shit really hit the fan, the only people we can count on are ourselves. Most of my friends and one of my sons-in-law thought I was 'chicken little' always crying the sky was going to fall.

My wife Lacy and I had a routine, we jointly went grocery shopping on Saturdays, By midweek, we'd usually used up our fresh veggies and salad. Since I was semi-retired one of my 'jobs' was to hit the food store on Wednesdays to pick up the items we either forgot or used up. Today I had a small list of five items to pick up. I think the total cost was only $12.00. After paying I walked over to the customer service desk and I handed the clerk my lottery tickets. I looked at the electronic display, which showed the Powerball was back to the basic prize. My hopes went up, someone had won last week's prize. My mind started to wander and daydream we were the winners. I daydreamed how we would live with the winnings. I smiled at the clerk while she ran my tickets through the lottery machine.

She smiled at me while inserting my ticket into the lottery machine. The lottery machine sucks down my ticket, it does down, back up and down again, the machine pauses a minute, the next instant the bells sound. I won something. Knowing my luck, it must be a dollar or two. I raise my head to look at the list of prizes, last week's grand prize was $42 million. The clerk is staring at me smiling and nodding, I look at her, clearly not understanding what she's trying to tell me. The store manager came over slapping me on the back, other shoppers gather around. It still hadn't registered on me. Slowly the fog lifted from my mind. The clerk was saying, "Sir, congratulations, you WON!"

"I won? How much did I win?"

"Sir, you won the big one, you won $42 million!"

"What? No bullshit. I won?"

The store's general manager smiled, saying, "Sir, may I offer you my congratulations too. You won the grand prize! You're the first grand prize winner the store's ever had!"

"You're going to give me $42 million?"

The general manager laughed, saying, "No, we only pay up to $500.00. Any prize larger than $500.00 is paid by the lottery commission."

"How much did I win?"

Laughing the General Manager said, "Why don't you come with me to my office? We'll call the lottery office together."

I followed the manager to his office in a daze. His office is the size of a large closet, he has a steel desk and one visitor chair which I dropped down into. His desk is covered with piles of paper, there's a bulletin board on the wall covered in notices from corporate. The office looks like a cave made from paper memos. It smells of old paper. I wonder *is this real or some joke? Have I entered the Twilight Zone?* I remember I left the bags with the five items I bought at the customer service desk. I started to look around, the manager smiled saying, "I think you're looking for your bags, here they are. I had a feeling you might forget them."

"Thank you, if I didn't bring them home, I'd have to come back and buy them again."

"You'll certainly be able to afford them. Let's see, according to the lottery, you won $42 million, which is spread over 26 years. You will receive a yearly deposit of $1,6115,384. Of course, you'll be responsible for paying all of the taxes on your winnings as regular income. You can also take a one-time cash payment, which, of course, is discounted. After tax you'll receive $28,770,000. You don't have to decide now. In fact, the lottery suggests you contact a tax advisor and a lawyer before you make your decision. You have one year from last Saturday to cash in your ticket. There are no exceptions. If you miss the date by even one day, you'll lose the prize. I had a customer who once won $5,000, he lost his ticket, by the time he found it, the time had expired, he was out of the $5,000. Be very careful with that ticket."

"Trust me, I'm not going to lose the ticket."

"If you want, we can scan a copy of the ticket and your driver's license which I'll be happy to send to lottery's office for you. We can call them to verify your winnings."

"Thanks, that's very kind of you." I still don't believe this is happening.

"Don't worry about me, the store wins a nice prize for selling you the ticket. This certifies we sold it and validates our claim. As the manager, I'll get a small part of the store's prize, so my family thanks you for buying your ticket in our store."

I nod my head, still not believing what's going on.

He scanned my license and the lottery ticket while I'm sitting in his office in a daze. He emailed it to the lottery, then he called them to confirm they received my information. He told me the manager at the lottery office would like to speak with me. The general manager handed me the phone, "Hello, this is Jay Tolson."

"Mr. Tolson, congratulations, we're happy to confirm you hold the winning ticket to the January 24th winning Powerball lottery of $42 million dollars. Please bring the winning ticket and two photo ID's to our office in Richmond in order to claim your prize. Do you have any questions for me at this time?"

"Not really, I'm still in shock."

"I'm sure you are. If I can give you a little bit of advice, try to contact a lawyer and an accountant before you start spending your winnings. We've seen many people go through huge amounts very quickly."

"Thank you. I think I'm going to need a few days to get my head screwed on straight. How much notice do you need before we claim our prize?"

"Twenty-four hours would be great."

"I can do that."

"Jay, again, congratulations. I'm sure we'll be seeing you soon."

The store manager padded me on the back saying, "don't lose that ticket, keep it in a safe place."

"I will," I said, walking out of the store with the manager chasing me with my two bags. I smile, shaking my head and thanking him. Getting in my car I call my wife, thinking, *I can't wait to tell her. Damn it, we WON, I can't believe it! We won, we really won! I still can't believe it.* People are honking behind me, they want my parking spot. I pull out of the parking lot while dialing my wife. "Honey, you'll never guess what..."

"Hon, I'm really very busy right now. Can I call you back?"

"Sure, but don't you have even one moment?"

"No, bye."

Guess she's really busy, I'll wait fifteen minutes. I don't want to tell our daughters before I tell Lacy, she'd kill me. Shit damn, we won! We can buy a house, a new car, she always wanted an SL, I can get one for her. Damn should we live here or move. I'll try her again. Her direct line rings twice before she answers it, "Honey, is everything OK?"

"Yes, it's just I want to tell you something."

"Honey, we're really busy today, I'll call you back as soon as I can. Bye."

Click.

Damn it, I have to tell someone. I'll drive to her office and tell her in person. Yeah, I'll get some roses and surprise her. I drive to a small florist in a strip mall on the way to her office "Hi, I'd like a dozen long stem red roses in the best vase you have."

"Sir, it's Wednesday, we only have those in the case. We usually stock up for the weekend."

"I'll take them. Do you have a box I can put them into?"

"Of course, I'll be happy to wrap them for you."

Lacy works in the rural D.C. office of a Dallas-based oil and gas fracking company. The high demand for oil and gas has kept her really busy. It's only a few miles from the strip mall to Lacy's office. Parking the car, I grab the roses and the copy of the winning ticket verification to show her. I ring the front door bell so someone will unlock the door, to let me in. Most of her coworkers know me because

I usually drive and pick her up on Fridays. It's our date night, after her work we go out to dinner. Joe, the receptionist, opens the door for me. "Hey, sport, what have you done now?"

"Huh?"

"Roses, the only reason a man hand delivers roses is cuz she's busted you doing something nasty. What did you do? You cheat on her? Oh, man, if you did, she's going to shove those roses up your ass. Man, I don't want to be you."

"Joe, no. I didn't do anything."

"Yeah right, no one hand carries roses unless they got busted."

"No, really. I have some great news to tell her."

"You got knocked up?"

"Joe, you're an asshole. Where is she?"

"Busy today, really busy. Something is going on at headquarters, they're driving everyone crazy. No one even had time to go out for lunch."

"Can you just call her and tell her I'm here?"

"OK, but it's your head."

Lacy comes out of the inner office looking both happy and tired. I jump up holding the roses, "Honey, you'll never guess what happened."

Lacy looks surprised seeing me in the lobby with the roses, "Hon, I love you, thank you for the roses, what did you do wrong? Did you break something at home? Didn't I tell you I'm really busy today?"

"Lace, just hang on a second, please give me just one minute. I promise just sixty seconds."

Getting annoyed, she crosses her arms across her chest, "Well, I'm waiting and very busy today, so hurry up. Everyone is waiting for me."

"We won!"

"We won what?"

"The LOTTERY. We won, we really won!"

"Slow down, we won? How much?"

I lean close, whispering to her, "We'll net around $28 million."

"NO SHIT!"

"No shit, really!"

She dropped the roses and jumped into my arms, the vase broke on the floor, sending water, glass and roses all over the foyer. "We really won?"

Joe looked up saying, "I'm not cleaning that mess up! You broke it, you clean it."

"Honey, look, here's the verification."

I show her the confirmation printed from the lottery machine. Her eyes get as big as the full moon. "Oh my God, we really won!"

"Yes, that's what I was trying to tell you."

"What do we do now?"

Her manager entered the lobby saying, "Lacy, I'm sorry to break up your little rendezvous, but we're really busy today. Jay, it's good to see you, however, I'm sorry, but I need her to finish a project that's on a time urgent status. Headquarters is screaming at us to finish it. I need her to write her section."

Lacy leans into me, "Honey, should I quit?"

"Not yet, we'll talk tonight. I'll see you later."

She reaches up to kiss me, Joe laughs, saying, "I told you, I'm not cleaning up the mess you made on the floor."

Lacy and I bend down to pick up the roses, she says, "I'll find something to put them in, you go home and rest. Don't lose that ticket. By the way, did you get the items on the list for tonight's dinner?"

"Yes, but don't you want to go out to celebrate?"

"No celebrating until the money's in our hands."

I leave Lacy with an armful of wet roses. Driving home, I listened, as I usually did to the all-news station. They reported on the election held three days ago in Greece. The announcer was saying, "If the new Greek government holds to their promise of not maintaining the current austerity programs, the German lenders are going to demand immediate repayment of Greece's loans. Other European countries are watching the events in Greece very carefully as many would like to renegotiate the loans which bailed out their failed economies." I thought to myself, *I wonder if the Greek's will try to write their debt off and if they do, I'm sure the other countries in Europe will do the same. If they do, it will crush Germany and Switzerland. This could be the spark that burns down the Euro, destroys the EU and ripples around the world causing a depression. Why worry about stupid shit, we won!*

A few minutes later I'm home. I pull out a pad and start making notes to myself, the first heading on the pad is, 'where to live.' *We could live anywhere. Where should we go? If the Greece elections are the first rock in the lake which is the world's economies, the coming economic tidal wave will impact where we live. If an economic meltdown is coming, we should prepare for it. We should live in a different location then if everything is going to be fine.* I got so wound up thinking what to do, I lost track of time. Before I know it, Lacy arrives home. I look at my watch, realizing I've sat at the kitchen table for five hours filling pages in my notebook with notes and thoughts.

Lacy calls to me, "Honey, what are you doing?"

"Huh? Oh, just putting some thoughts down on paper."

"Can you put it away so we can make dinner?"

"Sure. Are you sure you don't want to go out?"

"I'm sure, today was long and stressful. I just want to change and have dinner with a glass of wine."

"I'll start it, you go change."

"Thanks, please turn on the news, coming home, I heard something about a problem in Europe."

"Okay."

Turning on the evening news, the talking heads are all saying the same thing, "Greece couldn't just write off their debt, or could they? They wouldn't dare write it off. If they did, it would cause the EU to break up, the Euro would collapse. Europe's dream of a united continent could die because of a handful of selfish Greeks. Surely, cooler heads will prevail to avoid a worldwide monetary crisis." Every station reported the same story. Every reporter thought the Greeks would use their election to win some concessions from their lenders, then everything would return to normal. The world would move on to the really important stories, Kim Kardashian's new photos.

Lacy asked me, "Honey, do you think they're right? Will Greece screw up the economy in Europe? Why would the Greeks think they can just make their debt go away? Will it impact us?"

"Most of them are socialists, they live on the government dole. They have an entitlement mentality, theirs is worse even than what's developed here. They are used to having the government supply them with everything. Many in Europe never even try to find work, they're happy living on the government dole; that is until the various European governments had to start cutting back on their payments and benefits. The reduction impacted their lifestyles which is what led to the results of last week's election."

Sipping her wine, Lacy asked, "What happens if the Greeks decide to walk away from their debt?"

"Greece will enter a state of technical bankruptcy, they will have to drop out of the EU and revert to using their own currency which won't have any external value. Prices for everything in Greece will go up, the lives of the Greeks will be much worse than they were before the election. Store shelves will be empty even worse than they are now. Nothing will be imported because their currency won't be accepted by other countries. Millions will lose their jobs, Greek unemployment will skyrocket."

"Then why did they elect a Marxist?"

"Because they're spoiled children, they only know they don't like their current situation. They'd have voted for you if you promised them you'd restore their pay, jobs, and pensions. They want things back to the way they used to be. They want their lifestyle back."

"Well, let's forget Greece for tonight, let's talk about our winnings."

"Honey, what do you want to do with the money?"

"Jay, I want to give some to the girls, some to my family, I want to buy a house, a new car, maybe go on a long vacation. Why don't you give me a little time, I haven't had a lot of time to think about what I want since you told me we won."

"Lacy, do you want to continue to work?"

"I think so, I'd be bored with nothing to do, on the other hand not having to get up early every morning has a lot of appeal. I really don't know yet. When do we get the money?"

"We have to go to their office in Richmond to get it."

"Do they give us a single check?"

"We have a choice, either 26 years of payments or a one-time cash payout."

"I think we should take the one-time payout. No one knows if we'll be here in 26 years, or if the lottery will be able to pay it out that far in the future. Or what it will be worth if inflation continues to increase."

"I'm going to call Beth, our accountant in the morning."

While we're chatting, the talking heads on the news show a video of the newly elected Greek Prime Minister laying flowers on the World War Two Memorial. I look at Lacy, "Oh, oh, he's going to stir up problems now."

"Why? All he did is lay some flowers on a memorial."

"Honey, the German's are the leading lenders to the Greeks, the new Prime Minister said he was going to write off the debt, which means he doesn't plan on paying it back. By laying the flowers on the memorial, he's telling the Germans he remembers their atrocities from the Second World War. He's setting up a major confrontation between Greece and Germany. He was a communist in his early days. That may also have something to do with his actions how he acts towards Germany. There was a report on the news today that Greece is going to invoice Germany for damages done to it during World War 2. The damages exceed the amount of loans the Germans have given the Greeks, which has the effect of Greece not having any debt."

"Will it impact us?"

"My gut says the other European leaders are watching what Greece does. If they see Greece getting away with writing off their debt and not getting penalized, they will do it too. That will cause the EU to break apart. The value of the Euro will collapse and that will cause a massive financial stress around the world. It could even lead the world into a new depression worse than 1929."

"I didn't realize one country could cause another worldwide depression. Maybe we should ask the lottery to pay us in gold?"

Smiling, "Not a bad idea, but I don't think they will."

The next news report was about the war in the Ukraine. Lacy asks, "Is that still going on?"

I frown, not liking what we're hearing, "It looks like it's getting worse. Russia is saying they have proof NATO troops are fighting against their army in the Ukraine. If the Russians have proof NATO troops are fighting them, it will give Putin the reason he's looking for to expand the war and possibly implement sanctions like cutting off natural gas deliveries to Europe. The Europeans depend on Russian gas for their heat. This is a horrible winter, over a hundred thousand could freeze to death without heat. Putin could even declare war against NATO, saying Russia was attacked first. This could be the spark that ignites World War 3."

"Aren't we still in NATO?"

"Yes, but we have nothing to worry about. President Obama told us there isn't any fighting in the Ukraine, so how could the Russians have any proof we had troops there? Don't you remember, he reminded us just a week ago, the world is more peaceful since he became President?"

"Oh, you mean, just like he told us our health care costs were going to decline $2,500 a year and instead they increased, and we can keep our doctor, which we can't."

"But they increased at a slower rate. Doesn't that count?"

We both laugh while ignoring the news, returning to our chatting about what we are going to do with our new-found winning.

After exchanging a lot of jokes, I turn serious, "Lacy, I know I've asked already asked you, give serious thought to if you still want to work? You don't have to."

"What about the insurance?"

"I think we can afford to pay for it until you reach 65 and go on Medicare, which I hope will still be able to support us."

"I don't think money's going to be a problem for a while."

"Jay, I still can't believe it's real."

"I know, me too."

"I can't just quit, it would create a burden on my entire team. Let me have a couple of days to think about it. Although, something is happening at the office."

"Lacy, what do you mean something is happening at the office?"

"The big report we spent all day working on had to do with our financial future given the rapid decrease in the cost of oil. We bleeding cash like there's no tomorrow."

"Bad enough to cause layoffs?"

"That's my feeling. I heard a rumor that some staff are going to be released this Friday."

"Do you think you're on the list?"

"I don't think so. But these days, no one is really safe. I guess we don't have to worry about it now."

We both laugh.

After cleaning up from dinner, we sit in the family room watching television. Lacy puts on her programs while I surf the web and look at various posts on different forums I belong to. Many posters are very nervous about the implications of the Greek election and their new Prime Minister. I open a note file to start listing items we ought to purchase, now that we can afford it. We can finally afford to increase our supplies. We've been preppers for a couple years, we had three to four months of food, water and medications stored. We also have a couple of ARs, shotguns, and handguns, in addition to twelve thousand rounds of ammo. We have first aid kits and portable stoves for cooking. I also have six extra propane tanks which we could use for heat, light or cooking on our BBQ grill. Three hours later, Lacy asks if I want to join her upstairs, saying she's tired.

"Sure thing, be right there, just shutting down, I hadn't noticed how quickly time slipped by."

Turning off the light, I quickly fell asleep thinking about the prize and what to do with it.

Chapter 2

While we slept, the leaders in Europe were panicking over the Greek election results. The existing Greek Prime Minister, Antonis Samaras tended his resignation, saying, he didn't think there was any reason why the people's choice shouldn't take office immediately. The Leaders of Spain, Italy, Belgium, Austria and Portugal held a secret conference call to discuss the financial situation. Mariano Rajoy, the President of Spain, started off the discussion by asking the others, "If Greece can write off her debt, why can't we? Why do they get a chance of starting over and getting out from under the punishing payments and the restrictive controls the Germans have placed on all of us? I say if Tsipras gets away with restructuring or writing off any part of Greece's debt we all should get the same or a better deal. We've been making our interest payments while the Greeks haven't. I for one, am not going to explain to the Spanish people that the Greeks got a better deal than we did. I'm not going to accept any change in the terms of their loans without a better option for the Spanish people."

Charles Michel, the leader of Belgium, says, "I agree with you. The people of Belgium also won't accept they have to tighten their belts even more than they currently are, so the Greeks have an easier time of it. If Merkel gives the Greeks any relief from the agreed to spending controls, we should all stop making interest payments. Merkel controls all of the banks. I suggest we line up support from every member of the Union to pressure Merkel into giving all of us a better deal. If Merkel sees we're united behind Tsipras, she may blink. Tsipras is going to have to move very quickly to fulfill his campaign promises to the people who elected him. Does anyone think he'll succeed where we've all failed?"

Matteo Renzi, the leader of Italy, says, "I've spoken to him during the campaign. I asked him how he plans to succeed when we've all failed to win modifications in the restrictions on our government spending. He said if the banks and Merkel don't accept his changes, he's serious about pulling Greece out of the EU and a return to using the Greek Drachma. He also said he's got a surprise for Germany. He's going to bill Germany for damage done to Greece in the Second World War."

Werner Faymann, the leader of Austria replies, "Does he realize if Greece leaves the Union, others will follow. Our dream of a united Europe will come to an end because some fat, lazy Greeks wanted more. He'll hurt all of our people if he withdraws Greece from the Union. He'll take the Union down and all of us with it if he follows through with his threats. He could start another worldwide depression. His little stunt of threatening to bill Germany for damages done seventy years ago is a joke."

Mariano Rajoy sighs, "I think the Union is coming apart anyway. If Greece stays in the union, it will only delay the unenviable. Germany lost the First and Second World Wars, but now Merkel controls the banks who in turn controls the Union. She may have lost the military side of the battle, but she won the war. She indirectly rules all of us. She mandates what and how we spend."

Matteo Renzi asks, "Mariano, do you really believe the Union is doomed?"

"Yes, I do. All of our economies are weak, our people demand jobs and a brighter future for their children. When we tied ourselves together, we became only as strong our weakest member. Unfortunately, we have too many weak members. We have been at each other's throats for hundreds of years. In the last one hundred years Germany tried twice to conquer all of us, now because their leader controls the banks, she, they *have* conquered us. Our people resent it. I don't see Merkel accepting any changes to the bailout package she backed for Greece, that'll force

Tsipras to pull Greece out of the Union. Which one of us will be next? When the Union implodes how will Merkel get her banks repaid? She's not going to pay them back from the Germany's operating funds. Our people are tired of austerity programs, our people are burned-out being told they have to accept less and less. I think Tsipras might be onto something. If all of us unite, Merkel can't stop us."

Matteo shakes his head, "Mariano, I think pushing Merkel into a corner can be very dangerous for all of us. If she doesn't support us, we could be left without any operating funds."

Werner replies, "We can't continue on the current path, all of our people are unhappy. If Tsipras succeeds, our people will rise up and force a change across all of Europe. We could even end up at war with each other again."

Matteo whispers, "What if Germany decides to foreclose on her loans? What if she sends her military into our countries to collect what we owe her? Our people will go crazy, they'll see ghosts of the 1940s goose-stepping through Europe again. Are we ready to relive the dark days of the First and Second World Wars? Millions could die."

Werner says, "I don't think she would do that, the entire world will turn against Germany. The world fought Germany twice before, they won't want to go to war with her a third time, if the world does, they will completely destroy Germany so she never rises again. If Merkel resorts to military force, it will result in Germany's total destruction. Putin and Obama could be brought back into a cold war that can explode in Central Germany similar to our worst nightmares during the dark days of the Cold War."

Helle Thorning-Schmidt of Denmark says, "It's going to be different this time. The Americans bailed us out in the first two World Wars, this time they are tired of war. They've spent fifteen years fighting in the Middle East, their President has promised the people no more wars. If he hopes his party wins the next election, he won't send troops to our aid. His banks will demand if anything he sides with Merkel. I don't think we can count on America to come to our aid."

The five leaders agree to wait thirty days to see what, if any, progress Greece makes in their discussions with Merkel.

@@@@@

In the small town of Poltava, located in Eastern Ukraine, a squad of US Special Forces troops, wearing Ukrainian army uniforms is watching and reporting on the Russian army reinforcements moving towards the front. Sergeant Gray aims his handheld laser on the third Russian T-90 main battle tank in a line of the new Russian main battle tanks, he whispers into the radio, "Delta Foxtrot Two, lit. Bring it on."

His message is encrypted and burst to a US Military MilSat, which transmits it to Tampa, Florida, the home of SOCOM (Special Operations Command). The SOCOM commanding General responds, "engage."

Circling 45,000 feet above Sergeant Gray are five armed Predator drones. The pilot and weapons operator are sitting in a trailer in Germany receive the 'Go' command from SOCOM. The weapons operator says, "We're good to go, Hellfires are selected and ready."

The pilot confirms, "Good, we're clear to fire. All Predators are networked so each target is only hit once."

The weapon's officer smiles responding, "Roger, now firing."

The Hellfire missiles leave the Predators guided by the sensor in the missile's nose tuned to the frequency of the Sergeant's laser designator. The Hellfire follows the laser striking the top, the weakest spot on the T-90. The missile's first warhead blasts a hole through the T-90's thin upper armor and a layer of reactive armor. This allows the missile's body and main warhead to penetrate the tank. The explosion of the Hellfire missile inside the tank sets off the stored main gun rounds in the tank's turret. The explosion blows the turret off the stricken tank, killing the crew. Before the first tank's turret lands, Sergeant Gray illuminates the next tank in the line. The Predator weapons operator fires another missile, killing another tank. The Special Operating Force team moves their lasers from tank to tank, within six minutes the road is littered with burning dead Russian tanks. Hundreds of millions of Rubles worth of brand new tanks litter the road.

The images of the destroyed Russian tanks are reviewed in Moscow by the Russian Minister of Defense, Sergey Shoigu. He slams his fist on the conference table. "Damn the Americans. Only they could have done this."

Picking up the secure phone to the Kremlin, Shoigu says one word into the phone, "Putin." His call is instantly connected to the President's office.

President Putin answers his secure phone on its first ring, "Mr. Defense Minister what can I do for you?"

"Mr. President, the Americans have struck and destroyed a line of twenty-four T-90 tanks that were on the way to reinforce the front in Ukraine."

"How can you be sure the Americans destroyed our tanks?"

"Only they could have taken them out with such precision and speed. It had to be either one of their stealth bombers or drones."

"What proof do you have?"

"At this minute I have none. I've sent two experts to investigate the scene, they'll take samples and be able to determine which weapons caused the destruction. I'm willing to bet we find some missile residue proving it was the Americans."

"When you have the proof call me. What's your backup plan to replace the lost armor?"

"Mr. President, we don't have many of the new T-90 tanks available, I'm going to have to replace them with T-80s."

"Where are the balance of the T-90s?"

"Sir, they are with the Fourth Guards on the border with the PRC."

"Leave them there for now. If the yellow bastards see us withdrawing armor, they'll sense weakness and launch another series of cross-border attacks."

"Yes, sir."

"Send a few platoons of Spetsnaz to locate who destroyed our tanks. If they are Americans, keep some alive. I'll need them to pressure the stupid American President."

"Yes, sir."

"Increase the security of all of our bases in the Ukraine."

@@@@@

Lacy and I sit across from each other enjoying breakfast, sipping cups of rich freshly brewed coffee. Lacy smiles looking at me, "Honey since we can live anywhere, where would you like to go?"

"I was just going to ask you the same thing."

"Hawaii?"

"I knew you'd say that. I think Hawaii is out, it's too far for the kids to visit. Plus, if anything really bad happens in the world we're going to be stuck out there."

"Honey, the weather's perfect, if we bought some land we could grow everything we'd need. If nothing happens, we'll live in paradise."

"Do you really want to be so far away from everyone we know?"

Lacy smiles, saying, "No, you're right, we can vacation there, I know where I don't want to live."

"Me too, I don't want to move back to California, I don't want to live in the North East."

Lacy laughs, "But Jay, you were born in New Jersey, aren't we going to be buried in Jersey?"

"I was born there and got out as soon as possible, the only reason we're going to be buried there is, it's where the family plots are. Since I'm to the right of Attila the Hun, I don't get along with anyone there anymore. In addition, it's too cold. Same for the Mid West."

"Don't you get along with your cousins?"

"Only if we don't discuss politics."

We're interrupted by the television in the background, the 'News Bulletin' flashes on the screen. Lacy looked up saying, "Now what? What else can go wrong in the world?"

The 'talking head' reported the FBI arrested a Russian spy working for a bank on Wall Street.

I sip my coffee, telling Lacy, "Not good."

"What does it mean?"

"About the only reason I can think of for an FSB agent to be working on Wall Street is to screw with the market or to screw with our currency."

"Jay, what's FSB mean?"

"Sorry, the FSB is the replacement for the Russian spy agency which used to be called the KGB."

"You mean like the CIA?"

"Yes. They're similar."

"I thought the Cold War was over, why are they spying on us?"

"Honey, they're spying on us, we're spying on them. The Obama reset button with Russia didn't work, it was all a big PR bullshit event. Our relations with them are as bad now as when we were in the Cold War. Our relations may even be worse than during the Cold War. Russia is flying bombers towards Alaska and Europe again. They have developed new generations of weapons and all the while we've been reducing the size and strength of our military, Putin is rebuilding the Russian military. Putin is playing Obama like a fiddle. When they said Obama was the smartest man in the room, there must have been no one else in the room. He hasn't shown he knows anything about foreign relations. His policies are making things worse around the world. Our friends don't trust us and our enemies don't fear us."

"Do you think the arrest means anything of significance?"

"Depends what the agent was doing when he got caught. I don't trust Putin. He's never given up the goal of making Russia the world's sole superpower, he'd like to dominate the entire world. He's rearming the Russian military, he's waking the Red Bear out of its hibernation. He's never taken his eyes off of Europe."

"Does it impact our plans?"

"Let's assume nothing happens, everything in the world stays status quo for the rest of our lives, where would you like to live? If we assume something does happen, where would you like to live?"

"Honey, when you say, something happens, what do you mean?"

"Let's assume, the market melts down, a race war breaks out, or there's a major terrorist attack. And lastly, alien invasion."

Lacy laughed, throwing the crust from her toast at me. "Don't give me any of that science fiction bullshit." She continues, "What's the chances of anything bad happening?"

"I think there's a very real chance of a currency collapse, our debt is approaching $20 trillion, there's no way we can ever pay it back. Obama and Congress keep spending like drunken sailors. We're selling our bonds to the Fed, which is like me loaning you money to give it back to me. Sooner or later, and I think sooner, it's going to implode. Our currency isn't backed by anything except for the goodwill and trust of the USA government. I don't trust them to pay back what's owed. If the new government in Greece goes ahead and writes off their debt, telling Germany and the banks to screw off, the Euro will fail, resulting in the EU breaking up. At first our dollar will benefit. However, the dollar will fail when people realize we're not in any better financial shape as the EU. People will begin questioning how safe the dollar really is. I think if Greece goes through with their threat the price of Gold will soar. People will think it's the only safe financial haven."

"Why don't you do some research, we'll talk more tonight. I've got to get to the office. Maybe it's time to buy some gold. Are you still planning on calling Beth today?"

"Yes, she's an hour behind us. I have to speak to her anyway, I'm almost ready to send her our tax data for last year. We need to find out from her what the downside is if we take the lump sum payout."

"Love you, gotta run. Call me later."

"Will do. Love you too."

@@@@@

New York City's FBI Special Agent in Charge William Gray is frowning as he reads the arrest report of Evgeny Buryakov. He's thinking, *we delayed too long. We lost his two 'friends' who were able to leave the country. I tried to get D.C. to approve us picking them up three weeks ago. I've been doing this for 22 years, the assholes in D.C. are young pups. They think the entire world can get along by saying we're sorry and we love everyone. If Buryakov doesn't talk, it's going to take a lot of manpower to figure out the extent of the damage he's done. Just another day in paradise.* A knock on his office door breaks into his thoughts, "Come in."

"SAC Gray, we have processed Buryakov. He'll be in conference room number 3 in twenty minutes."

"Thanks. Don't let anyone near him until I question him."

"Sir, D.C. has said we have to transfer him to headquarters in two hours."

"How did they communicate this to us?"

"Via secure fax."

"You never saw it, pull the paper out of the secure fax machine. We'll transfer Buryakov when I'm satisfied we have all of the information from him we need to figure out what he was doing."

"Sir, D.C..."

"Said nothing because you didn't get a fax because we were out of paper."

"Yes, sir, you realize you could be fired for delaying to carry out HQ's order."

"Good. I'm ready to sit on my boat and fish all day."

"Yes, sir. I'll pull the paper."

"While you're at it, pull the telephone plug, some asshole may put paper in it. No one will check the plug."

"Yes, sir."

Damn D.C. They want me to transfer Buryakov so they can return him to Moscow. The screwed up State Department must be behind this bullshit. Stupid State Department and their damn phony reset button. They delayed us moving against Buryakov for weeks. If they'd let me move when I wanted to, we would have the entire team in custody and we'd have a much chance of knowing what they were doing.

@@@@@

I spent the morning making notes, talking with our accountant and sending her our tax records and previous year financial information so she could help us figure out the best way to handle our winnings. I didn't notice Lacy calling the house until the ringing brought me back to reality.

Lacy sounded concerned, "Honey, got a minute? Did you speak with Beth?"

"She's overjoyed for us, she said she's going to raise her rate to do our taxes to $27 million. After we had a good laugh, she told me to take the lump sum and put 25% away for any other potential tax issues. She's sending us some interest bearing account information we can stick the money in until this time next year. She reminded us that we have to spread the money around as soon as we get it. The Federal Deposit Insurance Corporation (FDIC) backs each insurer for only $250,000. Not per account, per person. After the 2008 banking meltdown, there is a hell of a lot less US banks than there used to be. There aren't enough US banks left for us to open accounts at each to cover our $28 million. Beth said she'd help us open accounts in banks around the world to spread our risks. She also suggested some high-grade bonds."

"What are we going to do?"

"I'm going to open accounts and you're going to open some. I don't intend to follow so many other lottery winners into the poorhouse."

"How long will it take to set up?"

"Only a couple of hours. We should be able to have everything set up so when we make the deposit into our primary account, we'll be able to instantly make the transfers into our new accounts to protect the money."

"When are we going to get it?"

"Most likely tomorrow, Friday, why?"

"I'm thinking of going with you, the office is a real zoo today."

"What's going on?"

"You may think the low oil prices are good, however, it's killing our margin. Do you remember me telling you last night there's a rumor floating up from HQ that there could be a layoff soon?"

"Yes, what of it?"

"It looks like 20 to 25% of the company is going to be laid off tomorrow afternoon."

"Do you think you're going to be one of the 20%?"

"I don't think I was on the list until Joe told Marshal about us winning. When I came in this morning, everyone was giving me a funny look. They think I'm going to quit, as such I think they will put me on the layoff list because I'm now an easy one to cut."

"Why don't you just ask Marshal? You two are friendly, you've done him a lot of favors before. If you're on the list, maybe he'll pay you off today so you won't have to go in tomorrow, Friday firings are depressing. There's no reason for you to stress about it. We'll go get the money, and then celebrate."

"OK, I'll let you know when I see you tonight."

"Love you."

"Love you too."

Hanging up, I hear on the news that the cost of a barrel of oil fell today to $42.00. I thought, *maybe the reducing oil prices isn't such a good idea. The timing of our win couldn't have been better if there's a chance Lacy is going to be laid off. With me out of work and semi-retired, we relied on her income and her medical insurance benefits.*

Lacy called at 4:30 PM to say she was on the way and could I meet her in the garage to help her. At 4:55 PM I heard the garage door open, I met Lacy as she pulled into the garage. She smiled while nodding to me. "You were right, I asked Marshal to be honest with me. He closed his door telling me I wasn't originally on the list, but after hearing we won the lottery, he added me because he felt I was going to quit anyway. It allowed him to keep someone who was a single mother. I told him I understood and took the rest of the day off." Laughing, she said, "I'm taking the rest of my life off."

"Honey, it's going to be OK. We'll get through this."

"You don't understand, I've worked since I was 16. This is the first time I haven't had a job. What are we going to do without insurance?"

"$28 million. Did you forget?"

"Why don't you take me out to dinner tonight? I think we can afford it. Did you call the lottery people?"

"Let me get my coat. Sure did. We're set to pick up the check tomorrow."

Over a glass of wine, Lacy tells me, "Honey, I think you may be right, the economy is sliding into the crapper. Marshal told me he and his wife bought a new house in West Virginia last weekend."

"Why the hell in West Virginia? It's going to take him 90 minutes to get to the office."

"He told me if oil prices stay below $50 a barrel the company will most likely close our branch and many others. At his age, he doesn't think he'll be able to find another job."

"He's only 57 isn't he?"

"Yes, but he said it's almost impossible to find a job that pays him similar to what he currently earns. He said the new house has enough land they'll be able to raise animals and grow their own food to be self-sufficient."

"How many acres did he buy?"

"Twenty."

"Marshal didn't strike me as a farmer."

"He's not. He said he's also going to cash in his 401K, for what he said is usable shit."

"What did he mean by that?"

"I don't know. I asked him, he said, he expects the market to crash within six months. He's going to cash out his 401K and IRAs before the market enters free fall. He agreed with you that Greece is going to be the spark that sets the Euro on fire, taking down the EU. He said OPEC is driving the cost of oil down in order destroy the fracking industry, it's sure taking a toll on us. He said he expects once OPEC buries our fracking industry, they'll bring the cost of a barrow of oil back to over $100. He said you should keep an eye on Russia and China, they're going to use the financial situation against us."

"I didn't realize Marshal paid that much attention to everything."

"Honey, remember he has two PhDs, one in economics, and one in math. He said he made a medium-sized fortune shorting the market in 08 and another fortune in 13-14 when he projected the market was going to jump. He said he's getting out of the market and suggests we not get in. He's converting everything he can to gold. He gave me a memory stick with some files for you. He said you should understand the math."

"That sounds scary. When is he moving?"

"He said in thirty days. I'll check the files when we get home. I was thinking if we're going to move, we should move closer to the kids. If we assume the market is going to crash, I don't like living on the outskirts of D.C. Remember the riots in Baltimore? I don't want to be anywhere near race riots."

"I told you, I won't move to Iowa, we visited there once, I hated it. Tell Sammi to move East, I also don't like Illinois, where Shelly and Todd live."

"Shelly can't move because of the custody issues, Sammi won't move because of Ricky's job. We could move someplace close to both, but still be in an area that we'd like."

"Like where?"

"Nashville, or some place close to it. I don't want to live in Ohio, there's also Kentucky?"

"I think I like Nashville better."

"I have an idea, why don't you pack a bag; we'll collect the money and we'll hit the road to investigate different areas. We can stop and see the kids while we're at it. Since you're out of a job too, what do you have to lose?"

Lacy laughs, saying, "I like it. By the way, Marshal did give me a little gift."

"Huh? What kind of gift?"

Lacy laughs, she hands me an envelope, "He gave me six months pay and my six weeks accrued vacation. It's a month per year, it's what everyone else is getting on Friday."

"Well, this is a nice surprise. When it rains, it pours, I thought they were going to give you two, maybe four weeks pay, and your accrued vacation. I didn't expect this."

Laughing, Lacy asks to see the desert menu, something she almost never does. I look at her in surprise. "I'm celebrating."

"I'll join you."

We return home and pack for a week before going to bed, we have a big day ahead of us. Early the next morning we drive the 2 hours to Richmond. We have our pictures taken, we sign a couple release forms, we can't stop staring at the check. I've never seen a check with so many numbers on it. $28,774,653.00. We're both shaking while holding the check. Next stop the closest Bank of America branch which thankfully is less than two blocks away. Walking into the bank, a woman says, "Welcome to Bank of America, how can I help you?"

"We'd like to make a deposit."

"I can help you with that, do you have your ATM card?"

"Yes, we'd like to split the deposit into two accounts."

"No problem." The teller looks at the check turning white and starts shaking. She calls out, "Mrs. Redding, may I see you, please?"

The manager joins the teller, I ask her, "Is there a problem?"

The manager looks at the check saying, "We're going to have to put a hold on these funds until the check clears."

"No, you're not. It's a certified check drawn on Bank of America, which is this bank. The lottery commission banks at this very branch, you can check their balance. You're not supposed to put a hold on certified checks, if you do, I'm sure Wells Fargo across the street would like our business."

Mrs. Redding looks at me saying, "I'll have to check with corporate, would you like to sit in my office. This shouldn't take too long."

"Don't go far with our check. I'd like it if you stayed someplace I can see you."

Fifteen minutes later, which feels like a year, Mrs. Redding returns smiling, "Would you like some coffee?"

Lacy says, "Yes, please."

Lacy opens a CD in the amount of $250,000, we deposit the rest into our normal checking accounts with the intent to start transferring to other accounts as soon as we're out of the bank. I figure if we find a place to live, we may want to bargain with cash in hand.

We left Richmond with $15,000 in cash and $28 million in different accounts. We started our journey to see our girls and granddaughters while thinking about where we're going to move. While I'm driving, Lacy logs onto and pays off everything we owe. Laughing, she says, "We're now debt free."

"I wonder if that was a good idea."

"Why?"

"If the market turns to crap, we might have been able to negotiate paying a lower amount."

"Honey, BFD, even with our two cars it was less than seventy thousand. We're free and clear. It came out of what Marshal gave me. We haven't touched our winnings yet."

We both looked at each other and laughed. Lacy logged onto the bank's website and started to transfer our funds to our other accounts.

We drove West on Interstate 64 until we reached Interstate 81 South, which we took into Tennessee, where we picked up Interstate 40. Lacy wanted to stop in Asheville, she'd heard it was nice, so we picked up Interstate 240 to State Route 74. By the time we arrived in Asheville, we were dead tired. We pulled into the Hilton Biltmore Park. We checked into a king suite, something we wouldn't have done before Wednesday. The Hotel General Manager told us they were booked for a convention starting on Monday. We figured a couple of days would give us the flavor of the area. After a nice dinner, we crashed for the night. We'd been driving eleven hours and were emotionally and physically drained.

I woke to a knock on our suite door, Lacy told me to stay in bed, she'd ordered room service for breakfast. I asked, "Why, it's free downstairs."

Lacy laughed, saying, "I think we can afford the $50.00."

"Too expensive." We both laughed. During breakfast, we called a real estate agent the Hilton's General Manager suggested. She met us in the lobby at 10:30 AM, we spent two days looking at the nicest homes in the city. At dinner Sunday night Lacy looked at me saying, it's very pretty, but I want to see Nashville. How far away are the kids?"

"Ten to eleven hours from here."

"And from Nashville?"

"Six hours, maybe less if we live on the North side of the city, which is where I think we should look."

"I like that. Close enough to see them when we want and not so close that we'll end up being a babysitter every weekend."

"Fine with me, we'll leave in the morning. Nashville isn't far."

As we're getting ready for bed, we watch the evening news. The reporter said, "The new Prime Minister of Greece announced today he wasn't able to reach agreement on renegotiating revised terms for Greece's $270 billion in German loans. Prime Minister Tsipras announced he was pulling Greece out of the EU and returning to the Greek Drachma. Tsipras said he expects to have new Drachma's in the banks within a few days. Most experts think this is the end of the European unity dream and the end of the Euro."

"Lace, I think the other shoe is going to drop very soon. I expect to see Gold soar."

"Why don't you buy some online right now?"

"Okay." It took me thirty minutes to purchase $100,000 in gold since we didn't have an open account with any of the brokerage companies. When the European markets opened gold jumped $100 an ounce as soon as trading started, the price of gold continuing to increase all night while we slept. In the morning, Lacy asked me. "Jay, if you knew gold was going to jump, why didn't you buy more last night?"

"I couldn't. The agent said the max they would sell me is $100,000. Even that took two discussions with his manager. I can buy more when the bank opens."

"Why not call BoA's special number they gave us, maybe they can help us."

"Crap, I forgot all about the special number, I told you I'm getting old."

I called the special high net worth customer service number the BoA General Manager gave us. They helped me purchase another $100,000 worth of gold. Our average price was $1,290 an ounce. By the time the Chicago gold market opened, gold was selling for $1,660 an ounce. We made over $28,000 by doing nothing. Gold closed the day over $1,920 an ounce, our paper profits were increasing by the hour.

Right after breakfast we left for Nashville.

Lacy kept checking the price of gold and silver on her phone, she was amazed how quickly the cost jumped. We kept buying as we drove to Nashville. We pulled into Nashville at midday. We checked into a suite at the Gaylord Opryland Resort. We had dinner while watching a live concert. We called the local real estate agent, one the agent in Asheville introduced us to. We agreed to meet her after breakfast the next morning.

Before retiring, the late night news reported that Italy and Spain were preparing to leave the EU and drop using the Euro, returning to their old currencies.

Lacy looks at me, "Think you should buy some more gold?"

"Why not, what do we have to lose?" Logging on to our account with the gold dealer, I purchased another $500,000 before shutting down for the night. I'd been able to buy it at $2,044 an ounce. In the morning, gold passed $2,400 an ounce when Spain, Italy, and Portugal confirmed they were writing off their debt and leaving the EU. Major banks were already warning they were going to lose billions on the collapse of the Euro. A few of the international banks said they might even fail. I'm happy we were very careful where we parked our money. *What happened to, 'too big to fail'?*

Lacy looked worried, "It's going to get much worse isn't it?"

"Yup, The EU is finished. It's going to fall apart within a couple of months. The US dollar is going to jump in value before it crashes. I think we ought to see what kind of deal we can cut while the market is going crazy, cash in hand is worth a lot more than any mortgage."

The New York stock market opened the next morning down 1,000 points and continued to fall even though the NYSE stopped trading three times during the day trying to cool the traders off.

Chapter 3

FBI Senior Special Agent in Charge Gray frowns as he reviews his notes from his last interview with Evgeny Buryakov. They reached an agreement that in exchange for political asylum and entrance into the witness protection program, Buryakov agreed to spill his guts. SAC Gray shakes his head thinking, *it's worse than what we thought, he was sent here to use automated trading algorithms to disrupt the stock market and our futures markets. He said the FSB's economic department sent him here to sow the seeds of our market destruction. He told us that when Putin devalued the Russian ruble, the ruble lost 50% of its value in only two weeks. The FSB thinks the USA dollar can be collapsed in a similar manner. Russia will be able to come back while we won't. Who in D.C. is going to believe this story? All of them have their heads stuck up their asses. None of them can see the real world. We're getting screwed while they play around sucking up to Obama. I think it's time to retire and prepare for the end. Buryakov told me he was able to upload his programs which are being remotely controlled from Moscow. The FSB has us by the short hairs. We're playing right into their hands. He said there's very little we can do now to avoid the collapse.*

@@@@@

A squad of Russian Spetsnaz arrives in Poltava to investigate the destruction of the Russian tanks, they investigate the burned out hulks that used to be new T-90 main battle tanks. Captain Second Rank Sarnoff looks at the ruins thinking, *it had to be the Yankees. No one else has the weapons to defeat our new T-90s. There has to be some proof let behind they were responsible.* While the Captain is looking at the destroyed tanks his sergeant yells, "Captain, I found something."

Captain Sarnoff jogs to the fourth destroyed tank in the row. "What did you find?"

"Missile pieces." Holding out his hand, he drops small pieces of burned circuit boards into the captain's outstretched hands. Looking at the small circuit board fragments, the captain sees the small "Made in the USA." Silk screened on the edge of one of the green boards. He smiles, "Sergeant, very good work. Let's go home."

Arriving in Moscow, the captain shows what he found to the Russian Minister of Defense, Sergey Shoigu. "Sir, you can clearly see the parts came from an American weapon."

Smiling an evil grin, Shoigu says, "Captain, very good work. Take your team to the Black Sea for a couple of week's vacation. You've earned it this time."

Captain Sarnoff smiles, nodding his thanks, he snaps to attention, saluting the Minister, who nods his head. When the captain leaves the Minister's office, he calls President Putin. "Sir, we have proof the American's were behind the destruction of our tanks in Poltava."

"Bring me the proof."

"Yes, sir."

Twenty minutes later the two men look at the small piece of a circuit board lying on Putin's desk. "Yes, that is the proof I need. Thank you, Minister. I'll get back to you on our next steps."

The Minister leaves Putin's office thinking to himself he should place the motherland's military on alert. Putin calls the Director of the FSB, "It's time to start the destruction of the American financial markets, is the embedded code ready to go?"

"Yes, sir. Buryakov was able to finish loading it before he got caught. The FBI thinks they'll be able to unravel the code since they have him. We never told Buryakov the program he loaded was really five different programs that once entered into the American financial network released hundreds of different worms. These worms found the data we wanted. Once we had that data, we can now control their markets. We can screw them up their asses any time you order us to."

"I think we should give the American's a special gift. One they aren't expecting. Spring comes on March 21, a Saturday this year. Launch the program on the first day of spring. When the brokers report to their offices Monday morning full of hope with the spring, we'll bring their markets down around their necks. Start short selling all of our shares. When we've crashed their stock market, we'll put our boot on their neck, crushing the life from them."

"Yes, sir, with pleasure. We'll be ready for March 21."

@@@@@

While the real estate agent takes us to see many different homes, the news from Europe continues to be bad. The agent is taking us to see a new housing development about fifty miles on the Northeast side of Nashville. We drive past a beautiful home set way back from the road with a for sale sign on the road. "Wait, what's that?"

The agent pulls over to turn around so we can pull into the house's driveway, "Let me check." She puts the address into her tablet, she says, "It's a custom built 7,000 square foot home with 6 bedrooms, seven baths on five acres. It's been on the market for six months. It's been reduced in price four times."

"Why isn't it selling?"

"It borders that farm. You can see the farmhouse is run down, not many people want to spend $690,000 to look at a rundown farmhouse."

"I'd like to see it."

Lacy asks, "Honey, what are you thinking?"

"Hon, give me a couple of minutes, OK?" I ask the agent, "How large is the farm?"

"Two hundred fifty plus acres. It's listed for sale, it's in foreclosure."

"Interesting."

The house is unbelievably beautiful, the home's detail takes our breath away. The agent tells us, "It cost the original owners a million dollars. They never moved in, one of them got ill just before the house was finished, they moved to Florida where they're children live. They're very open to offers."

Lacy says, "Honey, can I talk to you?"

"Sure, what's up?"

"Are you crazy? This house could hold all of our extended family plus some, it's crazy for the two of us."

"It is, isn't it? Honey, what happens if the economy fails? Wouldn't it be nice if the kids were safe and living with us? This house has three levels, plus the pool and pool house. If things really get bad, we could buy the farm next door and we'd have a built-in supply of food."

"What the hell do we know about farming?"

"Not a damn thing. Which is why I'm thinking of buying the farm and renting it back to the family living on the farm. They work it and give us a portion of the food."

"You think the dollar's going to collapse don't you?"

"Have you checked the price of gold this afternoon or how fast the market is falling?"

"No. Wait, I'll check it. Holy shit, it's now up to $2,850 an ounce."

"It's going to continue to climb as the EU unravels, when the EU is a memory in the footnote of history, the dollar will rise then fall harder than the Euro did."

"Hell of a gamble if nothing happens."

"Is it? What will it cost us? $600,000 for this house, maybe a couple of million for the farm, shit, that leaves us only $25 or 26 mil left. I think we can live on that. Don't forget, on paper, we've made over $200,000 on the gold we bought. How is it a risk?"

"Do you think the kids will come?"

"Not right now, they will when things turn to crap and they lose their jobs. Look, we can get the farmer to store fuel for his tractor and our cars for us. They must have storage tanks. We would have food, fuel, the house has two wells so we'd have water. Do you like the house?

"It's gorgeous, if the kids don't come, you better find a maid because I'm not cleaning a house this big for the two of us."

"What else is nice is this house isn't in a subdivision. It's not on a main road, and yet there is civilization only a few miles away so it won't be like living far out in the country."

"How do we furnish it?"

"We'll buy whatever we need."

"I think you're crazy, but I love you."

I kiss Lacy telling the agent, "I want the house inspected and I want the blueprints for it. I'd like to go meet the farmer."

The agent says she can get an inspector at the house this afternoon, and also should be able to get the blueprints from the original builders. She wonders why I want to visit the farm, but isn't going to say anything which might change my mind about buying the fifth house she showed us. We drive down the street to their house, pulling in their driveway a man in his forties meets us in his driveway, "What do you people want? You can't come in here yet, the date of the foreclosure isn't for another two weeks. I still own the house and farm."

I reply. "Hello, my name is Jay, this is my wife, Lacy. We're thinking of buying the house next to your farm. We thought we'd come over to meet our potential neighbors."

"Nice to meet you, sorry, I saw the realtor's sign on the car's door and assumed she was trying to sell my house out from under us."

"May we exit the car?"

"Of course, I'm sorry, my name is Fred."

Holding out my hand, "Fred it's nice to meet you. I heard you say you were having bank problems if you don't mind saying, what's going on?"

"Crop last two years wasn't the best. The damn bank wants to sell our land to a developer to build a hundred new homes here. Thinks they can call my loan and get my farm dirt cheap, sell it to the developer high and make a fortune."

"We don't want a hundred neighbors, we like it in the country. If you don't mind my nosiness, what does the bank want from you?"

"About $790,000."

"I see. Maybe we can help. Mind if we come in out of the cold and chat?"

"Not at all. Do come in. We have a fresh pot of coffee on the stove."

We sit and chat for a while, the agent is getting nervous, she keeps looking at her watch. I lean over telling her, "You told us you would take a couple of days to spend with just us, we're most likely going to buy that house. Do us a favor and just sit tight for a little while. In fact, why don't you start the paperwork on the house? I'll give you a number within an hour."

Fred introduces us to his wife Cheri and their sons, Mark, and Ryan.

Lacy talks with Cheri while Fred and I take a walk, "Look, Fred, I know what I'm about to say is going to sound crazy, please do me a small favor and hear me out."

"Okay."

"I have some money, we're going to move here from the D.C. area. I think the economy is going to go into the crapper when it does, it'll make 1929 look good. Europe's going to fail first, followed by us. When the banks crash, the depression is going to hurt everyone. I'm interested in working out a deal with you. I think when the banks fail, food is going to be a major problem. How about I buy the house next door, we add our acreage to yours, I pay off the bank for you, we work together to prepare for the fall. If it doesn't happen, you pay me back, I'm sure we'll be able to agree on an amount you can afford. You don't lose your farm, if I'm wrong, you can laugh at my loss, if I'm right, we'll both be laughing at the rest of the world."

"Jay, you are crazy. But I think I like you. I assume you know, you are plain nuts. I agree with you the market is going nuts, I think we can work something out. One big problem is we only have two weeks before the bank takes the farm."

"I can get the bank off your back next week. If we can work out an agreement, I'll get the bank paid off in a day."

Fred frowns asking, "So does that mean I end up working for you?"

"No, you work for yourself, you pay me back what we agree to. If I'm right, it'll be the best decision you ever made. If I'm wrong, what are you losing?"

"Jay, I think we'll be able to make a deal. How much are you thinking we pay you a month?"

"You know what you grow and sell, you tell me what you can afford, I'll give you until Tuesday. Here's my phone number. Call me."

We shake hands and go inside to break open a bottle of bourbon to strike the deal. I turn to the real estate agent, "Offer the owner of the house, $550,000 cash, we can close as soon as the title and inspection are completed."

The agent is surprised, she nods her agreement as she starts texting the owner. Later that night Lacy tells me, "You know you're crazy don't you?"

"Yep, I'm crazy, if I'm wrong, it cost us one point four. Which is next to nothing, and if I'm right we'll be set for life."

"When will we know?"

"I'd say by Wednesday. Worse case the house owners will want their full listing price, the house easily cost a million to build, the farm is only $790. We should be able to get the bank to discount the note for cash. I think we should head to the kids tomorrow, chat with them and then go home to hire a mover to pack and move us to Nashville."

"I hope they have a nice furniture store close by."

"Check online, I'm sure there are many."

The real estate agent called, interrupting us to tell us the owner countered our offer at $575,000. "Tell them OK. We're going to be leaving tomorrow, email us the papers. And the bank information to wire the deposit."

"Yes, sir. I'll do it right now."

"Lacy, we bought a house. I think we'll end up owning a farm on Wednesday. I can't believe we're going to buy the farm. Usually when someone says they've bought the farm, they mean they died."

Lacy laughs, "I want to see you in overalls and a straw hat."

"Don't get carried away."

Before retiring for the evening, we call our kids telling them we'll be at Shelly's tomorrow, asking Sammi to take two days off and meet us. She gives us a hard time finally agreeing that she and Linda will come to see us. Shelly is overjoyed saying she too can't take off of work, but she'll try to work from home.

We leave for Bloomington, Illinois Monday morning. It's a long seven-hour drive. Lacy says, "I thought you said it was a five-hour trip."

"How was I to know there was going to be a snowstorm and a ten car accident?"

"At least we're here. Where did you book us?"

"Crap, I forgot to book a room, log on to my Hilton account and see if the Hampton has rooms, better get two, one for us, and one for Sammi."

A couple of minutes later Lacy nods yes, "We're booked."

"Great, I need to rest, a hot meal and a drink."

Lacy laughs, "Whoever thought winning the lottery would be stressful?"

"Got that right."

We pull into the hotel finding Sammi and Linda, our oldest granddaughter waiting for us. Linda runs into our arms, Lacy exclaiming, "My word she's grown. She looks a lot older than the eleven she is."

Shelly pulls in right behind us with her entire crew. The kids run into my arms, knocking me over into a snow bank as all three of them hug me.

Over dinner, we tell the girls about the lottery. Both are surprised and cry with their happiness for us. We then drop the bomb that we're moving to Nashville, both girls are excited, it's a lot closer to them than DC.

Sammi asks, "Why not closer?"

"We don't like Iowa or Illinois, Nashville is a nice big city, yet we're going to live to the north of the city, close to you and also be close to civilization. We bought a huge home with room for all of you."

Sammi says, "Huh? What are you saying? Dad, are you asking us to move in with you?"

"Not yet, however, the time may come when we will be opening the house for all of you. I think the economy is going to tank, things are going to turn to shit. You may be safer with us than alone in your homes."

Bianca says, "Papa, that's not a nice word."

"OK honey, I'm sorry." I kiss and hug our youngest granddaughter. I continue, "Europe is all over the news, the market is entering free fall, things are going to get much worse before the economy turns around if it ever turns around. When things get really bad, you'll know it. When it does, come to us. Don't ask, just pack up and come. The rooms will be furnished and waiting for you. The house has six bedrooms, seven full and two half baths. We have a pool and a pool house. There's plenty of room for all of you."

Both girls look shocked, they don't know what to say. Shelly finally says, "Dad, what about our jobs?"

"If I'm right, they won't be there, most people are going to lose their jobs. We're going to have a worldwide depression that will make 1929 look mild. When it happens, pack your clothes, everything special to you and come south. Come before the roads get crazy. Here is a check for each of you. Don't use it to pay your bills, convert it to cash and keep it in a safe place. If I'm right, you'll need it to get to us. Gas and food will be in short supply." I hand each girl a check for $100,000. Each girl can't believe it. Sammi says, "Dad, please don't tell us you really think one of your crazy prepper stories is going to come true."

"Sammi, tell you what if in one-year nothing happens, I'll give you another $100,000 to say I'm sorry for scaring you. If I'm right, in a year you'll be with us. Fair?"

"Dad, that's more than fair. It's a deal."

Shelly says, "$100,000 for each of us?"

"Yes and we'll open a fund to pay for the kids college costs, we'll also pay for any special medical costs you or the kids need."

Shelly says, "I could really use a new car, mine is too small to cart all of us with us."

"Pick out anything you want, call me, we'll wire the dealership the money."

Sammi says, "Me too?"

"Yes, pick out anything you want."

Both girls hug us.

Chapter 4

While we sleep, France shocks the world when François Hollande, France's President announces he is withdrawing France from the EU and reissuing French Francs. He announces a return to full payments for all pensions, and a government hiring increase to hire the unemployed. Premier Merkel of Germany issues a statement to the members of the EU that Germany rejects the member nation's efforts to write off their debt and defaulting on their loans. She threatens to use military force if required to have the loans repaid. She announces a full mobilization of Germany's military. Waking the next morning, Lacy and I look at each other, she asks, "Is this the beginning of another European war? Will we get drawn in again?"

"I think Germany will move troops to her borders, I hope Merkel won't send her military across the border which will start another World War. Russia will sit on the sidelines waiting for the European nations to weaken themselves. When they're weak and their militaries are worn down, then the Russians will move in and take over Europe. We'll be powerless to stop them. Obama has reduced our military by a third. He's withdrawn our troops from Europe so we couldn't get to Europe in time to stop the Russians. I think Obama will do nothing and let Russia take over Europe. China will watch Russia make her move and while the world's attention is focused on Europe, China will make her own move in Asia. I think she'll take Taiwan, Vietnam, and maybe Thailand. If the dragon feels strong enough, she may absorb everything in the Pacific all the way to Hawaii."

Lacy looks shocked, "We'd let them do that?"

"How are we going to stop them? Do you think Obama will resort to using nuclear weapons?"

"Never happen. I don't think anyone will ever use them again."

"Then what is he going to do stop the Russians and Chinese?"

"Our military is the strongest in the world."

"Not anymore, plus, most of our equipment is run down from fifteen years of war. Obama keeps reducing the number of troops and retiring weapons systems. The average age of our Air Force fighters is 25 years old. While Russia and China are building and modernizing their military strength, we're reducing ours. We would suffer a very humiliating loss. Obama might send a token force, which will be crushed, it's how he's paying for his transforming America into a more gentle country. Without the strongest and most modern military, no one is going to take us seriously. We're no longer the superpower we were six years ago. Look at ISIS, Egypt and Jordan are carrying the water in attacking them. Before Obama became President, no one would have believed ISIS could have killed American citizens in cold blood live on the Internet without us teaching them a lesson. Most of the country is tired and war-weary, most of the country just wants to be left alone. Then there's the issue of the mainstream media, most of whom won't report a new war, they all but ignored Libya; because they don't want us in another war. The media loves Obama, they'll do anything to make his administration look good."

"I now understand why you want to get the farm with our home."

"Lacy, why don't you call a few moving companies, get quotes for them to pack everything, both of us hate packing. Even if it's an extra couple of thousand, it'll save us the pain of packing everything."

"How are we going to move both of our cars?

"Let the movers take mine, we'll drive yours."

"Where are you going today?"

"I think we'll hang around with the kids another day, we'll start to head back to Virginia after their school lets out. We can break the twelve-hour trip home into two days so we're not so tired when we get home."

"Sounds good to me."

We leave Shelly's at five o'clock and drive for five hours before calling it a night at the next motel we find. The next morning we leave after breakfast and thanks to the good weather we make it home before dark. We're tired from two long days of driving. The next morning, a full week after learning we won the lottery, Lacy looks at me with a worried look on her face. I ask her, "Honey, what's wrong, you look very worried."

"Jay, I'm not used to not working. I looked at the previous week as a mini-vacation, now I don't know what to do."

"Start packing your special items. I'll be back in a couple of hours."

"Where are you going?"

"I want to see about some things we might need if the crap hits the fan." Smiling at Lacy, I imply she should trust me and not ask.

"Can I ask where you're going?"

"I need to check a few things online before I go."

Logging onto a local gun trader site, I start looking for locals who are selling firearms and ammo face to face versus going through an FFL. I want to collect a number of guns that are off the record and can't be traced. The local laws enable face to face sales as long as the selling party checks the ID of the buying partner. I find four people within forty miles who have various AR 15s for sale. I contact each of them agreeing to purchase their rifles. When I return home at 6:00 PM, I have five additional AR 15s adding to the three we already have. I was also able to purchase an additional 25,000 rounds of 5.56 55g FMJ rounds. Lacy informs me tomorrow three moving companies will come by to give us a quote. She sees me carrying the boxes and smiles, saying; "I see where you went, how many are you planning on getting? Knowing you, you're going to arm us and our neighbors."

"I want to have at least twelve ARs, six shotguns and a dozen semi-auto side arms, two or three hundred magazines and at least one hundred thousand rounds of ammo. I'm sure I can fill out our armory in a day or two, cash speaks very loudly."

"Planning on starting our own small army? Who are you planning on invading? I hope it's Italy, I love their shoes and bags. I want you to know, I don't jump out of perfectly good airplanes. If you're going to invade Italy, I expect you to fly me to Rome first class." Lacy broke out laughing.

"When everything falls apart, this may be what stands between us and mobs trying to take what's ours."

"I hope you're getting them at a good price. Jay, I don't like the picture you're painting. Frankly it's starting to scare me."

"Lacy, I got them at a very good price, cash talks. Honey, I really hope I'm wrong. I'd rather have these and not need them than need them and not have them."

"I agree. But, I'm allowed to be nervous."

"Of course you are. Honey, I'm going to do everything possible to protect you and our extended family. Tomorrow, I'm going to call Fred and see if he can find a local company to install solar panels on both houses and a couple of windmills. I want us to be able to survive without relying on the grid. I want us to be able to generate all of the electrical energy we need. I'd also like a few more wells dug and a fire suppression system installed in our homes and Fred's barn."

Lacy sips a glass of wine saying, "What's next? Are you going to build a bunker under our new house?"

"Yes, I'm researching prebuilt shelters which only need a hole dug, they can be installed in a couple of days."

"Jay, you really are serious about turning the new house into a shelter, aren't you?"

"Honey, I'm going to have bars and heavy metal screens placed over the windows. I want a heavy duty fence built around us and a barricade to stop anyone from driving their vehicles into the front of our house. I want us to be self-sufficient and able to protect what's ours."

"How much do you think this is all going to cost?"

"I guess no more than another $500,000."

"What?"

"That includes a couple of jeeps and freeze dried food to feed twelve people for two years."

"Wasn't the entire idea of the farm so we had food available?"

"I like to have a backup to the backup plan."

"What else are you planning?"

"Since the house uses propane, I'm going to see about getting multiple tanks and also buried fuel tanks for our cars. I'd also like to have an external garage built for the kid's cars or any other cars we purchase so they're not kept outside."

"How long are you planning for us to be self-sufficient?"

"Years if necessary. If the market crashes, it could be a long time before things get back to normal. I'm not sure we'll ever get back to the way we are now."

"Why do you think that?"

"If my theory is correct, I expect Russia is going to move to absorb what's going to be left of Europe. Our currency is going to crash. The economy is going to have to be restructured in order to get our country back on its feet. If we go to war against Russia or China, we could lose many of our import and export markets. Think about the number of imported products which could have parts and support cut off. Almost all of our consumer electronics come from China or someplace else in Asia. If they close the faucet for parts and new products, no one will be able to get new TVs or computers until new factories are built here. When our existing products break, they'll be useless without parts. It could be years before new factories are built. Parts will be in short supply or simply not available. I want to make sure we have extra computers, televisions and two-way radios stored away. I also want to build a small Faraday cage to protect our spare computers and portable backup drives. I want to store replacement parts for almost everything we use."

"What are you going to do if nothing happens?"

"Then you get to laugh at me while we live in a 7,000 square foot house. One large enough we can play hide and seek in. We'll also have a basement full of parts we can sell on eBay for 15% of what we paid for them. Even if we lose another $500 to $750,000, we'll still have over $22 million left to live on. If everything improves and I'm totally wrong; say we end up throwing everything away, we'll still have more than enough to live on. We'll have enough that the kids and grandchildren will be set for life too. Frankly, I'd rather have something we need and not need it than need it and not have it."

"OK, I'm not used to having money."

"I know it feels strange to be spending as we are. Lacy, we're going to be OK. I think the timing of our win couldn't have been any better." The ringing phone interrupts us. I check the caller ID, smiling, I answer, "Hello Fred, what's new?"

"Jay, Cheri and I talked about what you offered us, how much will we have to pay you back a month?"

"Fred, nothing in the winter, since you're not growing anything, the spring, summer, and fall will be a sliding scale based on your crop yield and the market price."

"You know, you're one crazy SOB."

"Yeah, I am, what do you think?"

"I like it, it's the best deal and the most farmer friendly deal I've ever seen, we called the bank, we offered them $700,000, they turned us down."

"With your permission I'll call. I have a different tack I'd like to try with them."

"Go ahead. Have fun."

"Fred, I'd like you to check with local companies who can install solar panels on both of our homes and build a couple of windmills. I'd also like a few additional wells dug and security bars installed over our windows."

"Expecting a storm?"

"You might say, I'm expecting an economic storm from the European collapse."

"My sons say the same thing."

"We're going to get along perfectly."

"What else should I be doing?"

"I want to have an external four car garage built and, by the way, how's your barn?"

"I know people who can build the garage." Laughing Fred continues, "My barn is falling apart, I think it's forty years old."

"Get a quote to rebuild it, Fred, get quotes for a solid barn, based on a steel infrastructure and the walls made of preformed concrete or steel reinforced concrete. I'd also like to get quotes for fire suppression systems for our homes, your new barn, and the garage."

"You are expecting trouble."

"I just want to make sure we can't be burned out."

"Jay, I'll get right on it and call you tomorrow night."

"Night Fred, give our best to your family."

Lacy asks, "How did he take it?"

"I think he's smiling, sounds like his sons' are thinking along similar lines."

While we're getting ready for bed, 1,300 miles away in Sammi's house, Ricky was saying, "Did I ever tell you, your dad's crazy. He always thinks the world's going to end. His name should be changed to Chicken Little. All I hear from him is prepare for this or that. A year ago he was on a tear that the New Madrid fault line was going to cause a massive earthquake. It hasn't caused an earthquake has it? Then he was going on about a solar flare or EMP or something like that, I couldn't understand what he was going on about. I don't think there's anyway some sort of flare on the sun can hurt our power. He's always going on about some disaster or another. Can't he ever live in the here and now and be happy? Christ, he just won $28 million, all he shared with us was $100,000. He's buying a huge house he wants us to move in with him? Why would I give up my job to move to Nashville, we don't even like Country music. Honey, I hate to suggest this, but I think your father needs professional help."

"Honey, he's OK, he's always liked to stock up on things. He's always been worried about different disasters. He's always liked to be prepared. When we were young, after the divorce, he used to visit us every other week. He would take us food shopping and stock us up with food, even then, he stocked us up on a couple of months worth of food. He was always worried we'd be hungry. He didn't have to give us anything, but he gave us $100,000 plus any new car we wanted and don't forget he's paying for Linda's college education."

"I think he should have given us more. You're his oldest and we didn't get enough to buy a new house. I bet he's expanding the number of guns in his house too. I don't want our daughter staying in his house since he has guns in his house."

"I'll tell him we're thinking about it, it'll buy us time."

"You can tell him anything you want, I'm not moving and giving up everything we have here. He really needs some professional help. If I talked to Lacy do you think she will be able to guide him towards professional help?"

"Don't approach her about my dad. She will eat you up and spit you out. They've been together for 22 years, you didn't know him before Lacy. He's much calmer now. They love each other. If you go to Lacy, she'll tell my dad, you'll be driving a large divide between us. I love my father. He may be a little different, but he means well. He's trying to protect us. He wants to protect us if something bad happens and he wants us to know we have a safe place to go."

"He's so full of it, nothing's going to happen. President Obama has reduced our military, the rest of the world no longer sees us as the threat Bush made us into. Our relations with the rest of the world are much better now. If I can't talk to Lacy than I'm thinking of reporting your dad as an unbalanced person who owns guns."

"Ricky, please don't do that. It'll backfire. You don't want to piss my dad off."

"OK, but if he does anything to introduce our daughter to guns, I'm going to report him."

"You know how much he loves Linda, she's his princess, he would never do anything to put her in harm."

"He's too radical for my tastes."

"Ricky, he thinks the same about you. One day the two of you should sit down and try to clear the air."

"Not going to happen. He's everything I'm against. He thinks Obama is the worst President we've every had, I think he's the best. We're on opposite sides of every issue.

"I'm asking you, just please don't rock the boat between my dad and me."

"Okay, for now. As long as he doesn't place our daughter in a dangerous situation."

"Okay, Ricky, please, just go slow and don't piss my dad off."

Chapter 5

Three weeks to the day after winning the lottery everything we own in Virginia is on an Atlas Van Lines moving truck on the way to Nashville. Fred has been great in helping us move in. He lined up companies to install the fire suppression system, security bars, solar panels and the windmills. Three new wells have already been dug and plumbed. The windmills are going to be installed the week of March 23. I can't forget Fred laughing when I told him we got the bank to accept $650,000 to pay off the mortgage on his farm. Lacy and I now owned Fred's farm, he said he now had the best lender in the country. Fred told us his, and now our neighbors might be interested in doing a similar arrangement with us. I told him we'd to look into it sometime after we moved into our new home. I thought it might make sense to increase the size of the farm. The next day the EU officially died when the United Kingdom announced on Valentine's Day they were leaving the Union. The Euro will cease to be a traded currency on March 2. Since the UK's announcement, the dollar has increased in value by 30%. Gold is currently trading at $2,895 an ounce and with the average cost of our gold at $1,670, means we've made $1,225 per ounce! I requested the agents to convert our holdings into gold coins and send them to us. We agreed to purchase an additional $100,000 of gold coins and $200,000 of US Silver Eagles. The sales agent was so happy, he gave us a discount on the new purchase. Due to the quantity and high value of our purchases the agent kept trying to get us to leave our coins on deposit with them. We declined, demanding all of our coins be delivered to our new address. The dealer agreed and suggested that they send our coins in an armored truck. Lacy and I decided to purchase a couple of safes, ones we'll have bolted and then cemented to a secret sub- basement we had dug. It takes six people to manhandle the safes into the sub-basement.

Winter held on with a late winter storm that dumped nine inches of snow on us just as we finished loading our townhouse. The unexpected snowstorm delaying our exit from Northern Virginia for a couple of days. Interstate 81 runs through the mountains and the moving truck driver didn't think it was safe to continue the journey. We hung out at a Hampton Motel for a couple of days waiting for the roads to clear. We spent the time looking at the pictures Fred sent us, spring had arrived in Nashville. Fred started his spring planting which hopefully should yield us a good crop of peas, corn, soybeans, green beans, tomatoes, and peppers.

The moving van driver said it will take him two days to reach our new home. He laughed saying, it could have been done in one day. However, the new government regulations limited them to drive only six hours a day. Lacy and I drove without stopping for the night. We arrived in time to take Fred, Cheri, Mark and Ryan to dinner. Fred and Cheri brought us up to date on the work that was done on our house and their farm the previous three weeks. After dinner we checked into a local Hampton Inn, the Atlas Van Lines driver called to inform us he'll be at our home the next morning at 9:00 AM. He estimated he will have us unloaded in four hours. I agreed since we sold or gave away most of our furniture before moving. We figure we'll buy most of our furnishings new. We spoke with a furniture store manager who agreed to open early for us. We met him at 7:00 AM, he agreed to show us what they have in stock and what they can get in a very short time.

We ordered two sets of bunk beds for our young grandkids, two king bedroom sets, one each for Sammi and Shells, couches, love seats, a kitchen table and chairs, coffee tables, and lamps. We finished at 8:30 AM when we had to rush to meet the movers at our house. Pulling up, we were surprised to see the movers were waiting for us, as was Verizon and Best Buy. The Verizon installer asked us which number was going to be our prime and where we wanted the WiFi modem installed. The Best Buy installers wanted to get the large screen TV's wall mounted before the movers brought the furniture in. The first couple of hours were a mad rush of people running in and out of the house. At 3:00 PM, just as the movers are leaving, our new furniture arrived. By the time they left at 7:00 PM we were so tired, we couldn't even think about dinner. We were surprised when our doorbell rang, Fred and Cheri stood on our front porch with arms full of home cooked hot food. The four of us broke in our new kitchen table sharing our first meal in our new home. We spent the next three days unpacking and getting to know our new home. The solar panels had been installed, along with a battery room filled with large submarine batteries. We also ordered four multi-fuel generators which are going to be wired into the network powering Fred's and our homes. The windmills will be installed in three weeks, enabling us to completely live off the grid. Even without the generators we were creating more electrical energy than we used, our system automatically sold our excess back to the grid. We had a switch installed to block the transfer, allowing us to store the extra electricity in large batteries. We were now assured of electrical power even if the grid failed, our water came from our own wells, enough to irrigate our crops and provide both houses with all the water we'd need. We have our existing wells and the three new ones we sealed for future use. The new ones drew from different underground streams hopefully ensuring we always had water. Our windows are covered with steel security bars with the space between the bars covered in stainless steel heavy duty mesh. Construction people were coming to start building a patio/barricade in front of both of the homes. Our next major project is the fence around our land. Fred sent me a quote for the fence which almost knocked me out. I'd forgotten we now had over 250 acres. The fence was way too expensive, we'd have to think of another way to protect what's ours.

Early the next morning two large gun safes arrived with the crew to install them. They were installed in the secret sub-basement. Unless someone knew where the hidden access in the sub-basement was, no one would ever find the safes Lacy started to plan dinner, for the first time since we moved in, she's going to cook dinner for us and Fred and Cheri.

After dinner, Fred, Cheri, Lacy and I sat in our family room watching the news on our new 80-inch television. We had both cable and satellite TV services, figuring that if one went down the other would function as a backup. We also had both set up for internet support. The news was very depressing. China and Russia had started dumping their US dollars, pushing the dollar's price down and the price of gold up. Living conditions in Greece were quickly falling apart because no one outside of Greece would accept Drachmas in payment for anything. Italy, Spain, France, and Portugal found themselves in the same situation as Greece. Basic necessities like toilet paper, over the counter medications and spare parts which have to be imported from anywhere outside from the countries, were nonexistent. Fred asked, "Jay, how bad do you think things are going to get?"

"I think it's going to get much worse. When the US dollar collapses, it's going to be much worse here than what's going on in Europe. Many of the countries in Europe have had a year's experience living with shortages and brown-blackouts. They voted for the socialist government in Greece because they were tired of the shortages and having their pensions and pay cut. Had they thought through their situation they would have realized the only way out was for their government to cut spending, not increase it. They got what they asked for. Here in America, the current administration has created an entitlement mentality and the administration's pushing us to the edge of a race and class war. Our poor would be considered the upper class in many countries. What's going to happen when people's Obama phones stop working when their monthly government deposits aren't made? We have 100 million people out of work, they have no savings, when the government has to stop payments people are going to starve, they'll quickly turn to crime to feed their families. Things are going to turn bad very quickly."

"Jay, how quickly do you think this is going to happen?"

"Fred, Russia and China are dumping US dollars, they're destroying the value of the dollar by dumping it for pennies. They've declared financial war against America. Our problem is, the smartest man to ever be President isn't smart enough to realize they've already declared war. The Fed is buying dollars at inflated prices doing even more long term damage to the dollar. Can you imagine what would happen if China would demand immediate repayment of our debt?"

Fred frowns asking, "Do you think they would do that? It seems a little extreme to me."

"Remember, I said Russia and China have already declared war. If I were in their shoes, I'd crash Wall Street while I placed billions of dollars worth of short sales. That way, when the market goes into freefall, they'll make hundreds of billions off of our slide into hell. When the collapse of the free world happens, they'll be in a position to take over the world. There's no one who can stop them in Europe. Putin will move into Europe promising to restore order, promising to feed and care for the people. The people of Europe will welcome the Russians with open arms and lifted dress hems. When the dust settles, Russia will control all of Europe. Their empire will stretch from the English Channel to the Pacific. Their second goal will be to take over all of the oil reserves in the Middle East. They'll create wars among the various Middle Eastern countries when they're all weakened by the wars the Russians will just roll in and take over all of the oil. They'll kill the fanatics so they won't have to deal with any insurgency. They may leave Israel alone because they don't have any oil. While Russia is taking over Europe and the Middle East, China will absorb all of Asia and ultimately even absorb Hawaii."

Fred looks at me, "Holy shit. It's going to be World War 3."

"I don't think so because we won't have enough of a government left to order an attack on Russia or China. When the dollar crashes, the government will order the banks and stock markets closed so they can stall for time. Time they won't have. American's aren't used to shortages so when the market crashes and the banks close, they will get scared and panic. When the government welfare programs end, the people won't have any money. They're going to be hungry, tired and really pissed off. Almost no-one is going to know what happened to them. They'll riot. The rioting is going to make the worst of the race riots look like a college protest march. They're going to tear everything in their path apart looking for food and water. The cities are going to be burnt to the ground, tens of millions are going to die."

Cheri says, "Now it all makes sense. Now I understand why you're building all of the security features into our homes. I understand why you bought the house next to us, why you built a backup for the electrical system and dug the additional wells. Do you think the rioters will find us out here in the middle of nowhere?"

"Cheri, we're 43 miles north of Nashville. When the crash happens and Nashville is a smoking ruin, people will be streaming out in all directions. Most won't make it this far, those that do will be the ones who are survivors, ones who've learned how to adapt to the conditions. The ones who find us will be the hardened ones; they'll be the ones who've gotten this far by killing to take what they need to survive. There are three options I see. One, they're going to be hungry, begging for handouts or two, there are going to be mobs of college students who are used to handouts. They're going to be worst of the survivors, hardened criminals and gangs who survived by taking what they want."

"Would the fences you planned keep the refugees off our land?"

"I think they might have slowed them down, but not stop them, which is one reason I stopped the project. 250 acres is a large area to fence."

Cheri continues, "Jay, speaking of which, three of our neighbors would like to sell you based on similar terms as you gave us."

"How many acres do they have?"

"The three of them have a little over 700 when you combine their farms together."

Fred says, "That would give you 950 acres, not counting your 5 for a grand total of 955, more than enough to keep us self-sufficient forever."

Shaking my head, "If we can't fence 250 acres, how are we going to fence and protect over 950? We don't have the bodies to protect that large of an area. I like the idea of being self-sufficient, it's just, I never thought about such a large area."

Lacy responds, "Honey, we have time, maybe we'll think of an idea, Cheri, how much do your three friends need to join us?"

Cheri tried to whisper the answer, afraid the number will scare us away from the idea, "Lacy, it will take close to $2.5 million to acquire them from the banks."

I'm thinking of something nice to say when Cheri says, "Jay, I know that's a lot of money. Before you answer, think of this, the three farms are the ones on our other three sides, the four of us form a large box."

Thinking about it, I ask, "Does anyone have a map of the area to show me? I'd like to see what this box looks like. What's on the other side of the box? Other than land, what else would they bring us?"

Fred and Cheri smile, Cheri says, "When you two get settled, we'll arrange a dinner together. That way you can meet them, let them explain why they think they would be a good fit for our little group."

I'm starting to get angry, I'm afraid Fred and Cheri broke our security by telling their neighbors what our plans are. "Fred, Cheri, did you tell them why I helped you with the bank? Or what we're doing? Did you breach our security?"

Cheri said, "Jay, maybe just a little, they came over for lunch last week, they saw all of the activity, they saw the new barn being built. They couldn't help but see it's being built with steel and cement versus wood. They saw the solar panels installed on our roof and the windmill foundations being laid. They're not dumb, they know what our crop yields are. They wanted to know what changed. Just six weeks ago we told them we were going to lose our home and farm, now they see all of this money being spent. They knew something was different. I couldn't lie to them, we knew not to tell them anything important. We told them we couldn't tell them anything. Rich, one of our neighbors said our property looks like a prepper homestead. Jill, his wife, remarked she'd seen a program on TV about preppers who lived off the grid and she asked if we could tell them how we're affording the changes. They have been thinking of doing something similar too."

Trying to hold my voice under control, and hold my temper in check, I knew my face was getting red, I said as slowly and quietly as I could manage, "Cheri, what did you tell them?"

"I told them we came into some money from a family member who passed away. I felt so bad lying to them. I didn't know what else to tell them. The next day Jill called telling me she knows our mortgage was paid off, she said she was at the bank when the manager told her our mortgage was paid off. The manager told her someone bought our farm from the bank. They came over and asked me if our house and the work being done on your house were related."

"So they guessed the person who bought this house was also paying for the upgrades being done to your house?"

"That's what they think. Jill asked if they could meet the family that purchased the house. I told them we didn't know when you were moving in. Once you did, we'd check with you."

"I see, I want to think about it for a couple of days."

"Sure, no problem. I hope you're not angry with us. You've done so much for our family."

Before I could answer, our front doorbell rang. Since it was 7:30 PM, I knew it couldn't be any of the workers, we had everything that was supposed to be delivered. I looked at my phone which showed me the video from the hidden camera looking at the front door. I turn my phone to show Cheri, "Could this be Jill and Rich?"

Looking at my phone, Cheri nodded yes.

I open the front door to welcome our guests, "Hello Rich and Jill, welcome to our new home, I'm Jay."

Rich asks, "How do you know who we are?"

"Come in, I think a couple of your neighbors confirmed who you are."

"You have a camera by the front door? I looked for one and didn't see it." Rich said.

"If you had seen it, then the security company I hired should be fired. Come in, would you like some coffee and dessert?"

Rich and Jill entered our kitchen, they pause seeing Fred and Cheri sitting in our family room. Lacy smiles at our guests saying, "I think it's nice you came over to help us unpack with Fred and Cheri." I laugh, patting a very surprised Rich on the back. "Rich, I guess you stopped by to give us a pitch, something about a deal we can't refuse right?"

Fred and Cheri laughed at my attempted joke.

Jill handed Lacy a bakery box saying, "We come bearing gifts."

We all laughed, realizing the cake was going to cost me over $1 million.

Chapter 6

The 92-year-old King of Saudi Arabia suddenly died from natural causes, his brother became the Kingdom's new King. He announced he was lowering the price of 'sweet crude' to $39.00 a barrel. His intent was to force the American fracking industry into bankruptcy. Once the American fracking industry collapsed, he planned to increase prices again giving his family control over the world's oil industry. He could afford to take the financial hit as long as it drove his new competition out of business. The negative result of the reduced oil prices is the employment surge happening in the Dakotas, Texas, West Virginia and other states came to a halt. New unemployment claims in the first week after the King's announcement jumped by more than 600,000 new claims. Construction companies started failing as their orders were canceled. The unemployment rate multiplied. Since unemployed people don't go out to eat, nor do they purchase new cars or televisions, even unrelated companies like mom and pop dry cleaners failed. The Department of Labor reported new unemployment claims are running at a rate of 750,000 a week, home foreclosures are quickly rising to levels not seen since 2008. The banks that in 2008 and 09 were too big to fail started to fail. The only lesson they'd learned from the previous meltdown was the Federal Government would bail them out. Their investment portfolios were losing money, their mortgage-backed investments were losing money, mortgages, car, and personal loans are being defaulted on it numbers that exceeded 2008.

The US dollar, which had risen in value when the EU collapsed and was now in freefall. The dollar's collapse pushed up the value of gold and silver, By March 23, the cost of an ounce of gold was $3,800.00. An ounce of silver sold for $1150.00. Both continue to climb, setting new records every day, I internally laughed, because every penny the price of precious metals went up, the more our portfolio was worth.

March 21st, the first day of spring, was the date the Russian Federation launched their attack against the US dollar. The Russian Ministry of Finance had previously issued a short sell order for a trillion dollars worth of US public company shares, which went effect the moment the market opened on March 23rd. The New York Stock Market opened down 700 points, taking every broker by surprise. The market continued to fall for the following four days. At the end of the week, the market was down 4,800 points and in free fall. Other investors and countries also issued sell orders increasing the downward pressure on the market. At the close of the market on March 31st, the Dow Jones index fell from a high of 19,000 to 3500. The market continued to fall until it hit 1550 on Black Friday, May 17. Tens of millions of people were wiped out in the great market crash of 2015. Like the crash of 1929, investors jumped to their death from brokerage offices all over New York City. Average families lost their pensions and their life savings. There were so many foreclosures the banks couldn't keep up with the paperwork. Courts became backed up nine months hearing foreclosure cases. Shootouts took place among people who tried to stop repossession companies from taking their cars for non-payment of their loans. Stores closed at record rates, large shopping malls became empty spaces that were taken over by the homeless looking for places to stay out of the weather. Every day saw additional families move into the closed malls, the 'old timers' helped the new families settle into the malls. The 'to large to fail' banks were all begging the Department of the Treasury for a bailout, which the Republican-held Congress refused to pass. The Republican leader of the Senate, Mitch McConnell is quoted as saying, "We have to allow the markets to correct themselves. In 2008, the government bailed everyone out which caused today's meltdown. The markets never corrected their core problems and the bailouts only delayed the inevitable. The Senate today has taken action to send bills to the President's desk to cut all personal and corporate taxes to a flat 4%. The House has passed an emergency revised budget, which cuts Federal Spending by 30%. The President has vetoed both bills, saying his administration demands an increase in government spending. Congress and the President are at an impasse and we call upon every American to write to the President to tell him to sign our emergency budget and to cut taxes."

On March 31st, the modifications to our home and Fred's were finished. The hardest part of our independence was getting the local approvals for our fuel tanks. It took two weeks and a large monetary gift to a bureaucrat to get our permits issued. It took another week to get the tanks installed and a further five days to get them filled. I'd like to have more fuel on hand. However, we couldn't get permits for more than we had been issued. Lacy and I ended up buying the other three farms for just under $2 million. They were each only able to get permits for a 1,000-gallon propane tank and two 200 gallon tanks, one for gasoline, and one for diesel. Fred's farm has three 1,000 gallon underground propane tanks each holding 800 gallons of propane. We also had one 20,000 gallon tank of gasoline standing in Fred's new barn. In addition, we had two 5,000 gallon tanks filled with diesel fuel. I've reminded everyone not to touch the stored fuel until the town's fuel was gone. We treated the fuel to keep it fresh and we planned to check it monthly to ensure it was usable. The tanks are going to be our strategic reserve. I bought two tank trucks so we could keep our cars and equipment topped up from the stations in town. Every week one of us drove the tanker trucks into town to top them off. If we got overrun and lost the farms forcing us to bug out, we'd have our own fuel trucks to keep our vehicles fueled. The only real problem with us bugging out was, we'd be just another roving mob looking for safety and security. We started building reinforced concrete shelters around the fuel tanks so they couldn't be shot and explode. We needed a more secure place to stay if we got overrun. We needed a shelter, one that could protect us and allow us to remain hidden and secure for years if it came to that. Finding a company to sell us a shelter was another problem.

We all knew this was the end of the American dream. While Congress and the President argued with each other, the country was dying. As America died, so did freedom. Without a welfare safety net, 50% of the country will starve having nothing and no one to catch them when they were hungry. They will take to the streets using violence to take what they think they are entitled to. I tell Lacy, "This is the beginning of the end. This is how the American dream dies. The dream is going to die not with a whimper, but with violence and blood. Too many Americans don't know how to work, they have an entitlement mentality. They'll sit home waiting for their government check which isn't going to come. When they realize no check is coming, they'll turn to violence. They'll take what they want. They don't know any other way. Crime rates are going to soar, people will be afraid to go out, more companies and businesses are going to close. The closings will add to the unemployed who will be looking for help and handouts from the Feds who don't have anything to give. I'd be surprised if the Stock Market index isn't under 1,000 by July 4th."

President Obama responded to McConnell's speech by saying he was going to use his executive power to mandate welfare payments which he's going to fund through taxes on people's savings, checking and investment accounts. Any account with between $100,000 and $250,000 will have a special one-time tax of 10%. Those accounts with combined balances of $250,000 to $750,000 will be taxed at 12% and all accounts over $750,000 will be assessed a one-time tax of 15%." This was going to hurt our plans. When we won the lottery, we placed the bulk of our funds offshore but when the EU started to fail, we moved the funds back to US and Canadian banks. With the newly announced taxes, I had to quickly get as much of our funds out of US banks or converted into hard assets as quickly as possible. Our accountant convinced me to put more than half of our money in Switzerland. We also kept two large safe deposit boxes, each was filled with two million in cash. This we moved into a new hidden safe in our sub-basement. We recently added a second large safe in the sub-basement filled with gold and silver coins. We don't know what the coins are going to be worth in the future, we're just happy to have them. Lacy looks at me saying, "Jay, I know what you're thinking, stay calm. Most of our money is safe. Even if we end up having to pay the tax, we're going to be fine."

"I know, it's just that I hate that man. I worry he's going to force the Swiss into telling the Department of Treasury who owns accounts in their banks, then the IRS will tax us on our offshore holdings."

Lacy nods in her understanding, she says, "I didn't think he could issue an executive order taxing our bank accounts. I thought only Congress had the power to set taxes."

"Lacy, in normal times, I'd agree with you. He knows that any suits will take years to work their way through the courts, whichever way a judge rules, there'll be an appeal, it's going to take years before this is decided, during which he'll be collecting the taxes."

"Honey, what about an injunction blocking his Executive Order?"

"Good question, I think that even if different groups brought suit, a judge is going to say the case should be heard, thus taking years."

"So we're screwed?"

"In a word, maybe."

@@@@@

I had previously made an agreement with the Wise Company in Utah for the purchase of a year's supply of food for thirty people. It was very expensive since every survival food company was back ordered for over a year. They contacted me on

March 31st, telling me if I still wanted my order it had to be paid for up front and picked up right away. It cost me $75,000 to ensure we were moved to the front of the line and the promise we'd pay in cash. I asked Fred to send his two sons in a truck to Utah to pick up the food and drive it home. They made the 1700 mile trip in 30 hours. Due to bad spring storms, it took them 45 hours to return with the food. The farmers thought I'd gone crazy buying the freeze dried food, they argued the whole reason I bought the farms was to have a supply of food. I replied with the question, "What are we going to eat if the fields get burned or due to outlaws we can't harvest the crops? What about if the government shows up to take our crops? I like to eat, don't you?"

Fred and Rich asked if things were going to get that bad. I told them there was a good chance that law and order are going to break down, making the country like the old Wild West. I told them things were going to be worse than anything in our worst nightmares.

We've named ourselves the Portland Families, named after the closest town, Portland, Tennessee. The four families are, Lacy and I, Fred and Cheri, their sons Mark and Ryan. Rich and Jill, who have a son Jon, and a daughter Liz, they live next to Fred and Cheri. Randy and his wife Janice, and their teenage son Bob own the farm that borders Randy's. The last of our group is Paul and Flo. They have two teenage sons named Bill and Joe. Our group, without our kids, numbers seventeen. Seventeen people to defend over 900 acres. Working the acreage isn't a problem with the machinery we have. I'm not sure if it's possible to defend our land with such a small number of people spread out over such a large area. We need to build defensive positions and find a way to multiply our small force to protect us and what's ours. We need what the military calls a force multiplier, something that enabled the seventeen of us to defeat numbers ten or more times our numbers.

On the evening of March 31st, we invited our neighbors to a meeting at our house. We laid out cold beer, wine and sodas for the kids. Lacy prepared some snacks for everyone. I prepared a large map of our property. When everyone is seated with a snack and drink, I got started with the reason why I invited everyone together. "Everyone, thank you for coming over on this lovely spring evening. I hope you're all comfortable." Everyone nods their agreement. I sip my diet root beer, not wanting to drink until we've covered the key points of the meeting. "I'm sure everyone's heard the news about the economic meltdown. It's happening quicker than I thought it would happen. The economy and the country are on the way into the crapper. There are seventeen of us, we have over 900 acres of land between us." Fred laughs, saying, "Actually, Jay, you own 955 acres. We're your tenant farmers." Everyone laughs.

"Fred, thank you for reminding me. The very reason I asked everyone over tonight is to discuss how we're going to defend what's ours."

Jill asks, "Jay, do you think it's come to that? Do you really think people will come after us? We're north of Nashville, most people won't be able to walk this far or find us since we're not located on any main road. We have crops to get into the ground, we have farm work that needs to be done. None of us has any military training. We all know how to shoot, but we're farmer's, not warriors."

"Jill, I expect the economy and the country to collapse much quicker than any of us expected. The stock market is headed down faster than a crashing plane. I'm expecting the government to come apart within ninety days and when that happens, the entitlement class is going to realize there won't be any more checks coming. They are going to riot to get food to feed their families. When the cities run out of food, the hungry will flee the cities like waves of locusts stripping fields. They'll find us and they'll try to take by force what they want. Farms will be one of their major targets because they'll assume farms have food. The hungry will do anything to feed their families."

"Randy asks, "Jay, what are you proposing?"

"Here's a map of our area. At first I thought we could build a wall to surround our land, I soon learned that's out due to cost and manpower. I now think we ought to be able to string barb wire around our land. No one is going to bat an eye to four farms buying a lot of barbwire, you use it all of the time to keep your animals on your land."

Fred nods, saying, "Yes, we all have rolls of barb wire we use to close off the fields so our animals don't wander off. Since all of our farms are now one, we can use the barbed wire to string along the border of our land. If we need more, it's available at a number of local stores."

"Fred, I suggest we send a couple of the kids to town first thing tomorrow to buy up as much barbed wire as possible and anything else. We should get everything we can think of now before the prices skyrocket or the local stores run out of what we need."

Paul nods, "Great idea, we'll make a list of what each of us needs then we'll combine it into one master list. We'll send the kids into town tomorrow in one of our larger trucks to get everything on the list."

"Paul, great. The next thing I want to discuss is the second layer of defense. We have a couple of backhoes in our group. I suggest we dig a trench connecting each home. My thought is if we come under attack, we'll use the trenches for fighting positions, the trench will give us some protection from the invaders. While the trenches are dug, we can use the soil removed from the trenches for sandbags piled in front of the trench. I think the trench should be five feet deep and go from home to home and circle back. One large circle." I draw it on the map. Everyone stands up to look at the map I have on the wall. They nod in agreement. "We're also going to need a way to slow any attackers down before they hit the trench line. I suggest we dig trenches in our driveways to stop any vehicles coming to attack us."

Cheri asks, "How do we get in or out if we have trenches dug in our driveways?"

"Good question, we cover them with steel plates like the highway department uses. When everything is fine, we cover the trenches in our driveways with the plates, at night and in times of potential attack we remove the plates uncovering the trenches. In risky times, we cover the trenches in our driveways with painted bed sheets so anyone approaching us won't notice they're about to drive into a trench. I expect any attack will come at night so we should also rig up motion activated lamps to light up all around our homes and barns. A third line of defense I suggest is a series of small pits around the natural approaches to our homes. I'm hoping these catch the attackers after they've dismounted from their vehicles. These pits should be on the sides of the driveway and the approaches to our homes from the street. We should also remove any large trees from around our homes. Large trees can be used as cover for the attackers. We can use the wood cut for firewood and to build defensive positions. We want to have a clear field of fire in front of the trenches. We can't leave anything that could give invaders any cover."

Janice says, "My fruit and shade trees? No. I've been tending to those trees for fifteen years."

Flo says, "Janice, why can't we transplant them? The holes left behind could make good traps."

Janice isn't happy, but nods. "Flo, you better help me."

Flo says, "Janice, I know a company that plants trees, I'll call them tomorrow."

I continue, "I also suggest we circle our homes and property with hunting traps, this will stop many when they get their foot or ankles broken. If we can get enough traps, we should hide some along the inside of the barbwire. If people get through the barbed wire, they'll run into the hidden traps. If they get through the traps, they will have to get past the small pits. If they get through those, the motion-activated lights will go on. I'm expecting large numbers of people to try to attack, our goal is to be slow them down and stop them before they get close to our homes. Anything we can do to delay them, to reduce their numbers, reduces the numbers we're going to have to actually fight. We might even scare them enough to leave before they reach our homes."

Randy adds, "Jay, we should have an alarm system that goes off when anyone gets past the barbed wire. If we wait until the lights turn on, we won't have enough time to defend our homes."

"Good idea, however, I don't know how to rig an alarm like that."

Janice says, "I know a really good alarm company in town, I'll call them tomorrow."

"Perfect, thanks, Janice."

Matt says, "Can I ask something?"

"Sure, Matt, what's on your mind?"

"Let's assume people get through everything, what do we do?"

"Matt, then we fight. I should have asked this before, do you all have weapons?"

We go around the room, at the end of the count, which I mark on a large sheet of paper tacked to the wall. "We have between us, five shotguns, four hunting rifles and three Ruger 10/22s. I have twelve AR15s and four home defense shotguns, plus our semi-auto handguns."

Matt asks, "Jay, what's the difference in our shotguns and yours?"

"Good question. Yours are configured for hunting with a 26-inch barrel, mine are configured for close shooting with an 18 and ½ inch barrel. A last resort weapon. We're going to need additional weapons in order to arm everyone. I've asked a few people I know for help, we should get a response in a day or two."

Randy asks, "What are you looking to buy, I know the owner of the local gun store."

"He's not going to have what we want or need."

Fred says, "Huh?"

"You'll see."

We agree on the plans and the next day construction begins on our defenses. Matt and Ryan go to town picking up rolls of barbed and razor wire and hundreds of hunting traps. They purchase every trap within twenty miles of our homes. I get the call I've been waiting for. I call Fred, who agrees to take a trip with me. "Lacy, Fred and I are going to make a quick run to the border."

"Please be careful."

"I will be. I love you."

Fred and I leave on our clandestine trip to acquire additional guns. I got the name of a gun supplier from a friend of a friend of a friend. We exchanged messages through daily changed burner phones, we exchanged the numbers through encrypted emails. The contact informed me he could fill my order, as long as I agreed to a few conditions such as paying in gold or silver and doing the transaction in person. Each of us agreed to come to the exchange position with only one other person. I agreed to his demands because I had no choice. The meet and exchange was to take place in San Antonio, Texas, Fred and I swapped driving every three hours which allowed us to make the trip in 15 hours straight. We didn't want to spend the night anywhere with the amount of gold we were carrying. The exchange went off without a hitch. Our seller was very happy with the gold coins. I was very happy to be the new owner of two cases of US Army M4s (12 fully automatic assault rifles). One case of 6 fully automatic Uzi 9mm submachine guns and silencers for the rifles and Uzis. My big surprise was the seller was able to get us two RPG rocket launchers and 8 missiles, plus twenty-five hand grenades. He also had 50,000 rounds of 5.56 and 30,000 rounds of 9mm ammo. I asked for more, but that was all he could supply at this time. He told me, demand for weapons was the highest he'd ever seen, the reason he agreed to sell me anything was I offered to pay him in gold. We returned home 16 hours after leaving San Antonio, keeping our speed to just under the speed limit the entire drive home. The last thing we needed was to get busted with a truck full of illegal weapons. Our seller made his way back to Mexico. He promised to contact me if he was able to acquire additional weapons. On the way home, I converted an additional two million dollars into gold and silver. I was lucky to do so because the next day the Federal Government issued new tax rules that taxed all purchases of precious metals. Bars or coins with an excise tax of 20% of the value of the transaction. The stock market fell an additional 650 points before it was closed early for 'technical reasons' with the announcement of the excise tax. Fred asked me, "Are you taking a huge hit in the market crash?"

Laughing, I respond, "Nope, I never trusted the market. I invested in gold, silver and four farms. Do you think the farms will be a good investment?"

Fred smiles while nodding his agreement, "Best investment you ever made. Jay, why the automatic weapons and all of the trenches? Do you really think we're going to have to fight the people around us?"

"When people realize we have four working farms with food and fuel, I'm sure we're going to be close to the top of their places to visit. What really worries me is the people who installed our tanks will blab about them. When the government money stops, and it will stop, people are going to go crazy. When they get hungry enough, they'll kill for a gallon of fuel thinking the fuel will take them to a place they can find food. We're a farm, they'll assume we have both food and fuel. Which makes me 100% sure they going to attack us. Even if we had nothing, the rumor we do will be enough to drive them to attack us. The trenches will make it easier for us to go house to house without being seen. The trenches will provide us some cover when the attack comes. The automatic weapons will be force multipliers. The M4s will allow us to put down a lot of lead in a short time. I'm hoping they confuse the invaders enough that they won't know how few of us there really are. We have to learn to use automatic weapons which will rise to the right when fired. I have some new handguards and bipods to hold the rifles steady when we're firing. I would have loved to get a couple M249s or other machine guns, but my contact didn't have any. I bought a lot of small lasers which I plan to mount on sticks we'll stick around the trench in places we aren't in. The attackers will see the lasers, they'll think the lasers are us holding our weapons. Hopefully, they'll attack the lasers. The silencers will make it harder for them to figure out where we are. I also have two FLIR night vision handheld binoculars which will enable us to see them, hopefully before they see us."

Fred looks over to me, "Jay, I'm worried that you're convinced we're going to have to fight. You remember, none of us have experience fighting. If we get invaded by large numbers of people, there's a good chance we're going to be overrun. What do we do then?"

Before I can answer, Fred says, "Cop car behind us, been there for a few miles."

"How fast are you driving?"

"I'm within one or two MPH of the speed limit, sometimes under, sometimes over, never more than two over."

"He must be confused, he's not used to seeing someone on this deserted road going the speed limit. Just keep it up and don't look nervous."

"How the hell do I not look nervous? We're carrying a truckload of automatic weapons."

"Just chill, we'll be fine."

"Shit, his lights just came on."

"Put on your right blinker and start to move to the shoulder."

Before Fred can move to the shoulder, the police car zooms around us, speeding up. "Fred, I'd say, today is your lucky day. He must have gotten a call. He won't be back for us. As far as he knows we didn't break any laws. He most likely thought we were carrying drugs. I bet he called in our plates, the truck rental company told him they rented the truck to a farmer and he must have assumed we are carrying equipment for the farms. Fred, getting back to your question, I have a really out of the box idea. I'm working on a plan for a large underground shelter. Rich and Jill are going to have their barn rebuild like yours, I'm thinking of having a large underground shelter dug under the barn. We can dig tunnel entrances to the shelter from each of our homes. If we get overrun, we run into the shelter and hide until the attackers move on or they fight among themselves to the point we can come out and defeat them."

"With all of the defenses you outlined, do you really think we're going to need the shelter?"

"Fred, I'd rather have it and not need it than need it and not have it. If I can get my kids to come down and stay with us, the shelter is going to have to be large enough to hold all of us. Plus, it's going to need storage space for supplies to keep all of us going as long as it takes."

"Ah! That's why the freeze dried food."

"Yes, in case we're driven from our homes we need to eat."

Fred shakes his head, "I never worried about security or home invasions before. I have the shotgun for hunting and just in case someone tried to steal my animals. I'm really worried that you think it's going to get so bad we might have to leave our homes. I never thought I'd see the day when we living outside of Nashville think we're going to have to fight our neighbors."

"Fred, they won't be our neighbors, they'll be criminals or people so hungry they'll think nothing of killing us for a meal. I'm hoping we can hold off any attack but Fred, what happens if we get hit by a force of hundreds or even a thousand? Even with automatic weapons we would be overrun. Each layer of defense is designed to slow the attackers down and thin their numbers before they reach us. In the worse case, the defenses will buy us time to escape into the shelter. We need a place to hide until they leave, which hopefully they will when the supplies they find are used up. The refugees are going to be like waves of locusts stripping the land clean. I only hope we have time to build the shelter before we need it. I'd also like to find more people we know and can trust. Seventeen people aren't enough to defend what we have."

"Jay, why just one shelter? Why not build one behind your house and one in the middle field which is equal distance from all of our homes?"

"Interesting idea. I'll have to see how long it'll take to build. By the way, I ordered some personal defense items for us."

"Personal defense items?"

"Kevlar helmets and armored vests. Congress is about to outlaw the ownership of armored vests and helmets for any non-military and non-police. I called a couple of companies and bought what I could. I hope they ship everything I ordered."

"Will they work?"

"I pray we never have to find out. They aren't like the vests the police wear, these use thick metal plates, one in the front, one in the back, and two small ones on the sides. They are rated to stop all handgun and 5.56 rounds which the police use. They may save our lives when we have to bail."

"Jay, this brings up a question I almost hate to ask, what are you going to do if nothing happens? You've most likely spent $5million on your home, our farms, new barns, new equipment, weapons, food, fuel tanks and fuel. That's a lot of money, isn't Lacy going to skin you alive?"

Laughing, "Fred, we had nothing before we won the lottery. Lacy would have lost her job putting us into the group of those living on the government dole. We now own our house outright, we own a couple of year's worth of food and fuel, we own three farms, and a ton of weapons. Plus, we still have over $20 million left. Fred, I pray every day I'm wrong, my gut says it's going to be much worse than I think. I keep trying to think of what else we may need to keep us alive for the next few years if we don't have any outside help."

"What else do you think we need?"

"I'd love to have a doctor or an RN in our group. I've stocked OTC medications and many prescription medications which I got in Canada and Mexico. But if someone comes down really sick or gets wounded, we're going to need a doctor. A first aid book isn't going to cut it."

"I'll contact our local doctor, he's a small sole provider, he lives about five miles from us."

"I thought all of the small doctor practices closed up due to Obamacare."

"Most did, Dr. Basco refused to, he's sixty-eight. He said he's always practiced his way and the government can be damned, he's not going to change."

"Jay, what else can we do to keep what's ours?"

"The new barns are fire-proof, we should make sure all of the farming equipment is kept locked inside every night. When the locusts leave, we're going to need the equipment to start over. I've ordered sprinklers to be installed in the other's homes. Once the shelter is built, I want to move most of our stored crops into it."

"I'll talk to the others when we get home. I'll remind the others not to leave anything outside overnight. We're not used to having to think about security. Portland hasn't had any serious crime in many years. Jay, one idea I've been thinking about is cutting a trench on one or both sides of the barbwire to stop a car or pickup from driving through the barbwire."

"I like it, thanks."

"Jay, where are you going to get the sheet steel to cover the driveway trenches?"

"Local company in town sells sheets of steel up to one inch thick. That's too heavy for our need. I plan to buy some ½ inch thick to cover the driveway trenches. We'll drill holes in the corners so we can tie a rope to them, we'll drag them open and closed with the tractor or pickups. I want to see about lining some of our home walls with the ½ steel plate, it should make the walls bulletproof."

"How long have you been planning for this?"

"A couple of months. Anyone looking at the current situation could see the economy is going to crater. The election in Greece was the match that lit the fuse."

"Jay, how long do you think it'll be before the meltdown happens?"

"Look at today's announcement of the excise tax. That's a sign the government is panicking. The markets dropped over 50% of their value in three days and are still falling, unemployment is over 11% and increasing, it's only a matter of time before it all comes apart. The EU fell apart in less than three months."

While we're driving home, the news channel reports the President is closing the stock markets for two weeks to allow calmer heads to prevail. The President hopes traders calm down and don't pour gasoline on a burning fire causing it to burn out of control. The President also announced that he was going to help the recently unemployed by expanding the welfare programs to provide a safety net under those who recently lost their jobs. To pay for the increase in the welfare programs, he's increasing the taxes on the 1% to 40% of all income over $500,000 a year.

"Is this going to have a big impact on our plans?"

"I hope not, I need to see the details of the new taxes and when it starts. Our money isn't really considered income per say, plus we moved a lot of our money offshore or into hard assets. I wonder if Congress will sit still and allow him to raise taxes, the President doesn't have the authority to set taxes."

"Can they just take what you have?"

"Who's going to stop them?"

"This is beginning to sound a lot like the revolutionary war."

"Yeah, isn't it?"

Chapter 7

Captain Black, commanding the US Special Forces troops in the Ukraine led his teams to a hill overlooking a Russian Army forward operating base. He dictated out loud what he saw, so his radio operator could encrypt the information and bounce it off a US MilSat to the Pentagon. He sent images to the Pentagon with his notes. Sergeant Gray asked, "Captain, what are we going to do now?"

"Sergeant, how long have you been in this man's Army?"

"Sir, this April will be twenty-two years."

"Then you already know the answer to your question."

"Yes sir, we wait for further instructions."

"See, you knew the answer before asking. Before you ask, I have no idea how long it'll be before they respond."

"Yes, sir. I'll keep the men alert."

"Sergeant, rest a third of the men. I'll let you know when I hear anything."

"Yes, sir."

An hour later their instructions arrive. Captain Black taps Sergeant Gray on his shoulder, whispering, "Sergeant we have our orders."

"Sir?"

"Come with me." The two men quietly leave the tent where the other two sergeants are sleeping.

"We've been ordered to use the Russian anti-armor and anti-personal missiles to attack their base camp. We're supposed to wipe it out. HQ doesn't want any to escape."

"Sir, can we use the mortars?"

"Only if they're Russian or Ukrainian. We're not to use any NATO weapons."

"Sir, we're not carrying any. I check the men every day to make sure they didn't hide any side arms that we missed in the last screen. We have two Russian mortars with a total of forty rounds, HE, and WP."

"Excellent. Let the men get a little rest. We'll wake the camp at 0300 hours, feed them and attack at 0400. We'll fire 5 rounds of WP from the mortars followed by 5 of HE, followed by another 5 of WP. The secondary team will launch anti-armor missiles at the tanks when the first mortar rounds are in the air. If we time it correctly, we'll take them completely by surprise and cripple them before they know what hit them or where the attack is coming from."

"Yes, sir."

The American SOF camp quietly wakes, the men having cold MREs for breakfast. They take down their tents and police the area, removing every trace that they spent the night on the hill. At 0400, Captain Black says, "Fire."

Within a second the first rounds are dropped down the mortar tubes and are on their way to their targets before the captain completes the word 'fire'. Antitank missiles leave their shoulder-fired launch tubes as he finishes saying "Fire."

The anti-armor missiles arrive on target a moment before the mortar rounds explode. The missiles strike the Russian T-80 and T-90 main battle tanks on top of their turrets. The missiles' multistage warheads burrow into the body of the tanks where the main warhead explodes the onboard ammo and fuel. Tank after tank explodes, sending burning debris and shrapnel into the troop tents. The initial mortar rounds arrive as the line of tanks start exploding. WP burns through everything it touches. Water doesn't put the fires out. The Russian troops quickly come awake, racing out of their tents into the hell the American's released on their camp. Missile after missile strikes the lines of tanks as the mortar rounds explode over the tents. The American troops fire as quickly as the launchers can be reloaded and the shooter can lock a target in the missile. The mortar's first target is the ammo/supply tent, followed by the mess tent and the officer's tents. After the initial targets are destroyed, the mortars shift to the general camp, rounds land in the center of the camp moving out in an increasing circle. The Russians aren't able to immediately counterattack and by the time they are able to pick their heads up from the debris of their destroyed camp they discover all of their weapons are destroyed. The Russian troops looks for survivors, providing aid to the few wounded by setting up a first aid tent to replace the one destroyed by their attackers. They lay the wounded in lines in front of the new first aid tent, marking the ones who have the best chance of living when another round of mortar shells and missiles arrive killing everyone in the camp. Colonel Black tells Sergeant Gray to take a squad to the camp, "No prisoners and don't leave any proof behind of who we are."

"Yes, sir."

The squad walks down the hill carrying Russian-made assault rifles. Thirty minutes later they return telling the Captain, "Mission completed."

"Thank you Sergeant."

In Moscow President Putin is informed of the attack by the Russian Federation Minister of Defense, Sergey Shoigu. "Mr. President, there were no survivors. The attack was done with our weapons. Even the boot marks in the mud match ours."

"Minister, do we have a rogue platoon?"

"No Mr. President, my guess is this was an American Special Forces group operating behind our lines."

"How did they get our weapons?"

"Most likely grabbed them from one of our depots."

"Find and kill the Yankees. Send a squad of our best Spetsnaz to find these assholes before they do any more damage to us."

"Yes, sir."

When the Minister of Defense leaves Putin's office, he lifts his secure telephone which connects him to a special operator, "Get me the Minister of Finance."

Within twenty seconds, the call is connected. "Mr. President?"

"Complete taking down the American's economy."

"Mr. President, hurt them or take them down completely?"

"Crush them."

"Yes sir, I'll issue the trading orders and dump the rest of our dollars and I'll activate the last worms in the software we installed in their computer networks."

"Tell the world from now on we won't accept dollars in payment for our gas and oil."

"Yes, sir."

Twenty minutes later the New York Stock Exchange internal security department notices a huge surge in short trades, driving the market down fast enough that the stock market internal safeties are engaged to slow trading down. The safeties are designed to slow the sudden downward or upward pressures on the market. Many were put in place after the 1929 crash and improved after the 1987 crash. Even with the safeties engaged the market closed for the day down 600 points. While Russia is dumping all of their dollars, the Fed is trying to slow the fall of the dollar by buying dollars. By 2:00 PM, the Fed has purchased $1.8 trillion before the chairman of the Fed orders the purchase program shut down. The dollar continues to fall all night as the Asian markets open and China, followed by Japan, who has secretly signed a security treaty with China joins Russia dumping their dollars.

@@@@@

The world's economies are in free fall due to the collapsing value of the dollar and the stock market crash. By the end of April, most of the Western World is on the verge of another depression. Europe has to reduce or stop most of their government assistance programs pushing Europe into a state of upheaval and rioting. The central governments in Greece, France, Portugal, Spain, Italy, and Belgium have all resigned based on parliamentary votes of no confidence. Italy has governments form and collapse daily before the Mafia talks to the Pope. They jointly agree to govern the country. France breaks up into Muslim and warlord controlled areas. Paris is a burnt out shell of a once beautiful city. The kings of Spain and Belgium both disband their parliament, they rule by decree to pull their countries off the edge of the cliff. Switzerland closes their border, they expel all none citizens and lock their country down. Since every citizen is armed, they are asked to carry their weapons all the time to stop riots. Anyone without a valid ID card is deported.

Canada finds itself with French-speaking Quebec seceding from the Union of Canada, the large Chinese population in Victoria demand the right to turn most of Victoria into another Hong Kong. Alberta demands the right to either join the USA or go their separate way, they are sick of the high taxes and dual language laws. Alberta's economy has been damaged by lower oil prices. However, they are still viable due to a mix of high technology companies combined with their oil production.

The population in China's major cities demanded more freedoms. They demanded an end of the one-child rule and an end of the Army picking people off the street to work as slaves in factories. The economic slowdown forces many of China's ODM factories, like Foxconn, to be forced to fire over three hundred thousand workers. Most are tossed out of the factories without any sort of severance. China's new middle class takes a beating from the layoffs. People take to the streets demanding the Chinese government help them. The Communist Party of China deploys the Chinese army to stop the protests. China's army crushes the protests, China's communist party announces a new series of prodemocracy movements to calm their population. Putin watches China loosen the strings on their people. He waits for the right time to strike like a vulture waiting for its prey to die so it can feed. Putin knows in less than a year Russia could be the world's sole superpower, enabling him to rule the world. He decides to make an offer to China, one they won't be able to refuse.

@@@@@

When Fred and I return from San Antonio, we're surprised to find our neighbors fighting among themselves. Everyone in our compound is standing in the front yard yelling at each other. I try to stop the screaming and yelling without success. Fred leans on the truck's horn which finally stops the arguments. I yell, "What the hell is going on?"

Paul says, "We can't agree on the trench. I want it to be dug by the backs of our homes. Randy wants it to go in the front and then cut across the backyards of our homes. That's twice the work and it will cut into our fields, reducing our crop yield. Randy refuses to dig in the rear of our homes. Flo doesn't want her garden touched."

Randy yells, "If we cut the trench in the rear of our homes we won't be able to use it to defend the front of our homes which face the street."

Paul, yells back, "That's why we're cutting the trenches cutting across our driveways."

The yelling goes back and forth like a group of five-year-olds on a school playground that can't get along. I nod to Fred, who leans on the horn again. The yelling finally stops, everyone looks at me, "I thought I made the plan clear when we got together three nights ago. What the hell happened? Why didn't you call us?"

Paul replies, "We didn't get around to starting the trench until today. We knew you were due back today, so there was no reason to bother you."

"Why didn't you start the trench until today?"

Randy laughs, "Jay, we're farmers. Farms in the spring are very busy places. We have been working on getting our crops planted. We assumed planting was the most important job, which is why you bought our farms to begin with."

"You got me there, I forget about the work involved in farming. I'm afraid to hire people because I want to keep the trench a secret. Anyone we hire is going to talk, when they do, a smart gang leader may decide how to get around our defenses. We have to work out a plan that covers both the farming and the work on our defenses. Plus, I've been thinking of building underground shelters under the new barns."

Paul's son, Joe raises his hand. "Joe, you don't need to raise your hand, what's on your mind?"

"Sir, if we teenagers could skip school for a couple of weeks, we could dig the trench or work the fields while our fathers dig the trench. We skip school in the fall during harvest time, we're not doing much in school and many of the teachers don't show up anyway since the union couldn't get them a raise."

This was an idea that hadn't occurred to me. "Joe, I think I need to discuss this with your parents. It's an interesting idea. I tend to forget that on farms everyone in the family works."

Paul laughs, saying, "Jay, the current administration tried to stop our children from working until they reached eighteen and only then worked a limited number of hours a week. They were trying to put us out of the farming business. They wanted us to hire full-time employees, which we'd have to give benefits, sick days and vacation time to work our fields."

"I take it you showed them the front door?"

"We tried, but they kept coming back. Many of us got into financial problems last fall when we were forced to hire people and pay them $9.00 an hour. Many didn't last a day, we constantly had to train new people, cutting into our crop yields, our costs increased and our yields decreased. The local manager from the Department of Labor came around just before you arrived in town to tell us we had to hire more people this year. In fact, he's due to return within the next week to check on the people we hired this year. He told us he wanted to see the printed benefits program and make sure we hired a good mix of men, women and all races. We told him sometimes there's not an even mix looking for work. He told us if we didn't meet the government-mandated mix ratios for workers, he'd shut us down."

I shake my head saying, "Since the gates have been installed at our driveways, make sure the no trespassing signs are mounted today. If he still shows up, send him to me." I said, smiling like the Cheshire Cat. Everyone smiled and nodded thinking the government manager was about to get a surprise. "Now let's discuss the trench."

Paul said, "Jay, it's OK with us if Joe works here a few days versus going to school where he's not learning anything. We used to homeschool him until the local department of education told us we couldn't homeschool our children any longer."

"I'm not aware of any law to that effect. From today on, any of you who want to homeschool your kids can do so. Contact the school so they know, if you get contacted by the department of education, send them to me. With that agreed to, let's review the role of the trenches. They're to provide us fighting positions in case of an invasion of our farms. The trench in our driveways is to stop vehicles. It won't stop an attack by people on foot. We need the trench to go from the front of our homes, circle them and wrap around the back of the houses so we can fight anyone who attacks from the front or rear."

Rich says, "It's going to cut right through our fields."

"Rich, we'll lose a little yield, but it may save our lives, isn't that a good trade?"

All nod their agreement.

Paul asks, "What toys did you guys bring home?"

Fred answers, "Military weapons, you won't believe what we have."

Unloading the truck, everyone's eyes are wide in surprise. I tell everyone, "I think we need to arrange some range time to ensure everyone can fire every weapon we have."

Jill asks, "What about us women?"

"You also. When the time comes, everyone is going to have to fight."

Rich asks, "We're also confused how deep to dig the trench, some of us remember you saying five feet. That won't provide full coverage."

"Remember, the soil you remove will be made into sandbags which will be placed along the trench. We'll leave firing ports in the piles of sandbags. I forgot to mention, we'll need fire extinguishers, lots of them. We also need a few hundred empty glass bottles."

Paul says, "I guess we're going to be making Molotov Cocktails."

"Right you are."

Paul says, Joe, why don't you and Matt go to town, buy up all the fire extinguishers you can find."

"Dad, all of them?"

I reply, yes, all you can find while you're in town get a few bundles of steel reinforcing rods."

"Yes sir, we're going."

When the kids leave on the shopping trip, Fred looks at me asking, "Jay, why the fire extinguishers? We have fire suppression systems built into our homes and barns."

"Just in case, call it a plan B."

Fred says, "I understand. By the way, a friend of ours has a large field we use as a gun range."

"I'd rather no one know we have fully automatic weapons or even the types of weapons we have."

"Jay, I'll check, but I don't think he's back from Florida yet."

"Good, let's go in tomorrow at sunrise."

Everyone nods their agreement. We break up, Fred and I unload the weapons into my basement, Paul and Randy start spray painting the ground orange where the trench will be dug. When they've encircled our homes, Paul gets in one of the backhoes to begin digging the trench in the front while Randy starts digging the rear trench. I'm worried we're running out of time. I'm also worried about my kids and their families. As the American economy falls apart, I weekly call my kids begging them to bring their families to our compound. I worry when the shit finally hits the fan it won't be safe for them to make the trip. I'm worried the longer they delay, the more dangerous it's going to be for them to make the trip. I'm most concerned with Sammi since her husband Ricky always thought I was so far to the right I made Attila the Hun look moderate. I know he doesn't want to come here. He most likely thinks he's going to be safe in the middle of Iowa. My gut says, nowhere is going to be safe when the dam breaks. Sure enough, Sammi confirmed my worst thoughts, they aren't coming unless they're driven out of their home. Ricky still has his job, he thinks everything will quickly settle down and turn around when the President increases the welfare payments. I pray they wake up before the violence starts.

With the dollar in free fall, gold and silver's value increased almost every hour. When the violence started, it didn't take anyone by surprise. Welfare payments were cut and people couldn't put food on their family's tables. Different groups came together to march against the welfare cuts. Hundreds of thousands marched, tens of thousands rioted setting cities and towns on fire. Buses carried the rioters into middle and upper-class communities. Private security companies and police fought the rioters, running gun battles broke out between those trying to protect and those who want to destroy. The battles rage across the country. The violence became so bad, the gun fighting so intense, many first responders refused to enter cities and towns. Police refused to go to work, many are seen as agents of the government who reduced the welfare payments, the police are attacked wherever they were seen. Their homes are burned. Government workers are attacked for the reduction of welfare payments. Many towns repainted their police cars to look like regular cars. Marked police cars come under fire as they drive through neighborhoods.

@@@@@

Even with two backhoes it takes us three weeks working in two shifts to cut the trenches in a circle around our homes. Filling sandbags with the removed soil goes much slower; in fact, we give up the idea. We decide to push most of the soil into wooden forms that form 45-degree triangles in front of the trenches. I'm hoping the 45-degree angle and the densely packed soil will stop most bullets fired at us. We leave spaces for us to shoot out from the trench. We rigged strong lights on poles that can illuminate the area in front of our front trench which will shine in any attacker's eyes, hopefully blinding them from us.

We all spent time at an abandoned mine learning how to handle all of our weapons, with the exception of the RPG. I didn't want to use one of our limited rockets nor did I want the explosion to bring people to see what was going on. We taught the kids how to make Molotov Cocktails, they made 200 of them, most standing ready in wooden cases spread along the inside of the trench. We've also placed different types of acid in glass bottles. I've asked Paul and Randy to figure out how to make WP weapons. I was able to buy out a chemistry company's inventory of WP and other chemicals they usually sold to schools. With the economic downturn, schools didn't have funds to replenish their stocks. We have twenty pounds of it which ought to come as a nasty surprise to anyone attacking us. We store it in glass jars which will break when striking anything or anyone.

Being farmers, Fred was able to purchase fifty pounds of TNT to clear tree stumps. We're using it to make pipe bomb hand grenades. Small, thin pipes are filled with TNT, covered with nails and BBs held onto the pipe with either wax or glue. To light the fuses we bought over 400 electric fire starters. Paul's wife Flo somewhere found 500 pounds of barbecue charcoal that showed up in her new barn. I figured it would come in handy. I also bought each family a small four seat ATV, which can quickly move between our homes. The ATVs operate in any weather and they'll save us fuel versus using our cars. Each family member assigned to fighting was given body armor, a helmet, rifle, sidearm and 100 full magazines. Each family has a first aid kit and a FLIR portable thermal sight.

We contacted every company that sold underground shelters. The first five agreed to accept our purchase order and gave us a timeline, only to back out of the contract within 48 hours of when they were due to begin work. One construction company called to offer me what he said is an offer I won't be able to turn down. He told me his name is Franco, his two sons work with him. He tells me he has experience building storm shelters. I tell him, I'll listen to his proposal if he comes by in person to discuss the plans and his offer. While Fred and I were away, Paul and Randy placed an order for cows, pigs, chickens and four horses. The animals reinforced our need to expand our barbwire fences which we've finally succeeded in stringing along the front of our property along the street. We cleaned out all of the barbed and razor wire in the Nashville area that the police hadn't already taken for riot control so we could string it all around our property.

We installed motion activated lights and cameras on poles covering the fence. Each of our driveways has two covered trenches cut into them and we've dug hundreds of small holes which we hope will stop people on foot trying to attack us. Many of the holes have hunting traps placed in the bottom of them. Others have boards with large nails sticking up and a foot stepping into a hole will force the nails into any boot or shoe rendering the person unable to continue. The last item on my checklist is an alarm system that alerts all of us to any issues. Each family has different colored flares, I wanted some type of alarm that we can hear anywhere on the farms, an alarm that would also tell us which family was sounding the alarm. We were working on different ideas when we got our first uninvited visitor.

@@@@@

As the value of the dollar collapses, imported fuel begins to run short. The fracking industry was bankrupt due to the Saudi's pulling the price of oil down. There is a shortage of investment companies with available capital. The lack of capital further slowed domestic oil production. Specialized manufacturing companies that made the parts for refineries and oil drilling rigs were bankrupt meaning parts are almost impossible to locate. Domestic oil production sank to a forty year low, even oil from the Canadian oil sands dried up since the cost to transport the oil was too high without the Keystone oil pipeline President Obama vetoed.

As oil supplies dried up gas lines similar to the mid-1970s reformed. Many lines stretched three miles from any gas pumps that had fuel. Riots and flash mobs attack any station with fuel, stealing it to resell on the black market for $50.00 a gallon. Mobs hijack trucks carrying supplies. Cross-country truckers decide the risk isn't worth the reward so they park their trucks at home. Over a hundred thousand trucks are hijacked, their cargoes are stolen. By the end of June truck transport across the country ceases. Armed military convoys are organized to transport food, cargo and fuel across the country and into the country's cities. The hungry and angry target the military convoys. People quickly realize the military isn't traveling with loaded magazines in their weapon. The US Department of Home Land Security thought loaded weapons crossing the country were too dangerous. Mobs quickly attack the military convoys. Thousands of attackers hit the convoys before the military and National Guard get permission to load magazines into their weapons. Hundreds of Guardsmen and Army troops are killed before they receive permission to load and return fire. One convoy disobeys orders, they travel with their weapons loaded and ready for action. When attacked, they fight back. They kill forty people trying to attack their convoy. When the Department of Justice investigates why this one convoy beat off the attackers-they learn the convoy disobeyed direct orders, everyone in the convoy is court-martialed and accused of first-degree murder in civilian courts.

When word of the court-martialing reaches other convoys, many of the Guardsmen disappear in the middle of the night with their weapons.They refuse to be targets for a government that refuses to allow them to protect themselves.

Flash mobs break in and strip food stores before the stores are able to close or bring in armed security to stop the mobs. The shelves of food stores remain empty as their inventories are used up. Without trucks carrying food into cities and towns the food stores, once emptied, remain empty. Prices jump 50% in two weeks. Black markets are the only place many are able to buy food. Once food stores are stripped, flash mobs break into private homes looking for food. Companies with cafeterias are also struck by the flash mobs as thousands push their way into cafeterias. In many cases, large windows are smashed allowing the mobs entry. Those who still have jobs are mugged for their bagged lunches and briefcases. Flash mobs strike the few restaurants still open, forcing many of the restaurants to hire armed private security. Shoot-outs occur at some of the restaurants, twenty customers in different locations are hit in the crossfire. Fears of being caught in the crossfire take their toll as the number of customers going to restaurants drops by 80%. 95% of the country's restaurants close by the middle of July. Someone said America was nine meals away from anarchy and by mid-July it's becoming clear, nine may have been too high a number. In the twenty-first century, most people don't have the skills needed to survive without food deliveries, or know what to do when turning the faucet doesn't provide clean water. Most don't know how to live without electric power. The Bible says the meek will inherit the earth, most realize it's going to be the experienced, strong and those without a conscious who will inherit. The strong will end up fighting among themselves for limited resources until only the strongest or most prepared survive.

Chapter 8

April 27th turned out to be a beautiful day. We got a lot of work completed and felt good about ourselves. Just before we retired for the evening, we're alerted to someone trying to enter Fred's driveway when the motion-activated alarm and lights turn on. Whoever they are, they are blowing their horn to get Fred's attention. They obviously want Fred to open his gate. After a five-minute standoff, the car sounds its police siren. I say to Lacy as we're watching the ending of the evening news, "Shit, what do the police want with Fred at this hour?"

"Are you going to see?"

"I'm getting dressed in case there are problems. I think if we all show up the police will wonder what's going on and how we knew they were here."

"Good plan, I'll get ready too."

"Honey, I think we should err on the side of security, let's wear our body armor and take our helmets. I don't trust the local police showing up so late in the evening like this."

Lacy nods her agreement.

We both get dressed in our battle armor, Lacy takes one of the silenced Uzis, I take my silenced M4. We wait by the door for the second alarm which means Fred needs us, when the phone rings. "Hello?"

"Jay, it's Fred, I have a visitor who would like to speak with you. Is it possible for you to come by, dress blue."

Dress blue meant no hostile actions have been taken or threatened against Fred and Cheri. "Lacy, I'm keeping my body armor on so I'll wear a windbreaker over it. I'm leaving my M4 and sidearm. I'll leave my phone on, listen to the conversation. If you hear anything unusual, come armed for bear and sound the general alarm."

"Be careful."

"You too, I love you."

I drive our ATV to Fred's house trying to think what the police want with Fred at 11:35 PM. There's a single car sitting in front of his house. If it was serious, I'm sure they would have sent more than one car. My knock on the front door is answered by Cheri, "Jay, please come in."

In their living room are two sheriff deputies. Fred, knows the officers, saying, "Jay, I'd like to introduce you to Sheriff Grover and Officer Johnson of the Cheatham County, Tennessee Sheriff's Department. Sheriff, Officer, Jay is a close friend of mine. He recently bought the Gladstone home next door and he's the person who's bought my farm and the other local ones. If you're asking for something from the farm, you need to discuss it with the owner, which is why I asked Jay to join us. As I've told you, Cheri and I no longer own the farm."

Sheriff Grover holds out his hand, saying, "Hello Jay, a pleasure to meet you. We heard someone bought the Gladstone home. You got a hell of a deal on it, and the local farms. We came to see Fred and Cheri because I know them and we need your help."

"Sheriff, I'm listening."

"Jay, the town is running out of food, we haven't had a delivery truck in ten days. I know Fred and the other farmers store some crops to get them through the winter. This winter was very mild and the spring was a good growing season, we are wondering what you can share with the town."

"Sheriff, what are you offering in trade?"

"Jay, with lives in the balance, you want to bargain?"

"Sheriff, everything has a cost. I spent well over $4 million on my properties and improvements. One of the reasons why I purchased them was to ensure my family had enough food in the crisis that's now arrived. If I cut the supply of our available food without getting anything in return what does that say about my investment?"

"You'd be helping to save innocent lives. Many people in the local area are very low on food."

"I think my coming here has already saved the families I'm helping. All would have lost everything they own and their farms if I hadn't bought their mortgages from the local 'very friendly' bank. There's good will and there's being smart. We've prepared for the crisis. The town didn't prepare so it's the town's problem, why is it my problem? We no longer need anything the town has."

"Are you sure of that?"

"What are you trying to say? I find it easier if both sides plainly say what they want and what they're offering. I've asked you what you're prepared to give us for our food. I'm waiting for an answer."

Sheriff Grover stands up in anger, Fred says, "Sheriff, wait. Jay, can't you meet him halfway?"

"Fred, I'm prepared to meet him more than halfway. All I asked him was what he was prepared to give us for some of our stored supplies. He seems to think he's entitled to the fruits of our labor."

Sheriff Grover walks up to within a couple of inches of my face, "You had nothing to do with growing the food. You didn't sweat over it, you shouldn't have a say in it."

"Sheriff, I own it and everything else on the 900 plus acres around us. I'll repeat my question, what are you willing to give us for the grain?"

"My protection."

Thinking he made a joke, I smile, responding, "You're not even Italian."

"Jay, I just met you, I'd hate to have to kill you on our first meeting."

"Sheriff, you may kill me, but if you do, neither you nor your partner will leave this farm alive. Of that I can assure you."

Less than twenty seconds later Lacy kicks in the front door, holding her Uzi in front of her. "I'd suggest you not make any sudden moves, she gets pissy real easy and is a very good shot. By the way, that's a real Uzi she's holding."

"Where the hell did you get a real Uzi?"

Ignoring his new question, I look into the Sheriff's eyes saying, "I'll repeat my question for the last time, what are you offering for our grain?"

"I told you, my good will."

"Then, I bid you a fine evening. I suggest you leave my property. As no crime has been committed, you have no business here."

"I came to visit an old friend. I can stay as long as I'd like."

Fred responds, "Sheriff, I'm sorry, but I have to ask you to leave my house."

Grover looks between Fred, myself and Lacy shaking his head. "You haven't heard the last of this. I'll be back and we'll take what the town requires. You can't sit up here on this hill and dictate starvation terms to the town. The town won't accept it and as their Sheriff, it's my duty to provide security for the town. I don't understand why you don't want to be neighborly. You just moved here, you don't know sharing is the Southern way of life. Any of the good people living here can tell you that. I'll give you a day or two to sleep on my offer. Goodnight Jay."

"Sheriff this entire conversation has been recorded. Hence, let the record show that I haven't dictated any terms. I simply asked what you were willing to provide us with as a trade. If you take what's ours without payment, that's stealing. Stealing, by the way, IS a crime. With the shortages and rising price of food, it would be a felony. The only one making threats is you, the only one trying to commit a felony is you. I'd be happy to give the recording to the local radio stations, I'm sure the entire town would be interested in hearing their Sheriff trying to shake us down. Who in town will be next? By the way, Sheriff, as I'm sure you know. My property straddles the county line, my house is inside the county, most of the farm is outside the county. The farm is outside of your official area. You technically have no jurisdiction outside of my house. If you're willing to make us an honest offer, I'm all ears. If you're here to pressure us to give you what you want. You may leave the same way you arrived."

"By the way, the gate at the end of your driveway is a safety hazard. If the fire department had to answer a call for help, they couldn't quickly get in. If I were you, I'd remove it before someone does it for you. All in the name of safety."

"Sheriff we can open the gate remotely. Thank you for your concern for our safety."

After the two police officers leave, Fred asks me, "What do you think that was really all about?"

"He wanted our stored grain and anything else he could get from us. If we easily gave in, they would hit all of the other farms in the area. He most likely was going to take ours and sell it to the town, pocketing the sales price."

"Do you think they'll be back?"

"I'm sure of it, next time don't open the gate until you call me. We'd better warn everyone else."

Fred looks at Lacy, "Would you really have shot them?"

"If they harmed Jay or you and Cheri, I would have shot them dead."

Fred shakes his head saying, "Jay, by the way, would Lacy have fired on them?"

"In a flash, she would have killed them without blinking."

Jay, "You married a cold-hearted woman."

"You don't know the half of it. Don't ever piss her off."

"I'll remember that!" laughed Fred. Cheri and Lacy hug each other as we leave. On the way home, Lacy asks, "What do you really think was going on here?"

"Fred's friend isn't a friend. He wanted to twist his arm for our stored inventory of grains, which he most likely planned to rip the town's mayor off for a huge payment."

Fred asks, "Do you think he'll be back?"

"Yes, with force to take what he wants."

Cheri looking very worried, asks, "What are you planning on doing?"

"If he tries to take what's ours, I'll kill him," I said, walking to our ATV. "Come on, let's go home."

Cheri says, "Jay, you can't kill a police, sheriff."

"Why can't I? The rule of law is failing as we watch. When he came here tonight, he was the same as a common thief. I'll deal with him the same way we'd treat any thief we catch in the act. He thinks he can profit from the current economic crises by the fruits of your labor."

Fred nods, saying, "Think we should go on full alert?"

"Not yet, it'll take him a couple of days to get up the courage to return. We should make sure the lights that cover our front fence and the driveways are on in the evenings. We should also plan to meet them with some surprises for when he returns. He might send some thugs to convince us we need his protection. It's a racket that's as old as time."

Fred smiles nodding, "Jay, I agree, we'll be ready tomorrow night."

We went two nights without any uninvited guests. Late in the afternoon on the third day after the Sheriff tried to shake us down the company who offered to build our shelter showed up. He made us an interesting offer. He said he'd build the shelters if we took his family into our group. He said he had two sons, both in their twenties, his wife passed away a year ago. He has the digging equipment and other tools, plus the designs for shelters and access to steel plates. He and his sons have some food supplies and rifles, which they know how to use. I asked him why he wanted to move in with us and he said his home isn't in a good area, rioting had broken out a few blocks away from his home. He expected to shortly lose his home and he doesn't have any other place to go. He expected trouble sooner versus later. We took a vote; all agreed to take him in. I told him we had plenty of bedrooms he could stay in until we built him a house. He said he would arrange for their own mobile home to be delivered to a plot of land behind us."

The next morning I was woken at dawn by a truck's horn honking. I looked at the monitor to see a couple of construction equipment trucks waiting to enter our compound. I smiled thinking, *our new neighbor Franco and his sons, Lou, and Sandy are here.*

Franco sat at our table with Lacy, myself and our three neighbors, he said, "I've looked at your plans. Digging under the barn which is already up is too difficult. In addition, the shelter will not be large enough to hold everyone for more than a very short time. Everyone will have to be jammed into a single room. It's not going to work for a long-term shelter. Anything over a few hours and everyone is going to start going crazy."

"Franco, you're the expert, what do you propose? I'm all ears."

"Jay, my suggestion is, you drop your plan for a shelter under one of the barns. We think one shelter equal distance from all four homes may be a better idea. We propose a very large shelter, one with bedrooms, a large kitchen, living room, bathrooms, and of course storage space for the supplies required to keep everyone alive until we can surface. If we're going to be in the shelter for any length of time, we're going to need a lot of room. Room for our own privacy, room to breathe, room to be alone and to be together as a group. Without a lot of room, we're going to go stir crazy. We're also going to need an engineering room to make any needed repairs. Power will be supplied by the external solar panels and the windmills which will charge large submarine quality batteries. Water will come from your existing wells and waste will be pumped to a large underground cesspool field. In addition to the family's entrances, I suggest an emergency escape tunnel that will exit at the far edge of the farms." Everyone nods in agreement, "Jay, think about a Navy submarine, some stay underwater for seven months. They provide movies, they have workout machines and the best food the Navy can supply them with. Even with everything the Navy's provided to the submarine's crew, it still takes a special type of person to live in a metal tube underwater for seven months or longer. If we want everyone to end up sane, we're going to have to think of building a small apartment complex underground."

Franco's last comment stopped me in my tracks. I thought about a shelter as a last resort, I hadn't thought about living in one for any length of time. I hadn't considered the effects of living in a small box underground with all of us almost on top of each other, without daylight, without being able to go for a walk or the space to be alone. He was right. Our plans are going to have to change in a very big way. I should have studied how the submarine service deals with people being cooped up in a sub for months at a time. I didn't even consider some people may just go crazy being confined in the shelter. I also didn't consider the issue of food fatigue if we only have the same or very similar food every day. Damn it, there are basic things I should have thought about. I feel like a fool. "Franco, I blew it. You're correct, why don't you tell us what you're thinking?"

"Jay, don't beat yourself up over it. Most people wouldn't have thought about these issues. You were thinking shelter to protect your family and friends, not how they may respond to being in one for any length of time. I spent ten years in the Navy, eight of them in a submarine. I know something about how being in a small space for months effects people."

"Thank God you showed up on our doorstep."

Franco unrolls a hand drawn blueprint, "This isn't finished, it's not a full blueprint, but it should provide a good starting point. The foundation will be poured cement, the water and waste pipes and channels for wires buried in the floor. The walls will be preformed cement sections. The beams will be steel 'I' beams which will be load-bearing support for the roof. Fresh air will be drawn in from the tunnels and fans that open in the woods that surround the farms. The ceiling will be covered with soil that has crops planted so no one will know there's something out of the ordinary hiding under the crops. I'm thinking a group of bedrooms for the kids, a private bedroom for each adult pair, kitchen, bathrooms and storage rooms."

Paul says, "If you dig up our fields, we'll lose a lot of crops, we'll have food problems. We may lose most of our summer crop and since it's our main crop, we can't afford to lose it."

Franco says, "From the time we start till you have access to the roof for your crops will be less than four weeks. Is that workable?"

Paul thinks over the timeline, responding, I think we can make it work, if you start now, we're on a very tight timeline with the weather, crops need a certain amount of time to grow and mature before we can harvest them."

Fred asks, "How large a shelter do you think we need?"

Franco smiles, "How many people does it need to hold?"

I start counting heads, adding mine to the count and Franco and his sons, "I'd say we should plan for a space large enough to hold 30 to 40 people. This counts all of us, plus my kids and hopefully a doctor or nurse we can convince to join us, plus a couple of extra people, just in case I forgot someone."

"How long will everyone stay in the shelter?"

I nod smiling, "Franco, that's the key question. We don't know. It's supposed to be a last resort if we get pushed out of our homes. I hope the attackers take what they want and leave allowing us to reclaim our homes."

Randy adds, "Jay, what if they decide to stay, say for the winter or summer. We should plan to stay in the shelter for at least six months. Maybe they decide to stay and work our fields? We'll be screwed living underground while they live in our homes."

I nod responding, "Then we should move our stored food and other supplies into the shelter so if we're overrun they won't find anything useful. Maybe that will cause them to move along quicker. In the worse case, we can sneak out at night and take some of them down every night. We might be able to scare them into leaving."

Franco says, "The shelter has to be doubled in size to hold all of the supplies, what about the farm animals?"

We look at each other trying to figure out the answer out when our front gate alarm sounds.

We sprint to the kitchen to look at the monitor, we see three black SUVs slowly drive by all of our driveways. They turn around and drive back stopping at Fred's gate. A man dressed in all black gets out of one of the SUVs and walks over to inspect the gate. He pushes on it, he looks at the barbwire fence, he tries looking up Fred's driveway. He slowly walks back to his SUV. They drive to each gate doing the same recon at each house. I say, "It looks like we're going to have unwanted visitors soon. I don't like this. I think we should prepare for an attack tonight. Franco, why don't you park your equipment behind my house? Draw up some plans and show them to us tomorrow. We have some things to take care of."

"My sons and I are ready to stand by you in the defense of our new home. We brought our rifles with us, we have five AK47s."

I nod, saying, "We're standardized on the AR platform, I have some AK47 ammo put away if you need some."

"We brought 10,000 rounds for our rifles, we each have four seventy-five round drum mags. My sons and I can look at your defenses, we'll see what we can quickly do to help improve them."

We all nod our thanks. Everyone goes to their homes to grab their rifles, extra magazines, and their battle armor before we check our defenses. We can't afford to move around without our weapons in case we're attacked. Franco makes some suggestions to quickly improve our defenses, he suggests we add screens over our motion activated lights and move them further away from the barbed wire. He also suggests we dig more small pits while covering them with a thin sheet covered in leaves or sod that blends in with the ground around them. We agree with his ideas, tasks we will look at tomorrow, which assumes we survive our first attack tonight.

Franco's son Sandy asks, "Do you have any of the exploding gun targets?"

I reply, "We have a few, but not many, why do you ask?"

Sandy says, "I know where to get a lot of them. We can cover them with nails, place them midway between the fence and the trench when the attackers rush us, we shoot the targets, they'll explode like a land mine."

We smile and nod in agreement. I say, "Sandy, do you need money to get them?"

"I need money to buy cases of beer to trade for the targets."

Laughing, I nod my understanding, "How much is a case of beer going for today?"

"Between $100 and $150 a case. A couple of thousand will more than cover it."

I walk into my house. Opening one of the safes where I withdraw $3,000. Returning, I hand it to Sandy. "Please go make the trade, I like this idea. Can you sneak out and back tonight without being seen?"

"When they drive towards the house on the other side of the farms, I'll try to slip out of your driveway."

"Be careful out there."

"I will, I'll call when I return, if I can't call, I'll text the number 12378 which means everything is OK. Any other number means I'm under duress."

"Got it."

Franco starts digging holes, his older son, Lou works on improving our trench and removing any ground cover in front of the trench. Thus giving us an open field of fire the attackers are going to have to cross to reach us. I have another idea, "Lou, can you weld up supports that can hold a rifle? If we can strap or tie a rifle to a steady support, the rifle won't rise when we fire in the full auto mode."

"You have full-auto assault rifles?"

"You never heard me say that."

"How many do you need to be made?"

"I think six will do for now."

"I have some metal pipe on the truck, let me see what I can put together."

"Jay, when do you think they'll attack?"

"If they're smart, they'll wait until early morning, if it were me, I'd hit us between 3 and 4:00 AM. That'll give us some time to prepare."

"What if they're not smart?"

"Then they'll hit us as soon as it gets dark."

@@@@@

While working with Franco my phone pings with an urgent news alert. I look at the headline feeling a cold chill running down my back. The headline says, "Insurance companies announce stores, homes and offices damaged or destroyed by rioting aren't covered by existing insurance policies. The insurance industry says they consider the riots an act of war, domestic, but still an act of war, which insurance doesn't cover." This devastates most business owners. I think this is the straw that is going to break the camel's back with respect to our economy. Without insurance covering losses the stores aren't going to be rebuilt, no shelves are going to be restocked. I look at Franco saying, "Franco, the economy just took a swift kick to the balls. The insurance industry just announced they're not covering any losses due to rioting."

Franco shakes his head saying, "I was afraid of this. It means the riots will grow when they realize the shelves aren't going to be restocked. The rioting will expand as the mobs looks for food and water. That's why I came here. Our home wasn't defendable."

"I'm happy you came. I'm afraid we're going to need the shelter, plus we can always use more bodies for defense and work on the farms."

"My boys are young and very strong. They will help as needed."

"Thanks, Franco."

Franco wipes the perspiration off of his forehead while digging small holes asking, "Jay, how bad do you think it's going to get?"

"Do you remember the TV reports from Katrina?"

"Yes, why?"

"Katrina was one city, multiply that times thousands of cities and towns. At least in Katrina, FEMA, and the Coast Guard showed up, this time they're not going to be showing up. They don't have the resources to be everywhere at the same time. People will leave the cities looking for supplies. They may come in small groups or in groups numbering in the hundreds or thousands. Katrina showed us society fails very quickly, what's under the surface is very ugly. We're going to have to fight for our lives."

"Jay, we're ready. We came prepared to fight if need be. We saw the rioting only a couple of blocks from our house. We knew the rioting and destruction were moving in our direction. Your agreement for us to stay here is saving our lives."

"Franco, I'm glad we're able to help save your lives."

"Jay, you are saving our lives. We are going to build the shelter as if our lives depend on it because they do. My sons and I will man your front line tonight when the attack comes."

@@@@@

Two hours after leaving, Sandy texts 12378 to my phone letting me know he's close and not being followed. When I see the truck approaching our gate, we open it, hoping Sandy can sneak in without any uninvited guests sneaking in with him. He returned with five cases of exploding targets. Matt helps him spray paint them brown and green to blend in with the ground cover after Cheri and Lacy spray them with glue and cover them in nails and BBs. Two hours later the mines are finished. We hide them between the street and our trench, checking to make sure we can see them. Finding them difficult to see because of the paint, we spray a fluorescent orange spot facing our trench, hoping they aren't very visible from anyone coming towards us from the street. Now we could easily target them from the trench. All five families share an early evening meal together while we do everything we can to prepare for our visitors. We take turns spending two hours in the trench, so everyone can get a little rest and try to relax while we wait for the attack we think is coming. Paul asks me, "Jay, when do you think they'll attack?"

"The earlier they hit us, the less experienced they are."

We're as ready as we can be, everyone does their chores wearing body armor and carrying their rifles. At 10:00 PM our motion sensor alerts us that someone is pulling up to Fred's front gate. We watch video from our hidden cameras as they push against the gate. They get into the truck and slowly drive away. My phone rings, "Jay, Fred, do you think they're gone, did they give up?"

"Nope, they drove around the curve, we need to put some cameras there, we have a blind spot, somehow they figured it out. They're going to walk back to us. Just wait and keep your eyes open and don't make any sounds." I smile thinking of the little trick we set up in our homes. We have a couple of sewing models mounted on wheels that are pulled back and forth in front of our living room window shades. Anyone looking towards our houses will think the shadows they see are us and they'll think we're all in our living rooms.

Thirty minutes later we see eight bodies walking in a single file along the barbed wire fence. They're all carrying rifles. We can't tell by the thermal images what type of rifles they are. Two of them are carrying sheets of plywood which they lay over the barb wire fence. The sheets of wood allow them to walk over our fence. We'll have to find a way to make sure no one can use this trick on us again. Right after they cross our barbed wire, two of them step into one of our small punji pits, breaking their ankles and impaling their foot on the nails. Two are effectively out of the fight. The remaining six spread out slowly walking up Fred's driveway, so far they haven't seen us waiting in our trench. Their leader pauses, he kneels placing some type of device to his right eye. Damn it, he has a night vision device. We turn on our bright lamps which defeat his night vision and also momentarily blinds them, overloading their night vision.

Paul is our best shot, he looks at me, I nod. He aims and shoots a mine, it blows up in a bright flash, sending hundreds of nails out in all directions. We keep our heads down so any nails that come in our direction fly over our trench. The mini claymore surprises the hell out of our invaders while taking three of them out. Now there are only three people left. Paul aims, hitting the leader in his chest. Fred and I aim for the other two. I miss with one shot, hitting him with my second. Fred hits his target with his first shot. We wait to see if anyone else is coming. One of the wounded is crying out for mercy. We get up to see if any other invaders are alive. Of the eight who attacked us, three are wounded. They might make it, but it depends on if those who stepped in a punji pit get an infection and how serious the wounds of the others are. Fred asks, "Jay, should we call the police?"

"I think your friend Sheriff Grover sent them. Why don't you and Matt find their trucks and bring them here? We'll hide them at the far end of our property. I think the Sheriff will show up to see if his friends succeeded. We should act as if nothing happened. When dawn breaks, send the kids to police any brass they find. We need to remove the wood from the barb wire fence and remove any proof these guys were here. Strip the bodies, we'll bury them in a mass grave near the back end of our land next to the small hill."

Fred looks down at the three wounded invaders, "What about them?"

"Let's see if they have any knowledge we can use."

I bend down on one knee, "Any of you want to trade information?"

One of them men coughs up blood, asking, "What are you offering?"

"A quick, painless death, or we can cut your tongue out and drop you out in the back of our land, let the animals have you. You won't even be able to scream."

"What do you want to know?"

"Who sent you, what did they tell you about us?"

Cough, cough. "Sheriff Grover sent us. Told us you'd be real easy pickings, you have food, liquor, and women."

"Anything else you want to say?"

"He told us, he'll come by around nine in the morning."

"Thank you." Phuff. One silenced round to the center of his head sent him to hell.

Chapter 9

President Putin and Russian Minister of Defense Sergey Shoigu meet to discuss what else they can do to the Americans. "Mr. President, the American's economy is in the toilet, rioting is out of control, most of their cities are burning. Anything else we do will be considered an act of war, they may counter attack us with nuclear weapons."

President Putin laughs at his defense minister, "Sergey, the black Yankee President doesn't have the balls to use nuclear weapons. He lacks the balls to do anything except talk. He gives speeches how he wants the world to be, not how it actually is. How many lines in the sand has he drawn and moved in six years? He doesn't have one iota of guts in him. He's a pansy, we can do anything we want. As long as nothing can be traced directly to us, he won't do a damn thing. We are free to act in any manner we wish. I want some options that will destroy their economy for good. I don't want them to be able to quickly fix whatever we do to them. I want them to hurt. We are on the eve of the greatest moment in our history. We are about to capture Europe without firing a shot, if we manage the Americans right, we'll be able to control them forever."

"Mr. President, the only weapon in our arsenal which will destroy their economy is an EMP attack."

"Sergey, they'll see us launch it, their military may strike us on warning of our launch. I'd rather not use any type of tactical or strategic weapons."

"Sir, we can arm and train a lot of their protesters, they will keep the American police and military bogged down."

"I like this idea, how long until you can implement this idea?"

"I'll send a team to America, we'll ship the weapons in diplomatic pouches. The team will take a tour of the cities of America, dropping off the weapons and training their charges in how to fight the police."

"Are you sure you can ship enough weapons in diplomatic pouches to make a difference?"

"We can mark large crates as diplomatic pouches, the Americans do the same thing when they send equipment here."

You have permission to go ahead with your plan. Send me daily updates. Sergey, in order for this to work; it must stay a total secret. No one can know we're behind their next round of civil problems. Only use the best of your field people, people, you can totally trust."

"Yes, sir."

@@@@@

It took Franco and Fred three hours to dispose of the bodies. The two vehicles are hidden in a group of trees at the edge of our property. Franco's sons wore rubber gloves when they moved the trucks so no fingerprints could be traced to any of us. We retrace the invader's steps to clean up any brass and any signs they were here. At nine o'clock the next morning, like clockwork, Sheriff Grover shows up at Fred's front gate. Fred and I are waiting for him in Fred's kitchen. Cheri invites the Sheriff into their house. "Good morning, Sheriff. Would you like some eggs and bacon, coffee?"

"Just black coffee is fine, thank you."

Sipping my coffee, I look at the Sheriff, "Hello Sheriff Grover, what brings you back this beautiful morning? Have you decided to make me an offer for our grain?"

Looking at the front of the house, Grover says, "There were reports of gunfire last night I'm just checking to make sure everyone is OK."

Fred smiles at the Sheriff replying, "Well, that's very kind of you to check on us. As you can see, we're fine. We had a peaceful evening. We didn't hear any gunfire, Jay, did you and Lacy hear any at your place?"

"Nope, we slept like two babies."

We could tell looking at the Sheriff's face, he didn't believe a word we said, but he had no proof of anything to the contrary. He said, "Mind if I look around a little? Maybe someone tried to trespass on your property and got hurt in one of your illegal traps."

Fred looks hurt saying, "Sergeant, what traps are you talking about?"

"What about that trench that runs in front of your house?"

With all the strength I could manage, I say with a straight face, "Oh, that, it's the beginning of a new lawn sprinkler system."

"Isn't that a little deep for a sprinkler system?"

"Might be, we've never dug one before. Maybe we mixed up the instructions, you know like we converted the metric instructions into English wrong. Thanks for bringing it to our attention. I assure you we'll recheck the instructions as soon as possible. If there's nothing else, we're very busy today."

"Thank you for the coffee, I have nothing else to discuss with you today. As I said, there were reports of gunfire, I'm just checking on everyone in the area."

The Sheriff walked to his car while looking at the front of Fred's house. He shakes his head, he knows something's wrong. However, he doesn't have any proof what happened last night. When he gets in his car, he hits redial for the ninth time, the phone rings four times before going to voicemail. He curses to himself, thinking, *what the hell happened to George and his crew? He should have had an easy time last night. They wouldn't have been prepared for him. George and his crew should have been able to break in and show these assholes they need my protection. When I get my hands on George, I'm going to kick his ass. He must have picked someone up in the bar and spent the night with her. It's hard to find good help these days.* Fred takes George's phone out of his coat pocket, he and I look at the ringing phone showing the Sheriff's caller ID number and laugh. Fred says, "I wonder what he's going to do next?"

"He'll be back with some excuse to get a better look at our property. Later today, let's seed the plot where we buried our uninvited visitors."

"I'll get the boys on it later today."

"Thanks."

@@@@@

43,000 students attend one of the 36 colleges and universities in the Nashville area. As the value of the dollar crashes, the cost of each credit hour increases more than 50%. This forces many students to shift from full time to part time, extending their college education from four to six or more years. Many protest the quickly increasing costs, tens of thousands take to the streets protesting the rapid increase in their education costs. Thousands of students lose their part and full-time jobs due to the economy falling apart. Without a job, many students have to drop out of school. They begin the long trip home, most can't afford to pay the tuition without a job. Government student loans have dried up forcing many students to give up their education. Thousands of students sit in at their administrative offices in protest of the rising costs, lack of loans and lack of jobs.

@@@@@

Lacy and I are enjoying a cup of coffee after a long night, she says, "There's a truck at the gate." They're pushing the talk button. I get up to respond, "Hello?"

"Hello, this is Lowes hardware with a delivery. Franco ordered twenty pallets of Portland cement. Said to deliver it to your address."

"Please give me a minute to check with Franco."

"Lacy, please call up to Franco and see if he ordered a shitload of cement."

A minute later Lacy returns smiling, saying, "He said yes, more building materials are also on the way."

"Great, it would be nice if he warned us."

"Hello, I'm opening the gate, please follow the driveway, you can drop your load on the right side of the rear garage."

"Will do, we're going to need payment before we unload."

"I'm sure you do, how much?"

"Even with Franco's builder and quantity discount, it comes to $1,800."

"I assume you want cash?"

"If you want to pay with a credit card, we're supposed to collect a 3% processing fee."

"I'll pay in cash, I'll meet you at the garage."

Before I finish the discussion with the truck driver, Franco and his sons join me. "Jay, I'm sorry, I didn't check with you in advance, you said time was critical so I placed orders with my suppliers before they ran out of supplies."

"I don't disagree. In fact, I think you should order as much cement and reinforcing rods, sheet steel and sheets of plywood before they run out or the prices rise to a painful level."

"I'll place an order today."

"Might as well sign and pay for the cement. When are the reinforcing rods arriving?"

"Within an hour, they're coming along with 200 ½ inch sheets of steel and 400 sheets of plywood, nails, four air hammers and four small air compressors. If what we need isn't local we're not going to get it. I'm told the roads are too dangerous for any long distance deliveries. Most of the long distance truckers have gone home.

Either they can't afford the cost of fuel or they're worried about being attacked on the open road."

"Then order everything you can think of ASAP. I don't want to be caught at a loss because we need some small part that we can't get. Since the building materials are arriving, I assume this means you have the plans ready to show me?"

"Yes, we can review them right after the trucks make their delivery. We're lucky that there's a local cement plant, they were very happy to get our order. The manager told me he was going to close the plant due to low demand. With the stoppage of most construction, they have no demand for cement. We moved to the top of the line. As soon as you approve the plans and the hole is finished, we're going to pour the foundation as quickly as possible so we get our order filled before the plant closes."

"Franco, if you've found a local plant to provide us with cement, what's with the pallets of mix cement?"

"Odds and ends, plus for the tunnels between your homes and the shelter. If things are going to get as bad as you say, we can never have too much cement."

"OK, I'll give you that one."

Two hours later we have piles of cement, steel and wood stacked on the side of our garage. *I hope the Sheriff doesn't pay us another visit before the shelter is finished, we don't need him figuring out what we're building or where the shelter will be.* Looking at the plans Franco placed in front of me, "Franco is this real? Can you really build this?"

"It's going to be time-consuming because we don't want to disrupt the farms any longer than necessary, plus we don't want anyone knowing what we're doing."

"Did Lowes ask why you needed so much cement? Or why you wanted it delivered here?"

"I told them you were crazy rich, you wanted me to tear up your asphalt driveway and replace it with a cement one. Plus, you wanted a new parking area and a circular area built in front of your house. They laughed, saying I was going to need more cement than I ordered. I figured this was the safest way to respond to them. They ordered more cement which will be delivered here in two days from another one of their stores. I plan to build the shelter from cast cement forms and reinforced cement filled cinder blocks."

"I know I'm going to regret asking this, but where are the forms and the cinder blocks?"

"On flatbed trucks, I'm hoping they arrive within the next three days. I ordered them from different commercial suppliers, three of them are located south of Nashville, two are in Huntsville."

"Are the ones from Huntsville going to make the ninety-five mile trip here? Is it safe enough for them?"

"They're going to let me know. They told me, they've been making deliveries by sending their trucks out with armed security, if we elect to use their security, we have to pay their cost for the security people."

"If it comes to paying for the security or not getting the supplies, agree to pay for the security. While you're ordering supplies, I think you should order enough for your house foundation."

"I found a much cheaper home, I ordered a used mobile home, all we have to do is install the foundation it will sit on, then hook up the electric."

"When is this being delivered?"

"Next Monday. I thought you'd like us in our own home and out of yours as soon as possible."

"Franco, you move very quickly, I like that. Are the three of you going to be enough to build the shelter?"

"That's something else we need to talk about. I need extra hands."

"That's going to be a problem. I don't want strangers here seeing what we're building. When the shit hits the fan, they'll know what we have and try to take what's ours. There has to be another way. How many workers do you need?"

"It's different at each stage of the project. I could use ten right now."

"Damn it, ten?"

@@@@@

Due to the world's economies coming apart, millions of people leave their homes in Central and South America heading towards our Southern Border. They believe they'll be able to find a better life in America. They've been told President Obama will be granting amnesty to anyone who makes it across the border. Welfare, health insurance and free education for their children are all just across a line drawn on a map. Railroad trains are jammed with thousands of people traveling from their home countries to the southern American border. Many are carrying diseases not seen in America. A large number of the swarming young people are gang members. They know Americans are rich, and easy pickings to steal from. President Obama's DHS is running short on funds to process the waves of people. His administration promised to hire immigration lawyers for the poor people who are just looking to improve their lives. President Obama asks Congress to increase the budget for the DHS, Congress refused the request due to the stress on the economy. President Obama tries to shift money from the DoD and HHS to the DHS to pay for programs supporting the wave of immigrants crossing the Southern Border. Congress quickly passes a law, which the President vetoes, forbidding the President from shifting funds between federal departments. Congress is united behind stopping the President from shifting funds as he alone sees fit. Congress overrides his veto with a vote in the Senate of 75 to 22 with 3 voting present. The American people are behind the Senate's vote, which upsets the President who then announces he's going to withdraw all border patrol agents from the Southern Border, saying it's for their safety. Without sufficient funds to support the agents, he's pulling them back out of harms way. Without any border patrol, 2 million people swarm across the border overwhelming the towns along the border in Texas, Arizona, and California. Locals are killed, their homes looted and burned. The states lack the ability to process the immigrants. The states lack the funds to provide health care or provide education for the new immigrants. Thirty states pass bills that outlaw illegals from receiving healthcare, free education or any type of assistance. President Obama asks the Department of Justice to overturn the state laws as being racist. The immigrants are poor and hungry and without a job or welfare, they turn to crime in order to feed their families. Shoplifting, home invasions, rapes and robbery increase over 1,000 percent in two weeks. Battles break out between American citizens trying to protect their homes and the immigrants who are trying to feed their families. The governors of Texas and Arizona, call out the National Guard to patrol the border. President Obama federalizes the Guard, ordering them to return to their homes and armories.

Armed militias take up patrolling the border. Gun battles break out between the cartels and the militias, both sides crossing the border as the battle moves back and forth. In Texas, three families shoot illegals crossing the border on their property. The illegals fired on the homeowners who returned fire, hitting five of the illegals. President Obama ordered the FBI to arrest the homeowners. The FBI was blocked from issuing arrest warrants by the Texas Rangers. Upon hearing about the standoff, President Obama ordered the FBI to arrest the Texas Rangers and anyone else standing in their way to arrest the homeowners for murder. One of the FBI agents is shot by a homeowner who fired on the agent as he was breaking into his home. The agents behind the initial agent kill everyone in the house, later setting it on fire, burning it to its foundation. The media broadcasts the entire event live on the Internet and television until the FCC ordered the video taken off the air. The damage had already been done. Militias decide the Federal Government has declared war against the people. The militias attack Federal offices in revenge for the attacks on American citizens. America with a ruined economy is also on the edge of a civil war.

@@@@@

Matt and Lou pull two of the black pickups we inherited from the gang that tried to invade us into Fred's barn. The factory black paint is sanded before a gray primer is laid down in preparation for painting them white. I hope removing the window tint, and painting them white will hide them from the Sheriff's notice. Sandy offered to find some out of state license plates to mount on the two repainted trucks. He got one set of plates from New Jersey and a set from California for the vehicles. I decide not to ask where or how he got them. The plates are new and even have inspection stickers on them. Matt plans to change the wheels on the trucks so the vehicles look completely different from the ones George used to bring his men to our property. Tomorrow we'll drive one of them into town to see if anyone notices them. I'm still very concerned with supplying Franco with the number of workers he says he needs. Lacy spends every day converting more of our funds into precious metals and other assets we are going to need. President Obama announces the USA is stopping all interest payments in order to fund his social programs. Every week breaks the previous week's record for newly unemployed and lower tax revenue flowing into the government. President Obama refuses to stop spending, he's convinced he can spend the country out of its problems.

@@@@@

On Sunday, May 17th China dropped a financial bomb on America, it would have been more merciful had they dropped nukes, they issued a formal default notice to The Department of the Treasury. They demanded immediate payment of the $1.4 trillion debt China holds. China offers the Obama administration the option of seceding Hawaii and California to China as payment for the country's debt. China gave America ninety days to make payment in full. The world's economic markets are shocked by China's demand. The US dollar falls to an all time low. President Obama thinks China is bluffing. The Secretary of the Treasury informs the President not only can't America make the payments, but the country has also hit the debt limit and can't borrow any more money. With the national debt standing at $20.8 trillion, the Republican-held Congress refused to increase the debt limit. They inform the President he should cut spending because there's no way Congress is going to increase the debt limit. Most of the country agrees with Congress. President Obama goes on national television to announce he's going to issue an Executive order to continue to pay the country's bills and borrow money. China issues a press release saying President Obama may be breaking the US Constitution and they repeat their demand for repayment. With the falling value of the dollar, China demands payment in gold, sending the price of an ounce of gold to a new high of $4,000 an ounce.

@@@@@

The day after China's announcement has the entire world speaking about nothing else. A large and very wide flatbed truck arrives at our gate at two o'clock in the afternoon. Sitting on the truck is a steam shovel which Franco has been waiting for. I look at the monster machine asking,

"Do I want to know where this came from?"

Franco smiles, saying, "Not really and before you ask, I know how to use it."

"Can you tell me if I own it or did I rent it?"

"Kind of like you found it."

"Damn it, Franco, I don't want to give that asshole Sheriff any reason to arrest me."

"He won't, the shovel won't even be reported as missing. The construction company went out of business. A friend told me where to find it. By the way, a bulldozer will be here in a couple of hours."

"Why do we need a bulldozer?"

"The price was right."

Chapter 10

Paul, Randy, Fred and I are looking at Franco's plans for our shelter when our gate alarm sounds. We look at the monitor seeing an Army HUMVEE at our gate. I ask, "Does anyone have any idea why the Army would be paying us a visit?"

Everyone shakes their head no. "Well, I guess we ought to let them in and see what they want. Randy and Fred, grab your battle armor and weapons and hide in the rear trench in case they're not who they appear to be. Keep your phone on, I'll call you and leave mine on so you can hear what's being said."

Fred replies, "Will do."

A few minutes later the HUMVEE pulls up to my front door, two soldier's exit wearing ACUs, (Army Combat Uniform), one of them has a sidearm strapped to his leg. Paul and I meet them in front of the house, "Hi, what can we do for the US Army today?"

"We're looking for a Mr. Jay Tolson."

"That's me, what can I do for you?"

"Sir, I'm Sergeant Franklin and this is Private First Class Brown, we're on official business for the Federal Government."

"That doesn't sound good, would you like to come in? I think I'm past draft age, and if I remember right, I failed my draft physical back in the early 70's."

Sitting in our kitchen Sergeant Franklin hands me a sealed envelope with the seal of the DHS on it.

"I'm not sure I want to touch that envelope."

"Sir, my instructions are to present the envelope to you and wait for your response."

I look at Paul, who shrugs his shoulders so I open the envelope. Inside is a one-page letter addressed to me. I read the short note, handing it to Paul, who reads it, shaking his head. He slides it back to me, his eyes have turned cold, his fingers open and close next to his hip where his Glock 22 side arm is strapped to his leg. I look up at the Sergeant, "Sergeant, this is an unlawful order."

"Sir, as I'm sure you know the transportation network has been seriously broken, many cities and towns are very short of food. The Secretary of DHS, which has absorbed the National Guard for the duration of the national emergency, authorized the US Army and National Guard to purchase food supplies from farmers for the distribution to their surrounding towns. The records reflect that you purchased three producing farms, our assignment is to ascertain the amount of stored grains and other food crops you have. You are ordered to sell it to us at current market rates. Payment will be made to you within 90 days from when you present an invoice for payment."

"What if I don't want to sell it to you or anyone?"

"Mr. Tolson, per the President's order establishing a national emergency, you don't have the option of refusing to sell it to us."

"Sergeant, yes I do. Any unlawful order doesn't have to be followed and any law that violates the US Constitution is illegal."

"Mr. Tolson, the President has suspended the Constitution for the duration of the current national emergency."

"I haven't heard anything about that. When was the public announcement made?"

The Sergeant hands us another document, a copy of an Executive Order signed by the President. "Sergeant, the President, can't turn the Constitution on and off, it's not a light switch."

"Mr. Tolson, we're prepared to pay you the current market price for your stored crops."

"How would you be paying me?"

"We'll arrange a direct deposit into your account, less any estimated taxes due."

"Now, you're going to charge me taxes upfront?"

"Too many companies, large and small have been claiming losses, they're not paying their fair share so the President has decided that all government payments will be made net of tax."

"At what tax rate?"

"The rate depends on your income and combined savings and bank accounts."

"You're saying that you're going to tax me on the accounts we use for working capital?"

"All bank accounts are added together to calculate your tax. Based on the download the Department of Treasury has supplied us with, you are in the 75% tax rate, plus the millionaire 5% surtax. All accounts, both domestic and international are combined to calculate taxes."

"You're planning on stealing our crops. You're going to pay me only 20% of their value in dollars, which won't be worth the same amount by the time your deposit hits my bank. When you make the deposit, it may then trigger the President's special tax on bank accounts. In reality, I'm going to be lucky to see less than 5% of the net value of my crops. Nothing will be left to pay my staff and neighbors."

"Sir, would you rather the town's people starve?"

"They're not my concern, my family and the families of my neighbors are my concern."

"Isn't it true you're recruiting additional people? Didn't you just absorb a small construction company?"

"I don't know what you're talking about?"

"Care to explain truckloads of cement, rebar, sheet steel and plywood delivered to this address? Or what about the steam shovel and bulldozer?"

"I told the construction company owner, he could store his supplies and equipment here while his normal office is unavailable."

"Mr. Tolson, what are you building behind the house? Are you aware it's now against the law for anyone to damage or not use all of their available farm land to grow food crops? No one can let usable farmland sit idle. No one will get paid not to grow crops any longer. The country is hungry, we need to feed 320 million mouths as quickly as possible. We haven't been able to transport the food we have. We need local farmers to feed their surrounding communities."

"Sergeant, what I'm building is my business. I assume I'm still allowed to have some privacy aren't I?"

"Sir, you can as long as your privacy doesn't impact the production of food or interfere with the required support of the new national emergency orders."

"Is there a list of these national emergency orders?"

"They often change, we'll inform you if you're breaking any of the rules."

"Sergeant, are you telling me, I'm on 'double secret probation?'"

"Mr. Tolson, this isn't the time to be funny. The President is trying to save the country."

"I thought he did everything he could to destroy the country."

"Mr. Tolson, that's treasonous talk. I'd suggest you cease that kind of talk right now."

"Has free speech been outlawed?"

"Speaking out against the government is now against the law. Speaking against the President is classified as racist hate speech. Posts on the internet can also be deemed as racist or a breach of the federal hate crimes laws."

"I see."

"Mr. Tolson, what are your plans? If I have to, I can return with a court order, or with a platoon of armed men, or you can cooperate. Which will it be?"

"Sergeant, I already have contracts to sell my crops, as such you're violating my predated contacts. We're going to have a real problem, you see my sales agreement was signed before the President issued this executive order, and as such, my deal will stand. You should also know the local Sheriff also wants my grain, why don't the two of you figure out who's going to rape me, then I can set a fair price for my crops."

"Mr. Tolson, the price has been set by the Department of Agriculture."

"I'll be sure to let you and the Sheriff know if any grain is left after my existing buyer picks up his pre-ordered grain. Of course, it will then be sold at the new market prices and I don't accept dollars."

"What do you mean you don't accept dollars? You're an American business operating in the USA, dollars are the legal tender in America."

"As an independent business, it's up to me, the owner to decide how I want to be paid for my products. Not all business owners accept credit cards, not all accept EBT cards. I don't accept American dollars for any purchase over $10,000. The inflation rate is too high, the dollars devalue weekly."

"What do you accept?"

"Gold or silver."

"Sir, that's unacceptable, the President has signed a new executive order which will be made public very soon stating it's illegal for US citizens to own gold or silver."

"No such law currently exists, and until such an illegal law is issued, I only accept gold and silver as payment."

"Sir, we may be back to check your home for gold and silver. Soon all such private ownership will be collected. A truck will arrive in four days to collect your unsold crops."

"Better make it a very small truck."

The two soldiers frown, shaking their heads and the Sergeant says, "Mr. Tolson, we've tried to treat you as a professional and a patriot. I see we're going to have to change our approach, do I need to send an armed squad to take the crops?"

"If you do, it will get very messy."

"Are you threatening me?"

"No, I'm stating a fact. I own this land free and clear, the US Constitution provides me certain rights."

"I've already explained to you President Obama has placed the Constitution on hold for the duration of the national emergency."

"I don't accept illegal orders and unless you want to start a civil war, I'd suggest you leave my land and not return."

"We'll be back and we'll return with the force required to take what the town requires."

"Thank you for visiting, please leave my property. "The DHS has always been a pain in the ass, but this time the President has gone too far, he's setting up the country for a civil war. We the people aren't going to accept the President canceling the Constitution. We're not going to accept the US Army treating us like we're slaves. The farmers and landowners I know aren't going to accept the US government taking our crops while paying us shit and taxing the shit payments up front. Had they offered a decent price and terms I would have sold them some crops we have set aside just for this purpose. I won't allow the government or anyone else to steal from us. We're working too hard to allow them to walk in here and take what they want. This is still America. We're going to have to keep an armed, ready action force on alert 24/7 in case they return.

@@@@@

Both Sammi and Shelly called to say they were planning on visiting the third week of June when our grandkids' school was closed for summer vacation. Lacy and I are overjoyed. We're going to have a house full. It's also our chance to talk to them face to face about staying here. We bought the house with the plan of them staying with us. Sammi and Ricky drove to Shelly's house where they spent a night, then the two families caravanned to our house. They made it in one day. When they arrived, the grandkids ran wild around the house and yard after being cooped up in the minivans for so long. They loved their bedroom, with bunk beds and a tent that could be spread between the beds giving them a built in play area. Their room also had a large TV and a Xbox video game console with their favorite games. They couldn't wait to change and hit the pool.

Sammi, Ricky, Shelly, and Todd joined Lacy and me on the patio chatting over a bottle of wine and beers for Ricky and Todd while the kids splashed and played in the pool. I started off the discussion, "You know Mom and I love you, we worry about you. We think the economy is going to completely collapse and when it does, you may not be able to get enough gas to get here. It may not be safe to stay in your homes. We have everything you need here."

Ricky says, "Dad, what about our jobs?"

"Son, we have enough money, none of you needs to work again. If you don't like living under our roof, we can get you your own house."

Sammi smiled, saying, "We're not farmers, we don't want to play in the dirt."

"Honey, we're not farmers, we're farm, owners. There's a big difference. We bought the farms to ensure we have a steady food supply."

Shelly points to the large hole in the field, "Dad, what's with the hole? Planning on burying half of Nashville?"

Laughing, "Only the bad half. The hole's deep enough they'll never find the bodies."

Todd looks at the hole and the branches leading out from it, "Dad, you're building a large shelter with underground access from each home."

"Yes, you win the grand prize."

"How large is it going to be?"

"Large, Large enough to hold 40 people for months."

Ricky looks into the hole saying, "Why months? Are you again expecting the end of the world? More right wing bullshit?"

"Ricky, you and I haven't agreed on politics or our views of the world. I like to be prepared, you think the government will protect you from anything that may happen. You forgot about Katrina and Sandy or Three Mile Island. You forget that the government doesn't have the resource to help if something happens in the entire country. They had enough problems trying to support a small area of the country, there's no way they can provide support for the entire country. We're going to be left on our own to care for ourselves. Just a few days ago the National Guard showed up on my front door to demand I give them my crops to feed the local town. They were willing to use force to get what they wanted from me. Is this what you thought would happen?"

"Where's your proof this happened? How do we know this wasn't another example of your right wing bullshit?"

"Ricky, you can believe what you want, I'm telling you, and Mom can back me up, they came here to take my crops. They told me President Obama set aside the Constitution."

"Dad, that's a good thing, the Constitution is over 200 years old, it wasn't written for these trying times. The needs of the many overcome the needs of the one."

"What about my freedom?"

"Why should your freedom cause harm or the death of innocents? Why is your freedom more important that feeding the hungry."

"I'm not doing anything to cause the death of innocents."

"Yes you are, they're hungry, and you're refusing to give your crops to feed them."

"You agree that the government has the right to take what it wants?"

"If it's for the good of the people, yes."

"I see, well, I hope you enjoy living in a communist country. I know I won't. I expect to be paid for what people take from me."

"It's people like you that caused our problems. It's always been all about you, you don't understand sharing for the greater good. You don't pay your fair share so everyone is fed and healthy. It's people like you who have held our progress back."

"Ricky, it's impossible to hold a logical discussion with you. Why don't you leave Sammi and Linda here and you return home? You go ahead and be a good little commie and swear allegiance to the President while being part of the death of the greatest country in the world."

"Dad, you mean one of the most racist countries in the world."

"Please leave, I don't want to say something I know I may one day regret."

Ricky tries to get the last word in, "Dad, stop with the end of the world bullshit. You scared the crap out of Sammi for most of her childhood, EMP, sun spots, nuclear world war, global pandemics, no more scaring us or Linda. We don't want our daughter corrupted by your sick thoughts. You tried to scare Sammi and me into becoming preppers, you tried to convince us to spend more for a house that had a basement which you wanted us to convert into a shelter. We come to visit you to find you tearing up a perfectly good farm and making a shelter the size of an ark. Dad, you need professional help. You're right, we're not staying here, I wouldn't have even come, except that Linda wanted to see her Papa Jay. Mom, please take him to see a doctor. He really needs help. If you don't, Sammi and I may check into seeing if we can have him committed for observation."

The patio is silent after Ricky's outburst. I look at my son-in-law, lowering my voice to a whisper, I lean towards him, "Ricky, if you even try to have me committed, you will be very sorry. I think it's best if you and Sammi leave my house. I don't want you under my roof. There's a Hampton Inn about three miles away, I'll make arrangements for you to stay there until you're ready to go home."

Lacy pats my arm, "Honey, calm down."

"NO, Ricky, go upstairs and pack, I want you out of my house within fifteen minutes."

Sammi gets up, she comes to me, she hugs me saying, "Daddy, we love you, we're worried about you."

"Sammi, you are my firstborn, for years my world revolved around you. I told you, I would always be here to protect you. I'm trying to protect you now. What's my thanks? You and your husband want to put me in a mental hospital because I see things differently than you?"

"Daddy, we think you watch too much Fox news. We think you just need a little time to rest. No more of those crazy books you read, no more gun magazines, we think you just need a little rest. A man your age should have a hobby, something like golf, not playing with guns. Daddy, we're worried about you because we love you."

"Sammi, I'll love you forever, you're my daughter. But now, I have to ask you to leave my home." I get up leaving everyone behind on the patio. Shelly looks at me, "Daddy, are you OK?"

"I'm hurt and don't want to talk anymore. Sammi, Ricky, please leave my home ASAP."

Lacy comes after me, she pauses in the doorway. She turns to look at Sammi, "See what you've done? We were so looking forward to having everyone under one roof. You've ruined all of Dad's plans. I'm also hurt by you."

"Lacy, it's not like that. It's just..."

"No more, do as your father said. Leave our house within fifteen minutes."

Sammi and Ricky don't look into Lacy's eyes. They go to their room and pack. While they packed, I logged on and booked them a room at the Hampton Inn. Linda is upset having to leave her cousins. Linda's eyes are full of tears as she drags her overnight bag behind her. "Papa Jay, why do I have to leave?"

"You don't have to leave, your mommy and daddy are leaving. They don't like their room. They're going to a hotel. You can stay here if you'd like."

She runs over to hug me. Sammi comes into the room saying, "Come on Lins, we have to go."

"I said she can stay if she wants to."

Sammi looks up asking "Us too?"

"No, just her."

"Daddy, please?"

"No. You made your decision." I turn my back on my daughter leading Linda back outside to play with her cousins.

Shelly says, "Daddy, are you OK?"

"Yes honey, let me know when Sammi and her husband have left the house. I'll be outside."

@@@@@

In Moscow, the Russian leadership held a war meeting in the command bunker located three hundred feet under Moscow. The Minister of Finance stood and looked around the room, nodding at the ministers he knew he could count on. "Mr. President, Ministers, we are poised on the eve of a historic event. We're about to watch the Americans implode and collapse. Their economy is already over stressed. They're bankrupt and don't know it yet. We're going to help them over the edge of the abyss. We've spoken to the Chinese, who are also dumping their dollars. Europe is falling over the edge of a cliff, the EU will completely unwind within 90 days. The best way to cripple the West is to crush their supply chain. The American's invented the art of logistics, our financial attack surprised them. They counted on China buying a new series of bonds they announced they're going to issue. China surprised the hell out of the Yankees when they announced that not only they weren't going to be buying any of America's bonds, but they demanded full payment on all of their outstanding loans." Laughing, Putin says, "The little yellow bastards even offered to take Hawaii and California off their hands in exchange for the full payment. When their government isn't able to fund any of their welfare programs, their people will riot like nothing the world has ever seen before. Their people will tear their own infrastructure apart. When things reach the eve of a civil war, when millions are dying of starvation, then we'll move to help the poor Americans."

The Party Chairman says, "Mr. President, Minister, think of it, America in ruins. Party Chairman Nikita Khrushchev told them we would bury them. He told the Americans that Capitalism would be their destruction. After seventy years, we'll be enjoying a bottle of Vodka sitting in the President's Oval Office while the American elites in Washington run around trying to kiss our asses."

President Putin stands to address the Ministers, "Ministers, Lenoid is correct, we are watching America destroy itself. We won the second Cold War without firing a shot. I want the FSB and the Red Army to be ready to land in America."

The Minister of the Interior stands with a shocked look on his face, "Mr. President, are you planning on invading America? That would be very dangerous. The one thing that will unite the different people of America is an invasion. It may be the only time their left and right will agree to the same course of action which is to unite to push us off their land."

Putin laughs, "Ministers, please let me explain. We're not going to be invading as in the military sense of the word. We're going to land on America's shores to provide aid to the poor starving sick people who learned their government and Capitalism can't help them. We'll land with food and water in our arms, not assault rifles. We'll land with trucks full of medication in place of tanks. History has shown people will quickly trade their so called freedom for a full belly every day. We'll let the American economy fail, their logistics train will fall apart from the nonpayment and the people in their cities will be starving and begging for anyone to help them. When a few million of them die from starvation, lack of clean water and lack of medications, then and only then will we move in to provide humanitarian help to them. Of course, once we're in, we'll never leave. We'll control America."

The Director of the FSB stood asking, "Mr. President, what price did the Chinese ask to support us?"

The war room becomes totally silent. President Putin stood facing the Director of the FSB, "We agreed that China can try to take the states of Hawaii and California. They plan to force Korea, Thailand, Vietnam, Cambodia, Philippines, Singapore, Malaysia, and of course Taiwan to submit to their rule. They've already reached an agreement with Japan. The rest of Asia is ours, as is Europe." The Ministers are shocked by the news. None says a word, they can each hear their partner's heart's beating. They knew a deal with China was going to have to be cut in order for them not to lose their largest trading partner. None of the Ministers expected the price of the Chinese acceptance to be so high. Putin looked at the shocked and gloomy faces of his Ministers, "What the hell is wrong with all of you? China may end up with parts of Asia, much of which they are going to have to fight for while the Motherland ends up with our breakaway republics back, all of Europe and the largest prize of all, most of America. With America out of the way, Canada and England will fall our way as will New Zealand and Australia. The Chinese forgot to list Midway in their list. I want the Red Navy to send a task force to Midway to hold it against any attack from China. If we can hold Midway, Australia, and New Zealand, we'll block China's expansion. At the end of the day, we will rule the world."

Sergey stands, "I suggest we replace our glasses of tea with good Russian Vodka! President Putin has brokered a deal to make the Motherland the most powerful country and empire in the world's history. We're about to rule the world. We all know the Chinese are a generation behind us in weapon design. Once we swallow the American military, we'll add their technology to ours, we will easily be able to crush the yellow bastards at a time of our choosing. President Putin made an excellent bargain. The Chinese think we're allies. They are going to get bogged down in endless wars in Asia while our military will grow stronger. Once we have firm control of the northern hemisphere, South America, and Africa will come begging us to join our Empire."

Putin smiles, standing, he says, "I intend to treat Africa as a mine and a zoo. The only money we'll spend there is what's required to take their assets out of the ground, moving them to our factories. Let their people kill each other off or they can die of one disease or another. The Africans are not going to be allowed to leave their areas. We will enslave them, working them to their death. We'll own the bulk of the world's key minerals."

Sergey motions to an aide standing by, carts of fresh black bread, caviar, and vodka are brought into the war room.

@@@@@

That evening Lacy, Shelly, Todd, the girls and I are watching Survivor when the program is broken into with a special announcement. "Ladies and Gentlemen, we are interrupting your programming tonight with a special announcement. The talks between China and the US have broken down. China recently announced they are dumping their remaining holdings of US dollars. China currently holds over $1.4 trillion in US debt and they are demanding immediate repayment of the debt. China has also announced they will no longer accept our dollars in payment for their goods and services. Without an agreement, the US will have to find a way to repay China's debt. The Department of the Treasury announced that a series of special taxes will be implemented so the country can repay China."

Shelly looks at me, "Dad, what does it all mean?"

"Honey, it means we're in the crapper. China just drove the final nail into our financial coffin. Our dollar isn't going to be worth two cents in the morning. Inflation is going to become hyperinflation, the stock market has already crashed. I think the market will open down hundreds of points tomorrow. Honey, are you sure you have to return home?"

"Both Todd and I have jobs back home."

"Want to bet? I bet you'll both find out that you're going to be out of a job within 48 hours."

"I'll take that bet, what are we going to wager? The normal amount?"

"Yup, I win, you give me two kisses and a hug, you win and I'll give you a hug and two kisses." Turning to Todd, "We've been betting the same amount since she was three or four years old."

Todd smiles, "I like that, I think I'm going to steal it from you."

"Go ahead, it's free."

I turn to Lacy. "Honey, I think tonight's the perfect time to order anything online you ever wanted, I'm not sure what's going to be available for how long or at what prices. I'd buy more freeze dried food if you can find it."

Todd asks, "Dad, what about ammo?"

Laughing, "Todd, we have enough to support a medium sized army."

Todd replies, "You always said one can never have too much ammo."

Nodding, I tap Todd on the shoulder saying, "Come, I'll show you part of the armory."

Lacy shakes her head saying, "Honey, he believes you, let it go for now."

I think I understand what she's trying to say to me, "Todd, let's watch the news together, trust me, we're OK on ammo and supplies."

The rest of the evening's programs are taken off the air, reporters take their place talking about the hit to our economy and the potential implications for the future. A couple of the reporters say that all that's needed is for the government to increase spending and to reinstate the welfare programs. Others say the country is doomed, the country has already passed the tipping point, the country will implode before the internal and external pressures cause a mass explosion that will take the country down.

While we're talking, the phone rings. Lacy picks it up, she listens for a second saying, "Honey it's for you."

"Hello?"

"Daddy, I'm sorry, we were wrong. Can we come over? We're scared."

Lacy looks at me knowing what the call was about, I look at her, she nods. "Sammi, check out and come home. Just remind Ricky to keep his mouth shut around me."

Chapter 11

A furious President Obama is pacing the Oval Office, "I don't understand what the Chinese want from us. They know damned well we don't have the resources to pay them $1.4 trillion! We wouldn't have borrowed the money from them if we had it to repay them."

Jack Lew, the Secretary of the Treasury, watches the President pace. "Mr. President, we borrowed the money from China. The terms of our agreement are, we have to pay the loans back with interest on the agreed upon payment schedule. If we default on any terms of the loan, the loans are due when called, which China has just done."

"Jack, when did we default on any of the terms? What are our options?"

"Mr. President, we defaulted when we missed making the last interest payments. We delayed it and the Chinese are within their rights to call the loans. As to our options, we can ask the Fed to print a few additional trillion dollars, however, sir, by doing such will cause massive inflation. Plus, I'm not sure the Fed will do it."

"Jack, I've spoken to the Fed Chairwoman, she told me she's not leaning towards printing a trillion or any amount. She said doing so will completely destroy our economy. The crazy bitch said we might never recover. She reminded me that without the EU, there's no one else standing by to help bail us out of the hole we got ourselves into."

"Mr. President, there are a few things we could look at. Mind you, these ideas are very drastic."

"What are you thinking?"

"We can recreate the law outlawing private ownership of precious metals. We'll buy them back at a low figure and since the value of silver and gold has jumped, the metals we confiscate will be used to pay China. We can also increase the income tax rates to 75% on anyone earning over $250,000 a year. We can impose a federal property tax on every homeowner. We can impose a personal property tax on everyone's car and all boat owners. We could expand this to all commercial and farm equipment."

"These are some very interesting ideas. I like them, make it anyone earning over $120,000 a year. No one needs $10,000 a month to live. I really like the personal property tax and since no one needs to own a boat today, set the tax rate at 15% of the items book value."

"Sir, what about the tax on homeowners?"

"We'll hold this one in case we need additional income later."

"Sir, we can also increase the tax on corporations that hold dollars off-shore, we announce that taxes will be levied on dollars anywhere they're held. We'll tax them as if they were held in a USA bank, earned in the USA. They're owned by US corporations so it's really the same thing."

"I like this idea a lot, how long will it take to put in place?"

"Only a few days."

"Do it and hurry, we're running out of time to get the Chinese off our backs."

"Sir, one point you should consider, doing all of these tactics will do permanent damage to the dollar and our economy."

"The alternative is giving China some assets equal to the debt we owe them."

"What are they asking for?"

"Mr. President, first of all, they want Hawaii."

"Hawaii? No way, I plan to retire to Hawaii right after I sign the papers allowing Hawaii to become an independent nation."

Jack stops in mid-word staring at the President, "Mr. President, the people, will never accept that. You'll never get away with it."

"Yes, I will, you'll see. The press loves me, the people love me. It'll happen and no one will know until it's too late to stop it."

Unknown to either President Obama or Jack, an aide was listening to the entire conversation by standing next to the door between the Oval Office and the Executive Conference Room. The aide doesn't believe what the President and the Secretary of the Treasury are agreeing to. The aide texts a friend inviting them to a drink after work. At seven o'clock the aide enters a bar in Arlington, Virginia. He orders a draft while he waits for his friend who arrives within three minutes. "Sorry, parking's a bitch."

"I agree, I took the metro from D.C."

"What's so important you had to break protocol to ask for a face to face meeting?"

The aide slides his notes across the table folded in a newspaper. His friend's face turns white as he reads the note. "Is this really going to happen?"

"I stood by the door, I heard every word. Jack Lew is having the new tax rules drafted for release within the next few days."

"Christ, this is going to tear the country apart. I understand why the meeting couldn't wait. There are two girls coming in to join us in a couple of minutes. They're going to ask to join us, we're going to buy them a beer, laugh like we're having a good time. You're going to leave with one, me with the other. They're our cover story. Two old friends from college have a beer together, meet a couple of nice girls and leave for the evening. She will go home with you, she'll stay for a couple hours. In case you're being watched, it'll look normal enough."

"You mean she's going to sleep with me as a cover?"

"Don't get carried away, she works for me. If she went home with you and quickly left, it wouldn't look right. Make her dinner, have a drink, tell her your life's story. She's a good kid and also a black belt. She won't take any crap."

"What do you want me to do tomorrow?"

"Act normal, act as if you got laid tonight."

"OK, I'm supposed to be on call for a meeting of the National Security Council."

"Great, I can't meet with you tomorrow. If you learn something very important text the girl, you go home with tonight. She'll give you her number."

"OK, look here they come. Wow, they are both very pretty! Can I take the blonde home?"

"If you think blondes have more fun, you're wrong. She's a real ball-buster."

"I don't care, she's very easy on my eyes."

"It's your life."

@@@@@

While we wait for Sammi and her family to arrive Franco knocks on the doorframe, "Jay, got a minute?"

"Sure, what's up?"

"We heard the news report so we think we should work on the shelter around the clock. Do you have any objections? We'll rig the large construction lights to provide us with light. We ought to be able to finish the main opening tonight and if we can get help with the backhoes, we should be able to finish the tunnels to each home in six days."

"Franco, I hate to say it, but you may be right. Things don't look very encouraging. Please, go ahead. I also think you should rig a tarp over the hole so anyone flying a drone won't see what we're doing."

"We can do that. I hope everyone else doesn't get angry over the noise."

"If they complain, tell them to put ear plugs in. Our salvation is likely that hole in the ground."

Within minutes, we hear the steam shovel working on the shelter. We're watching FOX news, Lacy is trying to calm me down since I'm yelling at the TV. Sammi and her family return helping Lacy stop me from throwing something at the TV. Sammi runs into my arms, "Daddy, I'm sorry. We saw the news and a couple of minutes later, Ricky got an email informing him he's been laid off for the duration of the current financial crisis."

"Sam, I'm very sorry. This isn't what I wished for. Shelly and Todd are deciding if they should go home or stay. I think they're going to stay. You'll be much safer here than on the road. That's if you're able to afford to fill your gas tank. Inflation will start exploding and gas, which is in very short supply, is going to be almost impossible to find."

"Daddy, I won't doubt you again."

"Yes, you will, don't worry about it. I'll try to hold my temper in check."

Before we continue my phone pings with a message, reading it, my mouth drops open, Lacy says, "Honey, what's wrong? What's going on?"

"Lacy, we need to convert the money we have in the bank into gold and cash that can't be traced. Stock up on food, supplies, everything you can think of."

"Honey, what's going on? A forum I belong to just sent an alert message out, it seems someone got a hold of Obama's next plan. He's going to confiscate gold and silver in private hands, tax people like us at 75%. He's going to levy another tax on our bank accounts and bonds we're holding. He's also planning to place a tax on the personal property we own."

Lacy asks, "What property?"

"Our cars, the house, the farms and even the farm equipment."

"Oh shit. Can he do that?"

"Since there's no one with any balls in Congress, no one is willing to talk bad about him out of fear they're breaking the racist/hate speech laws. He's become more of an emperor than a President."

Sammi asks, "Dad, why is he taxing everything so much?"

"China wants to be paid back, he has to raise the money someplace. He figures taxing the rich is the best way."

Lacy shakes her head asking, "How do we hide our gold and silver? I've been converting money into gold and silver every week since we won the lottery."

"Lacy, where have you stored it?"

"In the safe." Smiling, she acts very proud of herself.

"Honey, we have to find another place to hide it. The first place they'll look is in safe."

Lacy starts to get angry, "Are you saying, they're going to come to our home looking for money? What are they going to take next, my jewelry? My gold fillings?"

"Don't give the government any ideas. I'm sure they're going to count our watches as gold, not jewelry. Sooner or later they may get around to taking our fillings."

"Jay, what are we going to do? I'm not prepared to lose our investment."

"I'll find a way." Thinking to myself, *Where would I look for gold coins? If I was coming into a house like this, where would I look?* "Honey, I have an idea, I want to sleep on it, if it still sounds good over coffee we'll discuss it. By the way, make sure you order twenty or so cases of coffee from the importer in Miami, I don't want to be without our coffee."

"Yes dear, I'm making a new list. I'll ask the girls if they need anything special for themselves and the kids. I don't know how they're going to get it here."

"Mail is still working, ask them to mail it. We should also make sure we have at least a year's supply of everyone's medications. I'd like to have two or three years supply on hand. I don't know where we're going to get the extra medications. After the damn Obamacare passed, every insurance company tells the others when drugs have been purchased. I tried to buy a six-month supply for cash, the drug store refused to fill my order because it was too early for refills. We've got to find a new source for medications. The Canadian ones I used have stopped shipping to the states."

Todd says, "Dad, should we take a quick trip across the border into Mexico?"

"If I can't find another source soon enough we'll have no other choice but to make a run to Canada or Mexico."

Shelly looks worried, "Dad, do you really think the trouble's going to last a year or longer?"

"Honey, I hope not, but you know me, you know I'd rather be prepared and not need it than to need it and not have it."

Shaking her head and smiling, Shelly nods her understanding while Sammi asks, "Is this going to be a yellow or red alert stock up?"

Lacy laughs, saying, "I think dad thinks this is a DEFCON 1 prepare. By the end of the week, none of us will be able to fit in the house for all the boxes he'll have."

Everyone laughs as we break up for the night.

@@@@@

As the dawn spreads over the country, millions of people wake, they read or listen to the news over their breakfast coffee. The stories of the new taxes and government confiscation scare most people. People log on to their bank accounts, where they try to transfer funds offshore. People line up in front of bank branches hours before they open. The Presidents of the largest banks reach out to Jack Lew asking for advice. The bank chairmen remind the Secretary of the Treasury they don't keep enough cash on hand to pay off all of their depositors. Jack orders the Federal Deposit Insurance Commission (FDIC) to issue an emergency order whereby depositors can withdraw only $250.00 a day. Banks are ordered to put up signs in every branch and place the emergency orders on their websites. These notices increase the country's financial panic. At 9:00 AM when the banks open, they are met with lines of thousands of people waiting to get into the bank. ATMs had been emptied of cash hours before the banks opened, increasing the panic. The initial people who made it to the teller demand to close their accounts but instead they are handed a notice from the FDIC saying a maximum of $250.00 withdrawal a day per person. Photo IDs are required to withdraw cash but by 9:30 AM the FDIC changes the rules mandating two photo IDs are required to withdraw cash. ATM cards are not accepted as an ID. At 10:30 AM, with thousands still in line, the FDIC orders the banks to close for three days to cool off the run on the banks. The FBC orders the country's banks not to refill the ATMs. The bank holiday increases the public's panic. People without cash don't know how to pay for whatever food they can locate. With the banks closed and the ATMs empty. Interest rates on credit cards are increased to 35%.

My entire family is having breakfast in the dining room. The television in the family room was placed is the dining room so we can watch the panic spread across the country. Shelly asks, "Dad, what do you think is going to happen next?"

"Honey, I think the stock market is going to crash when it opens, the real tipping point is going to be July 15th."

Lacy asks, "Hon, why July 15th?"

"The second Wednesday of the month is when the government makes their direct deposit for social security, VA, welfare, disability, you name it. If the government is really as broke as I think they are and having to scrape together every penny it can to pay back China, they are going to default on the July payment. If they default on their payments, there's going to be a panic that surpasses Black Tuesday, October 29, 1929, when the market lost 12% of its value. It was the 'official' start of the great depression. About half of the US population relies on some form of government payment program, 47% of families rely on food stamps. When the government defaults how are these people going to feed their families? They are going to tear every food store apart. People will swarm out of the cities after they strip the cities clean like hordes of locusts and since we're a farm, many will assume we have a supply of food. We have to be ready before it happens. We have five weeks to complete our preparations."

The table is silent as my words sink in. Sammi asks, "Dad, can we be ready in five weeks?"

"We don't have a choice. I may be wrong. Obama may find the money to make the payments. If he does, it will just delay the collapse for another month or two. It's going to happen. They've tipped their hand when they announced the bank holiday."

Lacy asks, "Honey, what are we going to do about our accounts? I don't want the government to take our money."

"Honey, how much do we have in the banks?"

Smiling, Lacy says, "Hon, we have $20 million in various accounts here and overseas."

"Good and bad news. I don't know where to hide $20 million."

"Honey, I think the accounts in Switzerland should be safe. Cash is going to become next to worthless. We should buy things that will be in high demand in a crash. Food, water, medications, cigarettes, beer and liquor, ammo, sporting equipment, toilet paper, and even diapers."

Sammi asks, "Dad, why not gold?"

"Sammi, people will be looking for goods to live on before gold has any real value. A family can have a million dollars in gold but with no food, they'll die. Food and life-saving medications are initially going to be worth a lot more than gold. I want everyone to search online for anything on the list and buy up everything you can find. I think we have only a couple of weeks before it turns to shit. I also want us to stock up on beer, wine, and cigarettes. I know none of us smokes, they'll make goof trading items."

Ricky says, "Dad, just another one of your typical end of the world bullshits, nothing's going to happen. You'll see I'm right and this is a total waste of money. It's your money, if you want to waste it, it's your decision. I won't help you waste good money. I don't understand why you don't willingly pay your tax? Its people like you who refuse to pay your fair share that put us in this situation."

"Ricky, you don't have to help, but do me a favor, keep your bullshit to yourself and your mouth closed."

Todd asks, "Dad, can you convert it into diamonds?"

"Todd, maybe but diamonds are not as easy to sell as gold and silver. Grading diamonds is much harder than determining if gold or silver is pure. Government coins are accepted as pure while diamonds are much harder to use as currency. Most people couldn't tell a real diamond from a cubic zirconia. Diamonds won't work. I think we should focus on what most people either want, need or just can't do without."

Todd asks, "Drugs?"

"Todd, if you mean drugs like coke or heroin, my answer is no. I won't deal with those kinds of drugs. They'll end up killing their users. I'll stock morphine and other pain meds because even we may need them."

Shelly asks, "Dad, can you transfer the money to Canada?"

"Ricky, all international electronic transfers are being watched by the IRS and the FDIC. I think I need to take a little trip to Nashville this afternoon."

"Lacy asks, "Honey, what are you thinking?"

"I know a couple of people I want to chat with. Todd, want to take a little ride with me?"

"Sure Dad, when do you want to leave?"

"Say 11, I have to call him to make sure he's in town and he'll see us."

Sammi asks, "Why Todd and not Ricky? Who is he?"

I look into my oldest daughter's eyes, "Because in a jam I know I can count on Todd. I don't have the faith that Ricky will know what to do. We're going to be crossing into a gray area. We're going to be making a deal with the devil. I want someone who will not be scared to hold a gun and know how and when to use it."

Lacy looks worried, "Jay, where are you going?"

"I'm going to see if we can cut a deal with Tony."

"Are you sure it's safe? Can you trust him in the current situation?"

"I can usually trust him to screw us a little, to him it's just business. I know what he's going to charge and I'd rather do him a favor than pay our money to the government. Having him and his friends as our friends may help us in more ways we can count."

Lacy nods her head in agreement with me. She says, "Make sure you tell him I said I'm looking forward to seeing Nancy soon."

Ricky asks, "Who is Tony?"

Lacy answers, "He's a member of what you could call the mob."

Sammi says, "Dad, you deal with gangsters? That's wrong. I'm against it."

"Honey, when it's your money you can deal with whomever you want. Todd finish up, then join me in the basement. We'll pack some heat in case we run into some unforeseen problems."

"Dad, give me a couple of minutes to finish my morning routine."

Laughing, I nod my agreement.

@@@@@@

As Todd and I are pulling out of the driveway, we pass five trucks with large preformed cement walls waiting to pull into our and Fred's driveways. Todd says, "Looks like the walls of the shelter have arrived."

"Looks that way, I wonder what the shelter is going to cost."

"You don't know?" Todd asks in a shocked voice.

"Nope, I just told Franco to get it done. I opened an account he can access to pay his suppliers. I told him to see me when the account balance falls under $10,000. He's stretching the original fund longer than I thought he would."

"Can I ask how much was in the original account?"

"$2 million."

"$2 million? You signed over $2 million to someone you barely know? What if he skims cash off for himself?"

"Very hard for him to do. He may be able to skim off some funds from payments he makes to suppliers, but not very much. Either I trust him to build our shelter, which is also going to be his shelter or I have a real problem. I have to trust a small group of people. I'm looking at the big picture. If Franco skims a couple of hundred thousand yet is able to finish the shelter, what do I care? If we need to use the shelter, cash is going to be worthless."

"Dad, how bad do you think it's going to get?"

"Todd, how bad do you think it's going to be when a hundred fifty million people have no money, no way to feed their families? When there are no deliveries to food stores, no food available even if they had the money? What would you do to feed your family?"

"Anything I had to."

"There's your answer."

"Is this Tony a real member of the mob?"

"So they say. Be careful what you say and do in front of him. He or his people will notice everything, anything that 'smells' to them could cost us dearly. Take your lead from me."

"OK. What deal are you hoping to cut with him?"

"A simple conversion of dollars to gold and silver that the government doesn't know anything about. We'll end up paying 35-50% over the current exchange, but I'd rather give it to Tony and his friends than to the government."

"They have untraceable gold?"

"So the rumor goes. Todd, the meeting is going to look very friendly, but one wrong word can cost us our lives, so don't say anything unless you think it through three times."

We park in front of a small Italian restaurant, the only one on a street lined with barbecue, bars and music clubs. The sign on the door says, "CLOSED."

I knock, saying, "Jay."

The door opens, a man I know as a friend of Tony smiles at me. He asks, "Who's the other guy?"

"Frank, this is my son-in-law, Todd."

"OK, come on in. Tony is waiting for you in the private dining room. He has Sal with him, so I guess you can bring Todd with you." I stop, reaching into my windbreaker, I hand Frank my sidearm and tell Todd to hand over his. Frank smiles, saying, "Excellent, you learn fast. I like that."

Entering the back room, Tony stands to welcome me with a hug and a kiss on both cheeks. "Jay, welcome, your message sounded very urgent. Who is that with you? Did you acquire another farm?"

"Tony, this is Todd, my son-in-law."

"Hello Todd, welcome to my restaurant."

"Tony, a pleasure."

"Jay, what's going on?"

"I'm sure you've seen the government's new tax and steal messages. I don't want to give the IRS half or more of my money or have them steal my accumulated gold. I know you have tons of gold coins stashed away, coins the government doesn't know anything about. I'd like to buy some from you. Before you ask, I'm willing to pay your price. This isn't the time for discussions and bullshitting over the quantity or price. My only questions are how much are you willing to sell me and at what price."

"Jay, as usual, you get right down to business. I have all you want. I'll sell them to you at a commission of only 35% because of all the business we've done in the past few months. You've always taken care of me, you've always kept your mouth shut and you arranged to share one of the gun runs you purchased from the cartel."

"Tony, thank you. I accept your offer. I want to purchase $15 million worth. The trick will be transferring the funds without attracting the notice of the FDC."

Laughing, Tony responds, "Leave that to me. I can have the coins here in three days."

"Sounds fair to me. Shall we say 8:00 PM? We can enjoy dinner while we make the exchange. I will need to bring some people to help make the transfer."

"As long as they're your family. No outsiders."

"I understand, when have I ever broken my word or your trust?"

"That's why I agreed to meet you and do business with you. I have a favor to ask you."

"You want something from me?"

"Yes, something very serious. I know what you're building under your fields. I know you're building a huge underground shelter for forty people and the supplies to hold the people for a year or more. I want in, for me and my family."

"Do you have a copy of the blueprints too?"

"To be honest with you, yes I do. I congratulate you, the plans are very good. I had two architects review the plans, they said the plans are good. Jay, I'll admit, I too think all hell is going to break loose. The best thing to do may be to bunker down and wait it out for a bit. My sources say the government is going to default on the July welfare payments and when that happens, hell itself is going to be let loose here. Millions are going to die when the existing food supply runs out because almost none knows how to farm or survive. Almost no-one knows how to live off of the land. So many of the preppers think they can bug out and survive. They're going to learn a hard lesson. When the end comes, waves, armies of people are going to be swarming out of Nashville and every other city. I thought we could fight our way out of the city, I've had my people look at the problem in every way possible. They all came up with the same answer. We have to hide, let the initial waves of hungry people wash over and around us and when they're gone we emerge and start over. There's not going to be a central government any more. My people think there's a good probability that near the end, Russia and/or China will invade to save us, only they won't be here to save us, they'll be conquering us.

"Jay, I have some assets you can use to help speed your project."

"What do you have?"

"We 'own' the construction unions. We can have hundreds of people on your property at dawn tomorrow helping finish the shelter."

"Why mine? Why not build your own?"

"I don't own a couple of farms, yours is already started and frankly, we reviewed your defense plans. Your shelter can be defended, you're far enough outside of town to buy a little time. We can expand your shelter and your farmland. I have the people who will help defend the shelter."

"Tony, how many people are we talking about?"

"Thirty, maybe forty tops."

"Tony, I know I don't have to ask this, I assume your people have their own weapons and ammo?"

Laughing, Tony responds, "Come, let me show you. I recently made a very interesting trade with an army supply sergeant."

Tony leads me to the basement under the restaurant, he turns on the light, I pull up short, in front of us are stacked cases of US Army weapons. M4s, Light anti-armor missiles, even hand grenades. Tony says, "Wait, here's the best part." He pulls back a curtain showing me stacks of uniforms, body armor and helmets, plus 400 cases of MREs. "It won't do me any good to have all this and no place that's defensible. We need to hide while the hungry pass by us. When they're gone, we surface and start over. I figure we'll have four to six months after the collapse before we're invaded. This is a good start, but not enough to fight off the Russians and Chinese. Can you get more from your friend in Mexico?"

"I'm still in contact with him. The problem is safely getting there and back."

Laughing, Tony pats me on the back saying, "You leave that to me. Remember, we own the Teamsters."

"I thought you guys would have your own sources for weapons and supplies. We're going to need security from the highwaymen and gangs stopping trucks to steal their cargos."

"We do, however, the demand for weapons and drugs is the highest I've ever seen it. I need enough to outfit an army. I want my team supplied with military weapons, but quantity and quality like that are hard to come by. Our usual contacts are being stressed to their max by the families in New York, Chicago, and Las Vegas, who are also now supplying Boston, LA, and Miami. They don't have the capacity to supply us little people in the woods. My contacts in the Army got transferred and they're watching their inventory like it was gold. Tell you what I'm going to do for you. I'll convert your cash into gold at the current exchange rate without a commission if you allow my people to help build the shelter and you make the call to your contact south of the border. I'd like to ensure we have enough weapons and ammo to control the area."

"Who's going to pay for the arms? They're very expensive right now."

"We'll each cover the cost for our own use."

"Tony, there's a couple other things I could use your help with."

"Let's order and discuss it over lunch. I have your favorite, fresh veal."

"Talked me into it."

Tony and I sit at our own table in the back corner of the restaurant while Sal and Todd sit at one near the front door. "Jay, what else do you need?"

"Tony, we're going to need a doctor and their medical supplies. I've talked to Doc Basco, our family doctor who's close to our farm. He said he would join us when the time is right, but I'd like to have a backup and more medical supplies. He's sixty-eight. I figure you have a doctor or two on your payroll."

"We do, that's a good thought. I'll take care of it."

"What else do you think we're going to need?"

"Lots of fuel and some vehicles which can be buried or hidden for use after the madness subsides. I have a couple of hundred gallons of diesel and gas in buried tanks and the two tanker trucks you know about. We're going to need a lot more since it may be a year or more before refineries get back up and running. I plan to park the tanker trucks in our barns, which are built with steel reinforced concrete. I'm hoping anything we park inside will be secure."

"I'll work on that, why don't we meet in two days at your home? I'll bring Nancy."

"Tony, a couple more things you should know, the Sheriff has been trying to get us to give him our stored food. He sent a group of fools to attack us and I think he'll go further the next time. To increase our problems, the National Guard paid me a visit. They demanded we sell them our stored grains. They gave me three days to hand over what we have or they'll take it by force."

"I was afraid of that. I'll look into seeing if there's anything I can do to keep them away from the farm. One thing you need to look into is if we dig up another few acres to expand the shelter, what is going to be the impact on this year's crops?"

"I looked the question of the shelter impacting our yield. I went to the county land office and found a plot of land behind our farms, it's over 50 acres. I've been trying for two months to find out who owns it. All I can find out is it's owned by a company based in the islands. If I could find out who owns it, I could buy it, those acres will make up for any loss the construction of the shelter causes."

Tony sips his wine, smiling at me.

I put my fork down, "Damn it, you own the land. The company is one of yours, isn't it?"

"Guilty. I own over 3,000 acres under different corporate names. I'll arrange to help you clear the land to expand the yield, but, I'm not selling the land."

"I can't see you as a farmer."

"It all depends on what one wants to bury."

Smiling, I got his message. "Tony, I'm worried that if hundreds of workers show up on my farm we'll be attracting too much attention, too many people will know what we're building."

"We'll provide security while your people do what you do best. Let the professionals build the shelters. I also have a security consultant who will help improve the security of the area."

"Tony, what kind of security consultant?"

"One that wore the uniform for 18 years. He and I have done each other some favors over the years. He will be one of the people I plan to bring into the group."

"I'll take it up with my extended family and neighbors. I think we'll be able to work out the details when we meet next. Are you sure you can move my funds without the feds coming after us?"

"Trust me, the feds won't bat an eye. I'll handle it, you just act surprised and hurt. Tomorrow, your home will be filled with agents from every three letter agency you can imagine and some you didn't even know exist."

"Tony, I guess we're going to have to trust each other if we're going to make this work."

We shake hands, "I better head back home."

"Jay, one final word. Don't mention any of what we've discussed with your other son-in-law, he's not to be trusted."

"I'm not going to ask how you know. I'll just accept you know. Trust me, I don't trust him either."

"Jay, don't worry, everything is going to be fine. I've never screwed you, you've made me a lot of money. You've turned into a good friend, plus Nancy and Lacy have become best friends. Jay, we're family."

Smiling, Tony and I hug our goodbye.

Chapter 12

On our ride home Todd looks over at me, I haven't said a word since we left the restaurant. Todd whispers, "Dad, can I break into your thoughts?"

"Sorry, Todd. Of course, what's up?"

"Are you sure we should be making a deal with the mob? Can we trust Tony?"

"They want the same thing we do, they want to survive. I've been doing business with Tony since the week we moved in. I ran into him one afternoon when Lacy and I were having a late lunch at his restaurant. We didn't know who he was. He introduced himself, he asked to join us. Said he heard we were moving in, he congratulated us on our winnings, he surprised me by all that he knew about us. He said he just wanted us to know if we needed anything he might be able to help, all we had to do was call him. He gave me his private cell number. When he left our table, Lacy asked who he was. I remember telling her that he was the local mafia, Don. She couldn't believe it. Then she remembered I once had a close friend who was, shall we say, very connected. When she met him, she realized who he really was. She thought back to that day and smiled. She told me to use my best judgment. Tony and I have done small favors and some business for each other. We've become friends and neither has taken advantage of the other. Lacy and I dine at his restaurant a few times a month, we always pay in cash and tip well. The wait staff knows who we are and treat us as friends of the owner. We always get the best service and the food is excellent. If you understand they're a business and you understand you can never break your word to them, you can do business with them. Just remember, when you break a contract with them, they don't sue, they get their payment one way or another. When you shake on an agreement, if the deal turns sour on your end, you live with it. They'll know it turned sour and respect you more for not saying a word. I can trust him. I'm not sure how everyone else is going to feel about them joining us. Lacy and his wife, Nancy, hit it off like sisters. Heaven knows we can use the bodies, we can use the assets he has so we survive."

"Dad, I'll trust your judgment. I never realized my father-in-law knew and dealt with the mob."

"I don't think it's a good idea to tell many people. However, if I'm right, very soon there aren't going to be many people left to tell. Turn on the all-news station, let's see if we missed anything."

"Don't you get auto-updates on your cell?"

"I don't carry my cell when I meet Tony, which is why I told you to leave yours in the car."

"I understand, the GPS."

"And the fearsome three letter agencies might remotely turn on the mic to listen to our conversation. When Tony visits us, we'll be turning off our phones and also every smart appliance we own. He knows I do this, He respects that he doesn't have to ask. On the first day, I met him at his office. His key man, Sal, the one you had lunch with searched me for my cell, I told them I left it off in my car's trunk. Sal nodded, he informed Tony who asked me why I left my phone behind. I told him my reasons, he smiled saying we're going to get along fine. He knows I have a friend across the border, the one I acquired the last batch of assault rifles from. Tony asked me to contact him to see if they have more weapons Tony can purchase."

"Dad, isn't that risky?"

"Not really, who's Tony going to talk to? If I can't trust the local Don to keep their mouth closed than the world is really screwed up."

"Has he come to the house before?"

"Yes, a couple of times. Mom's one of the few wives outside of their extended family Tony allows his wife to hang with. His wife Nancy really likes the time she's able to spend with Lacy, which is why I think that's why he's going to bring Nancy with him, it also makes for a good cover. Nancy isn't anything like Tony. When you meet her, you'll understand."

"Won't you attract the attention of the FBI?"

Laughing, "Most likely, then again, I already know I'm on the government's watch list so we try to keep strangers out of our house. Tony got us scanning equipment we use every few days to look for bugs."

"Ever find any?"

Laughing, I nod my head, "Yes, we don't know who or how they're getting in, but they are. We find a bug almost every week. Some are on the inside of the house, some on the windows of our bedroom and family room."

"Dad, do you think the Feds are using a small drone to drop them?"

"Shit, I hadn't thought of that. We'll have to add that to our list of things to be alert for." Looking into the rear view mirror, I see a police car has pulled in behind us, "Todd, I think our local not so friendly Sheriff is going to be stopping us. Don't get smart with him, don't give him any talkback, answer his questions, but only the questions he asks. I don't trust the thief as far as I can throw him. I expect that when we take the turn towards home, which is usually deserted, he'll pull us over. He'll be able to do it without anyone seeing him. It's funny, I can trust doing business with the mob and I worry about the Sheriff. Tony's trustworthy and the Sheriff's a crook."

"What do you think he wants?"

"Everything we have."

As soon as we turn off the main road towards our house the flashing lights on the police car behind us turn on. I pull over while rolling my window down. I have my license and registration in my hand out the window. The Sheriff walks to my window. I notice the flap over his sidearm is unsnapped. "Todd, there's a sidearm hidden under your seat. If things turn to shit reach down and grab it. It's loaded, there's a round in the chamber, so be very careful with it. All you'll have to do is flip the safety to fire and pull the trigger. I don't like that the Sheriff has his sidearm holster unsnapped."

"Dad, that's crazy, we haven't done anything wrong."

"Todd, just do as I say, we'll chat about it later."

"Yes. sir."

"Here he comes, look calm and smile."

"Hello Sheriff, is something wrong?"

"You took the turn too quickly, you almost lost control of your vehicle. I pulled you over to warn you. I wouldn't want one of our most famous people to be hurt, now would I?"

"Sheriff, that's very kind of you. What do you really want?"

"I had a strange call, it seems you had lunch with Tony the snake. Is that true? Are you hanging around with known criminals?"

"My son-in-law and I like Italian food. There aren't many good places close by to have lunch at. I really like fresh veal, the place we visited today makes it the best I've ever had."

"Jay, we both know who owns that restaurant. You entered it and had lunch in a restaurant that was closed? That's usually a pretty neat trick."

"I know the manager."

"You had lunch with the owner, one Tony the snake, the local mafia Don. The head honcho who calls the shots for all crime in the Nashville area. One word from him and people end up floating in the Cumberland River. I'd hate to see you be the next floater."

"Thank you for your concern."

"Jay, why don't you step out of your car so we can have a private chat, just the two of us? I may use words, by mistake, mind you, your young son-in-law shouldn't hear."

"I can assure you he doesn't have virgin ears."

"Jay, do me this little favor."

"Todd, stay here, watch us in the mirror. If anything happens, come out with a gun."

"Yes, sir."

Stepping out of the car, "Sheriff, what do you want to discuss?"

The Sheriff places his arm around my shoulder, "Jay, I want to make sure you understand how important your little farm is to the community. I don't like the idea that you're getting into bed with a slime ball like Tony. He'll corrupt you. He'll twist your mind and mess you up so you won't share your food with the town. I know you don't want a few thousand people to die from hunger, not when you have the means to feed them."

"Sheriff, I think we've had this conversation before. I don't have any stored food. The farms weren't doing well before I bought them which is why I could purchase them so cheaply. Even the National Guard showed up looking for stored grains. Don't you think if we had any they would have found them?"

"Son, don't bullshit a bullshitter. I know you have food. I know you're building something on your farm. I think it's a storage building. I'll wait till you're finished, then me and some of my boys are going to pay you a visit. You're either going to give us what the town needs or we're going to take it."

"Sheriff, my property is private property and unless you have a damn good reason and a warrant, you better stay off of it. It's not going to be good for your health."

"Son, are you threatening me?"

"No Sheriff, I'm just trying to give you some free advice."

The Sheriff punches me in the stomach, causing me to double over, "Listen to me, you little shithead. I'm the Sheriff around here. If I say you're going to be giving me what I want, you'll be giving it to me. The government is going to announce any farmer that doesn't sell stored food supplies to the local towns can be arrested for crimes against humanity."

"Sheriff, don't try it. I'm not threatening you. I'm trying to help you."

"Go home and get out of my sight. I'll be seeing you soon enough. I figure your summer crop will be ready for harvest in six to eight weeks and I might as well get the freshest. Now you be real careful taking turns."

"Goodbye, Sheriff."

"Goodbye, Jay."

Entering my car, Todd asks, "Dad, are you OK? I saw him hit you."

"Yes, I'm fine, just a little pain in the ass local Sheriff who thinks he can throw his weight around. I think the time's coming when he's going to make a mistake and the mass grave in the back is going to grow."

"Dad, what mass grave? Is there something I should know?"

Realizing I made a mistake, I tell Todd, "Son, just forget I said anything. There's also no need to worry everyone when we get home." When we enter the front door, Lacy runs into my arms, "Honey, are you OK? Where have you been all day?"

"I told you I took Todd to meet Tony. On the way home we got stopped by the pain in the ass Sheriff. I swear the day's coming when we're going to have to settle the score with him for the final time. He says he's coming to take our crop in six or eight weeks."

"Do you think he will?"

"He'll try. Honey, we need to talk. Tony has a suggestion I'd like to discuss with you and later on with all of our neighbors."

I explain the offer Tony made, she sits there with a surprised look on her face. "Honey, do you trust him?"

"Yes, he too thinks the shits going to hit the fan. He can provide us with the additional people and supplies we'll need to survive and prosper in the future. Lace, do you trust Nancy?"

"Of course I trust her, we're like sisters. However, I think you're going to have a hard time selling him joining us to our neighbors. Most of them haven't spent years palling around with a member of one of the families. How are you going to explain him?"

"I'm thinking of starting with Fred and Cheri. I'm going to tell them the truth."

"The truth? That's a strange way to convince someone. Do you really think the truth is going to work?"

"If they catch me in a lie like this, they'll never trust me again. Lacy, what would you do differently?"

"I don't know."

"Why don't we invite everyone over for a drink tonight? Since Tony is coming in two days, we should get this out of the way ASAP."

"Jay, that's a good idea. Why don't you send it to our group chat?"

"OK, the invites sent," I said after pressing send. The affirmative responses quickly came in, everyone eagerly accepted. We invited everyone to join us at 8:00 PM for small snacks, drink and discussion on our shelter. I asked our family, Franco and his sons to join us at 6:00 so I can break the news to them first. We grill a bunch of burgers, open sodas for the kids and beer for the rest of us. When everyone has a burger and something to drink, I stand up, "Thanks for giving me a couple of minutes. Something's come up today that I want to discuss before our neighbors arrive at eight." I explain the meeting with Tony and his offer. None of the adults in the room touches their food while I explain everything. Todd nods his head in agreement to everything I tell them. When I'm finished, Sammi says, "Dad, how long have you know Tony?"

"Since we moved here."

"Has he always been trustworthy in all of your dealings with him?"

"Sam, yes, he has. He's never cheated us or broken his word."

"I know you knew other people like him. I remember when I was young, you had a couple of friends who were in a so-called family. They were very nice to all of us, they used to bring me toys. If Tony is like them, then I say we should trust him. If he can supply additional people and equipment to speed up and ease the shelter construction, I'm all for it. I've spent the day studying the situation in the country. I think Dad's right, the situation in the country is getting worse almost every hour. The riots and the battles at bank offices are all over the TV. I think if the government cuts off welfare payments the country is going to spin out of control. I'd never have believed it. I thought logic would prevail. I admit it, I was wrong. Everyone's emotions are running wild. People are scared, thousands of people are being laid off every hour. China announced they're prepared to use military force if necessary to get their loans repaid. They've offered to take over Hawaii and all US assets in Hawaii. If they do this, it could lead to a world war. Every time a news banner blasts across the TV, I get more worried. I think anything that increases our chances of survival is a good thing."

Most nod their heads in agreement. Franco says, "We can certainly use his help, he controls all of the construction people and equipment in the area. I believe he can get us the people we need to complete the shelter."

I stand in front of the group, "My largest concern is the people he brings in to build the shelters will know where they are and how to access them. If he brings one hundred construction workers, when the shit hits the fan they're all going to be making their way here."

Franco stands to say, "Jay, I agree, but did you ever think that every truck driver who brings a load of equipment here isn't going to do the same thing? We should plan a false entrance, which would lead the people looking for the shelter into a maze."

I smile, thinking, that's a good idea, "Franco, can a maze be made after all of the helpers leave?"

"Yes, we would all have to agree and know where we moved the real entrances. If we're going to have a lot of help and equipment, I think my sons and I can build the maze at night."

"Franco, let's discuss it when the others join us. One other question concerns me, can someone explode TNT above us to break through the ceiling of the shelter?"

"Jay, the walls, and ceiling is made of steel reinforced concrete, the ceiling is going to be two layers each being twelve inches separated by twelve inches of compacted dirt. It's going to take a penetrating bomb to break into the shelter. We're going to be buried ten feet under the crops. Someone may know we're there, but getting to us is going to be a different story."

"I hope you're right."

At eight o'clock all of our neighbors arrived. I wasn't surprised to see everyone arrive armed. Everyone hugs each other and they all grab a beer and a couple of sliders and mini hot dogs I grilled. Everyone took a seat to hear what I had to say. I looked around the room. I've given presentations to corporate CEOs, to government multiagency working groups, to flag officers in the US Military and to elected officials; tonight for the first time I have butterflies in my stomach. I'm more nervous tonight than when I was asked to present to a group of fifty high-level Federal Government Department heads. "My friends, thank you for joining us this evening. Todd and I had a very unusual meeting today, one that has implications for all of us. We felt the best way to proceed is to call all of us together so we can discuss it in an open group. This way we can have an open and frank exchange of ideas." I pause to sip my beer and look into everyone's eyes. They can tell the subject is serious and I'm glad they're all paying attention to every word I speak. "Many of you know from various news reports of the person known as Tony the Snake. What you may not know is, Tony and I have done business together since we moved here." The mood in the room instantly changed, my friends start looking at me differently. Some have crossed their arms and legs, their body language changed when they heard that Tony and I have done business together. "Please bear with me a moment. I admit, I should have informed you of this before. Tony has arranged a lot of things in the background that have helped us get as far as we are. He has an interesting proposal for us. Before you explode let me quickly explain, he's offered to supply the manpower, and construction equipment to more than double the size of our shelter. He's offered to provide us additional supplies so we can last at least a year without touching our stored crops. He's also offered to provide us with the services of a military vet who specializes in security to improve our defenses."

Randy asks, "What does he want from us? I have only so much blood to give, Obama's already taking most of mine. Does Tony want the rest or something else?"

Every head in the room is nodding in agreement with Randy. I slowly respond, "He wants to join us."

That was the last answer they were expecting. Rich asks, "Jay, let me see if I understand what you just said because frankly, you just threw me for a loop. Tony the Snake is willing to help us double the size of our shelter in exchange for an entry ticket? What else does he want?"

"Rich, he wants to bring his extended family, his wife, children, brothers, and sisters and their children, plus a couple people he said we would find useful."

"That's all he wants? No other strings?"

"None, in fact, he asked if he can come by in two days with his wife, Nancy, to talk to all of us about it. He thought it would be good for everyone to get to know each other."

Fred stands up, surprising me by saying, "I know Tony, hell, I've borrowed money from him when the rotten banks turned me down. I've found him a man of his word, just never break yours. He's not the New York type of mobster. He runs Nashville, but he also draws the line at certain acts. He's going to surprise you when you meet him. If Tony thinks the shit is going to hit the fan and he wants to join us, I for one say we should listen to him. He controls the construction unions, he could have one hundred people here in ten minutes. Our shelter could be completed months ahead of our current plan. I for one say we should listen to him with an open mind. Anything that completes the shelter quicker is fine with me. I thank Jay for going the extra mile to try to ensure all of our security."

Randy stands asking, "Do we need his people? Didn't Franco say he could finish the shelter in a month?"

Jay smiles, "Randy, he did. However, I didn't believe him, look at the slow progress he's making. Can we afford to risk our lives on him or should we ensure the shelter gets built as quickly as possible?"

Everyone starts talking at the same time. After five minutes, I banged my hand on the table to get everyone's attention. "Please, let's settle down. Let's vote, all in favor of listening to Tony and Nancy raise your hand." Every hand goes up. "Good, now that that's settled, new business. I didn't want to mention this until we already agreed to listen to Tony. He has enough Army weapons, uniforms, and body armor to allow us to fight off an invasion."

Fred asks, "Do we want to know where he got an armory full of Army weapons and uniforms?"

I smile saying, "They fell off a truck in front of one of his warehouses." Everyone laughed. "Franco, how is the current shelter going?"

"Jay, everyone, you know my sons and I have been working in shifts 24 hours a day. The construction is going very slowly, we are only three people, at times Matt helps out. We have the preformed walls and panels for the roof, we need more bodies and more equipment. At the current rate, I project it's going to take us six to nine months to finish, it also depends on the weather. We have a large open hole. When it rains, we have to pump out the hole before we can do any new construction. The tarp we rigged over the hole only keeps some of the water out of the hole."

The room grows very quiet. Randy whispers, "Six to nine months? I don't know if we have six let alone nine months. The noise coming from China is scary, Russia dumped all of their dollars, inflation is out of control, gasoline is approaching $20.00 a gallon. We have the oil in the ground. However, Obama won't allow us to frack for it. Hell, we were offered contracts to frack on our land before Obama signed the damn executive order outlawing fracking. If he defaults on the next welfare payments, all hell is going to break out. We need help. I'd be willing to cut a deal with the devil himself to finish the shelter. I share the concern about the construction people knowing about our shelter. I don't want to have to fight the very people who helped build the damn thing."

I stand to reply, "Randy, I agree with you. Every person who knows about our shelter is one more who might and most likely will attack us. We can prepare some tricks for those that know where we are, however, it remains a risk, one we have to think about. I for one am leaning towards getting the shelter built quicker and taking the risk. We can make it very difficult for invaders to reach us. Once we know the world's burning, we can rig a lot of nasty surprises to hurt any attacker. Of course, we might surface to find others living in our homes and eating our food. Or we could surface to find our homes burnt to the ground. We're facing a risk either way we go. I for one think, we need more help in defending what we have. I think we should turn our border into a type of castle like in the old world. You know, like a moat around our farms, or guard towers."

Randy asks, "Jay, are you suggesting we build a wall around 900 acres? Do you have an idea what kind of resource that's going to take? We'll never get our crops in or out of the ground. There aren't enough trees close to us for us to use to build a wall with. Making it out of cement will require many thousands of trucks that aren't available. Where would we get so much in such a short time? I also think building a wall will cause everyone to wonder what we're hiding."

The discussion goes around the room three times before we find ourselves in agreement to listen to Tony while also trying to figure out how to improve our defensive positions. We agreed to meet in two days time with Tony and Nancy. Franco and his sons go back to work on the foundation of the shelter while our neighbors go home for the evening.

@@@@@

Spetsnaz Captain Second Rank Sarnoff receives new orders to report to the Russian Embassy in New York City for a secret mission. Sarnoff is instructed to pick five people from his team that speak perfect English and who have experience operating in America. Upon arriving in New York City, Sarnoff reports to the FSB head of mission, Demetri Darkenov, who instructs the captain on his mission. "Captain, in the basement of the Embassy, are eighteen crates of weapons, all of the weapons are from China. Your orders are to spread these weapons in the minority neighborhoods in America's major cities. You are to encourage them to attack the wealthy. We want you to start a race and class war. Such a war will divert the American's attention away from their other issues. Minorities across the country will take up arms in support of their brothers. When the arms are captured, they'll point to China's involvement in America's internal issues. This will increase the tension between the two countries. The drain on America's resources will force their President to enact even greater draconian tax and security measures quickly pushing the collapse of their economy and the possibly of a civil uprising. Here are your team's new ID documents and money to support your efforts. Do you have any questions?"

"None, sir. I assume once we leave the embassy we're on our own and we can't return here."

"Correct, you will work your way to Los Angeles, stirring up trouble across the country. Once you reach LA, you will call 619-555-5555, the code word is 'Bluebird'. Arrangements will be made for your return to the Motherland."

"Yes, sir."

"Captain, the highest office in the Motherland has their eye on you and this mission. Do well and you'll be promoted upon your return."

"Thank you, sir. I'm sure we'll have an enjoyable time sightseeing our way across America."

@@@@@

At 11:15 PM, I'm woken by my cell. I wonder who's calling at this hour, usually a call after I go to bed means bad news. "Hello, this is Jay."

"Jay, do you recognize my voice?"

"Yes."

"Good. You seem to have a problem. Our good friend the Sheriff of Nottingham has informed the feds that you didn't win the lottery. He's claiming you sold drugs to make the money. The feds are going to seize your accounts in the morning. First thing tomorrow the Sheriff is going to show up on your doorstep with an arrest warrant for you."

"I see, have the funds we discussed been handled?"

"Yes. I'd like you to call your bank to inform them someone stole your identity and they cleaned out your accounts. Claim you've been stolen from. Each of your accounts is insured for $250,000."

"I think I understand. I'm really pissed someone hacked my laptop and stole my passwords. I'll have to report this crime to the good Sheriff of Nottingham first thing in the morning."

"Excellent idea."

"So I assume everything else is in process."

"Of course. Sorry to have woken you."

"No problem."

Turning over, Lacy asks, "Who was that?"

"Tony, the Sheriff, has told the feds we didn't win the lottery, did you know we're drug, dealers? The feds are going to seize our accounts in the morning, except tonight a hacker raided our accounts and emptied our accounts."

"What? Why aren't you calling the bank's security department? If you know, this happened why don't you do something about it?"

"Honey, because Tony's people are the hackers. They will empty our accounts while also converting them into gold which Tony said is untraceable. By the way, expect breakfast to be interrupted by the Sheriff with an arrest warrant for me."

"He wouldn't dare."

"Yes, he will. As soon as he arrives to arrest me call Brad. He'll be at the court before the Sheriff is able to book me. He shouldn't have any problems getting me released. He has a copy of the certified letter from the lottery. Any judge that issued the warrant without checking the facts is about to be very embarrassed. Tell Brad that I want to file charges against the Sheriff that should keep him out of our hair for a while. Tell him about the when the Sheriff stopped me and punched me, Todd saw it."

"Honey, do you think it's wise to just wait and let all of this happen?"

"Yes, we really have no other choice. I didn't get a call tonight. In fact, I'm going to report the phone lost or stolen. I'll switch to my backup number, please make sure everyone has it."

"OK. Are you going to be able to get any sleep?"

"Yup, nothing I can do about it, plus it may be fun. Honey, Tony wouldn't have called unless he had everything already in hand."

"Are you sure he's not creating a problem, so he can solve it on the eve of the meeting?"

"The thought crossed my mind, but this does sound like our local Sheriff, who wants to find a way to take what's ours. Maybe I should have just paid him off when I had the chance to."

"That's not the answer and you know it. Brad is going to have to find a way to get the feds to investigate him."

"I like that idea, mention it to him when you call him in the morning. Goodnight hun."

"Night babe, I love you."

"I love you too."

Chapter 13

As usual, Tony was correct, our front door was kicked in at 7:30 AM by the Sheriff and fifteen heavily armed deputies. They ran through our house yelling for everyone to get on their knees with their hands held up. The deputies marched my family downstairs. "Officers, thank you for bringing everyone down for breakfast. How would you like your eggs, or do you want pancakes? Coffee? We have regular and decaf."

The Sheriff stood staring at Lacy and I in shock, "Jay, what the fuck are you doing?"

"Hell Sheriff, I figured even you could see we're having breakfast, would you like to join us?"

"I have a search warrant and a warrant for your arrest."

"Isn't that nice, you plan to arrest me before you search for whatever it is you think we're hiding. By the way, what is it you're looking for?"

"We know you're hiding gold and drugs in the house."

"And just how do you know that?" I ask while sipping my coffee. "I admit, I do have drugs here, would you like two aspirin? I have prescriptions for all of the other drugs. You'll find most of the pill bottles in the fridge, top shelf. Just don't mix them up. They're very expensive."

"Jay, you don't seem to understand. I've got you this time. You're in violation of the President's new executive order and you're a drug dealer."

"Sherriff am I a drug dealer because I offered you two aspirins? What else have you found?"

"Honestly, nothing yet but we will. If I have to tear your house apart, I'll find your hidden gold and drugs."

"Sheriff, my lawyer is on his way here. I think you will be served with court papers ordering you to repair any damage you do to my house. In addition, I'll be holding you and the county responsible for any damage you do to my home."

"Not if we find your hiding place."

"Sheriff, do you really think I'd be dumb enough to hide anything illegal in my house, knowing how much you'd love to nail me on something? Why don't you sit, share a cup of coffee with us."

The Sheriff pours himself a cup of coffee. He sips it, saying, "It's very good, it's a shame you won't get coffee this good in jail."

"Nor you."

"What the hell does that mean?"

"You lied to the judge to get the warrants issued. I plan to press charges as soon as you're done playing your silly games. In fact, since I'm Jewish, I'm planning on filing a Federal Hate Crime suit against you and your department. I have a press release ready to issue as soon as you're finished. Would you like to read it before it's issued?"

"Jay, we both know you converted your money into gold."

"Do we? With what money? Haven't you heard? We're broke. Someone hacked my bank accounts last night and drained all of our accounts. I've notified the bank of the issue, their lawyers are checking our claim. They've confirmed someone logged into our accounts in the middle of the night, they were able to trace the login. Whoever stole our login bounced the signal all over the world. You can have your tech experts check my laptop. You'll see I didn't use it last night after 8:00 PM. My laptop wasn't used to log into our accounts. Your experts will see our accounts weren't accessed by any of our devices or from our house."

"You're shitting me."

"Why don't you call the bank and ask them yourself? I'm sure their head of security is going crazy trying to figure out what happened to our funds."

Laughing the Sheriff says, "Jay, this is too funny. You got robbed? Your account is only insured for $250,000. You lost over $20 million, poof just disappeared into thin air. This is so funny. I love the irony of it. A thief robbed by another thief."

"I don't find it very funny."

"I don't understand why you're not panicking. I would be."

"Sheriff, you would panic because your money was gotten illegally, ours was won legally. Our money was deposited in many different accounts, in different banks. We may lose a million, the rest is insured. We'll be inconvenienced for a while, but only a while. The FDIC will return our funds very quickly, as will the other banks. They can't afford the bad press if they don't return it. Your people have been here for a while, have they found anything?"

"Not yet, however, this is a very large house. The largest in the area. If we don't find anything in the house, we'll start in your yard and then the fields."

Reading the warrant, I smile, "Sheriff, no you won't."

"What do you mean, no I won't?"

"Did you read the search warrant? You have permission to search my house. Not my yard, not the farm fields, only the house. If you do anything else without a valid warrant, I will call the State Police and say my rights are being violated. I'm sure the State Police would love to arrest you. Sure you don't want another cup of coffee or anything to eat?"

"Let me see that warrant again." I slide it across the kitchen table. My kids and grandkids are marching in and out of the kitchen getting breakfast, they nod and wave to the police officers who are dressed in black tactical gear running room to room in our house. Sammi asks, "Dad, why are they running around like clowns? Why are they all armed? We didn't do anything to interfere with them."

"Sammi, ask them."

Sammi looks at the Sheriff, "Sheriff, why are you tossing everything on the floor? A lot of that stuff is ours. Why aren't you putting everything back where you found it? There are young children in the house, one of them is my daughter, your people are scaring her by pointing your guns at her. When my Dad's done with you, I'm going to sue you."

"Young lady, I'd keep my mouth shut if I were you. Who the fuck do you think you are? And what the fuck are you doing with that cell phone?"

"I'm exercising my rights. I'm recording your cursing in front of my daughter, I'm recording your people tear my daddy's house apart and the way you're disrespecting him and all of us. I'm recording how you're scaring the young children in the house, how you're breaking items and pointing guns at unarmed people wearing PJs. I'm recording everything which I'm sure my dad's lawyer and a judge are going to be very happy to see."

"Young lady, you can't record a police officer. It's an obstruction of justice."

"Yes, I can. Google it yourself, it's legal in Tennessee. I checked. I'm not threatening you, I'm not interfering with your operation. My husband and I are standing at least five feet away from your people while we record everything you do."

Before the Sheriff can respond, our lawyer, Brad enters the front door. "Hi Jay, Lacy you're looking great this fine morning."

Lacy hugs Brad, "Coffee?"

"Jay's special brew?"

"Of course."

"Then yes. By the way, hello Sheriff, I think I have something here for you. Here it is, I have a court issued cease and desist order. It's signed by Superior Court Judge James, Brownstone."

"How did you get him to sign this?"

"By presenting him with the evidence this entire raid was bullshit. I showed him the certified letter from the lottery proving that Lacy and Jay won the money. I also have a certified email from his banks that his accounts were hacked last night. The bank's security confirms the access did not, I repeat, did not come from any device registered to Jay or Lacy. No device in this house accessed his accounts last night.

You're on a private witch hunt which the court frowns upon. You'll also notice you and your department are liable for any damage to Lacy and Jay's possessions. You invented this entire event because you're looking for something to hang on my clients. The Judge isn't very happy with you right now. In fact, I'm expecting you to be receiving a call to shut this investigation down."

"Councilor, I don't answer to you."

"You'll answer my questions when you're on the witness stand in open court."

The Sheriff's phone rings before he can respond to the Brad, "Hello."

"Yes, I understand. No, we haven't found anything yet. Sir, this is a very large house. We haven't checked the yard or the fields yet. I know what the warrant says. Sir, we only need a little more time. Yes, sir, I hear you. Thank you, sir."

Punching the end button, the Sheriff looks at Brad saying, "Councilor, it seems you've won this round, but one inning doesn't make the ball game. I'll be back."

"Sheriff when you return, you better have cause. Otherwise, I will take you to court."

"Counselor, I still have the arrest warrant for Jay."

"If you value your job, I'd suggest you forget it and leave the house. You and I both know you're here on a fishing expedition. If you arrest him, we'll add false imprisonment and false arrest to our charges."

"Mark my words, I'll be back. I'll get what I deserve."

"Sheriff, you may indeed get what you deserve. Did I tell you I've been recording everything you've said since I arrived? I'm sure the court is going to be very interested in hearing the recording as will the electorate in the next election."

"Counselor, what do you want?"

"Leave my clients alone."

The Sheriff turns around, storming out of our house after slamming the door behind him. Brad and I laugh as he orders his people to leave." I call over to Sammi,

"Sam, why don't you take some pictures of the damage they did to our front yard and anything else you see."

"Sure dad, happy to."

Shells sits down between Brad and me, "Dad, are you broke? Did you lose everything? Todd and I can help you. We have a little saved from what you gave us."

I hug my youngest, "Honey, it's going to be fine. Don't worry about a thing. Trust me, everything is going to be OK."

My phone pings with a text, it says, '245.' I smile and nod to Lacy. She says, "Good news?"

"Very good news." I show the text to Lacy, she smiles, saying, "Is that what I think it means?"

"Yes, that's pounds, not ounces."

She screams, "Really?!"

"Yup."

Shells looks at us like she just discovered her parents are crazy. "Can I ask what's going on?"

"Honey, just trust us, it's very good news." Todd enters saying, "Hey dad, the news just reported that gold broke an all-time record last night, it broke the $5,000 an ounce barrier. I bet you still have some you bought when it was $300 an ounce."

"Todd, don't I wish."

"Is the bank really going to pay you back for the theft of your funds?"

"They're security department confirms we didn't transfer it, they can't track where the money went or how it disappeared. I think they'll start paying off in a couple of days. They've offered us a line of credit until our funds transfer to us."

"Dad, how do you think the meeting tonight with Tony is going to go?"

"I think his wife Nancy is the one who's going to swing the vote. She's the convincing one in a social setting. She'll make the case very clearly and emotionally."

While we're talking, Ricky yells from the family room, "Dad, you should see this."

We move to the family room, the news reporter says, "The Department of the Treasury just announced that the July and August welfare, disability, and social security payments are going to be reduced and they may also be paid a week late."

I look at the screen saying, "I think that's the straw that's going to crush the camel's back. There's no way the majority that relies on the government's assistance can absorb a hit like this. The payments haven't gone up to cover inflations' smack down, let alone be late and reduced. I think the riots are going to start within minutes. Todd, do you remember how to send a general alert to the other families?"

"Yup."

"Please send one. Everyone needs to know what's going on. From now on, whenever we go outside we should be armed. Food is going to get even more expensive and may be hard to get. When hyperinflation strikes, all hell is going to break loose."

Ricky asks, "What's hyperinflation?"

"It's when prices jump so quickly you'd need wheelbarrows of money to buy a quart of milk. It happened after the First World War in Germany. It's one of the major reasons the German economy failed, allowing Hitler to take control of the country."

"Can that really happen here?"

"I'd say, it's not only possible, but I'd also say it's highly probable it's going to happen within the next three to six months."

"Is it going to hurt us too?"

"Not as much as others, but yes, everyone is going to be hit by it. Everyone in the country, if not the world is going to suffer. When America goes down, the world will follow."

Todd and Ricky both say, "Shit. That's not what we wanted to hear."

The entertainment segments of the morning news programs are all pulled so the networks can focus on the impact of the government's statement. A representative from the Department of the Treasury is trying to explain why there's going to be a delay. "...The country was surprised by the demands made by China. We didn't expect the People's Republic to call in the loans the People's Government made to the Government of the United States. We responded that we're not going to give the state of Hawaii to China, nor are we going hand over our national landmarks to meet the demanded payments. We want everyone to know we are actively working with the Chinese to get a delay in making the payments. If we can reach an agreement, we'll be able to meet our domestic obligations in a timely manner. The reason the Secretary made this morning's announcement is to ensure we can begin making the payments in case we have to. The delay isn't one hundred percent a done deal and we could reach an agreement with China at any time. We think it's a good idea if everyone tweets #Chinashoulddelay. We think millions of Americans messaging the Chinese government will have an impact on their decision-making process. We can get through this rough time if we work together. President Obama is asking those who have, help those in need. Check on your neighbors. If you have extra cans of food, offer them to your neighbors, if you anything you can share, you should do so. We are a country based on volunteering and sharing. President Obama will shortly announce he's signed a new series of executive orders giving everyone time to make payments on their rent, mortgages, credit cards, and other consumer loans. The President's executive order freezes all payments for all debts and rents for a period of sixty days. He said he's sure everyone will support his new executive orders."

I stand up in shock, shaking my head, "That's the end of America. Born July 4th, 1776, died Monday, June 29th, 2015. When the President mandated how private businesses should function. We've become a dictatorship. He was elected President, not King. He can't do what he just did."

Ricky looks at me saying, "Dad, I think he did a good thing. If the government can't make their payments, then the banks and other creditors should be forced to wait to collect their payments. What's fair is fair."

"Ricky, it's not an issue of fairness. It's an issue that the Federal Government can't dictate to private companies."

We're interrupted by a news flash, "Fox News is able to confirm that the previously agreed to deal with Greece and Germany has fallen apart. Germany has demanded Greece start making immediate payments. The Greek Prime Minister has said he is planning on resigning. There are reports of thousands of riots spreading across Greece, Italy, Spain, and Belgium. The problem in these countries is since the Euro collapsed no other country is willing to accept their original currency as payment for imports. There are mass shortages of most medications, even over the counter medications are sold out without any future supply in sight. People are dying all over Europe without medications. Even aspirin is impossible to locate. Every imported product has stopped flowing into the countries that once made up the European Union. Spare parts are impossible to locate, causing anything imported to stop when they break. Electricity, clean water, and even sanitation systems are breaking down in Europe. Today, the national police in Athens used live ammunition on hungry, sick crowds looking for help from the government. Hundreds are lying dead where they were shot in the central square of Athens. Twenty-eight blocks of Rome are burning out of control." Fox shows overhead images of Rome burning out of control. Flames are seen licking at the clouds, smoke covers the unburnt sections of the city. People can be seen rioting and stealing anything they can grab. The camera shifts to Athens, where people are fighting the police with rocks, Molotov Cocktails, and metal pipes. The police respond with live rifle fire. The more the police fire into the crowds, the larger the crowds grow. Fire engines are called in to use high-pressure water hoses to break up the riots. When the water spray starts, the people in the front lines hold up metal shields made from garbage can covers. The people behind the front line brace to hold up those in the front line, helping them advance towards the police and fire department.

I look at the screen, "It seems Fox has access to their own drones, there's no other way they could be getting these images. It looks like these countries are tearing themselves apart. Everyone, look at these images, this is a preview of what could happen here when people's money and food run out."

Ricky disagrees, "Dad, this is America, we're not going to act like a bunch of spoiled children. We'll sit down and discuss the situation. Those who have will share with those who need. It's always been this way, we're different from the Europeans. You'll see this shelter of yours is nothing more than a huge waste of money and resources. We should be using all of our resources to grow more food to help those who are going to be hungry."

"Ricky, whose going to pay me for the food you want me to grow and give away."

"Dad, it's the right thing to do. I'm sure once the government sorts out this little disagreement with China they'll pay you."

Laughing, "Ricky, tell you what. When the shelter is finished, you can stay up top and help those who come by looking for handouts. You decide how much each person should get while justifying your decision to those who think they're entitled to more than you're giving them."

"Dad, I'm sure nothing is going to happen. This isn't Europe. We're all Americans. We'll share. We'll work together until the government is ready to start making payments again. People won't be as bad off as you think because President Obama ordered everyone to put a hold on all payments. Dad, want to bet me that I'm right?"

"I'd love to bet you. I think I understand human nature better than you think I do. I know that not everyone is going to place a hold on payments. Many small and medium size companies need those payments to pay their workers. If I know your beloved President like I think I do, his next announcement will be to freeze prices and costs. When that happens, companies will stop making products, the shelves won't be restocked, once something is sold, it'll be gone. There won't be any replacements to restock empty shelves. Think about that a minute. When your peace loving, reasonable people realize there aren't going to be any more deliveries, watch how quickly every store is stripped bare. The black market will be the only place to get anything of value, the economy will collapse and it'll initially be replaced by one based on a barter system."

"Why do you think that?"

"Prize freezes and price controls don't work. The dollar is almost worthless and hyperinflation is starting due to the lack of goods and services, we're going to make Europe look like a grade school playground."

"Dad, why do you say that?"

"Because, unlike Europe, there are over 300 million guns in America, brother is going to fight brother over a loaf of bread. We lost the knowledge how to live off the land a long time ago. Most don't know how to grow food or hunt and trap. Too many think food comes from the supermarket, they don't know where food really comes from. Millions are going to die from starvation, exposure and fighting each other. That's why I'm building the shelter."

"I don't understand why we won't be safe here in the house."

"Even if Tony and his people join us, we'll be only around forty against thousands of hungry people who don't have anything to lose."

Todd nods his agreement, making Ricky even angrier. Franco enters the back door saying, "Jay, we've started pouring the cement floor."

"Franco, how thick will the floor be?"

"One foot of reinforced concrete. It has to cure for a few days before we start installing the preformed walls. There will be a steady line of concrete trucks in and out all day today as we pour the floor. I'm afraid that this may be the last shipment of fresh concrete we get. The general manager of the plant said he's going to close down as soon as he's done with our order. By the way, pray that it doesn't rain for the next three days."

"Just great, I assume there aren't any other concrete plants close by, are there?"

"No, I've been checking for days."

We spent the balance of the day watching a steady stream of trucks feeding the funnel that poured concrete over the reinforcing steel rods and PVC pipes laid in the floor. We planned to pump water into the shelter from our existing wells and pump waste out of the shelter into large septic fields. Electrical energy will be supplied by our large solar panels and the windmills charging submarine batteries. My biggest fear is the solar panels and windmills will be damaged or destroyed by fighting or the invaders will occupy the farms and disconnect the power feed. If we lose our outside electrical supply we'll be facing a series of major problems, one's I don't know how to recover from yet. I'll have to check if we can mount generators in the shelter. We have the fuel, but their exhaust could be a problem.

Chapter 14

The 7:00 PM evening news programs report that people and companies who deposited cash into their bank accounts have discovered their funds have disappeared without any notice. People and small companies are confused, worried and upset. Hundreds of thousands worry they won't be able to put food on their family's tables or pay their employees. Millions post on social networks their bank accounts are frozen or have been drained. None of the banks are able to tell their customers what's happening with their funds, except to say the IRS has seized all of the cash deposits. Calls to the IRS aren't returned. The IRS also doesn't return calls from Congressmen and Senators, whose offices are besieged with calls and emails from their constituents. America is panicking, everyone worries the IRS will drain their accounts. In the middle of the news programs, people log onto to their bank's websites attempting to transfer their funds and quickly learn their cash accounts are frozen. All cash transfers out of the country are blocked. The IRS and FBI inform the world's public and private banks that all accounts held by American citizens are to be opened for their inspection and possible confiscation. While most of America is watching the news, the IRS and FBI identify over a billion dollars whose origin is in their opinion questionable. These accounts are confiscated without notice to the account owners. Americans are watching their savings disappear in front of them. This evening's televised entertainment programs are interrupted to extend the news reports and the discussion on the confiscation of people's bank accounts. Rumors flash across social media that the IRS is breaking into people's homes looking for gold, silver and hidden cash. America is riveted in front of their televisions when the reporters announce the IRS has issued a press release saying, "Next year's tax refunds will be delayed until at least early 2017. No refunds will be paid out during the balance of the calendar year 2015 and all of 2016."

Fox's Megan Kelly breaks the news that the White House is going to announce that it's now illegal for the private ownership of gold and silver. All private holdings are to be sold to the government at the rate of $500 an ounce for gold and $30 an ounce for silver. Megan's audience is shocked into silence by the announcement. I'm happy we hid our holdings. I think to myself, *This time Obama hit his base, this time he went too far. He's screwed with the wrong people. He's going to lose the support from the media and the very wealthy. I laugh thinking how the mega-rich just got screwed by their messiah.*

Our neighbors start arriving at 7:20 PM to attend the meet and greet session with Tony and Nancy. All are concerned with the evening's news reports about the IRS confiscation of people's bank accounts and the report that private ownership of gold and silver is outlawed. Many want to know if we're affected too. I tell them, "Someone already emptied our accounts, we don't know who or how they stole our money. Even our bank security officer doesn't know what happened."

Fred asks, "Jay, does this mean we're screwed? Are you out of money to finish the shelter?" Everyone heard Fred's questions, all talking stops waiting for my answer, "Fred, everyone, we should be okay. The banks have acknowledged someone broke into our accounts, the FDIC and the bank's own security departments are working on restoring our accounts. In the meantime, they have extended us a line of credit without interest."

Todd laughs, saying, "Interest rates jumped to 20% yesterday, how do we go about getting an interest free loan?"

"Lose 20 million dollars through holes in your bank's security system."

Todd smiles, saying, "I think I'll pass."

"Please trust me, no one should worry. Really, everything is going to be fine. Grab a beer or a glass of wine and let's chat about what we want to discuss with Tony and Nancy when they arrive."

Our neighbors nod while downing a drink and grabbing a plate of snacks. As we start talking about the agenda for the evening, Todd walks back into the room saying, "Fox News just reported that worldwide, over forty central banks are hoarding gold, is this something important? Megan said something about the banks decided they're not going to sell their gold to the government."

Nodding, I say, "Yes, it is. It says the central banks are expecting a complete meltdown sooner versus than later. None of them trust their own or any other country's currency, they are hoarding gold as an insurance policy. Gold has always been used as an international currency." Before I can finish, the front door opens and Tony and Nancy enter with smiles on their faces. They're carrying three large boxes from a local bakery and Tony is dragging a case of wine behind him. Tony and I hug each other as Lacy hugs Nancy. The others in our group smile at the friendly welcome by both sides. Nancy says, "Hi everyone, we didn't know what to bring, so we asked the bakery to make up some different cakes and cookies for the little ones. We also brought an assortment of wine." The kids ran over, looking in the boxes, Linda says, "Cookies! Cool!"

After exchanging introductions, everyone grabbed a plate of cake and a cup of coffee, wine or a bottle of beer. Tony looked out of the rear windows, the large construction flood lights illuminated the shelter work site. He sees Matt spreading the fresh concrete on the floor of the shelter. Tony says, "I see you're working around the clock on your little construction project."

"Yes we are, we don't have a lot of resources so we work on it when we can. The floor will be finished in two days. You can see most of the preformed concrete outer walls waiting to be installed. When the walls are up and their steel support beams installed, we'll install the interior walls and the ceiling which is also preformed sections of concrete. We're going to use the steam shovel to lift the preformed sections into place. We'll bolt them to the steel beams. The roof will go on in sections to allow us to finish the interior rooms. The final roof will be the soil we removed from the hole. We'll cover the shelter so it's not visible. If we get overrun, we'll be able to survive in the shelter. Once the roof is covered, we'll plant crops in the soil so in a few months no one will know there's anything buried under the fields."

Tony doesn't take his eyes off of Matt working the fresh concrete. "Jay, how long are you planning on staying underground? How do you power the shelter?"

"Tony, we have external electrical power running into the shelter from solar panels and the windmills. I'm thinking about ordering some generators, that's if we can find any. We have wells providing us fresh water and sanitation pipes to move our waste into septic fields. We have food, weapons, medical supplies and clothing for different seasons. We're assuming that if we're overrun and have to hide in the shelter, our invaders will think we took off without realizing we're hiding right under their feet. How long we have to stay hidden depends on how long our uninvited guests decide to stay. I'm hoping that after they use up the supplies we've arranged for them to find, they'll move on."

"Jay, what happens if those who overrun you decide to stay around for a while? Maybe they know how to farm and like your homes? You'll be stuck underground, maybe without power or having to face the attackers who've taken over your own homes."

All of our neighbors are listening to our conversation, "Tony, we're assuming the shelter can remain hidden. We're assuming that whoever overruns us will do so like a swarm of locust, they'll strip the easy to find supplies and move on to their next source of food. We think we'll be able to hold our homes and land unless we're hit by a group of several hundred, which won't happen for a while after any collapse. I think most people assume the government agencies will show up to provide help within a day or two, just like Katrina and Sandy. I think what the news is reporting tonight is the next step in the collapse. I think if the market opens tomorrow it's going to crash like a lead balloon falling out of the sky."

Tony smiles saying, "Jay, you didn't answer the question."

"Tony, if the invaders stay, we'll have to sneak out at night to kill them. I don't think we'd have any other choice."

Tony also looks around the room, shaking his head saying, "Jay, that's a very big assumption. You're betting your life and the lives of your family, loved ones and neighbors on a theory that's never been proven. I agree that many people may wait for help to arrive but when a day or three goes by and they realize no help is coming, all hell is going to break loose. That's human nature. There's only a few days of food in Nashville or any city. When the food runs out, those in the city are going to do anything they can to find their next meal. They're going to loot every store, restaurant and home they come across." Tony pauses to look around the room, no one is speaking, some are holding their breath. Tony continues, "Any force that succeeds in overrunning the farms isn't going to be stupid. They'll have numbers and brains. They'll figure out you must be hiding someplace. They'll cut the leads from the solar panels and windmills cutting your power. Without the power you'll lose your pumps, you'll lose your freshwater and sanitation. You're going to be jammed together in the dark, thirsty and pissing on each other. You'll break out into the arms of those holding your property. When the waves of people hit, you'll be overrun, beaten and killed."

"Tony, we have automatic weapons, and some RPGs, we have the new supply that should be here in 24 hours or less. We have our trenches and..."

"Jay, families of the farms, you have nothing. You're building an underground shelter because none of you believe you'll be able to hold back the hordes of hungry, desperate people for long. You plan to attrite them and slow them down so that you have time to escape to your shelter. What if they follow you to your hidden entrances? What if they catch and hold a couple of your children and force you to open the shelter's hidden doors? Or maybe one of the wives? How will you react when your loved one's screams penetrate the ground and rip your guts?" Tony stands silently in the middle of our family room looking into our empty, ashen faces. "You all think you've got this figured out. I can tell you, you're going to be surprised by how violent the crowds will be. You're going to lose, you're all going to die."

Our family room became completely silent, every eye is locked on Tony.

"Maybe I can help you. I have access to a lot of construction people, they can be here tomorrow. Their bodies and equipment can finish your shelter in less than a third of the time you're currently looking at. We have people experienced in war and weapons. I have employees who are ex-military, many were Special Forces. They have the experience to improve the defenses. We can hide the solar panels in the woods and run their lines underground making them very hard to find. I think that by merging our families we'll have the numbers to hold off any swarm of people. Plus we'll be able to finish the shelter and improve it much quicker than you can without us."

Flo asked, "Tony, what do you want for the help you're offering?"

Tony smiled at Flo, "That's the easiest one to answer. All I want is to expand the shelter so my family and a few close friends can join you. We'll build homes on land I own that border your farms and we'll connect our homes to the shelter. I want a ticket on the ark."

Randy smiles, saying, "So you own the land behind my farm. You're the mysterious company that refused to sell the land."

Tony smiles, "Yes, that's my land. I held on to it and other patches as a just in case."

Nancy says, "We're really not any different than you, we all want the same things. When you get to know us better, you'll see we're the same as you. We want our family and friends to be safe. We want our children to grow up in a safe world. We hope they find people they love, they have a happy marriage giving us grandchildren. We don't want our family ever to have to go to bed hungry or afraid. Isn't this what all of you want? Are we so different?"

Most of our neighbors smile in agreement with Nancy.

Tony says, "My worry is when the shit hits the fan, and the people in Nashville realize there's not going to be any more food delivered they are going to look for any place there could be food. Farms are going to be a prime target. They're going to swarm over the land like locust stripping the land clean of everything edible. They're going to head for the farms, which is here. If the country is going to pull itself together, it'll do so by first feeding the people. The only way to feed the country's people is by protecting and expanding the family-owned farms so that they can provide food for the hungry. The large corporate farms are going to have their own issues since most large companies are going to collapse. The workers on those farms will most likely try to take over the land. Their issues are going to be similar to ours, fuel to run their equipment, manpower to protect them and work the fields. Of course, many of them are tens of thousands of acres so they are most likely going to break up into smaller farms. I can provide us additional bodies to work the farm and provide security. I have access to certain resources which might be the difference between survival and failure."

Randy says under his breath, "I take it failure results in our deaths."

Tony takes a minute looking around the room before he replies, "Yes it does. Failure means our death and the death of the American dream. If we fail, the country fails and the last hope of freedom in the world will die with us. We're all up to date with the news. We all know we're on the verge of the collapse of the country and possibly another world war. When Russia moves into Europe and China absorbs Asia no one will be left in the world to resist them. We as a country are failing, we're falling apart. No one can save us. We elected an inexperienced senator as President, one who grew up hating everything we stand for. He was raised by a communist and he sat in a church for twenty years listening to a pastor who screamed his hatred of white people and America. He thinks the world can be what he says it is, he thinks if he says something then it will happen. Everyone with half a brain knows he got elected because of his skin color. He made the inner city and minorities worse off than they were before he got elected and they still love him. They think he's their Messiah. He laid the foundation that destroyed America. Every time action was called for, he sat on his hands. He added more to our debt than all of the previous presidents combined. He sowed the seeds of our destruction. When he said he was going to transform the country, none of us knew what he meant. On the plus side, he's the only politician that kept his pre-election promises."

Paul says, "What about Bush, he got us into a war in Iraq for pure bullshit, we spent over $400 billion and threw away how many lives for a war over WMDs which weren't there. His tax cuts took much-needed money away from the government pushing us into the recession we're in. I think that Bush laid the foundation for the problems we're in now."

Matt responds, "Paul, do you really believe that?"

"Yes, I do."

"We can agree to disagree."

Fred says, "I think we need to return to the main topic. Tony, I think most of us agree with you on the current situation. None of us thought about what the future held outside of our group. Speaking for me, I agree with you that if the farms fail, the country fails. I'm sure we're going to vote you into our little club. I for one would like to know more about the people you plan to bring with you."

As Tony refills his coffee cup, he turns to face me winking. "Fred, I'll be happy to supply the group with a list of names and their backgrounds. None of them is what you would call typical gangsters, those kinds of people are most likely going to be the ones we're going to have to kill to hold the farms. As a quick summary, it's going to be me, Nancy, our two children, Nancy's younger brother and his wife with their three children. My security team is made up of eight ex-military people, all experts, and with hands-on experience in defending positions. I also have a doctor and his wife, a midwife, and two nurses on my payroll plus a couple of teachers which we're going to need if things completely fall apart."

When the group heard Tony say, doctor and nurses, everyone nods in agreement. All of us were worried about not having a doctor. With the country's logistical infrastructure falling apart, we worried some of us might die without proper medical support. People stand to refill their coffee cups or get another beer. Tony and Nancy work the room like the experts they are. The evening draws to a close at 10:30 when everyone except for Tony and Nancy has gone home. Tony refills his cup of coffee, "Jay, how do you think it went?"

Smiling, I pat Tony on the back, "I think it went very well. I don't see any problems. They'll all let me know their thoughts in the morning. As soon as I hear from them, I'll contact you. If we assume the answer is yes, when can you have construction people start working on the shelter?"

"24 hours after you call me. I think we're going to have to hurry. I'm concerned that tomorrow's unemployment announcement is going to be a shocker to the country."

"I agree. I hope the government releases the real numbers this time. Remember during the lead-up to the 2012 election when the Department of Labor released great job numbers which turned out to be false?"

"Yeah and no one paid by losing their job."

"Speaking of jobs, if everything collapses, how are you going to earn?"

"Don't worry about us. We've prepared for retirement. I didn't think it would come so quickly, but shit happens. We'll be fine. I make my living by providing people with what they want. People are always going to want things. It may be food, it may be weapons, it may be medicine. Everyone is going to want things and my job will always be here because of that."

"OK listen, we hate to throw you out, but we've got to get up very early tomorrow. Farm work is never finished. There's so much to do with the shelter and other preparations we wake up tired."

"No sweat. Jay, no matter how the vote goes thank you. By the way, how goes the bank situation?"

"The banks promised to start repaying us within 72 hours. All we can do is keep our fingers crossed."

Smiling, Tony pats my back saying, "Keep your head up, I think they'll repay all of your money, maybe even with interest. It's crazy how these hackers can steal people's money without them or the banks knowing it happened until it's too late." Tony winks while putting his arm around Nancy's waist, "Honey, I think it's time for us to go, these poor people need their rest."

Nancy and Lacy hug each other goodbye. Nancy says, "Lacy, call me tomorrow, let's have lunch soon while we can still enjoy it."

"That sounds good. I have to be in town in a few days to get my hair done."

"You're right, we have our appointments at the same time. Let's meet early for lunch and cocktails."

"Sounds good to me."

Lacy and I clean up saying, "Honey, do you think everyone liked Tony and Nancy?"

"Lace, yes, I think everything went very well. My only concern is will we have enough time to finish the shelter before it's too late."

Lacy pauses while placing the dishes in the dishwasher asking, "What are we going to do if we run out of time?"

I look into her eyes and lowering my voice, I respond, "We pray and we do whatever we have to in order to live."

Chapter 15

We wake early the next morning to the news reporters all worried about the newly released unemployment numbers. Lacy and I have breakfast while watching the Fox morning news. Looking at Lacy, "Crap, someone made a mistake, they just announced numbers which sound like they're the real numbers."

"Honey, can the numbers be real? 946,000 new claims in the past week? My God, that's worse than the numbers in the 2008 crash. The Department of Labor said the revised unemployment rate is 11%."

"I think the numbers of claims are correct, but not the percentage. My gut says the percentage is closer to 20%. The Department of Labor doesn't count those who dropped out of the workforce nor do they count anyone who used up their benefits. If you're unemployed for 27 weeks and used all of your unemployment benefits, you're no longer counted even though you're still without a job. Since they only count people receiving benefits the real numbers are much higher. If they're reporting 11%, think about how many people they're not counting. Call them the 'hidden unemployed.' Most of our economy is driven by consumer spending and without that spending the crash is going to be deeper and longer lasting than anything we've seen since the great depression. Even then we didn't also have to face the external forces dumping our dollar, crashing our economy. We have a president who thinks the only way to get us out of a recession is through government spending. The 'smartest man' to ever sit in the big chair doesn't understand how the economy works. He's never managed anything in his life. The 29 depression was made worse and extended because of the government's spending."

"A couple more weeks of numbers like this and no one will have any confidence in the economy. When people lose confidence in the economy, they don't spend and when they stop spending more people lose their jobs making the problem worse. It's a never ending cycle, like a snake eating itself. More than 50% of the country is dependent on government assistance which is stopping. There aren't any private industry jobs opening to hire these people, what are they going to do to put food on their table?"

We're interrupted by the Secretary of the Department of Labor making an announcement, saying, "My fellow Americans, we know that many of you are concerned with the new unemployment numbers. I want to assure you that the jump in the weekly unemployment numbers was expected. It's a seasonal blip, it's nothing to be concerned about. We are moving ahead with President Obama's announced immigration program. We believe increasing the number of immigrates will open new jobs for Americans, improving our overall economy. These new immigrates will pay much-needed income taxes. They will absorb the lower tier jobs that the average American doesn't want to do. Bringing these new people into our hearts will help all of us. I've heard the phony complaint that Fox News broadcasts, that opening the borders to additional immigration is taking jobs away from Americans. This simply isn't true. Most Americans won't take entry level jobs, jobs that are critical to keeping our economy moving. We're all aware of the current financial pressures on the government. China's demand for immediate repayment is delaying our payments, but this too will improve with the addition of millions of new workers paying taxes and social security into the system."

Lacy looks at me asking, "Is he, is all of the government insane? How the hell can they be opening the borders when millions of Americans are being fired? What brand of rose colored glasses are these people wearing?"

"None of them can face the truth that everything is falling apart, no matter what happens they hold onto the status quo. Holding onto power is the most important thing for them. They think they're above the people they're supposed to be reporting to. In the President's mind, he doesn't work for us, we exist to support him. Just like in the Dark Ages. He and his aides know what's best for us. With the left, it's always 'do what I say, not as I do.' None of the laws or rules applies to them. Congress passes laws which they exclude themselves from. Part of me thinks the coming collapse is going to be a good thing. It will give Obama the clean slate he needs to finish his transforming of the country."

Lacy shakes her head saying, "Jay, it's not a good thing, millions are going to die, we could see the end of America as we know it. We could end up with him as a dictator. If the economy collapses as most thinking people now seem to agree is unavoidable. The President might declare a national emergency, signing an executive order declaring martial law. He could postpone the 2016 elections until the economy picks back up, which we both know isn't going to happen. He could rule for life."

"Honey, if that happens, I hope the military takes their oath to defend against all enemies, foreign and domestic to heart and removes him from office. If not, I think we're going to see civil war 2.0 which is going to tear the country apart to such an extent, it'll never heal."

"Then we'll be no better than any other third world garbage pit, we'll be ruled by a military junta."

"Lacy, I wish I knew what was going to happen. I find it interesting that many illegal immigrants are leaving because they can't find a job while the government is opening the border, allowing more of them to enter. I think there's going to be a traffic jam on the border with thousands trying to enter as thousands try to leave. What a mess. Do you think I should call everyone and poll them on last night or give them time and let them call us?"

"I think we ought to give them a little time to digest everything. I'm sure they'll call us."

We sit at the table watching the talking heads report on the slowing economy when there's a knock on our front door. "Lacy, are you expecting anyone this morning?"

"No, are you? Did you forget something?"

Getting up to check I respond over my shoulder, "No, I'll see who it is."

Opening the door, I'm surprised to see the three families standing there. Fred asks, "Jay, mind if we come in?"

"Please do. Hon, better make some more coffee."

Everyone comes in, Flo asks, "Do you have any of the cookies from last night left over?"

Lacy says, "Sure, I'll get them for you."

Everyone sits at our dining room table, Randy says, "Lacy, Jay, we're sorry for dropping in on you without any notice. We all sort of chatted with each other this morning. We ended up meeting at Flo's for an early breakfast. By the way, Flo makes the best pancakes you've ever tasted."

"Flo, you didn't invite me? I love pancakes. I'm going to have to get even with you."

Flo smiles, saying, "I'll make you some." She gives me a hug.

Fred picks up the discussion, "We didn't want to waste any time so we decided to come over and tell you face to face."

I'm dying inside waiting for them to tell me what they decided. "Can you give me a hint?"

Randy smiles, saying, "How about we just tell you we're all in agreement that Tony and Nancy join us. Just having a doctor on his payroll pushed all of us over the edge. Those who didn't know them were surprised by them. We all voted yes. How soon can Tony have his people here to speed up building the shelter?"

"If I call him this morning, they can be here tomorrow."

Randy smiles, saying, "So why aren't you on the phone? We all heard the unemployment announcement, things are much worse than any of us thought. The government's announcements aren't making things better. We're all worried about the future."

Lacy carries a fresh pot of coffee into the dining room when the doorbell rings. We all look at each other trying to figure out who's at the door. Lacy says, "If none of you are going to check who's here, I will."

She opens the door, speaking to someone. She pauses saying, "Honey, I need you."

I join Lacy at the front door, there's a messenger with a dolly at the front door. "Mr. Jay Tolson?"

"Yes. I didn't order anything."

"I have a very heavy package for you."

"Who sent it?"

"It was sent by Four Clover Management."

I look at Lacy, shrugging my shoulders. I sign the electronic pad he holds out for me to sign. The driver says, "Be careful, this box is very heavy, the shipping label says the wooden crate and contents weigh 275 pounds." A "light" goes on in both of our heads. I ask the driver, "Can I borrow the dolly to move the box inside?"

"Sure, do you have to move the crate where you want it, or should I hang around a bit?"

"I have a dolly to move it, just need you to get it in the house."

Fred, Randy and Jill join us at the front door. Fred looks at the wooden crate, "Jay, what did you order this time? Something fun?"

"Something for later, could you help me move it inside? I have to warn you its very heavy."

"How heavy is heavy?"

"275 pounds."

"Christ Jay, what did you buy now?"

"Something small and very heavy, a cube of enriched uranium. I plan to make my own bomb."

Everyone laughs at the joke soon forgetting all about the box.

Lacy says, "Everyone, thank you for coming over and telling us face to face. We have some things we have to take care of this morning."

Everyone smiles and nods in agreement.

When everyone leaves Lacy looks at me with an evil smile on her face, "Can we open it?"

"Let me get a crowbar from the garage."

Breaking open the crate Lacy and my eyes grow wide in shock, Lacy says, "Is that's what $20 million in gold coins looks like?"

"Guess so. I feel funny pushing our neighbors out, but like you, I couldn't wait to open the crate."

"Jay, where are we going to store it?"

"We have space in the hidden space we built under the basement. Had I known it was coming today, I would have had a safe delivered."

"Think you can still find a safe for sale?"

"If not, we'll store the rifles someplace else and use the gun safe. Help me get this thing in the basement."

"I'll bring up the dolly."

@@@@@

Spetsnaz Captain Sarnoff and his team drop off two cases of AK47s to two different gangs in New York before doing the same in Chicago thinking, *Good, maybe they'll kill each other off so when we arrive we won't be facing our own weapons. I'd hate to be the cause of our troops getting killed our own rifles.*

He's interrupted by his first Sergeant, "Captain, we're finished here, our next stop is supposed to be St. Louis. We're ready whenever you are."

"Very good. Try to keep your speed down, we can't afford to get a ticket. One of their police may get curious and check our van, if they find our cargo, we'll be spending the rest of our lives in one of their jails."

"Captain, no we won't, our people will release us as soon as they arrive."

"Unless they kill us for getting caught."

"Good point. I'll drive slower."

"Da, very good."

The Spetsnaz team visits twenty-two American cities, dropping off weapons and ammo. They've sown the seeds and provided the basic equipment to enable the twenty-two cities to explode. Captain Sarnoff smiles thinking of the chaos he's spreading across America. When the weapons are discovered, the blame will fall on China

@@@@@

President Obama calls his Secretary of Defense, "Ashton, I don't care that you don't like my orders, all I require of you is to obey. We need to find at least two trillion dollars and one of the easiest places to find such savings is the departments with the largest budgets. Defense has the largest share of the pie so you're going to cut your share of the budget so we can get out of the jam we're currently in. I want you to cut 50% of the military. Start with those expensive and useless nuclear weapons. Then consider cutting the Marines. We don't plan on invading anyone so why do we need a separate 180,000 person military that copies the Army, Navy, and Air Force. If the Marines go away, the Navy can cut the number of ships they use to transport and protect the Marines. It's really very easy. If you cut the Marines, who are too right wing anyway, you'll have an easy time finding the balance of cuts I need."

"Mr. President, what about the people we'll be booting out of the military and the projects we'll be cutting? Over four hundred thousand people will lose their jobs."

"Since most of them are right wing nuts when they lose their jobs, their only available support will come from the government. They'll learn the error of their ways and vote for us to increase taxes on the rich so their benefits can be increased. Yes, I like it. Close down the Marines, cut 50 ships from the Navy and all of the Air Force's missiles and nuclear bombers."

"Mr. President, you're going to leave us open to attack without any way to protect ourselves."

"Ashton, I know you were recently appointed, however, you've just outlived your usefulness. I expect your resignation on my desk tonight."

"Mr. President, you'll have it. I disagree with what you're doing."

"Do you think I care? I don't have any other choice."

"Yes, you do. Just tell the yellow bastards to go screw themselves. They're not going to use force. They know we'll turn them into the world's largest glass slab. They know we'd nuke China back to the Stone Age."

"Ashton, I don't want to hear this type of talk. I told you, I'll never use nuclear weapons. History isn't going to report that I, the first African American President used nuclear weapons or started a war with China. A black man isn't going to nuke Asians. We need to pay them or they are going to take Hawaii."

"Mr. President, let them try, the Navy can stop any Chinese fleet before it comes into range of Hawaii."

"I already told you I'm not going to start another war. We're going to pay them."

"Mr. President the stress this is causing our people is too great, something is going to break. I'm pleading with you to reconsider your decision to pay them. Let us strike them, we'll put the fear of Buddha in them."

"Aston, I expect to see your orders reducing the military along with your resignation on my desk by 10:00 PM."

"Mr. President, I won't go down in history as the Secretary of Defense that left us defenseless."

"Ashton, I appointed you because you said you'd follow my plans and take instructions, you're not doing either. I'm very disappointed in you. You're fired. You can leave right now."

President Obama tells Denis McDonough, his chief of staff, "I just fired Ashton, I want you to take over Defense. Close down the US Marines, I want Defense's budget cut 50%."

US Marines Commandant General Joseph F. Dunford, Jr. receives a call from Ashton informing him of the upcoming orders. General Dunford is shocked at the news. He sends an urgent message to the senior Marine commanders to conference with him at 2400 hours.

@@@@@

Sean Hannity reports a flash news item on his show at 10:45 PM. Sean stands in front of the cameras shaking with hate. Sean announces the hot rumor the President is firing the US Marines and cutting the US Defense budget by 50%. Sean says, "My fellow Americans, this is pure treason. This is high crimes. I'd like one congressperson or Senator to come on the air and tell me why President Obama shouldn't be impeached. Fox News interrupts Sean's show with the confirmation that President Obama has ordered the Department of Defense budget cut by 50%. He also ordered the mothballing of all of America's nuclear weapons.

@@@@@

"Tony, are you sitting down? I'd like to talk about the meeting here at my place."

"Shit, Jay, wait one minute so I can go to my office." Tony enters his office, closing the door behind him. Tony sits down getting ready for bad news. He pulls a notepad out of his upper desk drawer to start making alternative plans.

"Tony, are you there?"

"Jay, before you begin, I want you and Lacy to know this won't interfere with our relationship. I'm ready, go ahead, tell me."

"Tony, I'm happy to say everyone has accepted and welcomes you, Nancy and your family with open arms."

Letting his breath out, Tony smiled, replying, "Jay, you owe me, you almost had me."

Laughing, "I just had to, sorry about that. Everyone would like to know when you can have the construction people on site."

"I'll be there today around 4:00 PM, I'll bring my construction foreman with me. Does that work with you?"

"Perfect, by the way, the kids want to know if you can bring some more of those cookies with you and Lacy wants to know if you and Nancy can stay for dinner."

"We'd be happy to. Even my restaurant is having problems getting supplies of fresh food and I'm paying through the nose for anything we can get. I think I'm going to have to close the place within a week or two. Eight of the restaurants on my street closed last night. Another four put up signs saying they're going to close tonight."

"Are you still packed?"

"I am, but the others aren't. The people who come to dine at my place can usually afford to spend whatever the meals cost. I've seen a large increase in the number of homeless in the city over the previous three days."

"Looking forward to seeing you at 4."

Lacy, who was listening to half of the conversation, asks, "Honey, you didn't thank him for the crate."

"Never on a phone. Never know who's listening. I bet a number of agencies have his phone tapped."

"You're right, I forgot about that little issue." Before we finish our home phone rings, Lacy looks at me asking, "Did you say something about phone taps?"

"Couldn't be."

Picking up the handset, "Hello, this is Jay."

"Mr. Tolson?"

"Yes, this is Jay Tolson."

"Mr. Tolson, I'm Steven Brown from Bank of America's security department. We have completed our review of the cyber attack on your accounts. Our analysis confirms someone outside of the bank and not from your location found a hole in our firewall. This party was able to hack into the bank. We found you were not alone in the attack, this party was able to empty 205 different accounts. Of course, I can't mention who the other account holders are but I can tell you the only thing all of the accounts had in common is all are in the high net worth department."

"So whoever hit us, also stole from 204 others?"

"That's correct, they made off with over $300 million. We've spoken with the FDIC and the bank's CEO. We'd like you and Mrs. Tolson to visit one of your local branches. If you can tell me which branch you'll visit, I'll arrange a meeting with the branch manager who will be waiting for you. Once in the branch, arrangements will be explained to you how Bank of America is going to support you."

"Mr. Brown, we can be at your branch in Nashville, the one on Main in two hours."

"Excellent, we'll speak again when you and Mrs. Tolson are with the bank manager."

"Honey, we have to go to Nashville, want to see if any of the kids want to go with us?"

"How much time do I have before we leave?"

"Ten-fifteen minutes."

@@@@@

The senior commanders of the US Marines agree to resign in mass before they can be fired. General Dunford knows once he and his staff leave there will be chaos in the ranks. He expects the mid-tier officers to quickly follow with their resignations as the snowball gains speed rolling downhill. President Obama wanted the military budget cut in half, General Dunford agrees to help him. He issues verbal orders that every Marine leaving should take their personal weapons with them. The General orders the armories opened to provide the leaving Marines with "sufficient ammo and weapons as may be required for self-protection." General Dunford's staff laughs at the thought of 185,000 Marines walking off their bases with their personal weapons and ammo. General Dunford says, "Think of the President's reaction when he learns everyone left with an M16 or M4, five thousand rounds, six grenades and in some cases, rockets. Many are going to be leaving in some sort of vehicle. They'll even take the tanks. He'll shit a brick."

Major General Smith, the head of logistics asks, "General, I don't want to broach the subject, but I feel I have to. Sir, have you considered removing the CIC from office?"

The room and conference call falls silent. General Smith breached the one subject that was on everyone's mind, yet no-one wanted to mention. General Dunford replies, "General, I know this question is on everyone's mind. I've fought with myself on the issue. We've all been in countries where the military took over the government, we've seen what happens, we've all seen the damage left behind when the elected governments have been overthrown. I don't think the American people will stand for a military coup. I think the economy is on the edge of a large cliff. The economy can't be saved, it's going to tip over very soon when it does we'll be needed to help our people put the country back together. I've spoken to the other Joint Chiefs, all are going to tender their resignation tomorrow. We've ordered a complete withdrawal of all of our combined people from every international OA. The recall orders will be issued in 55 minutes. We're bringing everyone home. We're going to release any who want to go with their personal weapons. A very well-armed militia is being formed whether the President likes it or not."

General Black asks, "General, we're just going to leave?"

"Yes, the President wants the budget cut, he'll get what he wants and the repercussions will be on his head. I suggest we plan to connect every Friday at 0900 which should allow those on the west coast enough time to get up and have their first cup of joe."

All agree and the recall orders are issued to America's troops around the world. Most are confused but obey. The world wakes to video of American troops leaving their international bases. The news is being watched in Moscow where the senior staff is horrified to see thousands walking off of military bases carrying their weapons and driving armored vehicles home. They know these armed soldiers and Marines are going to be a major problem when the time comes for the Russians to land on American soil.

@@@@@

Tony and Nancy arrive at our house at 3:30, "Tony, you're early."

"No one's on the road, the price of gas has stopped almost everyone from driving. I saw stations posting new prices on the way over, three stations posted a price of $30.00 a gallon, and signs saying, cash only, no credit. With the dollar crisis we can't import oil, we're not drilling a lot here at home due to the President's executive orders. We're running out of oil which is driving the price per gallon up. Station owners are raising the price and will continue to do so as long as they have gas and people will pay them for it."

"That'll be another nail in the economy's coffin."

"You're right, let me see the shelter."

We walk to the back of our homes where the large hole in the ground is open, Tony looks down saying, "The foundation looks good. It looks like it's cured, can I go down and see it?"

"Sure, when is your construction manager arriving?"

"Should be here any minute."

"Should we wait for him?"

"Good idea. Here he comes now, I see his motorcycle."

"No pickup truck?"

"Motorcycle uses a lot less gas than a large pickup. Jay, this is Jack O'Sullivan, my construction manager."

"Jack, a pleasure to meet you."

Jack is a large Irishman, dark red and gray hair. He looks like a football lineman, 6'7" tall, must weigh close to 275. Jack climbs down the ladder to inspect the Shelter's foundation. He walks across the entire foundation, looking at the pipes, wiring and metal brackets for the walls and support beams. "This looks very good. Frankly, I'm surprised. I was expecting to have to tear everything up and redo it. Why did you decide to build your own and not order a premade shelter?"

"Jack, none of the premade shelter companies I contacted could deliver a shelter within a year, they were all back ordered. I decided we'd build our own."

"I'd like to see the latest plans to ensure no one's made changes from the original ones I reviewed for Tony."

"Thought you would. Here they are, you can use my dining room table to review them."

After reviewing the latest plans Jack nods towards Tony saying, "These are good plans, you've caught some of the mistakes I was going to point out. I can help accelerate the building. Tony, for the second shelter I'd suggest you contact a couple of your friends, I'm sure one of them can break loose a premade shelter. I don't think we're going to be able to locally find the concrete and premade forms to finish a second one in a timely manner, or at all. I think every concrete company in the area has closed. Tony, one out of the box idea I have is, have you considered buying one of the bankrupt concrete plants?"

Tony looked surprised, "OK, give me a couple of company names, I'll make the calls. Why don't you locate Franco, who you've worked with before to see what support you can give him right away? After all, your family is going to be using one of the shelters if things get out of hand. Jack, while you're with Franco look at my land to check what you need to install the premade homes, I think we're going to need at least ten of them very quickly. The homes are in the parking lot at my south street warehouse. I'll arrange security to move them here."

"Yes, sir."

Jack leaves to find Franco, "Tony, where the hell did you find ten premade homes to install on your land?"

Laughing, Tony replies, "That is my secret. As are the solar panels for each roof and five additional windmills. I've lined up all of the available concrete trucks to start pouring the foundations in five days. Bulldozers are already clearing and leveling the land. Tomorrow a drilling company will dig a few additional wells."

"I see you don't let any moss grow under your feet."

"Jay, we both know time isn't a resource we have. Give me a minute to make some calls, Jack texted me the list of shelter companies and the name of the law firm to discuss buying the concrete plant. I'm about to steal a shelter out from under some of their existing customers."

Twenty minutes later, Tony returns to the kitchen, smiling, "Atlas Shelters just agreed to sell us eight 12' X 83' galvanized corrugated pipe shelters. They will be on the way from Montebello, California in a day after my deposit arrives which should be in three to four days. I have to supply security for the transportation which I'm working on. I'll hire a team from my counterpart in California, I'll pay his people and provide them with fuel and food to return home after the delivery is made. Each will have their own generator and air filtration system. We're going to interconnect them together and them with your shelter. We'll have our own underground city.

Each shelter is going to cost me a little more than three times their normal price. Shelter cost, transport, and a year's supply of freeze-dried food for forty people is setting me back a nice round $1.5 million for each shelter. I also have to pay double the fuel cost to deliver them and return the trucks to the factory, the fuel cost alone is going to be steep. I'm supposed to overnight prepaid fuel cards so they arrive tomorrow. I have to arrange $5million in gold to arrive before they ship the shelters."

"Frankly, it's not as bad as I thought it would be."

"The real problem is going to be the install. We're going to have to dig a hell of a hole. Your neighbors are going to be pissed."

"How long will it take them to get here?"

"Figure two days for the gold to arrive at the factory, a day to arrange their shipping paperwork and arrange for the in-transit fuel. They think they might have to send a fuel truck along with the shelters. I figure the trip from California to Nashville is going to take them five days, say they will be here ready to install in ten days. Which assumes they don't run into any attacks on the road here. I'm going to leave Nancy here to have dinner with you and Lacy. I'm going to my office to make the necessary arrangements."

"Ten days is good, it gives us time to bring in most of the crop before the holes are dug. Tony, I do need a favor before you leave."

"What do you need?"

"Can you get the sheriff off my back?"

"That's a hard one. He has a hard-on for me too. What's his problem?"

"He wants our crop so he can sell it in the city."

"That I can stop, I'll report him for black marketing supplies."

"Jay, we'll talk later, I've got to leave so I can make arrangements. I'll be back later to pick up Nancy."

"See you later, we'll keep your dinner warm for you."

Lacy says, "Tony wait, take this."

"What is it?"

"Fresh sandwich and coffee for your trip."

"Thanks."

Five hours later our phone rings, "Jay, Tony. I have a problem. I can't get out of my office, is it OK if Nancy spends the night at your place?"

"Don't give it another thought, of course, she can. We have one guest room unused, she and Lacy are close enough in size that I'm sure some of Lacy's stuff will fit Nancy. I promise you, we'll take good care of her. What about your kids?"

"I have two people taking care of them, plus they have a full-time nanny who cooks for them."

"If you want, send them here, just do it. Just give us a heads up so we won't attack the car bringing them."

"Thanks my friend, I owe you another one."

"Don't worry about it."

Nancy is happy to spend the night and she calls her children to assure them everything is OK.

Tony says he'll join us for breakfast with Jack and his construction people.

@@@@@

At dawn, we're woken by the sound of trucks and the alarm at our gate ringing. Getting up to check the monitor, I'm surprised to see Tony's black S-class Mercedes in front of a line of trucks at the gate. I hit the button to open the gates. Tony pulls up at our front door while the trucks and construction people continue on to the shelter. Tony and I grab a cup of coffee while walking out back to see forty-five men start working on building our shelter. A flatbed truck brought small cranes which lift the premade walls while Jack's people bolt them to the mountings embedded in the floor. The walls are going up right in front of our eyes, it's like watching a fast motion video. People are swarming all over the shelter. I can't believe what I'm seeing. Tony turns to me asking, "Happy?"

"Holy shit, I can't believe it."

"Told you I'd bring value."

"You did that with the small crate that arrived two days ago."

"Happy you got it without any problems, it's to your satisfaction?"

"Very much so."

"I'm not even going to ask where you put them."

"It's OK, wasn't going to tell you."

We smile at each other as we sip our coffee watching the shelter go up right in front of us.

"Tony, one other small issue we need to discuss, the National Guard was here for our crops if they return..."

"Don't worry about them. I think I've already taken care of them. I've spoken to their commander, who you'll be meeting shortly."

Chapter 16

With the people and equipment Tony's supplied, the main shelter is finished in three weeks. Most of the interior furnishings were installed before the roof was installed. Beds, tables, stoves, fridges and freezers and large crates of supplies were lowered into place. Last night we completed the last interior delivery. Many of the interior items have to be installed, but everything is at least inside the shelter. Today we start covering it with the soil that was removed from the hole. Next we'll plant crops on top of the shelter.

The bad news is Tony's purchase from Atlas shelters is taking a lot longer to arrive than anyone thought. The shelters weren't as ready as the factory led Tony to believe and the transport from California wasn't going smoothly. While the roads weren't busy due to the cost of fuel, if it hadn't been for the fuel truck accompanying the tractor trailers they would have run out of fuel a day outside of California. The convoy was attacked three times in transit, Tony's security people beat the attacks off with the cost of five of his people. Tony wants us to dig the holes to prep for the shelters so they're ready to install when they arrive. We want to wait until the shelters are here to give us the most time before we have to harvest our early crops. We reached a compromise, we agreed to wait for the shelters to arrive in case not all of them made it. My neighbors are happy with every day delay of the additional shelters, it gives the crops another day to reach maturity. Tony's worried the shelters won't arrive at all. He sends another security team out to assist the original team. We later learn if he hadn't sent the second team, he would have lost his shipment because they were attacked just outside Memphis by a well-organized, heavily armed group. John, Tony's security chief led the counterattack that broke the attacker's backs and secured the shelters.

July 8th, 2015 was a dark day for America. The government lied about making reduced welfare and social security payments. In fact, no payments were made at all, leaving over one hundred million people without any funds. Millions took to the streets protesting the lack of payments, they expressed their anger by destroying and burning everything in their path. The mobs are angry with the government, the banks, and every business. They think they've been robbed. There's no logic to the mobs destruction. What little fuel remained at gas stations is set on fire when the pumps are turned on and lit. The explosions destroyed entire city blocks. The riots causes hundreds of millions of dollars of damage. They stripped every food store bare, they flash mobbed restaurants stealing all of their food. Tony lost three people when a violent flash mob attacked his restaurant. The angry mobs in Nashville set the Grande Old Opry on fire, then they blocked the fire department from arriving to put the fire out. Lacy and I watch the smoke cover the southern horizon. Watching the news, we decide the bottom's dropped quicker than we expected. We're interrupted by our front gate alarm, we have uninvited visitors. "Shit!"

"Jay, what's wrong?"

"The army's back, this time with the sheriff."

Opening the gate a matte tan colored Humvee and the Sheriff's car drives up our driveway, parking in front of our house. The Sherriff looks at the back of the house where eight large holes are dug in our fields.

"Sergeant. Sheriff, how nice to see you again."

The Sherriff shakes his head, "Jay, what bullshit is this? What the hell happened to your fields? Who gave you permission to dig up your food producing land?"

"Sheriff, I'm sorry, I was under the impression I owned the land and I could do with it what I wanted. Did you happen to buy the land from me and forget to hand me a check?"

The Guard Sergeant replies, "Jay, under President's Obama's executive order 13891, it's illegal to damage any food producing land. You, sir, are in violation of said order."

"When did he sign this one? I've never received any notice about it. How can I be liable for committing a crime when I'm not aware something is a crime. In fact a minute before he signed this executive order, I owned my land and could do with it as I saw fit. You can't declare today something illegal which yesterday was legal."

"I have a copy of the executive order right here." Handing it to me, the Sergeant says, "You can see right here in black and white, you're in violation of the executive order."

"Sergeant, what's funny is when I went to school and studied civics I learned only Congress can pass laws, the President either signs or vetoes them, he doesn't make them. His executive orders apply only to his executive branch departments."

"This is a national emergency. The President has to do everything within his power to save the country. In extraordinary times, extraordinary actions have to be taken. We have a starving country. Fuel is too expensive to transport food across the country so we need every local farm to supply their local areas. You've been warned before. You've been told you have to turn over your crops for the betterment of the people living in the local area. By destroying your farm land, you have removed tons of food from the people who need it the most. Are you going to tell us why you've dug up your farm?"

"I bought a new toy, a metal detector. I got readings in those places, so I bought a backhoe and a steam shovel to find my buried treasure."

The Sheriff looks at the holes and at me, "Jay, you're nuts, completely certifiable. I ought to arrest you to protect you from yourself."

"Sheriff, I don't think you can do that. I haven't harmed anyone or myself, I own the land, I can do anything I'd like to on my own land as long it doesn't endanger anyone else."

"What about the families who used to own these farms, you've taken away their livelihood."

"Maybe I have, however, you're free to talk to each of them. I've given each family more than enough money to carry them until next fall."

"I thought you lost your money in some bank hack?"

"I did, most of it has been returned by the banks who admitted the hackers found a hole in the bank's security and I wasn't alone in the hack."

The sergeant looks disgusted, "Jay, when are you going to fill the holes and get back to farming?"

"A couple of weeks. By the way, would you like to try my metal detector?"

I hand it to the sergeant who waves it over the driveway, "Sir, you're a fool. You have the sensitively turned all the way up, it'll show a positive reading wherever you hold it."

"Guess that's what I get for not reading the directions."

The Sheriff and National Guard sergeant shake their heads in disgust as they get into their cars driving off our property. Lacy walks over to me asking, "Do you think they bought it?"

"Seemed like they did. The crazier they think I am, the more we can get away with."

"When are the shelters arriving?"

"Tony said tomorrow morning, it's a good thing the fools arrived today. It would be hard to hide the shelters if they saw them being lowered into the holes."

"Jay, aren't you worried the sheriff will see them on the road coming here?"

Laughing, I reply, "Tony is arranging a little something which will draw all of the police and the Sheriff to the other side of town, he'll drive them crazy."

Laughing, Lacy says, "I should have known."

"Which reminds me, Tony promised me he took care of the Guard. I better tell him he didn't get his money's worth."

Fred and Randy walk across the fields asking, "How did you get rid of them this time?"

I told them the story, showing them the metal detector. They broke up laughing. Fred asked, "Can they really be that dumb?"

"They left didn't they?"

"What's the next step?"

"The shelters are due tomorrow, I'm hoping the crews can get them inserted into their holes in two days."

"That's going to take a hell of a crew to move all eight into their holes."

"We'll have the people."

Randy asks, "Have you seen the news from Nashville?"

"Yes, we saw the smoke on the horizon, it's getting worse every day. I wonder how long it will be before Nashville and the other cities explode, forcing people to leave."

Fred responds, "I hope we get everything finished in time."

We all nod our agreement. Looking at the other two, I ask, "How's the hidden acreage coming?"

Laughing Randy replies, "Since that land hadn't been farmed for a very long time, our yields are surpassing our best estimates."

"Want to ride over with me? I want to also check on the new home development program that's going on behind the trees."

Randy asks, "Do you think it's going to stay hidden?"

"I hope long enough for our new neighbors to get settled and also give us enough time to get another crop in."

Fred says, "My fear is the windmills, they're visible for miles."

"I agree, I have no idea how to hide them. Do you?"

Randy says, "Plant some trees to hide them?"

"That won't hide them in winter and spring and will block the wind, plus anyone getting close will see them. If they find the power lines, we'll be in trouble."

"We'll just have to hope the lines are well hidden. Make sure they're buried deep, so they can't be easily pulled to the surface."

Randy asks, "Won't we be OK since Tony's shelters have generators in them?"

"Randy, I've ordered two generators for our shelter. The issue is fuel storage and exhaust. In the cool months, the exhausts will look like steam coming out of the ground. I've asked Jack if it's possible to cool the exhaust before it leaves the ground."

"When will we know?"

"I'll follow up with Jack." Todd joins us asking, "Christ, Dad, it looks like you guys are testing missiles out here. Didn't the Sheriff wonder what the holes were for?"

"He did, I told him I was looking for buried treasure."

Laughing, Todd looks at the holes, "Dad, where are the tunnels connecting the various shelters?"

"Christ, now you remind me we're missing something important, where have you been the past few days when the holes were being dug?"

"I've been sneaking people to the shooting range, making sure everyone can quickly aim and fire every weapon we have. Having the weapons won't help us if no one can use them or if they're not accurate with them."

"I was wondering where you've been, that was a great idea. How is everyone doing?"

"Ricky is not a bad shot when he allows himself to be OK with the idea of firing a weapon. Everyone else can score 8's or better. I'm using small targets, so in the real situation they should do well. I've had to remind most people to reload, they shoot up a magazine, the bolts slide back, but they continue to pull the trigger. It takes them a minute to realize they're out of ammo. Paul is a sharpshooter, he has the ability to be our sniper."

"Keep them practicing. You're right, most people are going to forget to reload. That's a good observation and one that may save our lives. Keep up the great work. The three of us stand in the warm air when two backhoes start digging trenches connecting the large shelter holes together. I smile, saying, "Seems someone else remembered to connect the shelters too."

Todd asks, "Dad, isn't this overkill? How many people are going to be sheltered here?"

"I really don't know. There's our group and Tony's group. I trying to arrange a joint gathering so everyone can meet each other."

Fred replies, "That sounds like a great idea, when are you planning it?"

"As soon as I can nail Tony and Nancy down. He's been very busy, he's been out of town most of the past ten days. I don't ask him where's he goes because frankly, I don't want to know."

@@@@@

At 7:00 AM on Monday, July 13th an unruly group of people starts to gather at the New York City side of the Lincoln and Holland tunnels. The mob starts with two hundred people gathering along the road at the exit of the tunnels. Within ten minutes, the mob swells to 500 people. By 7:30 AM the mob has grown to three thousand. Hundreds join the mob every couple of minutes, by 8:00 AM the mob is ten thousand strong and still growing. At 8:10 AM, the mob moves into the street blocking all of the traffic from exiting the tunnels into New York City. They block all traffic into the city with the exception of the George Washington Bridge. At 8:15 AM two large trucks run into each other on the upper deck of the GWB. Four minutes later, three cars run into each other in the middle lane on the lower deck completely closing the GWB. The two accidents block all access into the city from the GWB. Traffic at the three entrances into the city backed up for more than ten miles. At 8:45 AM the New Jersey State Police closed access to all of the exits leading to the tunnels and the GWB, diverting all traffic to surface streets, back to either the Turnpike or Interstate 80. At 8:50 AM a gasoline tanker truck just inside the Holland Tunnel explodes for no apparent reason. The explosion and fire spread to the cars waiting in the tunnel. The explosion roars through the tunnel burning everyone alive sitting in their cars and buses waiting to enter the city. At 8:55 AM a truck bomb exploded in the middle Lincoln tunnel destroying the tunnel and cracking the outside casing, allowing the river to flow into the tunnel. The raging river water drowned everyone waiting in the tunnel to enter the city. The water flowed out of both the entrance and exit of the tunnel causing flooding on the surface streets around the tunnel. The Fire Department couldn't reach the disaster sites due to the thousands of blocked cars and trucks. While the police started to move the wrecked cars off of the GWB, two truck bombs explode. They are quickly followed by twenty young men firing AK47s at the police and people sitting in their cars waiting for the bridge to open. When the police returned fire, the mob tossed pipe bombs and Molotov Cocktails at the police and the people trapped in their cars. The thick, burning black smoke blinded and choked the first responders who are trying to assist those stuck on the bridge.

At 9:00 the mobs started building barricades blocking all access to New York City. New York City Police are attacked when they respond to the closure into or out of the City. The mob is armed with AK47s. They open fire on the transit police and NYPD. The mob continues to grow as members send information across every social media website. When the mob reaches 10,000 people, they attack the stores and offices surrounding the tunnels. Large banners are attached to the buildings close to the tunnels and GWB saying, "PAY US."

At 9:05 AM television reporters from the three national and three local television stations have finally worked their way towards the front of the chaos to film and report on the mob. The reporters asked who the leader of the demonstration was so they could interview him or her. The front row of people responded, "We the people have had enough of the government's lies. There is plenty of money to pay us our social security, welfare and retirement payments. We're not going to allow access to the City until our payments are made. We also want the cost of a gallon of gas back under $3.00 a gallon. We want our food stores restocked, we want our lives returned to the way they were three months ago."

The socialist mayor of New York City decides to go to the Lincoln Tunnel to attempt to reason and find a way to compromise with the mobs. Mayor de Blasio approached the mob which has been separated from the rest of the city by police barricades and lines of armed, shield holding police. "Hello, I'm the mayor, please listen to me, I want to help you, I want to find a solution to your grievances. I want you to know I support you, I agree with your demands. Open the tunnels and bridges so we can work together on a solution that meets everyone's requirements."

Mayor de Blasio is pelted with rotten eggs and bottles of urine. The mob turns towards the police barricades pushing them away, thousands of people surge forward while thousands more surge towards the police from their rear. The police are pelted with bottles of urine and bags filled with dog and human feces. Others throw rotten fruit at the police. The on-scene police commander, NYPD LT Gray, orders his officers to fire tear gas into the mob. When the first canisters of tear gas are launched, most of the mob covers their faces with towels, a few put on gas masks. LT Gray is surprised when the mob throws the canisters back at the police mixed with bottles of acid which completely takes the NYPD by surprise. LT Gray orders live rounds to be fired above the mob's heads. The mob responds by drawing hidden arms, returning fire, aiming at the officers. Most are wearing armored vests, many are hit in the legs and arms. Those wearing vests are surprised the mobs' rounds are penetrating their vests. Penetrating rounds are illegal in New York State. The mob behind the police attach hoses to the fire hydrants, turning them against the police, who are again taken by surprise. LT Gray quickly realizes he's outnumbered. With the mob turning violent, he calls for reinforcements. Fifty NYPD police cars start to head toward the scene of the riot. Members of the mob run into the streets laying down sheets of plywood with large nails sticking up. These blow out all of the car's and bus's tires going over them. Hundreds of NYC taxis are used to block the streets leading to the tunnels and bridges. Manhattan is effectively separated from the mainland. The police reinforcement cars discover the booby-trapped streets too late. Only five of the fifty police cars that were sent as reinforcements make it to the scene of the riot. These five cars are taken under fire before they reach the intersection two blocks away from the riot.

LT Gray's officers are squeezed between both groups of rioters. He's about to order firing into the mob when his radio reports similar riots taking place at the Holland Tunnel along Canal Street, he's told there are over one hundred stores looted and burning out of control. He also hears reports that Times Square has been overrun by yet another mob. The hotels and stores are being looted by flash mobs numbering in the thousands. LT Gray calls for air support in the hope that dropping water on the mob will slow them down. The water might have slowed the mob down, however, due to spotty radio communications the helicopter crews only heard the call for help and the word fire. Five NYPD helicopters fly over Times Square firing into the mob. The NYPD by mistake fires on the people standing on the sidelines watching the flash mobs strip stores bare before torching them. The mobs reacts to the attacks by opening fire on the helicopters and every police officer and car they encounter. Anyone wearing any sort of uniform is shot at. The mobs begins taking over the key subway transfer stations completely shutting NYC down. They hang banners all over the city demanding payment. Mayor de Blasio calls a press conference to announce he's calling upon President Obama to reinstate the welfare payments to the poor people of New York City. He says most are suffering because most New Yorkers only have a couple of days of food in their homes.

New York City's electrical workers union demands an immediate pay increase to cover their loss of buying power due to hyper-inflation. Mayor de Blasio issues a press release stating the City can't afford any pay increases due to the high number of unemployed in the City and loss of tax revenue. He also publicly reminds the unions the terms of their contract are fixed for an additional two years. The electrical workers union President responds by cutting electrical power in New York City, saying, "Maybe after two years in the dark the Mayor will reconsider his decision."

People are trapped in high-rise apartment buildings, thousands are stuck in elevators and subways when the power is cut. Tens of thousands of street gang members use the power outage to loot all of the stores in their local area. Many plan attacks against their rival gangs knowing it's going to be very hard for the police to stop their battle since they're already tied up with the existing riots and now the blackout.

Two days into the power outage, large sections of New York City are burning out of control. Mayor de Blasio begs the federal government for help putting down the rioting. The Department of Home Land Security sends twenty MRAPS loaded with armed security officers to assist the NYPD. The convoy is attacked at exit nine on the New Jersey Turnpike just outside New Brunswick, New Jersey. Members of militias standing on overpasses fire stolen anti-tank missiles at the convoy, destroying it on the New Jersey Turnpike. The militia members wait for the undamaged MRAPs to stop and dismount their troops before they open fire with AR15s and AK47s, hundreds of the DHS security troops are killed. The militia leaves them lying on the Turnpike. The attack forces the NJSP to close the turnpike stopping all movement along Interstate 95. When the NJSP approaches the scene of the attack, they come under the militia's fire stopping them 200 yards away from the location of the attack. Mobs in Newark hear about the closure of the Turnpike, they attack the New Jersey Parkway, closing it just before exit 14 for the Newark Airport. All North-South Traffic through New Jersey is stopped.

Hundreds of thousands of people watching the news reports coming out of New York City are motivated by the scenes, they too take to the streets. The people are scared and depressed, they are afraid and angry at the system for letting them down. Cities across America watch what's happening in New York City, they watch the mobs close the tunnels and bridges, they watch the mobs tear the city apart, they see large sections of Manhattan on fire and the flash mobs taking what they want. People copy the tactics used in NYC in their local cities. 165 cities across the country are set on fire from unhappy, scared, hungry people demanding the government live up to their commitments.

President Obama orders the US Army to bring order to the country. The Chairman of the Join Chiefs of Staffs (CJCS) General Dempsey looks at the written order from the President, his aide hears him explode in anger. "Damn him, he caused this mess. If he'd let us take on the Chinese before he shrank our forces, we wouldn't be in this vise. I'm not going to order US troops to fire on US citizens. We're the protectors of the people, not their murderers." General Dempsey composes a message back to the President informing him that US troops are not going to patrol or fire on US citizens. The President sends back a one-word reply, "RESIGN." General Dempsey looks at the message and smiles, telling his aide to call the remaining chiefs together so he can inform them he's been fired. Twenty minutes into the meeting with the remaining service chiefs, President Obama receives the resignations of General Dempsey and the resignations of the chief of the US Army, Air Force and the Chief of Naval Operations. President Obama smiles thinking to himself, *that's one way to get rid of these right wing nut jobs. I'll simply promote someone who agrees with me to run the military and who knows how to take orders.*

President Obama asks the Secretary of Defense for suggestions on new chiefs. The new Secretary informs the President he can't accept the US military being used against US citizens. He's fired for his honesty. The President appoints his National Security Advisor to the position of Secretary of Defense. He does so without the consent of Congress, telling Congress he doesn't care what they do. Susan Rice becomes the first woman Secretary of Defense and the only one not approved by the Senate. Her first order is for the US Army to put the rioting down in New York City. She orders the 10th Mountain Division located at Fort Drum, in Jefferson, New York to mobilize and move into New York City. The 10ᵗʰ's commanding general, Major General Stephen Townsend and his executive officer, Lieutenant General David Baker, both refuse the order. They demand it be sent in writing from the President. Secretary Rice fires both senior officers for requesting a written confirmation. The troops of the 10ᵗʰ Mountain Division, one of the US Army's Light Infantry Division, watch their senior officers are fired for not obeying the Secretary's order to fire on Americans. The troops fight among themselves whether to obey the order or not. At the end of the day, only 2,500 troops out of 12,000 agree to follow the orders. Unknown to the 2,500 troops, militias in New York City have broken into Fort Hamilton, where they were able to convince the commanding officer to open the armory. The militias oppose the orders sending the army to restore order. They arm themselves with M16s and M4s, Army body armor, hand grenades and anti-armor and anti-air rockets. They dig trenches along the road the 10ᵗʰ has to use to reach NYC. They're in high spirits while they wait for the arrival of the army. Thousands of cases of liberated MREs are distributed to the hungry people. First aid materials found in the armory are used to set up mobile aid stations to provide a small degree of medical support for the city's people. Mayor de Blasio orders the militia to disband. He's rewarded by having himself dragged out of Gracie Mansion. He's stripped naked, tied to a pole as hot tar is poured on him and he's covered in chicken feathers. The militia dumps him at the Holland Tunnel, telling him not to return. The militia opens Gracie Mansion to the homeless and needy. The flash mobs continues to strip the city bare of food while the militia are arming people they trust with the weapons they stole from the armory. The New York City militia leader, John Green sends messengers to invite all of the gang leaders, two hundred citizen leaders and leaders of the mobs to a sit down to discuss the defense of the city before the Army arrives.

Green breaks into Madison Square Garden to hold his city leadership meeting. The militia strings generators to provide cooling and lights for the meeting. Leaders of fifty different gangs and twenty mob leaders arrive to hear what the militia leader has to say. John welcomes everyone to the meeting. Outlining the situation, he shows them images some of his people have taken at Fort Drum of the troops moving towards the city. The room explodes with threats, claims of false bravado and joy they were going to get the chance to kick the government out of the City. John fires his sidearm into the ceiling to get the attendees to quiet down and listen to him. "Listen up assholes, this isn't the normal army coming here. This isn't some video game, these people will shoot back, in many cases they will shoot first. The best troops refused to obey the order, the troops coming here are ones who shouldn't have been accepted into the army. These people are going to enjoy killing and raping us. We have to work together to prepare for them. If we work together, we can defeat them and teach the government a lesson. I know that usually the gangs would rather kill each other if one stepped into the other's territory, the mobs just want to take what they want, and the average citizens want law and order restored. The only way we're going to survive is for us to find a way to work together, or we're going to hang together."

Two of the mob's leaders stand saying, "Who made you mayor? We don't want to trade one asshole for another. Why should we do anything you want? What's in it for us and our people? Our people are hungry, we're tired of having to obey, we want to rule ourselves."

"Then go, pick an area, move your people there and rule yourselves. I won't stop you, nor will I aid or support you."

"What about food and clean water?"

"You want to rule yourselves, you figure it out. Either you can work with the rest of us or you can leave. We don't have time for silly games. I think a third maybe up to a half of the NYPD are going to join the army to fight us. I wouldn't put it past the government to use air strikes against us. They're worried if the rest of the country sees us beat them back, the country will explode in insurrection and revolution, something that we should have done years ago."

Three people representing five multistory apartment buildings say, "We're not an army, most of the people in the city just want things to return to normal. Why can't we offer to sit down with the Mayor to negotiate a truce and return to the status quo?"

John shakes his head responding, "There isn't any more status quo. We tar and feather the mayor before kicking him out of the city. The government is out of money, China is making plans to invade the west coast. It won't surprise me if Russia invades the East Coast. Millions of us are going to die from starvation and a lack of medication. Forget the way your life was two months ago. It's not returning for a very long time if ever. If you don't have the stomach to fight for your rights, you can join the flash mobs and try to rule yourselves, we won't help or support you either. Life is hard, our time is short. How many of those stuck in the upper floors of the apartment buildings are going to die? How many people are too scared to venture outside? They're going to die in their apartments, aren't you here to help them?"

The citizen representatives sit down confused and worried about their future.

John is able to work out a temporary truce between all of the parties. He partitions the city on a large wall map which will be the responsibility of each of the groups. John assigns one of his militia members to assist each group. John announces his plans to feed most of the people in the city. He sets up feeding locations that are protected by armed members of the different groups pledged to protect the city. The food comes from warehouses and surviving food stores. John is smart enough to know even with a reduced caloric intake of 1,500 calories a day he's going to run out of food in four or five days when he knows the city will really explode.

Chapter 17

Nashville is known as the center of country music. Country music performers are known to be more conservative than many of the other musical performers. Many country music stars help open soup kitchens similar to those who helped feed the hungry during the Great Depression. The largest common kitchen is set up in the Nashville Music Center, which takes up an entire city block between Demonbruen Street, also called the Music Mile and Korean Veterans Blvd. Twenty-five country stars support forty cooks from local restaurants feeding Nashville's hungry. Tony and I are proud of them stopping everything so they can help feed the hungry. With the stars feeding the hungry, most people delay leaving Nashville. This gives us time to complete our shelters and the homes for Tony's extended family who moved into their temporary homes three weeks ago. Tony and Nancy moved into our house until his was completed. We moved Sammi and Ricky to the pool house until Tony's home was finished. While Ricky was happy, Sammi was disappointed in moving out.

My largest concern is fall will soon be on us. The weather will change, the evenings are starting to cool down. Even Nashville gets cold in the winter, the city gets its share of snow. I'm very concerned that as the weather cools people will use fires to stay warm. These fires could easily catch homes on fire, which could spread uncontrolled through the city, creating a firestorm which will destroy many blocks making even more homeless.

Tony's security advisory Ex-Marine Captain John DeFranco smiles looking at the progress we're making in finishing the shelter complex. The main shelter's shell is finished and covered with the removed soil, new crops have been planted on top of it. People are still working on the inside of the shelter, building rooms, adding plumbing and moving supplies to the storage areas. John inspects the fighting trenches, making notes for the changes he wants to make. John calls Tony asking, "Tony, can you get your hands on a couple of mortars?"

Tony shakes his head, "Any particular type?"

"I'd love to have three or four 81mm tubes, I'd even be happy with a few of the small 60mm ones. In reality, I'd be happy with any mortar we can get. I'm worried that if we're attacked by a large number of people, our numbers aren't going to be enough to repulse a human wave attack. Not everyone is a fighter, some are going to freeze, some are not going to aim to kill and some just don't have the fire in their belly. We need a force multiplier if we're going to win."

"Aren't the full auto weapons going to be enough? I have enough trouble getting ammo, we're paying five dollars a round for whatever we can find. Finding mortars right now is almost impossible."

"Tony, I note you didn't say it's impossible, what about the contacts in the cartel?"

"John, no go, they're trying to buy every weapon and round they can find from different National Guard armories knowing we're going to collapse, which will cut their supply of weapons off. Where does one find mortars?"

"National Guard, Army? If you can't find any mortar tubes, see if you can find the mortar rounds. If you can find the shells, we can make the tubes. The IRA has been doing it for over thirty years."

"I'll let you know what I find. What else do we need?"

"Can you find any flame throwers?"

"Why not just ask for a nuke."

"Cool, I would have if I thought you could get one."

"John, don't you think untrained people using a flame thrower are more of a danger to us than to anyone attacking us?"

"Are you saying, me and my people aren't trained?"

"You know damn well what I'm saying. If something happens to you and your crew, the farmers could roast my ass with the flamethrower as easily as anyone else's. Can't you make a portable flame thrower?"

"Tony, I have a good friend who's in the Army Reserve, mind if I give him a call and see if we can broker a deal?"

"Go for it, just tell Jay or I what we need and where you want us to be, to pay for whatever deal you make."

"Will do."

John calls his friend in the reserves with whom he's done business with many times. Aaron is a Master Sergeant in the Army Reserve who manages two National Guard and Reserve armories. There's been time's equipment has been signed out of the armory, handed to John and never returned. The missing weapons were marked as damaged during training. "Aaron, how are you and the family? Have enough to eat?"

"John, we're getting along, the Army is supplying us with MREs for our families, not great, but better than nothing. Gas is too expensive so I spend 4 days a week in the armory as do many others. We're getting by, better than most. What can I do for you?"

"Is it possible for us to have lunch? I can arrange to have you picked up."

"Can you have someone at the Armory at 11:30?"

"Sure, look for a white Chevy Tahoe, I'll be in the back seat.

Arron's picked up at the armory, he settles in next to John.

"Hi Aaron, we're going to visit another close friend of mine. He owns a restaurant downtown."

Aaron nods at John. They're dropped off at the back door of Tony's restaurant. Aaron says, "I thought all of the restaurants on this street closed a couple of weeks ago."

John smiles responding, "They did. This one is owned by my friend. Name of Tony. He has enough supplies to provide meals for special meetings and for his very close friends."

Walking in the back door, Aaron's jaw drops when he meets the owner, he's thinking, *oh crap, Tony is that Tony. I'd better be on guard. He can make me disappear.*

John says, "Tony, this is Aaron, in the past Aaron has supplied me with some special goods. He might have some items you're looking for. I thought the two of you should meet."

Aaron shakes Tony's hand. The three sit around a table. Tony starts talking about their specials, "Tony, you didn't bring me all the way here to chat about food, why don't you tell me what you'd like me to make disappear for you. I should tell you right up front. Demand is very high as are the prices."

Smiling Tony replies, "Right down to business, I like that. I'd like to know the going price for mortars and their shells."

Aaron stops chewing his bread and butter looking at Tony, "Mortars? Jesus Tony, they're not easy to make disappear. Rifles and ammo are always checked out for training or security operations, but mortars are only checked out for the summer two-week training or an actual deployment. Christ, this could get me caught."

"So the price is high?"

"High? Tony, I'm not sure it's possible. Heavy weapons are kept in a different section of the armory, they're under a different security system. The heavy weapons are guarded 24/7, it's not like I can just walk in and forge an officer's signature to sign them out for a training mission. Expensive doesn't begin to cover it. We're talking hard time in jail if I get caught. They'll open an investigation and check everything in the armory. I could get busted for all of the exchanges we've done. They'll send the ATF after you. It's not just me who could end up in jail."

"I'm sure you can set it up so if an investigation happens, you'll be able to lay the blame at someone else's feet. You've done it before."

"Tony, I've only gone into the heavy weapons armory four times a year to take inventory, opening it without the right codes sets off an alarm. Tony, can't you pick something else you'd like to buy? How about a couple of nice Humvees? A case of

M4s? I can get you 50,000 rounds of 5.56 ammo real cheap or how about a couple of cases of hand grenades? I can slip you fifty cases of MREs."

"Aaron, I'll take all of those, but I still want the mortars."

"Tony, not easy. I have to spend some time thinking about how to get into the armory without setting off the alarm. Can you give me a few days to investigate?"

"Aaron, when can I pick up the M4s, ammo, and grenades? I'll take the Humvees too."

"Today's Tuesday, how about Thursday. Have John arrange the transfer. He knows how to do it and get people onto the base and into the armory. John, send the same three people to drive the Humvees, make sure they're wearing the uniforms I gave you with their ID tags, no one has ever questioned them before. We'll do it the same way, they walk in the base, I'll meet them at the armory, we'll load the weapons in the Humvees, and your men drive them from the base. I'll expect to see the payment in my Swiss account when your men leave the base."

John asks, "Aaron, have you ever had a payment issue before?"

"Never which is why I continue to do business with you."

Laughing Tony responds, "Aaron you'll do business with me because I'll make you a very rich man."

"Tony, I've done okay working with John. I've been able to pay off two ex-wives, buy my house for cash and own two very nice sports cars. I expect you'll follow the methods John and I have proved work with almost no risk to either party."

Tony smiles, "Don't worry, you'll be paid in the usual way. Don't cross me. You can guess what'll happen if you screw with me. I want my mortars and while you're at it, I want a few cases of missiles."

"Missiles? Christ Tony, why don't you ask for a nuke?"

"I didn't think you stored nukes on the base or I would ask."

"We don't. What kind of missiles?"

"What have you got?"

"Look, I wasn't joking, if you think sneaking mortars out is impossible, getting missiles out *is* impossible. The brass is scared a MANPAD could end up taking down a passenger plane. They are RFI chipped, if one goes through the doorway without the correct codes, it sets off an alarm shutting down the entire base. Forget missiles."

"Can't you get the RFI codes?"

"No, only certain officers have them. I can't buy them off."

"Give me his contact information, I'll see what I can do."

Finishing lunch Aaron leaves Tony sitting at the table. Tony's thinking, *I might not be able to get the mortars, but additional rifles and ammo are always welcome, I'm sure we can find a use for the Humvees. Dressed in Army uniforms riding in Humvees we can pass for army soldiers, never know when this might come in handy.*

@@@@@

The Nashville Music City Center has lines of hungry, scared, tired people that go around the building three times. If the lines of people were straightened out, there would be a line exceeding two miles long. None of the Country Music stars expected to see so large a number of hungry people. Alan Jackson remarked to Reba, "I'm shocked at the number of hungry, depressed people. Most of these people have no hope, no dreams, and no future. Many are going to be waiting an entire day for the chance to get something hot to eat. I hope we don't run out of food before everyone gets something."

"Alan, it's hot outside, the sun is strong. I'm going to take some cases of bottled water out to them. They must be really miserable waiting in line."

"Reba, don't go out alone, make sure you have security with you, some of those people have no hope, they have nothing to lose. They may attack you in order to get the water."

"I'll be careful."

"Reba, I thought it over, don't go, I'm worried about your safety. The line of people rings the building three or four times, many have been standing outside all day. They are hungry and angry. When word spreads of water, they will turn into a mob fighting everyone for a bottle of water. I'm surprised they haven't rushed us to break in here already. The only reason that may be keeping them at bay is they remember us, they enjoy our music, many hold us in a special place. If we weren't here, I think they would rush the soup kitchen, many would be killed."

"Alan, I don't believe they will act like animals, they are still human, I'm sure there is good within them."

"I pray you're right, the supplies we're serving are running low. When we run out of food, there is going to be a panic that'll spread like a wildfire. I'm going to take my family and leave the city tonight."

"Where are you going?"

"I'm hoping we can make it to Canada."

"I thought Canada closed their side of the border with us."

"The northern border is the over 3,000 miles long, the Canadians don't patrol all of it. Before the time of troubles started the Canadians didn't have a large military. Since then they've been expanding their military. Canada's worried about their future since China demanded payment from America and Obama went crazy. Canada worries what the Chinese or Obama may do. They don't want to be caught in the crossfire."

Reba says, "Alan, I think Obama was always crazy."

"Reba, when the food runs out, Nashville's 1.7 million are going to tear the city apart looking for food. Hungry people will do anything to feed their families. Wouldn't you do anything to feed your family?"

Reba says, "I have some supplies hidden in the basement."

"I wouldn't say that out loud. Why don't you leave when I do, I'll make sure you get home safe and sound?"

"The shelter's not going to stay open all night tonight?"

"Reba, it'll stay open. However, the kitchen only has watered down soup left to serve. It's more water than anything else. I'm going to try to slip out when the sun sets. I don't want to be here when the people learn what the real conditions are."

"Thanks, I'll be happy to go with you."

As the sun sets and the sky darkens, the people waiting in line for food and water wonder if they will ever reach the end of the serving line. Many are restless after having waited all day for something to eat. Alan and Reba trade coats with a couple of the serving staff, they slip out of the Music City Center through the basement which exited into a parking garage two blocks away. They found a car that Alan could start by twisting the ignition wires under the dash. He looked at Reba, "We have half a tank of gas, we're going to try to slip out of the city without using headlights. If we're lucky, we'll be able to reach our homes without getting stopped by the crowds of people."

"Thank you for taking me home, what about our cars?"

Alan replies, "I don't care about mine, I have others. I don't want to be anywhere near the soup kitchen when the food runs out."

Reba nods, "I'm getting very worried about the situation. I thought the government would ensure delivery of food and gas instead they seem have stuck their head in the sand hoping everything will get better if they just ignore it. I don't think FEMA or DHS has done a damn thing to help out. I haven't seen a single FEMA truck since the crisis started."

"FEMA is most likely waiting until we're all tearing each other apart, DHS is most likely trying to figure out what color code to use for starvation."

Reba laughs, "Thanks, I needed that."

"Reba, are you going to be OK?"

"I have some people who help out around the house. I have a safe room, actually a safe section in my basement, and it's large enough to hold ten people for a week. We have food, water, and weapons. I hope it doesn't come to us having to fire on our own neighbors."

Alan says, "Frankly, I never thought we'd make it to September. The feds missed the July and now the August welfare payments and if they also miss the September payment next week, nothing is going to be able to hold back the people. Seventy percent of the country is broke, hungry, tired, and scared. At this point in time, they'll do anything, attack anyone to get a slice of bread."

"That's another thing I'm concerned about, prices are jumping every day."

"You mean the loaf of bread that this morning cost $22? Or a gallon of milk, if one could be found, is selling for $45? My wife is going crazy trying to feed us. We're lucky that money isn't the problem, finding the food is. My wife told me last night that she saw four people attacked outside of a supermarket. They were pushing their carts out of the store when they were attacked in the parking lot. The store was almost empty. The thieves stole their carts which had only a few items in them."

"I didn't think many people would be in the parking lot, not with gas selling for $50 a gallon."

"She told me the store's shelves were almost empty, there was no meat, chicken or pork, just a handful of canned goods, many of them were out of date. The bread was locally baked, the freezers were empty. The store manager told her he's going to close the store in a day or two, there's nothing left to sell. Fewer and fewer people can afford to buy gas enabling them to drive to a store. A few customers rode bikes with a wagon attached to it."

"I have a lot of freeze dried food stored away. If I have to, we'll be able to live on what I've stored for almost a year."

"I've been fishing for most of our food."

"That's a great idea."

Before Reba can finish, they see the road is blocked ahead of them with four men standing behind burnt out cars holding ARs or hunting rifles. Alan says, "Not good. Is there another way to your home from here?"

"Yes, but it's a long ride. Will we have enough gas?"

"I don't think we have another option, we're going to have to try it."

"What do you think those people want?"

"Anything we have, if they recognize us, they may try to ransom us."

"I never thought of that. I'm getting scared, I never thought it would get that bad in Nashville."

@@@@@

By the third week of September, the American dollar is worthless. None of America's international trading partners accepts it. Every industrialized country has seen their currency and banking system crash or they are experiencing hyperinflation due to the collapse of the dollar and lack of trade. Most governments are watching their people struggle with hourly price increases. Businesses laughed at President Obama's executive orders freezing prices. The Russian Federation easily moved into every European country with the exception of the United Kingdom bringing food, medical supplies, and hope. Russia placed a friendly national leader in each European country. President Putin conquered Europe without firing a shot. The Russians started to move the European undesirables into forced labor camps, where no one left alive. They were either worked to death or executed in the camps. The Russian leadership decided the best way to improve the lives of the average Russian citizen is to reduce the number of unproductive people looking for government handouts. When the labor camps are filled to capacity, undesirables are shipped to Africa where they're dumped on the shore and forgotten about. It's cheaper than shooting them.

@@@@@

In Nashville, small numbers of people gather together, five become twenty, which quickly become two hundred, the number quickly expands to thousands, which multiplies to tens of thousands, all of whom share a common trait, they're hungry. Tens of thousands demand government help. They realize burning large areas of Nashville didn't do anything except burn their own neighborhoods down so they decide to change the method of getting their message heard. Thousands march to the exits of Nashville pushing cars and trucks that are abandoned on Interstate 40 and 65 into blockades closing access into or out of Nashville. They loot sporting goods stores for tents. Large tent cities are formed that quickly fill with refugees. Mobile outhouses are placed in a line along the freeways and trees along the freeways are cut down for makeshift shelters and firewood. Many of the campsites resemble those on the reality television program Survivor. Families are scared, they're hungry and they've watched their life savings disappear. They can't afford to feed their families or pay their mortgages. They demand action from a government that responds with speeches and soundbites. Thousands of people sit down on the Interstate highway blocking traffic into and around the city. Usually, the only traffic is the military escorting or carrying supplies into the cities. The thousands of refugees attack the military convoys stealing the small amounts of food the convoys have. Civilian traffic has all but come to a halt due to the price and scarcity of gasoline. The only civilians on the roads are those walking, riding bikes or motorcycles trying to escape the cities. They're looking for a safer place for their families. Thousands join the protesters surrounding the cities every day. Others are looking for farms which need manpower in exchange for food. Many small farms have already been overrun by refugees looking for or demanding food. The protesters thought if the fire didn't bring them help, shutting down access the city will get their message heard. Shanty towns and tent cities spring up at the highway entrance and exit ramps leading into and out of every American major city.

Hoping to stretch the limited amount of food, President Obama uses an executive order signed in 2013 which gives the Federal Government the power to ration food and water. The average American daily consumption of 2500 calories is reduced to 1200 for adults and 1800 for children under the age of 15. Even at these levels there isn't enough food to go around. The President faces his cabinet saying, "We don't have sufficient food to feed everyone. We have to do something very drastic. We have to protect the young and potentially the most productive if we're going to have a future. In order to provide for the most productive, we are going to reduce the calories to anyone over the age of 70 to 900 calories a day." His cabinet debates the President's suggestion for three hours before they finally agree since they can't find any other solution to the current crisis.

MSLSD, the progressive channel news station fully supports the President's new plan. Their newscasters take to the air to spread the President's message. Their guests spend hours talking about how the rationing should have been done years ago to ensure American's ate healthily and lost the extra weight so many American's carried. MSLSD debated among themselves wondering why no one had had the guts to tackle the poor eating habits of the average American. The First Lady went on MSLSD to brag how she and the President were transforming America. She tells the station and their viewers that following the President's new diet would help American's live longer and be happier. At the same time, Fox News Network was reporting the President and First Lady was starving America. They were taking another freedom away from the people, they no longer had a freedom of choice of what to eat. Fox reported that even the reduced caloric meals weren't going to feed all of the hungry people. Fox news questions why the government hasn't farmed as much of the available land as possible to grow as much food as possible. President Obama responds to Fox by saying, "If we farmed all of the available land, it would increase global warming. We're saving the planet."

Many who were given half an MRE for a day are depressed and hungry. Most felt that something was better than nothing but the majority of people were constantly hungry and getting angrier by the day.

@@@@@

US Military convoys bringing food to the shanty town camps outside the cities are attacked by gangs and mobs that steal the MREs in the trucks knowing they won't be fired on by the US troops. Those waiting in the shanty camps for the food grow desperate when the food convoys don't arrive. Many decide to leave the camps, they head towards farms which they hope have food and water. Farms have animals to slaughter for meat. Farms have water for their crops. Farms will have barns they can stay in so they can get out of the weather. Hay which is softer to lay on than the cold hard ground. Tens, hundreds, thousands leave the cities looking for food and protection from the elements. The refugees making their way on the nation's highways are attacked by gangs who steal anything of value the refugees have. Thousands are killed and left to rot on the nation's roads. The rule of law has broken down across the land of the free. Most of the country's first responders have left their job to protect their families.

@@@@@

Starting in mid-July when the welfare payments were cut off we kept a four-member team on alert 24 hours a day. When we finished the shelter complex, two watched from the security shelter. The security shelter was a separate one built between the main shelter and Tony's. All of the video, IR and motion activated cameras were wired to display on a bank of monitors watched by two people 24 hours a day. The security shelter had its own generator to ensure the monitors always functioned. Two people made the rounds in our fighting trenches, one walked to the right while the other walked towards the left both completing the entire circle every forty minutes. We couldn't count on the town provided electricity which became very erratic. We switched our electricity over to that supplied by our windmills and solar panels. We disconnected the junction which transferred any excess power we had to the grid. We learned the grid was sucking most of our generated electricity. Two hours after cutting the line to the grid we got an urgent call from the Nashville power company asking what happened to the electricity we had been supplying. We explained that our windmills were down for repair. The generating manager asked if he could send a repair team to help us, he explained our electricity was very important to the available power in the area. We told the generating manager we were working on it. Randy and Fred asked. "Jay, how long can we go bullshitting them? Sooner or later they're going to figure out we've just cut them off. Isn't there a way to send them a small amount of power, maybe a fraction of what we used to? What are we doing with the power we're generating, there's no way we can be using all of the power we're generating with the windmill farm."

"I'll talk to Eric."

"Eric?"

"You know Eric, he's the electrician who's supervised installing the windmill farm and solar panels. He's the one you saw wiring the shelters. Let's check with him. I for one, worry the power company will suck all of our power to feed the city."

Fred laughs, saying, "Oh, that Eric, the guy with the mustache and ponytail. Why can't he set up some phony problem to fool the idiots at the power company? If we don't give them access, they'll just show up to see for themselves why we cut power to their grid."

I figure there's nothing lost by talking with Eric. "Let's see if we can find him, see if he has any ideas to keep these assholes off our back. The last thing we need is for the power company to be looking all over our property."

The three of us set off for the shelter complex to locate Eric when our alarm sounds, People drop everything they're holding to grab their rifles, body armor, and helmet. Bags of extra magazines are carried to the fighting trench. Todd runs towards me, "Dad, John said a large group of people is on the road heading towards us. Over two hundred and still counting. He wants a full mobilization."

"Shit, don't stand here talking to me, GO! Get everyone!"

Lacy runs out of our house carrying my AR and dragging my armor and helmet, "Jay, put this on! Hurry, John said they're very close, the frontline of them should be here within ten-fifteen minutes."

"Got it, thanks. Did he say if they're armed?"

"Don't know, he sounded the general alarm for a full mobilization. He wants everyone armed on the front line."

"I'm coming! I wish Tony had been able to get us a couple of mortars, we could stop them before they got close to us."

Lacy looks at everyone running towards their fighting positions. "Is this going to be bad?"

Pulling on my vest and helmet, I check my AR to verify it's loaded. I pull the charging handle to chamber a round and placing the selector on safe, I reply, "It depends on what their intentions are."

Our second alarm sounds which mean they are within five minutes of us.

Chapter 18

The small road that borders our farms is not the easiest to find in normal times. There's not even a road sign to say the name of the road (we took it down three months ago). Our road is falling apart due to a lack of maintenance and overuse by the heavy delivery and concrete trucks making numerous trips to our complex. We're happy that we've been forgotten and left alone for months, it's given us time to complete our shelter construction, get our crops harvested and plant our fall crops. We haven't been bothered because of the general lack of fuel. Most people had a hell of a lot more important things to do than bother with four small farms which most people forgot about or didn't remember where we're located. Today, hundreds of refugees are walking towards us. The road that runs along our farms is covered in refugees, they are spread out over half a mile. I ask John, "Do you think they're coming for us?"

"Jay, either they're lost or they're coming for us. There's nothing else on this road, our road loops around and merges with the main road a few miles past us. If they're not careful, they could be walking in a circle for a very long time."

"John, our road is pretty hard to find, it's almost hidden from view by the overgrown trees. It's even harder to locate since we removed all of the local street signs. Even if they had our address, we would be hard to find unless someone knew exactly where we're located."

"Jay, some good news, if anything can be good news. Given the number of refugees, the videos show almost none of them are armed, or at least no weapons that we can see."

"John, we have to assume the worst. How long until they reach us?"

"If they're coming for us, their front line of people will reach your gate in less than three minutes."

"John, is there anything we can or should do at this time?"

"Make sure everyone is ready. If they're hostile, we're in for a hell of a fight, look at their numbers, there must be a thousand of them. We could kill every other one and they'd still reach us. Quantity is its own quality."

"I heard that was the Russian's operating line from the cold war."

"Sure was. Their tanks and planes might not have been as good as ours, but they had something like a ten to one advantage. Even if we'd nailed a Russian tank with every round our tanks fired, we'd still have lost the battle due to their numbers. Our tanks would have run out of ammo and the Russians would still be coming. Yeah, quantity is its own quality. This group is so large they could easily overrun us. If we shot every one of them with each bullet we had, some would still reach our trenches. We have to stop them before they can get close enough to hurt us."

Before I can respond, John's iPad receives the video from our cameras mounted in trees covering the lines of approach to our property. The video shows the front line of the mob. John looks up saying, "They're here, they're milling around the front gate. They look confused. Wait, two are climbing over the gate, we'll have to do something to make that harder. Let's see what they want before we open fire."

Two refugees manage to climb over our front gate, bringing tools to take apart the hinges so they could open the gate, allowing their people to swarm in. Five, twenty, one hundred, three hundred, more keep coming, starting up our driveway. John hands me his binoculars, "John, they look dirty and tired. They look defeated, but it doesn't mean they won't fight. We have to assume they'll fight because they have nothing to lose."

I ask John, "Is the driveway trench uncovered?"

John replies, "No, whenever the alarm sounds the driveway trench covers are automatically uncovered, however, when I saw who was coming, I stopped the process. They have no vehicles, I thought there was no reason to give away one of our secrets."

John picks up a handheld microphone, "STOP where you are. You are trespassing on private property. STOP or we will open fire." John fires three shots into the air. The front line of the mob stops when they hear the gunshots, two men walk towards us holding a dirty white/yellow t-shirt over their heads, "We want food and water."

John responds, "I'm sorry, we don't have enough to share."

"You're not going to shoot us, we're unarmed, we mean you no harm. We're hungry and tired. Feed us and let us rest in your barns, when we've eaten and rested, we'll move on."

"There's too many of you, we can't feed all of you."

"You can and you will. We knew there were groups of small farms up here that aren't sharing with the city. You're not doing your fair share and leaving us to starve. It's your shared responsibility to help your brothers and sisters. You have all of the food you need, we have nothing. If you won't or can't feed all of us, give us enough to feed the children. You don't want their lives on your conscience do you?"

"How many children do you have?"

"A little over two hundred. If you can't feed all of us, you must have wells with fresh water for us."

"If you don't come any closer, we'll bring you food and water enough for the children."

I look at John, "Can we afford to feed the children?"

Lacy says, "Jay, I'm ashamed of you. Of course we can feed the children, we have to. I'm not going to go to bed worried about the children. We have plenty of wells, we have more than enough cows, we can give them water and milk, plus some food."

"And what about the next group and the next?"

"We'll deal with each when they get here. I'm not saying we feed them to hurt ourselves, but we have plenty, it's the right thing, the Christian thing to do. We have to share what we can afford to. There's no reason to touch our stored supplies in the shelter, but I won't allow the children to go hungry."

The eight of us in the trench all nod at Lacy's comments. John yells back, "Sit down where you are, we'll bring you some food, water, and milk. Do not advance up the driveway."

I guess what John said was repeated because we heard cheering from the crowd. Five of the community's teens gathered drums of water and milk, which they rolled down the driveway into the crowd. They returned telling us the crowd looked tired, hungry and very dirty. They were sitting or lying on the grass between the barbwire fence and the street. Matt said, "There are hundreds of them, they look like they've lost everything, they are overjoyed at the water and milk. Jill, Flo, and Liz took some paper bowls and cereal to the children, they also brought three cases of protein bars to the adults". Flo told them, "I'm sorry, this is all we can afford to share. We haven't harvested our crops yet. We hope this helps you. For your safety, slowly and carefully move off the grass, stay on the driveway, there are booby traps in the grass."

The crowd screamed in fear. Flo said, "Everyone on the grass stands up, don't move, just stand where you are. If you can see your footprints in the grass, step on them until you reach the driveway. Don't wander into the grass." Five didn't listen, they stepped into a hunting trap which broke their ankles. They screamed in pain. Flo thought to herself, *Shit, now we have to use some of our first aid supplies to fix them up.* Flo used her handheld radio, "John, have a problem down here, five stepped into the hunting traps, broke their ankles, we're going to need some tape and splints."

"I'll send it down to you, do you require other assistance?"

"I'm OK, condition purple."

John nodded his understanding, that purple meant she was OK.

The crowd had tears in their eyes. One of the women hugs Flo saying, "Thank you for your kindness. Do you mind if we rest here on your driveway for a little while?"

"No, that'll be fine, is there anything else we can share with you?"

"Some bottles so we can carry some water with us."

"We can do that, where are you going?"

"West, towards Memphis, to the Mississippi. There's good land there, we heard the government set up a few refugee camps on the banks of the Mississippi. We're going there if we can make it."

"We hadn't heard that."

"Someone told someone who told one of us, we have no place else to go, so we're going to the river."

"Good luck and God bless you."

"Thank you for your kindness."

Flo, Matt, and Jill carried two cases of empty plastic bottles to the crowd, which they filled with water from one of our wells. They used the outhouses we'd set up on the edge of our property which we used when we had to go and didn't want to go back to one of the houses. Three hours after they arrived the last one was gone. A sense of sadness and a sense of relief flowed over us. We met the hordes and they weren't evil, we shared some of our resources with them. We never learned if they made it to the river, we never heard about any refugee camps. We wonder what happened to the people who wandered past our farms in the early days of the crisis, we wonder if they lived or got caught by the roaming gangs who prey on the refugees. The highwaymen who rob and rape are the worst. We know one day they will find us and the end result is going to be very different than the initial group who came by asking for charity for their children. We know it's only a matter of time, we don't know how long it'll be until they arrive, but we know they're coming. We've heard the HAM reports of the roaming highwaymen who attack anyone they encounter, the gangs who broke out of the cities looking for food and valuables. We got off easy in our first encounter, we know the next won't be as painless. It seems the roads between the cities are dangerous, the inner cities are death traps. Anyone entering the inner cities, not in a heavily armed group will come under attack, even larger groups are attacked. The cities have deteriorated into active war zones, no one willingly enters them anymore. Tony told us that there's nothing left of the music center area. Every building was looted and burned until all that remains are the building's steel skeletons. He said it reminded him of the pictures of Hiroshima. All of us feel a loss of Nashville's music center. We wonder what happened to most of the country music stars who live just outside Nashville.

@@@@@

"Jay, we have a problem." Said Tony.

"Add it to the list, it should be number nine hundred and something, sooner or later I get to it."

"Jay, cut the bullshit, we have a serious issue. This morning Jack died."

Jack was our construction manager, he was overseeing the building of our shelter.

"What happened?"

"You know Jack rode his bike everywhere, this morning he rode into a trap, around fifteen punks tied a rope across the road, Jack didn't see it, he hit the rope, it almost cut him in half, the punks finished him off, they stole his bike."

"How do we know this?"

"One of my men was a few hundred yards behind Jack, by the time he arrived, Jack was already gone."

"Shit, I hope Franco can pick up the slack and finish the shelter. Damn it, I'm really going to miss Jack."

"Me too."

@@@@@

In order to protect as many people as we can, we rotate people in and out of the shelters and their homes. We usually try to keep 50% of us in one of the shelters, that way some of us will survive in case of a surprise attack. The main shelter turned out to be 100 feet long and 50 feet wide, it's buried ten feet under our crops. The ventilation pipes are mixed in with our crops, hiding them in plain sight. Most of the interior space is made up of small rooms. The kids share bedrooms sleeping in bunk beds, usually six to eight per room, the adults sleep in rooms that are tiny, usually only 8X9 feet, a couple are only 8X8. Some jail cells are larger, but it was the only way we could give every couple their own room. Storage space in the bedrooms is very limited, each person gets two drawers and a small section of one of the closets. There are also pull out storage under the beds. Most of the bedrooms have windows painted on the walls so we feel like we're spending time above ground. Every bedroom has reading lights and a ceiling fan to help circulate the air. Body armor, helmets, weapons, and ammo are stored in the armories. Everyone has an armored vest, a helmet and shooting gloves. There is one large kitchen with six restaurant ovens, ranges, and microwaves and there are also four restaurant size dishwashers. Since Tony owned a restaurant, it was easy for him to arrange the kitchen equipment for us. The most popular place in the shelter is the serve-yourself drink station where the coffee machine runs 24/7 and we also have Tony's soft drink machine for the kids. Most people also liked the self-serve soft ice cream machine, the ex-military called it a dog machine, the rest of us were confused until it was explained to us. There's a single very large dining room with cafeteria style seating, long tables, and chairs. We try to mix up the seating so everyone gets a chance to sit with everyone else. We don't want small cliques forming. The main shelter has six small bathrooms and a medical/first aid room which also serves as a small surgical room.

Every inch of open space in the shelter is filled with supplies. The shelters are connected together with tunnels separated by steel blast doors. We've spread the supplies through the different shelters in case one is overrun. This way the people in the others will have a chance to survive. The security room has its own small generator and air supply separate from the other areas. This way if our power is cut the security room will still be operational. The security room has two walls covered with monitors with a server room tucked behind the security room. Every camera and sensor we have are fed into the security room. The room is manned 24 hours a day, usually by two people. Even though the sensors will sound the alarms automatically, we want to have a person in the loop. Our main armory is next to the security shelter. Each shelter has its own armory, the main one is centrally located. We store our extra assault rifles, parts, and ammo in a central location, we have AR15s/M16s/M4s/RPGs/hand grenades/side arms/shotguns and of course ammo. We recently received a present from Tony's contacts in Miami, four full automatic Thompson submachine guns each came with four 50 round drum magazines. These will be perfect for in close-in combat, as will our 12 gauge shotguns. We have over 400,000 rounds of ammo for each caliber weapon we have. The floor under the armory is filled with 50 caliber steel ammo cans stuffed with ammo. We have cleaning kits and oil so we can keep our weapons in good shape. We've also recently completed our goal of acquiring a silencer for each AR/M type rifle. We purchased eight the legal way, we paid the ATF their fee of $200 per silencer, filled out the paperwork and waited four months before our permits and tax stamps arrived. The others we picked up from our contacts in Mexico. In additional to stocking rounds for our weapons, we've also stocked 40,000 rounds for AK47s and .308 rifles, plus 5,000 rounds for 40 Cal handgun rounds. We think we're ready for any extended battle. In addition to the firearms, we have ten crossbows and over 800 bolts. We have these for quiet hunting or just in case we get attacked by zombies. At this point, anything is possible, plus, we got them free so why the hell not stock them?

I was curious how Tony's pre-made shelters would work out. I wasn't sure if large sections of steel culvert pipe would work. I have to admit I'm pleasantly surprised, each came out very nice. I wish they could have delivered when I contacted them, it would have saved us a lot of time and expense. Since each of Tony's shelters is circular, a floor is laid in each pipe, under each floor is storage space for supplies. We've tried to make the shelters more pleasant to live in by painting the walls in light, cheerful colors. We let the kids paint their own bedrooms, and we've hung pictures on the walls, all to make living in them feel a little bit like a normal home. While Tony's are smaller than the main shelter, he has eight of them buried under the farms, all are connected to the main shelter which we use for cooking and eating. While we have completed the shelters, all of us hope we never have to use them. No matter how much we make them like home, we know we're going to be very crowded and stressed if we have to retreat into them. Retreating to the shelters means we've lost the battle for our homes. It means we're being overrun and have taken losses. Losses we can't afford. The shelter is our life insurance. A policy we hope we don't need. However, as the country falls apart, we know the day is coming when we might have to move into the shelter to save our lives. Many of us worry about how the kids are going to handle living in the shelter for a long period of time.

@@@@@

The third week of October began with beautiful fall weather, sunny, dry, temperatures in the mid-60s. It was perfect weather for us to harvest our crops and start canning them as soon as they were out of the ground. We began the harvest with the farthest acreage. As soon as the crops were harvested, the soil is turned and our fall/winter crops are planted. Thanks to almost perfect summer weather our crop looked to be a record breaker enabling us to survive for another couple of years. Farmers know not to get overly optimistic. One season's good weather usually meant the next was piss poor. We all knew our luck couldn't hold out forever. The country had broken apart into sections. While we still had a central government in Washington D.C. they were further removed from reality than ever before. None of the states or locals paid D.C. any attention. They passed laws and rules all trying to centrally manage an economy that had fallen apart. No amount of income redistribution was going to fix this flat tire. We were done. Banks were open only five hours a week, (one hour a day, Monday–Friday) even then, they were empty. Barter replaced cash and credit transactions. Credit was what one person was willing to extend to another, usually based on how well each party knew the other and the number of transactions completed with each other over the previous few months. Credit cards disappeared, their only use was as pocket ice scrapers in the Northern States. As the Federal Government became more useless, the states and in many cases the local community governments became only government most people followed. Many areas set up their own government, which covered the spectrum from warlord to full democracy where everyone had a vote on everything. In our case, Tony and I tended to make the important decisions together that affected our community. We won the right to decide due to us investing in the infrastructure to bring everyone together, provide the shelters and most of the supplies. This isn't to say we didn't seek advice from the community. In order to keep the peace, we tried to hold weekly full community meetings so everyone could discuss our plans and major decisions. In order to keep everyone up to date and share news, we tried to gather at my house or in the main shelter's dining area to share drinks, coffee, and talk. With each of us being so busy, this allowed us to get together and share news and exchange thoughts.

Saturday, October 17 started with a cold rain falling from a cool gray sky, but it wasn't hard enough to keep us out of the fields or stop patrolling. In fact, the rain felt good on our faces. The cool rain is projected to continue for another two days. We'd agreed to meet at my house this week. We laid out extra mats to catch the rain and mud on everyone's sneakers and boots. Everyone was happy to get together once a week. We had a long table set with coffee, tea, soft drinks, wine and, of course, the bar was fully stocked, but our custom was not to consume hard liquor until after the meeting concluded. Tony and Nancy were in a very good mood, they hugged everyone as they arrived, I guess we'll find out why soon enough. The kids were in the home theater watching some movie Tony was able to get on the black market before its official release on DVD. They had plates of cookies and popcorn to keep them happy and out of the adult meeting. Everyone took off their rain gear, most were holding an umbrella which they left leaning against the corner by our front door. It must have been a very good week, everyone looked genuinely happy.

We'd just sat down in our family and dining room and gotten comfortable. Tony asked to go first which was fine with all of us, he stood smiling, but just as he opened his mouth to start speaking, our intruder alarm sounded. Our heads went up, we nodded to each other. I said, "No time for everyone to get home and return, hit the gun safe downstairs, grab a rifle and ammo, let's go! Lacy and I grabbed our personal weapons, our neighbors followed me downstairs. I opened one of our gun safes handing out AR15s and M4s, each person also got a bag of ten or twelve 30 round magazines, some of the bags held a mix of 30 and 42 magazines, mine held ten of the new PMag 60 drum style mags. I sent Todd to the armory to get some grenades. Opening the front door, we run for the trenches through the rain and wind. A cold front was moving in, we felt the temperature dropping. The wind is driving the rain almost horizontal at us. I'm happy we had the time to line the trench with cement and install water runoff drain holes so we weren't standing in ankle deep muddy water. We heard the motorcycles and a truck before the second alarm sounded, Fred said, "Sounds like a hell of a lot them."

Randy responds, "Sounds like Harley's, lots of them. Must be a biker gang from the city or south of Nashville."

Before Randy finished speaking, John's voice came through my radio, "RED ALERT, a biker gang, fourteen bikes, two pickups, they're ARMED, SAY AGAIN ARMED."

Our motion-activated lights turned on when the bikers got close, the lights illuminated the street and driveway for us while at the same time blinding the attackers. Unfortunately, our lights became the gang's first target. Each of our construction lights was shot out. The alarm connected to our gate sounded a moment before the sky in front of us was lit by a large flash of light, we were shaken by the explosion's overpressure blast wave. The few of us who were wearing night vision yelled, pulling off our NVG's. The explosion's flash overloaded the NVG's sensors hurting our eyes. After our lights had been shot out, everything went quiet. We don't hear or see our attackers. They're acting very smart, they shot out our lights, then they paused or they've figured out a way to advance very quietly. We don't have any idea what they're planning. I'm just about to say something when we hear a single gunshot and Fred screams, falling over. I yell, "SNIPER, get down."

The bikers came prepared with tools and C4 or something like it to blast open our front gate.

"John, please tell me the driveway trenches are uncovered."

Jay, they are. The steel covers have been removed.They are covered with thin camouflaged sheets, a step will cause anyone to fall into the trench, we've added some surprises for anyone who lands or steps in the small holes."

"What did you do?"

"We turned them into punji pits. We have lined the bottom of the trenches and small holes with plywood holding large spikes, they will cut right through sneakers and boots. Once in, the heads of the spikes open like hunting arrows. They're going to be very painful to remove, plus they'll leave a very nasty infection behind. Anyone who steps into a trench will be out of commission for a very long time. They'll most likely die a very painful death."

"John, you're a cold-hearted bastard, I like it."

Smiling an evil leer, John says, "Wait, I have a few more surprises waiting for anyone who breaches our walls meaning to do us harm."

Looking at the driveway, I see a white shirt in the air, "Look."

Two bikers walk a few yards up our driveway, they're holding a large white T-shirt on a pole. "You up there on the farm. We know you're there. Here are your options, we want 300 pounds of food, 250 gallons of clean water, all of your beer and liquor, and any pain medications you have. We also want two of your women, they must be under the age of 40. If our demands are not met, we'll kill all of you and take what we want. We've done it before. We've been raiding farms and subdivisions between Nashville and here. You have five minutes to decide."

John replies, "If you kill all us, you'll never find the fuel tanks, which are diesel."

"Don't care, our truck uses diesel, you have less than five minutes to decide. If you agree, send a child out with a white flag, if we don't see the white flag, we'll attack and kill all of you. We've wiped out many other small farms and housing developments, in the end, we always get what we want. Some of us have military training. A bunch of farmers aren't going to do shit to us. Your five minutes is slipping away as you try to bullshit us."

I whisper, "John, what do you think?"

"If they do have members who are ex-military, they're going to try to surround us, take us out in one hard, fast attack. Some will most likely have NVG."

"What do you suggest?"

"As quietly as possible, spread our people out in the trench. The gang has to work their way through our traps and booby-traps, we have the explosive targets sitting along their most likely path to us. We can negate their NVGs with flares. I suggest we open fire at 4 minutes 30 seconds, they will most likely wait till the clock runs down. We need to use whatever surprise we can against them. When I give the word, fire four flares, I'll set off the exploding targets, everyone else should take down anyone they see. When we start firing, turn on the lasers mounted on the poles, it'll confuse them as to where we are. Make sure everyone has a silencer mounted."

"Okay, I'll pass the word down the line," I turn to whisper to Todd next to me, he taps Randy repeating the message. Our people silently start spreading out preparing for the fight of our lives. Lacy, Cheri, and Flo dragged poor Fred out of the trench and into the shelter so the doc could work on him.

At the four-minute thirty-second mark John nods to me, I fire four bright flares into the air between us and the bikers. The flares wash out the biker's NVG, at the same instant John triggers four of the exploding targets/Claymore mines. The small cans are covered in nails and BBs, when they explode they send a wave of metal out in all directions, catching the bikers completely by surprise. The homemade mini Claymores cut down a number of attackers and while they're still reeling from the shock of the attack, our people pop up in our trench and open fire with three round bursts. Tony and his sidekick Sal are firing full auto, they are burning through their ammo in seconds. Todd sees their truck coming up the driveway, the driver doesn't see the trench which cuts across the driveway because it's camouflaged. The gang's truck noses into the trench and before anyone can escape it, Todd hits it with an RPG, blowing the truck apart with everyone in it. Tony switched from an M4 to one of the Thompsons, he's firing short bursts from the submachine gun so he can control the bursts. The heavy 45 caliber bullets are tearing the bikers apart. Two of us each throws a hand grenade into a group of bikers. A group of six bikers stand to rush our trench, five of us open up with M4s, the closest a biker reaches us is twenty feet from our trench. I'm thinking to myself, *We have to do better than this, we have one person down. One I can't forgive myself for, we're not going to be the same without Fred. They were able to get too close to us. We have to keep them further away from us. Even with all of our firepower they managed to get within twenty feet of us. Not acceptable at all.*

We wait five minutes to see if anyone else attacks us, holding our breath as each of the minute's counts down to zero. There weren't any incidents in the five minutes so John sounds the all clear. We start to climb up out of our trenches when a shot rings out, it creases Todd's leg. Tony and I spin around to where the shot came from, both of us burn through our mags on full auto, we're rewarded with a scream to our rear. Tony and I nod at each other. We hold our weapons at the ready while we load fresh magazines and begin to check out the bodies of our attackers. Some of the gang are wounded. John says, "Keep two alive for questioning, kill the rest of them." The quiet of the rainy evening is broken by the sounds of single muffled shots, each shot putting a gang member out of his misery. Some of us couldn't look the wounded in the eye when we pulled the trigger. A couple of our neighbors couldn't bring themselves to kill the wounded, I told them, "No problem, I'll do it." I walk to each of the wounded where I fire a single round into their heads. I try to make sure no one sees I'm feeling sick with each shot. It's one thing to shoot someone at a distance and another to stand over them, looking into their pleading eyes and pull the trigger. We found their bikes in front of our gate. I said, "Everyone take a bike, we can use them for later, push them into the barn. I need two to help me check their trucks."

Randy and Matt join me at their damaged truck, there's nothing left but a burnt out shell. When the truck struck the trench, four teenage girls were throw out of the back of the truck which saved their lives when the truck exploded. All four of them are in rough shape. "Matt, I'll help the girls, check to see if anything else got thrown out of the truck. Put the truck with their bikes in the barn. Randy, go down to the gate and check out their other truck."

Matt and Randy nod their agreement, I help the girls, who are in shock. Picking up my handheld, "Flo, need your help by the truck in the driveway, we have some teenage girls in shock or drugged."

"On my way. Jill's coming to help me, are any badly wounded?"

"I don't know. They fell out of the truck, they were lucky, another moment and the RPG would have struck them. All would be dead. Flo, don't leave the girls alone and don't show them anything outsiders shouldn't see. We shouldn't trust them yet."

"Okay."

Randy inspects the gate on the way to get the undamaged truck, "Jay, need to see you at the gate. It took a lot of damage, I'm not sure if we have the parts to repair it."

My driveway is littered with shell cases and blood, we hear crying and begging for help from locations between the gate and the house, *I think we caught some bandits in our hunting traps. I'm happy its bandit hunting season.* The hinges on the front gate are toast, they were destroyed by the C4 explosion. "John, do we have any other hinges?"

I inspect the gate with Randy, who says, "We can't repair it. However, we can change the gate. For now, I suggest we just weld it shut. When we replace it, we'll cut the welds."

"Do it, no reason to fool with it now. We might as well deal with it in a couple of days."

Randy nods saying, "OK, I'll weld it shut, at least no one else will be easily getting in tonight."

John listens to the crying and begging, "What do you want to about them?"

"Nothing tonight, we'll check on them tomorrow. I don't feel like wandering around our own minefield in the dark. If they moved a trap, we could step in one."

"You know most of them will bleed out."

"Less for us to deal with. We have three to question. I don't think any of these assholes is one of the leaders."

A biker says, "Please, I can hear you, you have to help me. I can't move, my foot is stuck in a damn hole with spikes through my foot, I'm bleeding, it hurts. You have to help me."

"Why?"

"It's what you're supposed to do. It's the Christian thing to do."

"You mean like attacking people you don't know, like kidnapping teenage girls? Do you mean those Christian things?"

"You don't understand. We have the right to live, we have the right to happiness. We've got all sorts of rights."

"You stay there and think about those rights you have, oh, and if a wolf comes by, be sure to tell the wolf about your rights. I'm sure he'll be happy to listen to you as he eats your leg."

"NO, you can't leave us here."

"Shut up or I'll shoot your kneecaps out."

John looks at me saying, "Jay, you're a cold-hearted bastard. I like that about you."

"Thanks. Right now, it's Miller time. I'm dirty, thirsty and tired."

John and I walk home while Randy begins welding the gate shut for the evening.

Ricky yells, "Dad, you're not just going to leave the wounded out there are you?"

"I sure am. Ricky, leave them be. After you help Randy weld the gate, do NOT talk to them, don't go near them. They'll tell you anything you want to hear to get you to release them. Weld the gate and come home. Don't pass go, don't collect $200, just weld the gate and come back to the house."

"Dad, I don't agree with you."

"Ricky, I expect you don't agree with me, but I still make the rules, so just follow them."

Unknown to us, thousands of people from Nashville are heading in our direction. They are heading north out of the ashes of Nashville. They are comprised of eight thousand college students, plus four thousand members of various mobs who agreed to work together to find food. Thousands of tired, hungry and angry people pulling wagons and pushcarts filled with their belongings. They knew the city didn't have any food, they knew farms were their best chance to find something to eat and feed their children. The mob included thousands of people who are used to taking what they wanted. The mob moved like a swarm of locusts that stripped the land as they moved. They stripped stores, homes and farms bare as they moved north. While they moved north, fourteen thousand hungry people are moving south. They started as a handful that left the ruins of Indianapolis picking up people from every town and city they passed through. They are heading south looking for warmer weather to spend the winter, they are looking for good farmland to grow crops to feed their families. Both groups are traveling on Interstate 65, and we're located smack in the middle of both groups.

Chapter 19

It took us until 4:00 in the morning to clean up from the battle. We all agree to take a couple of hours off to get some rest before the sun comes up. I can't rest until I check on Fred, who's in the infirmary, but the doc won't let anyone see him since he's still working on Fred. Cheri jumps into my arms, her face is covered in streaks from her tears. "Cheri, how is he?"

"I really don't know. The doc's been working on him since he was brought in."

"Was he awake?"

"Some of the time, he knows he's been hit."

"Cheri, do you need anything?"

"Other than Fred?"

"Yes, want me to send over some coffee?"

"I have some, the doc has his own coffee machine."

"If you need anything or when the doc finishes, please call me. I'll send Lacy down to be with you."

Hugging me, Cheri says, "Jay, thank you."

"Cheri, he'll be OK, you'll see. He's too hard-headed to go and die on us."

"Jay, he knows better than to die on me."

"I'm going back to the mess hall, anything you need, just call."

Walking into the mess hall, I run into Lacy, I ask her to stop in and spend time with Cheri, "Jay, I was just heading to the infirmary. I have a change of clothing for Cheri and some breakfast."

"Honey, you're the best. If Fred comes around, or when the doc tells Cheri how he is, please call me."

"We will."

The rest of us meet in the main shelter's dining room at 7:00 AM for breakfast. Sipping a large cup of coffee, I look at John who also hasn't gone to bed yet, "John, is it possible to make more exploding mines? If we had lines of them, we should be able to surprise the hell out of the next wave of attackers without us risking our lives."

"It's possible, we have everything we need. I'll look into it."

"Great, I'd like us to make and bury as many as we can build."

"The ground is soft which will make it easier to bury them. How soon before you can make more? I'm concerned about another attack."

"I'll start after I get a short nap in, I haven't gone to bed yet. I wanted to review the battle and try to figure out where to move our sensors and cameras so we get a better indication we're going to be attacked. Had we all not been in your home, we wouldn't have made it to the trench in time to stop the attack. We need better advance notice. We need the time to man our battle stations."

"Jay, we're going to be limited in our mine production by the limited chemicals we have. I know a plant not far away. I'm not sure if they still have any inventory, but it would be a good place to check out."

"John, if you know of a plant close by, I think we ought to send a team to grab everything they have. One so it can't be used against us and two so we can ring our property with mines. Get all of the material you can find, we can make hand thrown pipe bombs and rig a lot of surprises for attackers."

"Damn it, you're not going to let me take a nap are you?"

"Nope, last night scared me. It showed me we have too many weaknesses in our defensives. We got lucky."

"Jay, every battle plan goes out the window when the enemy is engaged. We won last night."

"We won and we lost. What about Fred and Todd?"

"Todd just got creased, not in the least serious. Even the bleeding stopped. Fred's going to make it, the bullet struck him in the shoulder. A real lucky shot, it struck him through a gap in his armor. Our body armor isn't magic. It's designed to block a kill shot. Nothing is going to block a shot that causes a serious wound. We're very lucky we suffered only one casualty."

"John, we can't afford to lose many. We're not starting out with many people. We can't afford to lose even one if we're going to survive. We need numbers to fight off a large attack."

"Jay, we are in a war. Call it anything you want, but it is a war. Think in terms of the Middle Ages, you're the local landowner. Instead of a castle, we have barbed wire."

"Which didn't keep the gang out."

"It slowed them down, which is all barbed wire is supposed to do."

"I wish we had a twenty-foot wall around us."

John laughs, "There aren't enough building materials around to build a wall like that."

"It'd be nice."

"It would take years to build a wall like that, years we don't have. Have you seen the last reports from the HAM operators?"

"No, what do they say?"

"Complete meltdown across the country. I don't think there's a city that isn't burning. People are starving to death, they're fighting for a slice of moldy bread."

"Crap, I'd hoped we could get to winter before it turned this bad."

"Why winter?"

"Cold will keep people off the streets. It's still warm enough that people will be out looking for food and supplies."

"Jay, with the cities destroyed, I estimate the country is going to lose over a third of our people by the time spring comes around. There's not going to be enough food located where the people are. There's a lot of food in the country, it's just not where the people are."

"John, I've said for a long time the country is going to tear itself apart."

"Jay, it's going to be a complete disaster. I'm worried about next spring when the weather warms and all of the bodies that were left where they died will rot and spread diseases. We could be seeing the spread of diseases, unlike anything the world's seen since the black plague."

"Shit, what can we do to protect ourselves?"

"Stay clean and be careful of strangers who might be carriers of whatever bug that spreads across the world. While the doc is good, we don't have access to the CDC or anything like it anymore. All kinds of diseases are going to make a comeback. Stuff we thought was gone will be making a comeback."

"You're always full of good news. By the way, who's watching the cameras while you scare the shit out of me?"

"Your son-in-law, Todd. I trained him to be my primary backup."

"Good, John, how far can we place cameras or sensors so we get as much advance notice of uninvited guests?"

"I'm looking into that right now, I'm planning to test small radio-controlled drones."

"Will they work at night or in bad weather?"

"We can mount one of the FLIR cameras on the drone, but I don't know how the drone will operate in bad weather. We need more tests."

"Please remember we only have a small number of FLIR cameras."

"I know, but it's the only way I can think of to give us the range we need and also function at night."

"I know you'll keep us informed of the tests."

"Why don't you join me for a test tonight, around 10?"

"I will, I'll ask Tony to join us."

Tony walks over saying, "Did I hear my name taken in vain?"

I laugh, "We were just talking testing an RC drone with one of our FLIR cameras mounted on it. John invited us to see a test tonight around 10."

"Count me in. I agree we need as much advance notice as possible, last night could have ended differently had we not all been together when the alarm sounded."

John replies, "The issue is even with forty people, we don't have enough bodies to operate over 1,000 acres of farm and provide security. We should be operating random patrols around our perimeter plus have a ready forcefully armed and ready to respond to any incursion to our property. A large force can overwhelm us before we can respond, we have too large an area to defend. It can take ten minutes or more for people working in the fields to arm themselves and arrive at the fighting. They could come under fire in transit to the main battle area. Anyone who is serious about attacking us can watch us for a couple of days, they'll quickly learn our routine. If I were leading an attack against us, I would watch our routine and I'd attack when I saw most of us in the far corners of the fields. I'd know how long it takes us to respond. I'd place snipers in position to take down our people when they try to make their way from the fields to the front line. I could reduce our numbers by 15~20% with a couple of good snipers."

Tony and I sit down in surprise and fear. We look at each other asking John, "What should, what can we do with our limited numbers? We can't stop working on the farm, it's how we feed ourselves."

John sips his coffee, "I've given this a lot of thought, we can't reduce the numbers working in the fields or we won't get the yield of crops we need. We can't keep a large number of people in the trenches 24/7 because we could be attacked in a different position. We need advance information, and we need to slow down any attack, we need to keep them tied down at our perimeter before they can get close enough to us to hurt us. I want to increase the number of hunting traps and mines along our border. I think we should dig more pits, and increase the depth of the barbed wire fence. We have enough wire to add another layer in the sections near our gates."

Tony replies, "Don't forget about the gates, we thought the locks were secure, last night we learned they weren't as secure as we thought."

"I'm going to increase the number of locks and also add some steel rebar poles to block the gate from opening. If we assume most of the attacks against us will occur at night, we can add spikes and barbs to the ground which will slow the invaders down."

John, "I think we need to add barbed wire or something on top of the gates to slow down anyone trying to climb over them. My other concern is anyone checking us out will see our defenses in the daylight, they might map them to know the areas to avoid."

John responds, "We'll let the grass grow longer, the spikes and barbs don't have to be high, just enough to slow them down. I wish we had some bouncing Betty's."

"Huh?"

"Land mines, when triggered, they bounce up and explode."

"I like that, can we make some on springs?"

"Too much work for the return, we can make regular mines and spikes much quicker. We're going to need thousands, over ten thousand of them to cover the area from the road to our homes. I know where to find the rebar, we can cut and weld them into "X" shapes. I also want to look at cutting more trenches and vehicle traps just behind the barbwire."

Tony asks, "John, all well and good, however, how much time do we have before we're attacked again?"

John lowers his coffee cup, he looks at Tony and me, his voice lowers to almost a whisper, "Tony, that's the real question. Isn't it? I don't know. The reports we've picked up on our radios tell us a story I wouldn't have believed six months ago. Hundreds of thousands of people are wandering around the country looking for help, hundreds of thousands are either fighting over scraps in the cities or they're dying from starvation. Bodies are lying where they died."

"Shit, I built the shelter as a last resort, hoping we'd never have to use it."

"Jay, I think we're going to need the shelter sooner versus than later. I think the only way we're going to survive is the shelters. We were lucky last night. We've talked many times that if we're hit by a large group, they'll overrun us, it's all a question of numbers. Even though we were lucky last night, one of us got hit, this proves no matter how well built our defenses are, there's always a risk. A lucky shot can get any of us. If we assume the reports are correct, everyone with half a brain is leaving the cities, the government stopped sending military convoys into the cities with food and water. Those people have nothing to lose, they're not going to be as easy to negotiate with as the first group. When we get hit, we'll have to retreat to our shelter to live to fight another day."

"John, how long do you think we have before a sizeable group hits us?"

"It could be at any time, which is why I want to expand our eyes ASAP."

Tony smiles, he pats John on the back, "So why are you wasting daylight talking with us, get going. Set up new cameras. I hate surprises, especially surprises that want to kill me."

"I'm going, I stopped here for coffee."

"Excuses, excuses."

Tony smiles at John, who nods his head at us. "I hope I'm wrong, but my gut says we've been lucky."

Tony gets very serious, "How many people do you want to accompany you?"

"Four shooters in case we run into trouble, plus four to help install the cameras."

"They'll meet you at the warehouse in fifteen minutes."

"Works for me. Gives me time to have another cup."

Tony and I walk towards the infirmary to check on Fred. The doc meets us before we reach the ER, "Guys, he's sleeping, please don't wake him."

We nod in agreement, "How's he doing? I swear when he got hit, it felt like I did too."

"Jay, we got the bullet out, he should be fine, the only potential issue is an infection, I've given him a strong dose of antibiotics to counter the possibility. If he doesn't develop an infection, he can go home in two or three days."

"Thanks, doc."

Tony and I turn to leave when I get a brain flash, "Tony, if John hasn't left yet, I think we need to see him."

"Let's hurry." We catch John and his team as they are loading into two pickups, "John, before you go, can we see you?"

John laughs, saying, "First you tell me to go, and then you ask me to wait."

"John, how much mace or pepper spray do we have?"

John stops mid-step, "Damn it, I think I see where you're going. Why didn't I think of it?"

"We can rig a remote sprayer of pepper spray. It may break up a large group. If we can get or make tear gas, we could mix the two together, the gas will surely break up large attacks without us killing them."

"Tony, you brought a college chemistry teacher with you, didn't you?"

"Yes, Jeff Stone. I'll find him."

Jeff was found in the small lab looking at fertilizer. "Jeff."

"Tony?"

"Can you make tear gas?"

"Sure, it's an easy formula, I was afraid you were going to ask for VX."

"What's VX?"

"Forget it, you don't want it because I won't make it."

I nod responding, "It's nerve gas, very deadly shit. The wind could blow it back at us, killing all of us."

Tony frowns, "You guys win, just tear gas."

"To repeat, yes, I can make it, anything else?"

"Explosives. You've got fertilizer, and diesel we need to make thousands of land mines."

"Harder than large bombs, I'll see what I can develop. I'll need some supplies."

"Give the list to Matt, he's going to take a team into town."

Twelve hours later Matt and his team return with most of John's list. John's team mounted Pan/Tilt/Zoom (PTZ) remote control cameras on existing telephone poles a mile from our gate. He wired them with small amplifiers to ensure the images were good quality and he could control them from the security shelter. At 7:00 PM, many people complained about a buzzing noise over the farms, people even shot into the air, trying to hit or scare away the buzzing. Todd laughed at the shooting, he landed the small RC drone in front of a group of our people who now realized what the noise was. The video of our neighbors scared by the buzzing was enough to make most of us laugh for the evening. Our spirits lifted thinking we had a handle on our security. We felt we'd be able to see anyone attacking the farms before they could close enough to harm us. We were wrong. Dead wrong.

Chapter 20

Captain Black taps Sergeant Gray on the shoulder whispering, "Sarge, we have to get out of here. The Russians have almost closed their circle with us in the middle, I don't think they liked us taking out three platoons of their tanks. Our orders are not to get caught and leave nothing behind which they could use to prove we were here.

Wake the men, we'll try to slip out in this heavy rain, we won't leave tracks in this weather."

"Sir, where's our pick up point?"

"Sarge, about ten klicks from here, a Pave Low helicopter will be waiting for our radio call."

"I'll get the men ready to move."

The Russian Spetsnaz captain whispered to his team, "The Yankees are two klicks in front of us, I want them alive. Our orders are to bring back live prisoners who can prove the Americans attacked our troops. Putin wants to use the prisoners to force the Americans to pay for the damage they've done. Tell the men to wound, not kill. If they kill all of the Americans, I'll kill them. Am I clear?"

"Yes, sir. Sir, the Americans are broke, they don't have anything to pay us with. China is pressuring them into giving up their state of Hawaii."

"Maybe our dear leader wants New York City."

"That would be interesting."

"We move out in thirty minutes."

"Yes, sir."

The American Special Forces team quietly breaks their cold camp, moving towards their pickup point in a driving rain. They move in single file with their fingers hovering over the triggers on their Russian-made AK74 assault rifles. They're wearing NVGs, which enable their transit through the dense woods which have heavy ground foliage. They move almost silently, unaware there is a Russian Spetsnaz team following them. Captain Black took point at the start of the march. His sixth sense kept telling him something was wrong so he drifted back to the rear kneeling in the mud listening. He felt in his bones something was wrong. He heard a branch snap, he tapped the last soldier in line, holding up his hand to tell his squad to pause. Each troop paused in mid-step. Captain Black motioned to his men to take up an ambush position. His men dropped to the wet ground, covering themselves with the ground material. They waited for the people who were following them to reach their position. The Russian Spetsnaz team was very good, they were almost silent following the Americans. They had intercepted the American communication figuring out where the probable pickup locations were. They were lucky in picking up the American's trail, they decided to follow the Americans to their pick-up point, where they would capture the Americans and their helicopter.

The Russians walked in single file on the same trail the Americans used. Unknown to the Spetsnaz the Americans had lined the curve of the trail with Claymore mines. As the Spetsnaz entered the turn on the trail, the Claymores exploded, sending thousands of steel BBs into the Russian Spetsnaz team tearing most of them apart. The surviving Spetsnaz were taken under fire by the Americans firing silenced AK74s into the Russians. Sixty seconds after the firefight started, it was over. None of the Russians survived. Captain Black checked each Russian, he took their IDs and any paperwork they had. He told his men to take the firing pins out of Spetsnaz's rifles so they couldn't be used against them. The American team reached their pick up point without any other incident and boarded an Air Force rescue Pave Low helicopter that is equipped with special mufflers making it almost silent. Once onboard Captain Black is handed a radio transcript with his new orders, "Men, we're going home. There's been a lot of civil unrest, we've been tasked with a special mission, helping our people who are hungry, fighting warlords and gangs."

The sergeant asked, "Warlords in America? Captain, you're kidding me, right?"

"Wish I was, conditions back home are a mess. China is moving towards Hawaii, it looks like there's going to be the largest naval battle in the Pacific since the Second World War. The seventh fleet is moving into position to block the Chinese from landing in Hawaii. Two or three carrier battle groups are going to take on the entire Chinese fleet. The Pacific is going to be the world's largest live shooting gallery."

"Captain, I hope they don't go nuclear."

"Sarge, I don't think either side will let that genie out of the bottle."

"Cap, I didn't think they were serious about taking over Hawaii in exchange for their loans."

"I didn't either, however, most of their fleet is moving east toward Hawaii. The intel says they're deadly serious. I didn't think the President had the balls to put up a fight."

"Captain, did the President order the Navy to respond or is the CNO issuing his own orders without the White House's knowledge?"

"Sarge, I hadn't considered that I'll think about it on our flight home."

"Cap, are we going to be flying home in a C17?"

"Sarge, we won the lottery, we're going to Kiev where we're going to board a commercial flight to London and another commercial flight all the way to Chicago. If it weren't for the military, there wouldn't be enough flyers to keep any airlines flying. Most of the existing commercial planes have been reconfigured with all coach seats. They're cramped, but they beat sling seats."

"Captain, someone in high places likes you. I don't think I've had the luck to fly half way around the world commercial. Anything beats getting beaten up in a C17 for twenty hours."

"Got that one right."

"Cap, I don't know about our next mission, fighting other Americans isn't something any of us signed up for. I have some serious negative thoughts about this. I'm not sure the men are going to like it either."

"We're not going to fight normal citizens, only the bad guys."

"Captain, who says who's the bad guys? The current administration thinks anyone on the right is a bad guy, hell, they think we're the bad guys. I won't fight my brothers and sisters."

"Sarge, I agree with you. Our orders came through SOCOM, I'm hoping they're putting us into the heartland to help hasten the recovery. I promise you, I won't accept any order that tells us to fire on unarmed or armed normal citizens. They can court martial me, but I won't do it. I swore an oath, the same oath as you, I intend to keep my oath. I'll do whatever is required to defend America from all enemies, foreign and domestic."

"Cap, thanks, I know the men will appreciate that."

"Sarge, I'm very concerned about the word warlord in our orders. I'm worried some of my brother officers decided to use their troops to set up feudal systems in the heartland."

"Cap, I agree that's going to suck. With your permission, I'll check the men."

"Yes. Good idea, I bet you find most of them sleeping."

"Cap, to be truthful, I can't wait for the ride home. I intend to sleep on both flights."

"Sarge, always sleep when you can. I envy you, I have paperwork to catch up with. You'd think in the twenty-first century the damn Army would dump some of the stupid paperwork."

"Captain, just be happy they don't ask you how many rounds we fired."

"Crap, I think there is a form asking how rounds we expended."

"Why, they didn't come out of our inventory."

"Doesn't matter, this man's Army runs on paperwork."

"Glad it's you and not me."

"Asshole."

@@@@@

The group moving north out of Nashville is being led by a small group of Iraqi war veterans who took their families out of the city looking for a safer location to make a new home. The veterans are followed by two waves of people. The first wave is made up of four thousand college students and other teens. The second wave is made up of three thousand adults and families. They're pulling wagons, pushing supermarket carts and even wheelbarrows overflowing with large black plastic bags that hold the most valuable items they were able to take with them. The bags usually hold photo albums, jewelry, a few toys for their kids and whatever food and bottled water they had or could find. They're tired, but also in good spirits since they're out of the tinder box of Nashville. The walk is very hard, the sun is warm for October, most of the people are thirsty and bone weary tired. Almost none of them have an idea where they're going. They've become lemmings, following the person in front of them. They spend nights along the side of the road, they fill rest areas to overflowing. They drink from streams without considering how pure the water is or even that some of the refugees are using the stream to relieve themselves further upstream. Hundreds have come down sick from drinking bad water. They lay on the sides of the road throwing up and fighting stomach torturing diarrhea. Many are too ill to move, laying in their own filth looking up into the sky asking for help. Help no one is able to provide. Those who live alongside Interstate 65 have barred their windows and doors with wood or metal bars to keep the refugees away, refusing to provide any help because they have only a limited amount of supplies. Small farms and towns are stripped bare of anything usable. Stray animals and pets are captured and eaten.

Following the waves of refugees are gangs who are waiting for stragglers to fall out of the group. When someone falls out, the gangs pounce on them, they steal everything the stragglers have, sometimes raping the women and children, sometimes killing the adult men just for the fun of it. There are rumors of cannibalism from different places in the country.

@@@@@

Our community celebrated Fred's release today from the medical shelter. While he can't work the fields or stand any security watches, at least he's out of the infirmary. His right arm is in a sling. It may be a couple of months before he regains full use of it and that's after rehab. I count my lucky stars that Fred is going to live. I've come to trust Fred and count him as one of our closest and most trusted friends and advisors. I don't know what I'd do if he were lost. I know Cheri would have been beside herself. I wonder if she'd have blamed me. Our arrival here has changed so many things. We've turned Fred and Cheri's lives upside down. Our arrival didn't cause the economic meltdown, our arrival didn't cause the destruction of Nashville and most of the country's other cities. Our arrival did save Fred's farm and their home, we stopped their eviction. If anything, our arrival here saved them from total economic loss. We've developed a strong bond together, we've shared our plans and dreams with Fred. The only thing we haven't shared with him is what really happened to our money. Only Tony, Lacy and I know the real story about what happened, it's not something we'll ever tell another soul. We've dug under our home's foundation where we had a couple of very secure safes buried. The safes hold over $20 million in gold and silver. The safes in our basement hold an armory's worth of weapons. Weapons we acquired through both legal and not so legal means. We have enough weapons to equip a medium size army. I still wish we would have been able to make a deal for mortars. Even with the economic meltdown, we weren't able to find a source willing to sell them to us. Even offering huge bribes to a couple of supply sergeants we'd previously acquired M4s and M16s from couldn't get us mortars. It wasn't a question of price, they just refused our requests out of fear they'd be caught. They sold us grenades, body armor, helmets, ammo, and MREs, they even sold us C4, but no missiles or mortars. I want the mortars because I know it's only a matter of time before we're hit by a group numbering in the thousands. The mortars would give us the range to reach out to them before they got close to us. John said he'd try to build one, so far he's been busy with other tasks. I'd give my right arm for weapons that will give us a standoff range to attrite the enemy before they can get close enough to hurt us.

We split our days working the fields and doing security rounds, and building additional defenses. We all wonder what happened to the National Guard and the US Military. We haven't seen them in months, not since they tried to steal our crops. The HAM reports we hear scare us. Thousands of cities and towns have been destroyed, millions are dead. We've heard odd reports of Navy battle groups leaving Pearl Harbor and San Diego. We've had reports of contractors working 24/7 getting ships ready for sea. The strangest report of all, we heard that five thousand people are working around the clock to make the USS Missouri ready for sea again. Why in the world is the Navy trying to make the Battleship USS Missouri ready for sea? Today there was a report saying hundreds of Patriot missiles were bring installed around Honolulu. Raytheon and Lockheed announced their latest quarterly results are going to exceed Wall Street's estimates due to the increased demand from the US military. It almost sounds like we're preparing for another World War or an alien invasion. I'm not sure which would be worse. Maybe that explains why the military has disappeared, maybe they have a more important mission than providing food convoys to the country's hungry citizens. I asked Tony to check with his contacts to see if the underworld, which usually knows what's going on has any usable information. My gut says something big is going on. Based on the new taxes and special fees, I thought we would have easily paid China most or all of what we owed them. Somehow none of this adds up. The feds stopped making all welfare and other benefit payments so if we didn't pay China, where did the money go?

@@@@@

The thousands of people traveling south on Interstate 65 have been walking for months. These were some of the first to see the problems brewing in the cities and their bedroom communities. They gathered their families, their special mementos, all of their supplies and left their homes as quickly as they could. Most have worn out at least two pairs of boots or sneakers, all have lost at least 15% of their body weight from lack of food and constant walking. As they pass the beltways around other cities and their bedroom communities, they've picked up additional people who are looking for a safer place for their families. Their numbers grow every day. At first they ignored the new people but as the days turned into weeks, which turned into months, they built new relationships, making new friends among their neighbors who are walking with them. After months of walking, they find themselves forty miles outside Nashville. There are five thousand people spread over miles of the freeway. They strip the land and everything on it bare as they move south. Wood buildings are burned so the mob is warm, flowers are pulled up and used in soup, tree bark is removed and chewed, every stray animal is killed and eaten. The group moving north from Nashville and the group moving south are within four days travel of each other. We're in the path of both groups.

Chapter 21

Both groups of refugees surprises each other when the leading scouts from each group run into each other two miles from our complex. At first the front line of both groups fought with each other, they fight over the meager small animals the northern group is cooking over campfires. The southern group which has been moving north smells the meat cooking. Their noses pick up the faint smell as the wind blows the smell towards the refugees. They pause mid-step looking at each other, they share the same thought, "Grilled MEAT!" Most are tired of looking for editable plants and a handful of the group has gotten very ill from eating the wrong plants. One member had a copy of a document called, "Plant Warning Signs." He passed it person to person until the document reached the front of the line so those looking for edible plants could make the right choices and not kill any more of the group. The scouts, the Iraqi veterans tells the rest of the refugees to wait, they are going to find the source of the meat. They promise to return with food.

The rest of the refugees are hopeful they'll be eating this evening, stopping where they are. They make camp on the center median and shoulders of Interstate 65. They roll out their sleeping bags, those who have tents pitch them, those without walk into the woods that line the interstate gathering tree branches and anything else they can use to make a shelter. Animal scavengers who've been following the crowd for any remains left behind are careful since it's a contest every day between the humans and animals to see who catches whom. Any animals that get careless are caught and made into dinner for the crowd. Any small children, elderly or any who are too weak to continue are usually dragged away into the underbrush along the freeway where they become the animal's dinner.

Members of both groups push themselves to the front lines trying to stop the fighting. When the leaders of the groups realize they're really the same, they want the same things, they are both trying to find a safe location for their people, the fighting slowly winds down. The fighters in both groups stare across at their counterparts. They pause, looking the other side in the eyes. They slowly lower their weapons, they stop fighting and begin talking. The leaders of the two groups agree to merge the groups together forming one 'super crowd' as they exchange information on what they've seen and news they've picked up on their march. News is hard to gather, most of what spreads as news is really rumors and hearsay. The group that was heading north realizes there's nothing to the north for them. The land has already been stripped bare, those heading south learn Nashville is in ruins, there's nothing left in the cities the groups can use to survive or make a new life. The two groups sit around a giant bonfire talking about their various options. The leaders of the groups agree to wait where they are while they send scouts out to see if there's anything useful in their proximity. Scouts are sent five miles in all directions to look for a farm or any food. The two groups discuss if they should turn east towards Knoxville or West towards Memphis and the Mississippi River.

Three hours after leaving the super crowd's camp site three scouts find our road. They are surprised to find a road without any road signs. None of the scouts knows where they are, or what's ahead of them. Our newly installed cameras see them make the turn onto our road. The alarm in the security shelter alerts the on-duty team that someone is close by. John calls my cell, "Jay, three people starting down our road. My gut is screaming, there's more here than three people."

"John, what's your gut tell you?"

"It says DANGER WILL ROBINSON. It's like when I was in Iraq just before my team walked into an ambush."

"You just said there are only three people."

"Forget what I said, something is wrong, my gut hasn't been wrong yet."
"What do you suggest?"

"Be on guard."

"Will do."

Six of us wait in the trench for the three lost souls walking towards us. Six others are arming themselves to join us in the trench just in case there's a couple more behind them.

After twenty minutes and no visitors, just as I start thinking they turned back, our gate alarm sounds. They're here. Our cameras send their videos to my iPad, I see the three looking at our gate. One of them is pushing on our gate, another is looking at the barbed wire surrounding our property line, the third walked along the road trying to see up on our property. We wait and watch them on my iPad. The three men walk along our barbed wire looking for a weakness in our defense line. They take some pictures with their cell phones before leaving. They return the same way they came, back down our road. Thirty minutes later they disappear around the turn on the main road that connects with our street. My gut is screaming at me, now I understand what John was saying. Something is definitely wrong with this situation. I think our three visitors were a scout group for a much larger group. I call John, "John, do you see anything on the cameras?"

"I saw the three return the way they came, they looked like they were checking us out. They looked experienced at it. I think they'll be back with a lot more people than three of them. These guys knew where to look, they are experienced scouts, my bet is they are ex-military."

"Any idea how long we have?"

"I'm going to guess between one and three hours."

"Why do you think that?"

"I think they were a scout group, they were checking us out. I don't like the way they were taking pictures of our gates and barb wire. I think they will return and report to their leader who will return in force."

"Shit."

John says, "I'm going to call an all hands alert."

"I agree, send the kids to the shelter now, it may save us time and their lives by getting them there before we come under attack. I'd suggest two of the women accompany the kids."

"Good idea, it'll help control the kids. Who do you suggest?"

Thinking about who to send with the kids so it doesn't look like I'm playing favorites or giving my daughter's any special treatment, I pause before responding, "Nancy and Jill."

"OK, I'll send the message so everyone knows. I'll sound the silent alarm so if there is a mob getting ready to attack us around the corner, they won't hear us."

"John, I hope you're wrong. My gut says you're right. My gut is screaming at me."

"Mine started as soon as I saw the scouts and I think we're in for a major battle. I'm going to ask the kids to move the boxes of canned crops into the shelter with them. I don't think we should leave much behind when we seal the doors."

"John, you think this one is going to be *the* attack?"

"Jay, I do. With your permission, I'm going to leave Todd behind to watch the monitors, I think my experience can best be used on the lines with the rest of us pulling a trigger."

"John, I disagree. I think your best spot is behind the monitors telling us what's happening. We need your experience watching the entire battle. If it's as bad as you think, we're going to need eyes on the entire front."

"OK, I'll send Todd up to the front line."

"John, before you send him topside make sure he's wearing his body armor and helmet, I can almost feel it in the air. I swear I smell the order of their unwashed bodies, they must be close."

"I know what you mean, I feel it in the air too."

@@@@@

The scouts returned to the campsite of the combined two groups. They reported to the leaders they had stumbled on a complex with barbed wire fences and welded shut gates. One of the scouts sips water while telling the leaders, "From a distance it looks like a large farm. I can't think of any other reason someone would go to such trouble as stringing barbed wire around their property."

"Jack, how large did this farm look like?"

"Robert, I'm only going to guess."

"Your guesses have been good, you've been the scout leader who's found us food and water so we've been able to make it this far. Tell me, what's your guess?"

"Maybe a thousand acres. The barbed wire went further than any of us could see. Near the road, it's double layered. If there's no food there, why the welded gate, why the double row of barbed wire? There has to be something very valuable at the end of the driveway."

"Robert, do you want me to go back to the location to keep an eye on them?"

"No, I'm worried they may have eyes on the road. I'm betting they already saw you and your scouts. I'm betting they're getting ready for us. If it comes to a battle, we don't know anything about them or the weapons we'll be facing. I'm worried about this farm. I think it might be better to pass on this one."

"Why? This farm could be the one that takes us through the winter. We can't pass it up. Robert, I feel this is the one we need. There are so many of us now, we have to find a large supply to carry us through the winter. I don't think we should take a pass on this farm. I'm not sure when we're going to find another."

"I understand your feelings, I am going to accompany you back so I can take a look at his farm myself."

"When do you want to leave?"

"As soon as you're rested."

"Robert, I'm ready to go now."

"Then let's go."

Robert and Jack nod to each other, they slip a handgun into their fanny packs, they each grab a bottle of water before they leave the rest area to review the farm

Jack and his team discovered. The two men walk with their eyes and ears wide open. They pause every few hundred steps to listen and look for anything out of order. They make sure no one's following them, nor is there anyone in the woods that line the road. They reach the intersection of our road and the main road. Robert whispers, "Jack slow down, pretend you're taking a drink from your water bottle. I need a few minutes to look around so I can see if anything is unusual. Jack lifts the closed bottle to his lips, pretending to take a drink while Robert sits at the intersection. He looks around checking the area. He's about to leave when the sun reflects off the lens of a hidden camera on a telephone pole, catching his attention. He looks down smiling to himself thinking, *Gotcha, think you're so smart don't you?* Robert nods towards Jack, who walks over to him, Robert whispers, "We're being watched. There's a camera on the telephone pole to our right, I saw the sunlight on the lens. I bet whoever is on the farm is watching us right now. Let's slowly walk towards the farm. You said the road continued past the farm, keep walking on it, we walk past the farm to see if we can see anything on the other end of the road."

"OK, I'm ready, what do we do if they come after us?"

"I don't think they will. I think the barbed wire and welded gate means they don't want to come out. They're worried someone is going to gain access to their farm, which means to me they must be sitting on a ton of food. They want to be left alone. With hundreds of thousands of people starving, people don't feel charitable. They should be sharing with those who have nothing, however too many want to keep what they have for themselves. I think we may have to teach them how to share."

"Shit, I sure hope so, I'm so tired of eating flowers and roots as a salad. Maybe they have cows, which means steaks!"

"Don't get ahead of yourself. Let's take it nice and slow, we're just two guys looking for some food and water. We don't want to get them to get worried when they see us."

@@@@@

John studies the images the cameras at the intersection where our road and the main county road meet. He calls Jay, "Jay, two men are at the intersection, one of them is one of them who was here a few of hours ago."

"Are you sure it's one of the same people?"

"Yes, ran face recognition, came back as the same person."

"I guess we don't have a file on those two so we know who they are, do we?"

"No only that we've seen him before. I don't know who he is, but he seems to be taking instructions from the other person. I think the other person is a leader. If they're back in only three and half hours, however, many there are in this group aren't that far away, I think less than two miles."

"Shit. Not what I wanted to hear. Isn't there a chance there was a leader group closer than their main body?"

"Do you feel like risking everything on that assumption?"

"No, you're right, we should be ready. What are they doing?"

"I'll forward you the live video, you'll see they're trying to look like they're out for a walk, except look at their body language and look at their eyes. They're paying too much attention to our fence and gates. They're trying to see what's beyond our driveways. I bet you they are going to walk past us to the next hill to see if they can get a view of us from the hilltop."

"How many of us will they be able to see?"

"They'll see our fields on that side and might get a glance of Tony's housing settlement behind our fields."

"Crap. We should have dug trenches around Tony's homes."

"We didn't have time."

"Pass along to Tony he should make sure anything of special value they have should be moved to their shelters. My gut says these two will scope us out, return to their main group and come back to demand we feed them."

"I agree, if we assume they're one to two miles away, we can expect the main body to arrive between three and five hours."

"Sun will be setting, do you think they'll attack at night or at dawn?"

"If they're well armed, tonight, if most of them are average people, then I say dawn."

"I agree, let's send half of everyone to get something to eat and rest, we'll rotate our alert groups so everyone gets some hot food and rest. John, what about the kids?"

"I'd keep them in the shelters until at least midday tomorrow."

"Agree, please issue the instructions."

Todd walks to me asking, "Dad, what's going on?"

"Two guys are checking us out, one was one of them who was here before. John and I think they're scoping us out before they bring their main body to demand food and water."

"Dad, what if we left some food and water outside the fence? Do you think they'd take it and move on?"

"Todd, no, I think they'd take it as a sign we have a lot more here. They'll see it as an invitation to hit us harder and quicker, we'd be giving them hope. Hope is dangerous, the more hope they have, the harder they're going to fight us. If they're not sure if we have a supply of food or not, they'll most likely save some of their strength in case we don't have supplies."

"I understand."

"Check on your kids, get something to eat and get some rest, we're going to alternate people on alert. John and I don't think we're going to be attacked until tomorrow morning."

"Dad, are you sure?"

"No, which is why we're going to keep half of us on alert."

@@@@@

Robert and Jack walk past our main gate, following the road up a small hill to our left. From there they can see our fields. Robert says, "Jack, look at those fields, many still have crops in them, I bet they must have barns or silos filled with food."

"Robert, look to the right. I see a person walking around, he looks like he's carrying a rifle and is in body armor."

Robert places his right hand over his eyes, blocking the sun. "Shit, you're right. Black rifle, can't make out what type from here, it does look like he's wearing a bulletproof vest. These people may be heavily armed. We should go back and talk to the other vets, we need to think this over. If they're heavily armed and have defenses, we might have to pass them by, most of our people aren't armed. We could lose a lot of people if they're able to bring the battle to us before we even get through their barbed wire fence. Let's turn around and head back. We need to think this one over."

As the two follow the road around another curve they see two small farms, both only have horse fences along their property lines. Robert smiles, "Well, look at this. We'll take these first, we may be able to feed everyone from these farms. We may be able to leave the other farm alone for now. I don't like the idea of charging a defended location with untrained people."

"I'm with you."

"We should be able to take them with our veterans and armed men, we'll hit them when the sun sets and we'll spend the night on the farms enjoying their food."

Four hours later it's over. The veterans in the crowd and the 500 who are armed easily surprised and took over the two small neighboring farms across the road from us. The two farms had only twelve people between them. Even though each person was armed and a good shot, they didn't have a security system or cameras to alert them to the mobs that completely overwhelmed them. The mob was attacking the farms from all directions before the farmers could respond. There had been relative peace for a few months and the two small farms had become complacent. They didn't worry about invaders, they had only a small number of people wander by asking for handouts which the farmers gave them. They didn't expect to be overwhelmed by hundreds of armed people who wanted everything they had. The farmers' families were struck down as they were heading to their homes from the fields for dinner. Most never made it. They didn't carry their arms in the field, they felt they were safe on their land. The mob shot them while they were walking out of the field, then they rushed into the homes, killing the women who were preparing dinner. The battle was over quickly, none of the farmers were prepared enough to get a single shot off to defend themselves. They'd stopped carrying weapons two months ago. They felt safe and they realized just how wrong they were when they saw hundreds of people rushing them from all sides of their farm. They realized they were dead wrong too late to protect themselves.

The mob was overjoyed with their success. They took over both farm houses, the fields, crops and barns full of animals. The slaughtered cows and pigs, they dug pits where they roasted the animals while one hundred returned to escort the main body of the large group to the farms. Thousands of hungry and tired people pitched tents and lay their sleeping bags in the fields of the farms. For the first time in months, everyone had a hot meal of fresh meat and roasted corn and peppers. People lined up to shower with hot water and use a flushing toilet for the first time in a long time. People were happy for the first time in months. The leaders took turns staying in the homes they'd conquered. They sent scouts to look for stored food on the farms. The wells provided them with all of the fresh water they'd need. The leaders agreed to spend a couple of days investigating the two farms before they planned their next move. Some of the people wanted to stay on the farms for the winter.

We saw smoke from their campfires on the horizon and we wondered whether our two neighbor's homes had caught fire or they'd been attacked. John tried to reach them on the radio we'd given them, no one answered. John called their phone which was answered by someone John didn't recognize, "Hello, Dan are you OK?"

"We're fine, who's this?"

"Dan, this is Frank, don't you remember me? Three farms over on 127th street?"

"Oh yes, Dan, how's everything with you?"

"Fine, we saw some smoke on the horizon, just checking that you're OK."

"We're fine, we're burning some of our fields, nothing to worry about."

"OK, great, thanks. See you soon at the monthly get-together."

"Sure thing."

John calls me, "Jay, the two farms were overrun, I told them I was Dan from the farm on 127th Street."

Laughing, I respond, "John, that was a good one, they'll go crazy looking for 127th street since we removed all of the street signs. Considering those farms were sold to a developer, all the attackers are going to find there is the start of a new housing subdivision."

"We now know they're violent. I think they'll stay there for a few days, rest and eat everything they find. They'll most likely slaughter and eat their animals before they try to locate the three farms you told them were on 127th street. Once they realize there're no farms there, they'll realize they were suckered and think about us again. I'd say we have maybe five days before they hit us."

"In the time we have left, let's see what we can do to make it harder for them to reach our homes."

"I agree. I'll come to the security shelter."

"I'll be here trying to get as much information as possible about what happened at the two neighboring farms."

Chapter 22

Robert and the other leaders relaxed in one of the captured farm houses. They drank beer they found in the basement of one of the farmhouses, they ate fresh steaks from the cows they recently butchered and grilled. They discussed their next actions.

Jason, one of the oldest and most experienced said, "Guys, my people have been on the road for months, this is the nicest place we've found. I'd say we stay here except the crops we've found and the animals are only enough to feed us for four to six weeks."

Robert looks around the comfortable living room responding, "Jason, I think we might be able to harvest some more of their crops which should let us make it through the winter."

Len, the youngest shakes his head, he says, "Guys, we won't make it through the winter, there's not enough shelter for all of our people. Most of our people don't have winter clothing, they'll freeze to death the first night the temperatures drop below freezing. We need to move someplace further south, someplace we can be safe and find enough food to live on while we start again."

Jason looks at Len thinking about what he said, "Len, you might be on to something there. Let's do a census of our people, we need to figure out what they have and need before we decide where or when to go. When our two groups combined, we lost track of the condition of everyone. I think we should spend the next few days checking on everyone. Everyone is resting, they have enough to eat and clean water to drink. Everyone is going to shower, they'll be in a much better frame of mind after a couple of days rest and having enough to eat."

Robert says, "Guys, we came from Nashville, there's nothing there. When we left, the city was in shambles, most of it was burning out of control."

Jeff, a leader of the northern group, says, "I think we should pack up all the food and water everyone can carry and head south towards Mobile. Being along the coast where's it's much warmer is going to do everyone a lot of good."

Jason replies, "Jeff that means we'll have to make our way around the three major cities, Nashville, Huntsville, and Birmingham. I think Huntsville might be OK, the military had a large presence in Huntsville, and they may have been able to hold control of the city. Birmingham, on the other hand, could be a real mess. I wouldn't want to go there in normal times. The city was famous for race issues and riots before things got crazy."

Jeff asks, "Can we reach Mobile without going through Birmingham?"

"There's a highway that goes around the city, however, I think it's going to be a fight anywhere near the city."

Jeff asks, "Is there anywhere between Huntsville and Birmingham we can find a place to stay?"

Robert says, "Maybe we can find a place to stay in Huntsville or near the river like in Decatur. The last time I was in Decatur, there were many farms."

Jeff says, "I like being next to a major river. It could provide us water for farms and transportation like our ancestors did. Based on the distance between here and Huntsville I think we're going to need sufficient food to keep us going for at least thirty days."

Robert says, "I agree. There are three bikes in the garage, why don't we send three scouts south to check the conditions."

Everyone nods their agreement to Robert's idea.

@@@@@@

Tony is sitting across from John in the security shelter, "John, we know our neighbors have been overrun, do we know anything else?"

"Unfortunately, we don't. We don't have any cameras with a field of view that far. All we know is when I called, someone else answered."

"We need information to have some idea of what we're up against."

"Tony, I have one out of the box idea, it's a little dangerous, but it's the only way I can think of without putting any of our people at risk."

"What are you thinking?"

"We send one of our drones over their farms."

"Can we do that?"

"I think we can. If we lose one, we'll be down to only seven. Our camera wouldn't be able to transmit to us, but the camera will record on an SD card, which we'll review when the drone returns."

Tony looks concerned, "John, so if something happens to the drone, not only are we out the drone, but also the camera and the SD card."

"Tony, you see the problem. We only have a limited number of cameras, drones, and SD memory cards."

"I can't believe we missed stocking drones and cameras."

"Yes, we blew that one. I don't think it occurred to you or Jay cameras or drones were a high priority item. You were focused on stocking food, weapons, computers, medications and farming equipment. You guys did better than I thought possible. We have enough food that if we had to move to the shelter and live off of our supplies we could do so for a few years. I'm amazed you two pulled it off."

"What we didn't think through was the need for information."

"Why should you? Neither of you had the experience to protect a facility. I used to have to design security for fire bases in hostile areas. The Indians were always looking for ways to get to the good guys. They surprised me with the number of ways they thought of to get to the good guys. We needed information, such as how many people we're facing, how're they're armed and how they're treating the farms they conquered."

Tony looks at John and back to the monitors, he's very concerned about the group sitting less than a mile away. Tony's thinking to himself, *I knew we should have either purchased that land or found a way to bring them under our umbrella. They didn't think they were in danger, they lowered their defense, it got them killed.* "John, since I can't think of any other way to get information, you have my support. I do, however, have one suggestion."

"Sure, what is it?"

"I suggest you paint the drone. Currently, they're dark gray and black for night operations. If we're going to perform a daylight mission, I suggest we repaint it so it doesn't stick out against the sky if they look up."

"Damn it, great point, I forgot all about that. I'll get right on it."

At 5:30 PM with the sun setting John and Todd launched the drone. Tony, Fred with his arm still in a sling and I crammed into the security shelter with John. We tracked the drone, we watch it cross our front boundary when our RF signal strength falls off cutting the live video stream off. John says, "That's the end of our live video until it returns."

Fred asks, "John if you can't see how do you control the drone?"

John smiles responding, "Who said anything about flying it? We programmed a course into it and let it go. We sent it to GPS points we know from visiting the farms. We instructed the drone to fly to the first GPS location, fly four increasing circles, then move to the second GPS location and repeat the circles. It should repeat to the third and fourth GPS waypoints before it returns home."

I ask, "John, why only four GPS locations?"

"Jay, it's really five, we have to enter our location since we can't fly it in the normal manner. The drone will only store five locations."

"I should have gotten better drones."

"Jay, you wouldn't have known. I was surprised to see you even had drones."

Fred asks, "If I understand what's going on correctly, we won't know if the drone operated correctly until it returns. We have no way to control it or see what it's recording until it returns. If it doesn't return, we lose a drone, camera, and memory card."

John nods, saying, "Fred, you got the key issues correct."

Tony asks, "John, how long will the mission take?"

"Thirty minutes. I hope."

"What do you mean, I hope?"

"I hope it doesn't crash or get shot down."

The drone flies over the two farms without incident, when the clock reaches 27 minutes we run through the tunnels to exit in the field looking for the drone. None of us sees it when it drops out of the sky by our feet. John picks it up saying, "You're a good little drone, you came home to your papa. Now show us what you saw."

We run back to the security shelter with the SD card we removed from the camera and inserted it into a laptop which displayed the images on a large wall screen. The image starts blurry, it quickly clears up. What we see stops us in our tracks, our mouths hang open. We didn't expect to see rows and rows of tents, sleeping bags, and campfires. John said, "Looking at the tents, I'm going to estimate there are a few thousand people in the camp."

Tony replied so softly we had to strain to hear him, "Thousands? My God, it's worse than I thought. Can we beat them back?"

John looked at the video before speaking, "Tony, we can slow them down with mines and traps, we can shoot the hell out of them. However, if they keep coming up our driveways, they will overrun us. We don't have enough people to take them all down. If everyone hits a person with each round in their magazine, which you all know isn't probable, in fact, it's not even possible. We have to change magazines after 30, 40 or 60 rounds. Which means if I use 40 rounds as an average, times the 30 adults and teens we have trained to fight, then we can hit 1,200 of them before we have to change magazines. That assumes every shot equals a person hit. Let's also assume we can stop 300 of them with our mines and traps before they reach our trench line. If 3,000 people race up our driveway and lawns, they can reach us before we can take them all down. We'll be lucky to take 20% of them down. Many of our people are going to be stressed out, they will miss most of their shots, they may hit one person more than once. A single attacker may be struck by more than one shooter. Our people may fumble their reloading or because of the stress, forget to reload. Frankly, we're screwed. If we had air support we could win, if we had mortars which could reach out and strike them before they can close to us we would have a chance. The distance between the road and the trench is to close. Running people can and will reach us."

None of us spoke. We sat in the security shelter staring at the display. Tony and I are sitting in front of John in shock. After a very long and silent three minutes, I break the silence, "John, isn't there some way we can take more of them down? If we hit them hard enough won't they retreat?"

"Jay, you'd be correct if we were an army fighting another army. Usually when an army unit reaches a 30% casualty rate, they lose unit cohesion. A regular army would withdraw and regroup. A mob has nothing to lose. Worse, they're families, hitting a member of a family will push the other members onward wanting revenge."

"John, we have to find some way to stop them, or at least slow them down enough so we can force them back."

"Jay, I'll put my thinking cap on. Let me review our armory. Can we get together tonight at 7?"

Tony and I nod in agreement. Tony says, "I'll volunteer Jay's house for the meeting."

@@@@@

Captain Black was shocked when he and his team landed at Chicago's O'Hare International Airport. The runway was littered with trash, large areas of the terminals were closed due to disrepair. Empty airplanes sat in a parking area of the airport. Captain Black stopped counting when he passed twenty-six parked airplanes. The inside of the terminal reminded the Captain and his First Sergeant of a third world country. Most of the restrooms were out of order, the terminal smelled of urine, feces, vomit and rotting meat. Sergeant Gray looked around, he whispered, "Cap, there must be thousands of homeless living in the terminal. What the hell happened here? We were only gone three months."

"Sarge, it's pretty clear the economy took a dump and took millions down with it. I worry what we're going to see on our mission."

"Sir, that still bothers the men. None are happy about peacekeeping inside America."

"Sarge, look around if we don't do it, who will, Notice the only people flying today are wearing a uniform? Usually, we're in the minority, today we're all that can afford to fly because our uncle is paying."

"Sir, there has to be a better way than sending SOF to police America."

"Sarge, you signed up to be all you can be, now let's collect our bags and locate our transportation."

"Yes, sir."

The troops found a bus painted in Army green outside waiting for them. The bus took the team to Soldiers Field, which has been taken over by the US Military. Captain Black checked in. He was given food vouchers and directed to the armory to pick up more ammo. Afterward, they were directed to their vehicles, eight LAV (light armored vehicles) and a map of their AO (Area of Operations). Their area was a vertical slice of the country, from Chicago to Mobile. Sergeant Gray said, "Sir, that's a huge AO, are they crazy?"

"Sergeant, we're short of people, heavy on criminals so we'll do the best we can with what we have."

"Yes, sir. Sir, I have a list of known HAM operators in our AO, plus a list of known radio intercepts. I guess this means people are alive in these areas."

"Sarge, we don't have enough people to spread out while moving south in a line. I think we'll split the team into two squads, half will head south on Interstate 55, the other half will head south on Interstate 65, we'll meet back up In New Orleans."

"Sir, split the team? We only have a few LAVs."

"We're getting reinforced with two hundred National Guard troops. You command the west group down Interstate 55, I'll take the other half south on Interstate 65. I'll meet you in the 'Big Easy.'"

"Yes, sir."

@@@@@

At 7:00, John joins Tony and me in my kitchen over a cold beer. "John, did you come up with any new ideas?"

"Does pray count?"

Tony smiles, shaking his head no. I laugh saying, "I really hope you have a better backup plan than pray. Mind you, I do believe in God, but pray?"

"Happen to know where we can find another few hundred heavily armed people?"

Both Tony and I shake our heads no.

"Either we need bodies or we need to mine the hell out of the entrances. The problem with mines is they are one-time use. I think it's time for Todd to show you some of the toys he's been playing with."

"Huh?"

"Jay, your son-in-law, designed and built a catapult."

"I plan on firing large Molotov Cocktails at our uninvited guests."

Tony is surprised, asking, "Will it really work?"

"Oh yes, it will toss cocktails from behind the trench across the road."

"How come I didn't know about this? He's my son-in-law."

"I suggest you ask him."

"I will, when will you test it?"

"Already have. It works like a charm. I wish we had more of them."

"Can we make more of them in the time we have left?"

"Jay, since we don't know how much time we have, I'd say we should try."

"I'll get a hold of Todd right now, maybe he can get a team together to start building another tonight."

"If he can, it will help."

"I suggest we keep every adult and teen who can fire an assault rifle on the front line. I'd like to arm everyone with either an M4 or M16."

"John, I thought you didn't like full auto rifles."

"Usually I don't, right now we can and will use every force multiplier we have."

Tony and I nod to each other. "We agree."

Todd walks by, I yell, "Todd, please join us."

"Hey, Dad, Tony, John, what's up?"

"We heard you built a catapult."

"Yes, it's kind of cool. Tosses a rock across the road from the back yard."

"Can you make another or two?"

"Sure, since we have the plans, they're not too hard. I can have the parts ready to assemble by midday. The CNC machine is already programmed, all I have to do is feed it wood."

Tony says, "Don't let us delay you. Great job, grab your construction team and get it going. We may need to use them in combat sooner than later."

Todd leaves to start the CNC machine making another catapult.

Tony, John and I continue discussing plans until 11:00 PM when we call it a night.

@@@@@@

The People's Liberation Army, Navy (PLAN or PLA Navy) had never been in a real battle. Fleet Admiral Zin wanted to drill his various ships before he faced the mighty US Navy in battle. He issued orders for China's three fleets to meet in the South China Sea off the coast of the port at Haikou. The Liaoning, China's only carrier which can carry 33 fixed-wing warplanes was the queen of the Chinese fleet. Admiral Zin ordered his submarines and cruisers to mock attack the Liaoning and in four battles, the Liaoning lost two mock attacks and won two of them. Admiral Zin informed the Premier he needed three additional months to prepare China's three fleets to enter battle against the US Seventh Fleet, which is being reinforced with the US Navy's Third and Fourth Fleets. Admiral Zin told the Chairman, "Sir, we're going to be facing six of America's Nimitz-class nuclear carriers, each capable of carrying more than twice the number of planes as the Liaoning."

"Admiral, the Americans have been asking for a delay in paying us back, I'll agree to give them a short delay so you can have a little more time to prepare."

"Thank you sir."

Three months of practicing mock attacks have given Admiral Zin more confidence. He called his captains together for a meeting. Admiral Zin had an ace up his sleeve, one he doubted the US Navy knew about. He addressed the captains of his ships, "Captains, we have been practicing for three months. In that time, 75% of the time we have failed to take out the Liaoning. If you can't sink the Liaoning, how are you going to handle one of the American CVNs? Each is 100,000 tons, each carries 75 warplanes. Submarine commanders, you are supposed to be able to sneak up on the carrier, penetrate her screen and hit her with a full broadside of torpedoes. In the previous six encounters, only three out of thirty of you have made it inside the Liaoning's screen. Two of you ran into each other at 100 meters, you caused enough damage that your two boats will miss the encounter." Admiral Zin asks the two commanding officers to join him on the stage when they join him he draws his sidearm shooting both captains dead. "Let this be a lesson to the rest of you. Don't let the people down. Learn how to command your ships in battle, our time is running short. The Premier has given us only three more weeks before we are to head towards Hawaii. The next commanding officer who fails will join these two as shark bait."

The rest of the commanding officers snap to attention. They salute the fleet admiral, who orders them back to their ships.

The American Navy surged every warship it could to the Pacific. Ships that were in dry dock for repairs are quickly refloated so they can join the upcoming battle. The US Navy has twelve experimental F35C stealth fighters. The CNO orders the training squadron to join the USS Ronald Regan. Every F/A18E and F are sent to the Pacific Fleet while their F/A18C and Ds are sent to the Atlantic carriers. The Navy's plan is to use the airfield at Pearl Harbor to operate P3 and P8 anti-submarine planes. They also plan to base F/A 18s providing CAP (combat air patrol) over Hawaii, plus replacement fighters for the any the carriers lose in the upcoming battle.

All of the ship's weapon systems are checked while each ship's armories and vertical launch cells are fully loaded with war shots. In Hawaii commercial and navy technicians are working 24 hours a day to bring the USS Missouri back to life. Cranes move equipment while others remove museum displays. 16-inch shells and powder are trucked to the ship. Fuel oil is pumped into the ship's tanks. Nine weeks after the China crisis began Captain Jefferson orders the ship's boilers lit for the first time in twenty years. Thirty minutes after the boiler ignition the USS Missouri is generating its own power. Captain Jefferson informs the crew he wants to leave port in three days so they can join the Seventh Fleet. No weapon in China's arsenal, except for a nuclear weapon can penetrate the Missouri's 16" thick armor. The CNO plans to use the Missouri to lead the American battle fleet. She'll be escorted by five Virginia-class fast attack submarines. The CNO plans to have the Missouri launch 32 Tomahawk anti-ship missiles while her 16" guns fire. Her 2,800-pound shells have a range of 30 miles. Battleship sailors volunteer to take the Missouri into battle since it will be the first battleship to fight a fleet battle in the largest sea battle since the Second World War. It's also most likely the last time a Battleship goes in harms way.

Chapter 23

An hour before dawn finds every able-bodied adult in the front yard digging new trenches and placing as many mines as we can build. We placed our entire inventory of mines, including our reserves hoping they will be able to slow down the mob who will sooner or later come across the road to investigate our farms. Looking at the lawn, I don't think anyone is going to be able to set foot on our property without setting off a mine. The problem is once a mine goes off, it's gone. People coming in behind the first wave won't be slowed down by the mines. While we're planting the mines, the older teens are helping make pipe bombs which we'll use as hand grenades. John is turning two backpack water sprayers into flame throwers. We also plan to dig a trench in front of our fighting trench which we line with straw and jellied gasoline. We plan to light it if we're getting overrun. Our defense plans are starting to resemble the dark ages, we're only missing the castle and boiling pitch to pour on the attackers.

@@@@@

The mob across the street is happy. They are well rested and for the first time in months they are resting with full bellies. 180 miles away in Knoxville eight motorcycle gangs merged to form a new club they call the Son's of the Devil MC. 375 hardened men and women had finished raiding the outskirts of Knoxville before 1,200 armed citizens drove them off in a battle that went back and forth for five days. The citizens greater numbers won out over the gang's mobility, the gang was forced out of Knoxville. The leader of the combined gang, Big Dutch, decided they should move towards Nashville. The 375 survivors ride west on Interstate 40 towards Nashville. They stop at every town along Interstate 40, where they rob to take what they want. Houses are robbed of their food and water, women are raped, hospitals and doctors' offices are broken into for drugs. In normal times the trip between Knoxville and Nashville takes less than three hours, the gang is taking their time to stop at every town, and rest stop. Big Dutch decides to spend the night on the outskirts of Cookeville, the largest micropolitan area in Tennessee with a population of 106,000. Big Dutch figures Cookeville is large enough to have food, fuel and water and also spread out enough, it will be hard for the people to come together to put up a fight. The gang picked up 20 additional people as they rode on Interstate 40 West. There were almost 400 heavily armed gang members who entered the southern subdivisions of Cookeville. The gang took the town by surprise. They rode into small subdivisions, right up to people's front doors or rear sliding doors which they kicked in, taking what they want. They left subdivisions in ruins, many burning out of control with many families trapped inside after the gang stripped the homes bare. They captured twenty young women aged between 16 and 30. The gang plans on using the women before they sell them to other gangs for drugs and gasoline. Big Dutch looks at a map before retiring for the evening. He decides their next stop will be a rural area about 40 miles north of Nashville, an area of small farms that should be able to supply his gang with food and water until their next stop. His goal is to reach the coast at Mobile, Alabama.

@@@@@

We worked 18 hour days improving our defenses. We used the last of our barbed wire to increase the depth of our fence, we placed over 900 land mines, we dug up all of our front yards with punji pits and buried hunting traps. Our two backhoes dug a trench in front of our main fighting trench which we planned to set on fire, hopefully trapping people between the barbed wire and the trenches. We flew our drones over the farms across the street to keep track of the mobs. So far, they haven't moved from their tent city, which is good and bad news. Good in that they haven't moved towards us, bad in that every day they don't invade us, our nerves are getting worn thin. We've even started to fight with each other. Our tempers have grown short, we're sensitive to everyday comments, we're overly sensitive to everything due to our general lack of sleep and extremely high-stress levels. None of us knows how much longer we can continue this way. On the fifth day of nothing happening, Fred had an idea. He suggested we pause and have a community barbecue suggesting this was a good time to allow each adult three beers out of our strategic alcohol supply. At 7:00 PM we started grilling one of the cows that we planned to slaughter two months from now to help take us through the winter. We allowed everyone to leave the trench for a couple of hours while John and Todd took turns manning the monitors in the security shelter. Eric dragged out some speakers which enabled us to have music at the barbecue. Everyone's mood started to increase as the fresh hot beef and beers mellowed them out. We sat in folding chairs around long folding tables, taking a break. Our stress started to melt away, we smiled for the first time in five days. The beer hit some of us harder than normal since most of us worked through lunch and we haven't had any alcohol in a week. We didn't realize our music and the smoke from our BBQ pit drifted across the street to the mob. Robert's ears heard the music, he knew someone was having a party without inviting them. When he smelled the grilling meat, he knew the complex across the street was larger than he thought. He called the leaders of the mob together for a council meeting.

"That farm Jack found across the street is having a party, music, grilled meat, they might even have beer. I don't think it's nice of them to have a party without inviting us. We're right across the street from them. I'm sure they know we're here."

Jack asks, "Why do you think they know we're here?"

"Because I've seen a small drone flying over us twice. The only place it could have come from is across the road. Those small commercial drones don't have much range. The only location close enough to have launched the drone was across the road. They know we're here, they know how many of us there are. They most likely don't know how we're armed or any other resources we have."

Drew, one of the other leaders asked, "Robert, what do you suggest we do? We all saw their barbed wire fences and their welded gates. How do we get into their complex?"

Robert smiled, "We're on a farm, there are plenty of sheets of wood here. We can lay the plywood over the barbed wire, we can walk across their fences. We don't need to break through the gate. There can't be as many of them as there are of us."

"Drew shakes his head, "Robert, maybe they're armed and waiting for us or someone else like us to attack them. If it were me, I'd have spent the last few months building defensive positions. Before we attack them, we need information. We need to know what we'll be facing when we cross the barbed wire."

"Drew, how do you think we can get the information?"

"Can we capture their drone? The farm houses have laptops, if we can capture it, maybe we can figure out how to use it to get a look at their location."

"Drew, good idea if we had a controller and the way to change the frequency so we control the drone and use it against those who are spying on us."

Jack smiles, saying, "We can do this. I found an X-Box in the basement, it has controllers, I'm sure we can find the circuit board controller. If we change the switch settings, we'll be changing the frequency. If we can connect the drone's PC board to the laptop, we might be able to look at the flight program and just reverse it."

Everyone nods, Robert says, "Worth a try, they usually send it twice a day."

While the mob leaders discuss what to do, Todd prepares to send the drone across the street, he calls to John, "John, do you hear me?"

"I'm 5 by 5, what's up?"

"Winds are a little strong today, think we should launch her?"

"Yes, we need to make sure they haven't moved or changed anything since this morning. The drone should be fine. I'm ready here, pick it up and send it flying."

"Roger, here goes."

Todd lifts his arms as high as he can with the drone in them, the drone's four small motors are spinning, the drone rises from his hands and starts flying across the road.

Robert and the other leaders hear someone yell, "Drone."

Robert says, "Let's go, this is our chance to capture it and turn the tables on those across the road." The leaders run out of the farm house as the drone begins to slowly circle the farm house. Jack yells, "I found a long handle fishing net, I think we can grab the drone with it." Jack runs after the drone failing four times to capture it. On his fifth attempt, he gets the drone into the net. He gently brings it down to the ground. "I got it! I got it!"

Robert and Drew run to where Jack is holding the drone. He hands it to Drew, who says, "Jack, let's see if we can reverse this sucker's course and turn the tables on the assholes across the road."

A thin teen walks out of the crowd watching them, saying, "I know how to reprogram it. I used to make drones like this in my basement. I can help you."

Drew says, "Everyone, make a hole, let the drone expert through. Son, what's your name?"

"Scot, most of the friends I had called me Scotty."

"Well, Scotty, I think we'd like you to take this drone to engineering and reprogram it. Make sure it's disrupters are set on stun and don't enter warp speed inside the atmosphere."

Scotty's face breaks out into a huge smile, "Captain, yes sir. Right away sir."

Scotty grabs the drone running towards the farm house to reprogram it.

Robert smiles, "Drew, how did you know to address him as Scotty in Star Trek?"

Laughing, Drew responds, "Any geek who's named Scotty is going to be into Star Trek. I bet you he'll be back soon with the drone programmed and running better than we got it."

"No bet. I think you're right. Did you know he was in the group?"

"No, I sometimes wonder who else in mixed in with the people we don't know shit about. I wonder what other skills we're overlooking by not getting to know everyone just a little bit."

"I think you're right. While Scotty is reprogramming the drone, let's start with the group in front of us."

Smiling Drew nods his agreement.

@@@@@

Big Dutch is leading the gang towards Nashville. He figures they could have been there yesterday, but every town they stop in seems to have food, liquor, and nice women. They party in every town they come to. Big and his gang are happy. Their bellies are full, they've all had sex as often as they've wanted, their numbers steadily increase, the club is now approaching 450 riding all types of bikes and 15 trikes. Big is thinking this crisis has been the best thing that's ever happened to them. No police, no bullshit lawyers and judges, no having to kiss anyone's ass. So far, it's been pure pleasure.

@@@@@

An hour after receiving the drone Scotty returns with the drone and a huge smile. "It's ready and better than new."

Robert, who's been sitting in a large group of people chatting about their backgrounds, asks, "Scotty, how did you improve it?"

"The drone we captured from the Klingons couldn't transmit, they flew it over us, when it returned home, they had to load the memory card in a laptop to view the video. I found some laptops and PC boards, I amplified the WiFi signal so that we can stream video from the drone when it flies across the road. We'll see them in real time."

Robert asks, "Will they be able to control the drone away from us?"

Smiling Scotty shakes his head saying, "Nobody is going to hack my programming. I used to be able to hack almost any system. All we need is to watch and control it from this laptop using the controllers I have plugged into it."

Drew smiles, saying, "Scotty, you are hereby promoted to LT Commander and placed in charge of all electronics and programming. You are also hereby named as drone controller, we're ready when you are, let her fly."

Scotty smiles, saying, "It's easier from inside the house so I can place the laptop on a table. I can connect the laptop to other displays so others can watch at the same time."

Robert pats Scotty on his head saying, "Commander, lead on."

Scotty launches the drone. Drew, Robert, and Jack look over his shoulder as he pilots the drone across the road. He flies the drone up the driveway, making sure they get a good view of the fighting trench. Drew says, "Whoa, I don't like that. It looks like a fighting trench from the First World War. It looks very well protected. If they have machine guns, they could cut us down before we even got to the trench. Look at the walls in front of the trench. They have firing slots in them."

Robert points to the first trench, "What's the other trench?"

Drew asks Scotty, "Can you move the drone to look at the other trench?"

"Sure, watch this." The new trench appears on the display,

Robert says, "Shit, that trench looks like it's designed to stop us. It's got hay in the bottom of it, I bet they are going to pump gas into the trench and set it on fire, along with any of us that get caught in it."

Drew nods his agreement, "I wonder what other traps and tricks they have prepared for us."

The drone flies over the back yard where everyone is sitting around the fire pit drinking beers. Robert points at the screen saying, "Look, they have M4s or M16s ready, they also have magazine belts next to the rifles and helmets and armored vests. These people don't fool around. They're armed to repel an armed attack. I think we're going to have to think how we attack these people."

Jack asks, "Scotty can you show us their fields and other parts of the farm?"

"Sure." He increases the height of the drone while slowly spinning it around, they see a large farm and the other homes. Jack says, "The barns are made of cement, not wood. This is going to be a hard nut to crack."

Robert shakes his head, "No, it won't. Notice almost all of their defenses are pointed towards the front of their property? If we cross onto their property from the sides and come at them from their rear, I think we can surprise them and possibly take them without losing a lot of people."

Drew says, "We're going to have to send some people directly up their driveway, it's what they're expecting. If we don't, they may increase their security in the rear, which might catch us out in the open."

"We'll have to ask for volunteers, I don't want to order people to their certain death."

The other two nod their agreement.

Robert says, "I think we should toy with them for a day or two before we attack, run them down. They must have an alarm system so let's keep them up all night, tiring them out before we attack."

The other two nod and smile their agreement.

@@@@@

The Chinese Navy is composed of one carrier, surrounded by one hundred and two cruisers and destroyers, forty frigates, and one hundred twenty submarines. They've turned northeast heading towards Hawaii. The American Navy renamed the Eight Fleet since it combines elements of three different fleets. The lead ship is the USS Missouri, the very ship the Japanese signed the instrument of surrender ending the last Pacific War. The Missouri still has workers installing and testing equipment as she heads into war. The two fleets are heading towards each other at the best speed their slowest ship can sustain which is 22 knots for each fleet. The two fleets are moving towards each other at a combined speed of 50 MPH. If each Admiral's plan goes without a hitch, the battle will open near Wake Island, the location where the Pacific war against the Japanese seventy-three years ago was turned in America's favor.

@@@@@

Todd approaches the party with a frown on his face. "Dad, we lost the drone. We think either it crashed or it was captured."

"How the hell could they have captured it? I thought they couldn't see it."

"Guess they knew about it and waited till the winds blew enough to have pushed the drone low enough for them to grab it."

"Todd, can they discover anything about us from it?"

"John said, no, the memory stick in the camera was clean. They can assume we sent it, but couldn't prove it."

"Todd, can they reverse the programming to send it to look at us?"

"I don't think so, we couldn't. But none of us have the programming skills, one of them might."

"Shit. Everyone listen up."

Everyone stops drinking and talking, "I think the group across the road grabbed our drone to spy on us. That means they'll be planning on paying us a visit."

Everyone starts to move towards their weapons. We didn't know that every move we made was being watched by the very group we had been spying on.

Robert watches saying, "They're well drilled, that young man who's waving his arms around must be their drone controller, he most likely told them he lost control of the drone. The man he spoke to was one of their leaders. He told them what happened. Notice how they didn't panic, they quickly dropped what they were holding and doing as they moved to their weapons while pulling vests and helmets on. Everyone knows what to do and where to go. The only way we're going to break into this farm is by surprise. None of these people looks hungry. They're sitting around eating steak and drinking beer. BEER did you hear me, they have cold beer. They have generators. This is where we spend the winter. This farm is large enough for all of us, there must be enough food here to feed us for months."

The others nod. Drew reaches into his backpack, he pulls out half of a candy bar handing it to Scotty. "Commander, you earned yourself the last of our emergency candy. You did more than great."

"Thank you, sir."

Robert watches Scott leave the farmhouse saying, "Don't lose that young man. When he collects the drone, assign protection to him. He's going to be our eyes from now on. We'll have him use the drone to scout in front of us. We won't need to risk our scouts."

Jack replied, "We can use the drone to make sure we're not being followed too."

"Great idea. Let's get to work planning our takeover of that farm."

Chapter 24

President Putin reviews the intelligence images showing the Chinese and American fleets steaming towards each other. He smiles thinking to himself *when they engage each other maybe the perfect time for us to land in New York City offering food and medical support. The Americans will welcome us with open arms, once we're in, we'll never leave. The American's focus will be on the battle in the Pacific, they won't have anything positioned to stop us. I'll give the orders to Sergey so he'll be ready to execute the plan, very soon we're going to rule Europe and America. I'll allow the yellow bastards to have Asia while we incorporate America's technology into our military making us the strongest force in the world.*

@@@@@

Robert and his advisors study the images sent back by the drone. Robert points out the path that looks like the best for attacking the farm. "We split the people into three groups, a small group of volunteers will attack up their driveway, I don't expect more than 10% of them to make it. While they hold the farm's focus, two other groups will lay wood over the barbed wire on the sides coming in behind their trench. They won't expect a three prong attack. In case they have an alarm system, the flanking attacks can't kick off until the front one has started. I asked Scotty to make smoke bombs for our frontal attack group. Hopefully, the smoke will mask their approach, giving them some time and a small chance of making it."

Drew studies the plans, "I agree with your plan, I worry about the frontal attack, even with smoke, I don't expect to see any of those people tomorrow night. Isn't there some other way?"

"I've reviewed the images, I can't find another way. If we don't send some people up their driveway, they will grow suspicious and keep a sharper eye on their flanks. If they catch us out in the open, they'll cut us down before we reach them. We need the distraction of the frontal attack, which is what they're expecting. We should give them what they're expecting so they don't look on their flanks."

"Robert, I agree with you that it's the best plan, I just wish there was another way."

"Me too, but I haven't been able to find it."

"When do we kick off the attack?"

"In two days, we harass them with the drone to keep them off balance, on the morning of the third day we'll attack an hour before sunrise."

"Let's do it."

@@@@@

Big Dutch walked around his campsite, his gang now numbers 532 people, all are heavily armed. They have two school buses and a 32 foot Ryder truck filled with supplies and slaves following the bikes. Dutch studies the map on his lap, deciding to spend two nights in their current location resting and partying before they move into the northern suburbs of Nashville. He nods to himself thinking he's going to grab a slave for some relaxation for the night.

@@@@@

Our own drone which was captured by the group across the street buzzed us day and night for two days, every time it came close John sounded our alarm. I'm worried that this is all part of a master plan to make sure we don't get any rest. I think it's all part of their plan to keep us off balance pending an attack against us. I ask John, "Buddy if you were commanding the other side what would you do?"

"Jay, I'd do what they're doing, I'd keep us confused and unbalanced, I'd screw with us until we're tired and confused. When we're worn out always responding to the alarm, I'd attack."

"That's what's worrying me, I think they're going to attack us very soon. I'm sure the drone showed them our trench and other defenses."

John nods, saying, "Jay, I agree which is why if I were them, I'd attack three fronts, one up the driveway where we expect it. And two on our flanks where our defenses are the weakest. I thought about digging additional pits on our flanks. The problem is our flanks are so large if we dig everywhere we won't have any crops left. We don't have any idea where they'll be coming at us from. Without knowing their avenue of attack, we don't know where to build defenses. You had a good idea when you dug the fighting trench around the houses so we can fire in 360 degrees around the houses."

"Thanks, you're saying we're going to have to wait and see what happens."

"Unfortunately, you're right."

"When do you think they'll attack?"

"If it were me, I'd attack at dawn tomorrow or the day after. They're ready to go, you can't keep an attack group wound too tight for any length of time.

"Yeah, that's what I thought too. I'll pass the word to everyone to go to bed early tonight, we'll get up at 4:00 AM to man the trench by 4:30. Since the trench circles our homes, I'm going to spread out our people so we have some ready for action on our flanks."

"I agree."

I spread the word about the revised plan. Everyone agrees that the attack will come very soon. We hit the sack early so we're all up and manning our fighting positions by 4:30 AM. The attack started at 5:00 AM with smoke bombs being lobbed over our barbed wire fence.

"Everyone, be ready, they will most likely be coming in behind the smoke."

The wind pushes the smoke in our direction when it covers us, we start coughing, our eyes tear up. They made a form of tear gas. We didn't bring our gas masks with us. We start trying to rinse our eyes with water and putting wet towels on our noses to block the gas. As we're trying to recover from the tear gas, we hear the yelling from our front. Hundreds of people are screaming, they're coming in our direction. The attackers have laid sheets of plywood over the barbed wire allowing the invaders access to our property. The first attack wave begins running up our driveway and front yard when they run into our mine field and punji pits. The mines blow apart the first fifty attackers, the pits stop another thirty, the screaming of the wounded is horrible, they cry, they beg, they scream in horrible pain. The second wave enters our property right behind the first wave, they're able to reach further than the first wave which is down to only ten unharmed people out of the one hundred fifty that started. The second wave reaches the next line of our mines which cuts them down to only five people who with the ten from the first wave turn around to return to the farm across the street. We think we're winning when shots ring out from our flanks, my iPad pings with a message from John, "LARGE ATTACK COMING FORM BOTH FLANKS!" Before I can respond, a third wave starts running towards us from the front while over five hundred are attacking us from our left and right-hand flanks.

I text "John, get the kids in the shelter! This doesn't look good."

"Roger."

"Everyone lay down fire on our flanks, there's five hundred coming in from both sides."

Before I finish, hundreds of shots are striking all around us. We're firing in three directions trying to slow down the attack to buy us time.

We don't know that there are another five hundred across the street waiting for the word to go and Big Dutch's gang is only five miles away from us. The attack on us is working, their numbers are allowing them to soak up our mines and still advance. Each wave gets closer to us than the previous and once the mines explode, there isn't any more to stop the following waves of people. It's like the human wave attacks the Chinese used in the Korean War. The attackers surprise us by throwing Molotov Cocktails at us. The initial flaming cocktails burn the grass and camouflage sheets covering the punji pits, some of the fires set off our makeshift mines allowing the attackers get closer to us. The people assigned to protecting our flanks are firing on full auto, they're burning through ammo at a crazy rate. Magazines are burned through, empties dropped while new ones are inserted and the firing continues. The piles of bodies around us are increasing as we burn through ammo.

We've beaten off four attacks when there's a pause in the fighting. I'm guessing the other side is regrouping. We have only one minefield left between our trench and the road, one minefield and the trench filled with straw and gasoline. All of our rifle barrels are smoking, a couple have changed color from the extreme heat generated by firing so many rounds in so short a time. The bottom of our trench is filled with spent brass and empty magazines. We start to collect the magazines so we can refill them. I'm worried about the barrels of our rifles, we've each burned through over five hundred rounds in a very short time. *We don't have enough extra barrels to put new ones on each lower. It's something I should have stocked but didn't. That was a dumbass move on my part.*

Flo and Jill are walking through the trench handing out bottles of water, which we really need. We're starting to relax when we hear hundreds of motorcycles and gunfire, AR, AK, and shotguns. I text John, "Do you see anything? We hear motorcycles."

"Can't see the road, our cameras must have been shot out."

"K."

Damn it, we lost our eyes on the road, we don't have any idea how many or who's fighting with whom. We're shocked when we see motorcycles driving up our driveway. They must have ridden over the sheets of plywood laid over the barbed wire. I yell, "FIRE."

We open up firing full auto, we're moving our rifles left and right, trying to spread as much lead down range as possible. We're cutting down the riders, but there are more behind them, four of us are throwing hand grenades towards the bikers. Some of the bikers are advancing while firing at us. We were taken by surprise when two missiles strike the bullet traps built in front of our firing trench. The RPGs blow the packed soil all over us and blow holes in our wall. We toss grenades towards the bikers when we start receiving heavy fire from our flanks. I think I understand what happened. While the group across the road was attacking us, a large biker gang heard the firing. They came to investigate and they must have cut a deal with mob's leaders. We're under attack by both groups, the bikers have heavy weapons and their bikes give them mobility which is starting to take its toll on us. We've taken eleven casualties, none of them are life-threatening, thank God for our armored vests and helmets. We've got people hit on their arms and sides, we've got some who stood when they shouldn't have, catching a round in the legs or lower back. We have less than 30 uninjured against a thousand or more. My iPad pings with a text, "Got another drone up, hundreds of bikers, heavy weapons, get out before too late."

The gang's motorcycles are giving them an advantage we didn't count on. We built our defenses on the assumption we'd be attacked by people on foot. We blew it in not considering a biker gang would attack us. We thought bikers would have left the city area for greener pastures. We didn't consider any sticking around Nashville or coming our way. Our mistake is costing us dearly.

Four of them ran into our trench in the driveway which only alerted the others to where it is. Their frontline is almost upon us. I light the fuse to the trench in front of us, it lights with a boom and bright flash. I pass one word to everyone, "SHELTER."

While the fire in front of us holds the closest attackers at bay, we slip out of our trench to the hidden shelter doors. After the last one of us enters, I close and lock the door sealing us in and the attackers on our farm. I left a group of mines behind us. Hopefully, this will slow down the attackers and give them pause so they won't be able to follow us too closely. I'm hoping they don't know we have the shelter complex.

The doctor and nurse Tony brought with him are already working on the wounded, they've asked for volunteers. The medical lab is overflowing with the wounded, most have parts of their clothing cut away so the doctor and nurse can gain access to their wounds. I'm surprised to see Lacy and Nancy covered in blood, helping the nurse work with our wounded. I'd sent them to check on the kids. I yell, "Doc, any word?"

"Go away, I'm busy. If you're not wounded, get out of here and let me save these people."

I can take a hint. As I'm leaving, Tony and John are walking towards the medical lab. I stop both of them, "Don't, the doc just ordered me out."

Tony asks, "How bad did we get hurt?"

"At least eleven caught a bullet someplace, plus we lost the surface. We're all underground. Whoever the bikers and the mob are, they now have our homes, barns and everything that was on the surface. I'm afraid we should consider everything up top gone."

"I agree with you. How long do you think we're going to have to stay down here?"

I'm already depressed, I say, "Until the people up top who beat us leave."

"Shit." Says Tony

"Tony, you've got that right. We blew this battle."

"Jay, don't be upset, we'll return to surface soon enough. We'll teach the bikers and others they shouldn't have screwed with us."

"Tony, I know you're right, but look at us, we have eleven plus Fred wounded. We're down to less than 20 people who are able to fight, we're now trapped in our own shelter."

"Jay, this shelter just saved all of our lives."

End of book one.
The Shelter Book 2, "A Long Days Night is now available on Amazon Kindle.

SPECIAL PREVIEW
"In the Year 2050."
"America's Religious Civil War."

Author's note

This story started with me reading a report, "The Future of World Religions: Population Growth Projections, 2010-2050. Why Muslims Are Rising Fastest and the Unaffiliated Are Shrinking as a Share of the World's Population" By the Pew Research Center. They published a chart which woke me up.

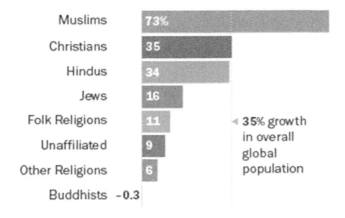

Islam Growing Fastest

Muslims are the only major religious group projected to increase faster than the world's population as a whole.

Estimated change in population size, 2010-2050

Muslims	73%
Christians	35
Hindus	34
Jews	16
Folk Religions	11
Unaffiliated	9
Other Religions	6
Buddhists	-0.3

◄ 35% growth in overall global population

Source: The Future of World Religions: Population Growth Projections, 2010-2050

PEW RESEARCH CENTER

When I read the report, I thought, what would happen if a radical Muslim was elected President? How would one get elected? Since the report made it's projections in the year 2050, I choose that as the year to place this story. Rather than turn the story into a "SciFi" story focusing on the advances of technology in the next 35 years, I made very few technology projections used in the 2050s, I wanted the story to be about the 'What if' America elected a Muslim as President. Since technology plays a major role in our lives, I did project that our televisions and gaming will be replaced by 3D hologram technology which seems to be a logical step in entertainment devices. If anyone is interested, the full report is available on line at the Pew Research Center site.

Prologue

In the year 2050 the world's population based on their religious beliefs, is almost equally split between Christianity and Islam. The high birth rate in the Islamic communities combined with the much lower birthrate in the world's other religions laid the foundation for Islam to pass Christianity by the early 2050's. By 2050 Islam controlled most of the European Union states. The shift started in the late 1990s when Europe's open borders allowed large numbers of Muslims to relocate to Europe. Instead of assimilating into the existing population the Islamic immigrants separated themselves into Islamic ghettos where they followed their own religious practices and practiced Sharia law. Infidels were not welcome in these ghettos, the Muslim immigrants patrolled their ghettos which over time grew to encompass entire cities with their own government, police, and fire departments. In order to be competitive local banks were forced to follow Sharia law, which outlawed charging interest. The Islamic cities formed roaming religious police, who were called the Mutaween. Their job was to ensure the population followed Sharia law. The Mutaween ensured that no remnants of the 'Western lifestyle' remained to pollute the followers of Allah. With high birth rates and high immigration, the size of the Islamic cities and communities grew, as did their political power. The Muslim's voted in an Islamic block. By 2020, they were running their own candidates for public offices. In 2022, Muslims held the offices of the mayor of London, Birmingham, Paris, Berlin, and over 200 smaller towns and cities. In 2050, the Islamic Caliphate covered all of Europe, the Middle East, Africa, (with the exception of South Africa which after numerous race wars was a devastated battle field of ruined cities) and a third of Eastern Russia. The Chinese Communist Party fought the expression of all religions. Australia and New Zealand outlawed radical Islam, they deported any who tried to overthrow their democratic lifestyle.

In 2015 America and Iran signed the worst treaty in modern history. America agreed to release all economic sanctions against Iran in exchange for Iran agreeing to not produce a nuclear weapon for ten years. Iran laughed at America's stupidity in accepting their word without a backup plan. Iranians chanted "Death to America", "Death to Israel." While their government signed a worthless treaty.

In 2020, Iran launched a surprise attack against Israel with fifty nuclear-armed missiles. Forty-six of the missiles were intercepted by Israel's expanded anti-missile shield. Israel struck back at Iran with 200 nuclear missiles and bombs. Tehran was struck by six 350KT Israeli weapons, the capital of Iran was vaporized, the city ceased to exist. Saudi Arabia also struck Iran using their secretly developed nuclear weapons. Israel had secretly traded nuclear assistance to Saudi Arabia in exchange for them attacking Iran if Iran struck Israel first. Israel also shared with Saudi Arabia various technologies. The two entered into an uneasy peace. Saudi Arabia knew Israel had enough weapons to destroy the Kingdom if Saudi Arabia moved against Israel. With the destruction of Iran, Saudi Arabia took its place as the leader of the Islamic world. The King of Saudi Arabia signed an agreement with Israel agreeing to recognize the right of Israel to exist in exchange for Israel agreeing not to attack Saudi Arabia. The treaty allowed Saudi to focus on converting the rest of the world to follow Allah. The Saudi Royals knew that when Islam was strong enough, they would return to the question of Israel.

While In the United States, twenty Muslims were elected to Congress in the midterm elections of 2020. In the 2024 elections, Muslims won 55 seats in the House and 6 seats in the Senate. In 2026, there were 102 Muslim members of the House and 16 Senators. They formed a powerful congressional group, the Congressional Islamic Group, (CIG). The CIG pressured the liberal media to suppress any story which didn't reflect Islam in the best light. Any Story about an Islamic attack on an infidel was suppressed. The CIG understood that most Americans got their news from fifteen second sound bites, they knew, who ever controlled the media, controlled how the average American thought. Their antagonists were the right wing talk radio hosts who had the largest share of the radio market. The CIG pushed the equal time rule through Congress. Any media that broadcast a right wing radio or television program also had to broadcast an opposing program for the same amount of time in a similar time slot that had a similar number of listeners or viewers. The new law doomed talk radio. If Rush was on for three hours in mid day, then the same station had to broadcast an opposing view program in a time slot that had the same number of listeners. Since Rush had the highest rated radio program, there wasn't another time slot or available program that provided an opposing view. Talk radio's success was its own downfall.

The right wing talk radio and television hosts, Rush, Glen, Sean, and Mark were all kicked off the air. The four of them merged their networks into a new Tea

Party/right-wing network they called the EIBLAZE network. They quickly learned, regardless of their number of viewers and listeners, due to the equal time rule, no commercial station could host them. They began broadcasting on the Internet. The CIG brought suit against the EIBLAZE network and Google saying Internet providers, under the FCC's takeover of the internet in 2015 were covered by the equal time rule. The FCC sided with the CIG. The EIBLAZE found no provider would host them due to the fear of being sued by the FCC. The EIBLAZE's only option was to move offshore so they could continue their broadcasting. The CIG and FCC pressured service providers in the EU and Asia to block the EIBLAZE network, which left the hosts having to fund their own Internet provider based in Israel. The CIG filed suit against the new network and all broadcasts originating in Israel. Israel refused to hear the lawsuit. The CIG pressured Congress to cut all aid to Israel until they followed the equal time rule. Israel had sufficient support in Congress to block the CIG from cutting aid. Israel continued to host the Tea Party/right wing broadcasts which became the only voice of logic and conservatism available to the American public.

When the 2052 Presidential election process started, the CIG offered their own candidate for President. Their candidate, Senator Osama bin Mohmand won 274 Electoral College votes. Becoming America's first openly Muslim President. President elect Mohmand promised America a new generation of peace, an end to the various wars which had gone on for fifty years. The American public was tired of and fed up with two generations of wars. They elected Mohmand thinking he would bring peace and since he ran as a Green Party candidate, the public expected him to protect the environment.

Sitting President Jackson tried to take some of the glow off of President elect Mohmand by releasing President Obama's sealed records. The unsealed records showed what many on the right had long suspected, President Obama was a Muslim. President Jackson hoped that by releasing President Obama's records, he would defuse those who were worried about a Muslim President. He hoped that like most candidates who won elections, once in office, they realized if they wanted to get anything done, they had to move towards the center.

President elect Mohmand promised he would sign an executive order marking President Obama's birthday as a national holiday. Thus celebrating the birth of the person who started the transformation of America towards becoming an Islamic country. The new national news station, Al Jazeera, renamed the transformation of America as the jihad of America. Al Shihabi was granted a daily interview time every day with President Mohmand. Al Jazeera was the only media to have total access to President Mohmand. AL Shihabi helped script a wide-ranging jihad of America, one which they hoped would fully transform America into a devoted Islamic country which will proudly take its place within the worldwide Caliphate.

Chapter One

Amid the loud cheering and chanting at the Mohmand election headquarter hotel, the CNN reporter looks into the camera saying, "Good evening America, tonight, November 17th, 2052 history has been made for the third time. We're all witnesses of this historic event. In November 2008 we elected the first African-American, Barrack Obama as President. He started the transformation of America to make us a more peaceful, caring country. As everyone knows, President Obama served two terms, he left a legacy of accomplishing more than any other President prior to him. In 2016, the conservatives' voter ID laws blocked many minorities from voting thus allowing the radical Tea Party candidate Ted Cruz to be elected as President. President Cruz defeated Mrs. Clinton who performed horribly in the debates. Many said that President Cruz pushed her buttons causing her to lose her temper in every debate. Some say the 'real' Hillary Clinton was seen during the debates. Everyone may remember when she lost it in the second debate when Ted Cruz held up recovered emails showing Mrs. Clinton sent Ambassador Stevens to Benghazi to ship illegal weapons to the Syrian rebels. As Secretary of State, she not only knew the attack was a terrorist attack, she turned down his request for additional security. She stood by, doing nothing allowed Ambassador Stevens to die a horrible death. Ted Cruz repeated during the debate, Clinton's hands were covered in blood. At the end of their third and final debate, he showed emails proving she ordered the military to stand down dooming the Ambassador and his staff to death.

The CNN reporter continued, "Fulfilling his campaign promise President Cruz started dismantling President Obama's vision of America starting with his first day in office. We in the media didn't agree with President Cruz, we made our thoughts very public. When the economy didn't recover from the recession, which was caused by the Republican tax cuts and President Cruz throwing the country into confusion when he, by Executive order overturned President Obama's signature bill, Obamacare. The country spent four years trying to figure out how to replace Obamacare with a health care system that covered everyone. The confusion cost President Cruz reelection. The presidential election of 2020 saw Elizabeth Warren beat Ted Cruz to become the country's first woman President. She followed in President Obama's footsteps. She was even more progressive than President Obama. She brought back Obamacare, further confusing the public. President Warren forced a restructuring of Wall Street, which pushed the economy into a deeper recession. In the 2024 election, President Warren ran against Rand Paul, who she beat claiming it was the conservative wing of the Republican Party which pushed the country into the recession. President Warren won reelection but the people handed both house of Congress to the Tea Party. The country suffered deeper divisions than under Presidents Obama and Cruz. President Warren and Congress couldn't agree on any issue. The country suffered an additional four years of deep recession due to the Tea Party refusing to work with President Warren.

The election of 2028 saw the emergence of a third and fourth party which further broke the country apart. A little-known Congressman from West Virginia won the election by promising the country a return to old time values. President Frankfort won both of his elections. The elections in 2036 and 2040 went back and forth between the right and left. While Washington D.C. argued with themselves, the country was changing. The birth rate of the Islamic population grew quickly while the birth rate of other religions dropped to a point where they didn't cover the replacement of their existing numbers. The number of Catholics, Baptists, Mormons and Jews declined while the number of Muslims exploded."

The CNN reporter paused to look into the camera before continuing, "In 202, the Islamic community formed their own party and started running their own candidates. By the election of 2052, the majority of people who actually voted were Muslims. Tonight we celebrate our first openly Muslim president. Osama bin Mohmand easily defeated the other two candidates. The Tea Party candidate was so radical that we and the other networks didn't carry his message. This was also the first election cycle in one hundred years when there weren't any televised debates. President Mohmand refused to take the stage with a bacon eating infidel. We join with all Americans and the world in celebrating the election of President-elect Mohmand. We thank Allah for sending us such an intelligent guiding leader as President-elect Mohmand."

MSNBC's reporter says, "Who is Osama bin Mohmand? He started his career as an investor in companies that supply Muslims with items they use in their everyday life. Mohmand made over $50 million when he sold his company to Amazon. After selling his company he turned his energy to politics. He moved to Michigan, which has a large Muslim population. He became the Mayor of Detroit, where he developed the bailout that saved the city from a second bankruptcy. He parlayed his fame into the Senate race where he became the junior Senator from Michigan. He served three terms in the Senate, his most notable accomplishment was authoring the law that made Muslims a protected class of people in America. He's also known for putting the deal together which enabled Muslims to pay fees on their credit cards in place of interest since interest is outlawed in the Holy Quran. Mohmand has been quoted as saying he's the moderate Muslim who wants to make peace with the different people of the world. We warmly welcome Osama bin Mohmand as our new President."

@@@@@

Monday, January 20th dawned bright and warm for January in Washington D.C. The sky was crystal clear without a visible cloud. At 7:30 AM President-elect Mohmand was led into the Oval Office to meet his predecessor. As the custom, both men met in private to discuss issues between the outgoing and incoming Presidents.

President Jackson welcomed President-elect Mohmand to the Oval Office, "President-elect, welcome to the White House. My family and I will be moved out by the time your inauguration service concludes. Per tradition, I'm pleased to host you and answer any specific questions about the House and the position as I can. I thought we would have breakfast together while we chatted."

"Mr. President, I truly appreciate you taking the time this morning to host me. I'm sure my family will be happy to move in and start the cleaning and remodeling as soon as possible. I will be happy to have a cup of tea while you eat breakfast. I've already had mine. I can't eat in the House until the kitchen is cleaned and restocked with Halal food. I'm not permitted to eat non-Halal foods or eat foods prepared in a nonconforming kitchen."

"I see. Are you planning on changing all of the House staff?"

"Yes, I'm in the process of having the staff replaced as we meet. My temporary Chief of Staff is going to oversee the White House is cleaned, all traces of non-Halal food will be removed, the kitchens cleaned the bedrooms cleaned and all of the linens and towels changed. We're bringing our own China to replace the existing White House china, silverware, and cooking equipment. We plan on disposing of all of the existing White House kitchen supplies. If we didn't do this, Allah would frown on the Muslim State of America."

"President-elect, I'm sure you know that America isn't a Muslim State. Our constitution forbids us having a state religion."

"Mr. President, I wouldn't worry yourself about such things. In less than two hours, none of this will be your concern. You served for eight years. Eight years which saw increased discrimination against Allah's faithful. You didn't raise your voice in protest while Allah's people suffered under your administration. I'm going to ensure my people don't ever suffer the same discrimination again. As soon as I take the oath of office I'm going to start ensuring my people are protected."

"Mr. President elect, may I give you a word of advice?"

"Of course, please, I'm all ears."

"If I were you, I would take it slow. You won the election by four Electoral College votes. A little over half of the popular vote was cast for your opponents. You won the election with a minority of the popular vote. You're not entering office with a strong mandate. I'd advise you go slowly with any sweeping new programs. Build a strong working relationship with Congress. Get Congress on your side. No one believed a third party could win, let alone your party."

President-elect Mohmand smiled, he sipped his tea while he looked at President Jackson. "Mr. President, I do have a mandate, over 99% of the Muslim population in America voted for me. I have a duty to follow the wishes of those who elected me. I'm going to carry forward the bold promise made by President Obama, I'm going to complete the transformation of America into converting America into an Islamic country. In fact, my staff has designed a new flag I'm going to shortly unveil. Would you like to see it?"

"President-elect Mohmand, do I understand you plan to change the American flag? You plan to transform America into an Islamic country? A country that follows Islamic law?"

"President Jackson, its called Sharia law which is soon going to be the law of the land. Today is going to be a day remembered forever. The day the green flag of Islam finally flies over this great land. The day when America takes its place among the followers of Allah and Mohmand his the messenger. Today America is going to be the next country in the formation of a worldwide Caliphate. Under my administration, a worldwide Caliphate will finally become a reality. You should be proud that you're able to watch the formation of the worldwide Caliphate. Today we will begin the process of having a common law across the entire world. For the first time, Allah's word will become the common law of the world." President Mohmand smiled an evil grin as he paused to sip his tea.

"President-elect Mohmand, I'm sure you know that half of the country are Christians, Jews, or nonbelievers in any religion which is why our founding fathers saw fit to ensure we never have a national religion."

"President Jackson, you're familiar with the process to modify the constitution. When I was elected, my party, the Green Party, won control of the House and Senate. A bill will be passed, a bill, I'll sign, sending the amendment to the states where my brother and sister Muslims will make sure it gets passed. President Jackson, when one has the numbers and the support of the people he represents, anything is possible. The simple truth is a higher percentage of my people vote than yours. Getting bills passed and changes to the foundation of America isn't going to be as difficult as you may think it's going to be."

"It was genius to rename your party the Green Party, many citizens thought they were voting for environmentalists. You mixed in just enough technobabble about saving the planet that many people supported your platform because they thought they were voting for people who supported clean air and water, slowing global cooling and finding alternative power sources. Frankly Mr. President-elect, you lied and deceived your way into this office."

Smiling an evil smile, President Mohmand grins saying, "President Jackson, every politician lies. I did nothing different than you or anyone else who got elected. By the way, we *will* clean the air and water. We're going to reduce the population stress on the planet, hence we are green. I will complete the transformation the late President Obama started."

"I'm sure you know that the previous four administrations spent sixteen years undoing the damage President Obama did to the country. I'm proud of my record which lowered the tensions between the left and right. My administration got the real unemployment rate down to 9.8%. I improved the security of our people."

"President Jackson, you may have lowered tensions between the left and right, however, you allowed an increase of tensions and discrimination against the followers of Allah. Your security measures were targeted against the followers of Allah and Mohmand his messenger."

"Mr. President-elect, I tried to calm the tension against Muslims. If Muslims hadn't attacked innocents around the world, if Muslims didn't kill women and children of other faiths..."

"There are no other faiths. The only faith is Islam. The only true religion is to follow the word of Allah as recorded by his messenger, may peace be with him, Mohmand. Allah and Mohmand his messenger have laid out the way to honor and serve Allah. Those who practice false faiths, serve Satan, it is the duty of every Muslim to either convert nonbelievers or kill them because they pollute the minds of the true believers. Nothing will be allowed which may lead the faithful away from the love of Allah. I'm honored to have been selected by Allah to protect the American people. I've been selected by Allah to bring America to its rightful place in Allah's world. Some may not agree, some may try to fight my plans, these poor souls will quickly realize they can easily convert to the one true faith or they will have to pay the Jizya. Infidels won't be allowed to hold certain positions in my administration."

"I know the American people, they won't accept these changes. The Tea Party, which holds over 125 seats in the House won't accept any new taxes or your new policies. They stall your policies."

"President Jackson, the average citizen WILL happily accept my changes. They will accept them because the media supports me and my changes, they will spin the changes so that the average citizen will be happy to accept the changes. The media will fill the people's heads with sound bites that support my cause and quiet the voices of any dissenters. Infidels will be silenced one way or another. None will be permitted to speak out against the word of Allah, any who attempt to, will find they don't have access to the public airwaves. They won't be able to publish their lies anywhere people could read or hear them. When President Obama led the government takeover of the Internet, he laid the foundation I'll use to crush all dissent voices. If the Tea Party gives me any problems, I'll go around Congress by using the limited executive orders that are left to the office. I'll have my agencies levy fees on nonbelievers, these don't need Congressional approval."

President Jackson looked at his watch, he nodded towards his guest, "Mr. President-elect it's almost time we begin making our way to the podium. The Chief Justice, Ms. Hillary Clinton is waiting for us. I understand she plans to resign right after she swears you into office."

"It was another stroke of President Obama's genius that he appointed Mrs. Clinton to the Supreme Court shortly after she lost the election to the infidel Cruz. Her Presidential aspirations were doomed when her story of cleaning her server turned out to be false. When Rush got his hands on all 30,000 of her emails from her server her run was finished. President Obama appointed her in a recess appointment to get around the Senate, hence protecting her from prosecution. While Obama had no love for Clinton, he knew if he didn't find a way to support her he'd bring him down with her. She's going to resign so I can appoint her replacement."

"How did you manage that? I assumed she would never leave the court. If I had know of a way to get her to resign I would have used it in my first term."

"She and I had a couple of meetings after I was elected."

"What did that cost you?"

"Only a small donation to her charity. $75 million is a small price to pay to have her resign. My friends wired her off shore accounts the money, hence she'll resign this evening."

President Jackson sat back on his couch in surprise, "You bribed the Chief Justice to resign."

"Yes, as you know the Clinton's have always had a price on everything. Hillary was harder to buy after Bill's unfortunate heart attack in bed with those two young women. His passing was such a loss. President Jackson, I'd be happy to appoint you as a special advisor. I'm sure we can come to agreeable financial terms. I can make you a fantastically rich man, you'd never want for anything for the rest of your life. Your son, Robert would never have to work a day in his life. After helping me, you could buy yourself your own country where you could be President for life. You could be King, which will enable you to hand your crown to your son. Your family can rule forever. All I ask is for you to remain silent and disappear, quietly leave the country."

"Mr. Mohmand, I'm not interested in being part of your administration. I don't believe in kings or dictators. In fact, I may lead the voices speaking out against your administration. You may have been elected by the people. You don't understand America or Americans. Your plans are not going to be accepted by the good people of America. They are going to fight you for every inch of their freedoms you try to take away from them. You're going to quickly learn America doesn't want to be part of your Caliphate. Middle America doesn't understand what you really stand for, or who you are. Once they figure out who you really are, they are going to fight you. If you go too quickly, you're going to find the military won't support you. They may even remove you from office."

Laughing President-elect Mohmand says, "You forget, as commander in chief, I get to appoint the service chiefs, they will be totally supportive of me. All military officers will be, or they'll be looking for new jobs outside of the military. Any officer who doesn't support me will have their career cut short. I plan to bring in military advisors from members of the Caliphate. They will help train the US Military how to deal with domestic terrorists. They will train the military how to suppress any civil unrest."

"What about their oath of office? What about your oath of office, do you intend to openly break your oath? The military isn't going to follow instructions from your imported advisors."

Smiling an evil grin, "President Jackson, the Holy Quran instructs us to lie to nonbelievers to further Allah's cause. I'll lie, I'll deceive, I'll do anything that pushes the Great Satan to recognize the true word of Allah. I won't stop until America becomes an Islamic country and a member in good standing in the Caliphate. Nothing is going to stop me. Allah is my light, he is smiling on me, he has shown me our time has arrived. I will take my place in the history of the Quran."

"Maybe I will stop you."

Smiling President-elect Mohmand said, "President Jackson, if you like living, don't try to oppose me. You won't enjoy it. Your reputation will suffer, you may even lose your loved ones, in fact, it would be a loss to the country if you were to meet with an untimely accident. Accidents happen so often these days. The country will mourn you, I will use your death to further my goals. Even in your death, you will help me. Your only option is accept my offer and quietly slip away."

"You shouldn't threaten a sitting President, it's a crime. The secret service doesn't have a sense of humor."

Smiling, Mohmand says, "In a few minutes the secret service will report to me. In a few minutes I will be the leader of the free world, the most powerful man alive. Allah's will, will be done. If I were you, I'd retire in silence and follow MacArthur's advice and just fade away. Mind your own business and disappear so I don't have to make you and your family disappear. Don't make waves, go along to get along. It'll be healthier for you."

"Mr. President-elect, don't ever threaten me or think you know everything. I'm warning you to go very slow or this country will rise up and bring you down."

"The people won't revolt, because like a frog placed in a pot of water, they will sit in the water as the temperature is brought up enough to boil the frog. The average American citizen is going to be happy to have what they have. They're not going do anything to upset their comfort. They won't even try to speak out because they won't want to rock their boat. The average American is more interested in who in Hollywood is sleeping with whom than the loss of a few of their freedoms. Soon, the water they're sitting in will boil and they'll cook themselves alive. It's going to be so easy leading America down the path I want it to go. Look at history, look at how easily President Obama started the transformation of America. The press could have ensured he wasn't elected, yet they fawned all over him. They saw him as their Messiah. I'm going to show them, I AM their Messiah. I will lead America to a new brighter future following Allah. If the people don't follow the laws of Allah, they will lose their heads. Millions may lose their heads. America's great rivers will run red with the blood of infidels and the worshipers of the cross and the six pointed star. America will learn, there is only one God and that God is Allah."

President Jackson slowly shakes his head saying, "We'll see about that. I think I can promise you that America isn't the same as a third world country. The people of America will fight you with every asset they have. Most of the country isn't like Detroit. The people aren't going to rush to switch religions. 277 years ago, the people stood up to the world's mightiest military to form this country, they are not going to allow you to walk into America and change it into an Islamic country."

"President Jackson, they won't be able to stop me. A handful of citizens armed with hunting rifles against the strongest army in the world won't stand a chance. We will easily crush them. Their blood will join the blood of other infidels who've tried to stand in our way. Nothing can stop us now. Our time has come. We've waited over a thousand years for this moment."

President Jackson remembers his history of the previous one hundred years, the holocaust of the Jews in Europe, the holocaust of the Armenian Christians, the holocaust of the Middle Eastern Christians. He frowned knowing there was only one way to stop Mohmand's plans. His thoughts are broken by Mohmand's words, "President Jackson please put a smile on your face before we face the people. I wouldn't want them to worry something is wrong." Mohmand laughed knowing he'd already won. He looked at President Jackson, "Remember your history, no one stopped Hitler, no one stopped ISIS, no one stopped the Turks, no one will stop me. The media will cover up the truth. You should join us, fighting us will cost you everything you hold dear. Come, let's uphold tradition of a peaceful transfer of power."

A secret service agent knocks on the Oval Office door, he sticks his head in the Oval Office saying, "Mr. Presidents, it's time. We should be leaving now."

The two men stand, they face each with hate filled eyes before they walk side by side towards the front door of the White House. The secret service leads them to the front of the House while other agents fall in behind them. Agents on President Jackson's protection detail kept one eye on their counterparts who are on President-elect Mohmand's detail. Neither side trusted the other. Everyone has been cleared from the White House halls, the two men walk from the Oval Office to the White House front door where a podium has been set up for the swearing in ceremony. Each of the two secret service details are worried because they've received many threats against each president. Many people realized too late, President-elect Mohmand is a fundamentalist Muslim. One who has plans to transform America into an Islamic country. Some reborn Christians worry that Mohmand is going to try to outlaw all religion except for Islam. There's many within the secret service and the military who have concerns about the new president. They worry the new president is going to try to turn America into a Muslim state, one where non-Muslims won't be welcome, or will be treated as second class citizens. Their fears are well founded. The secret service has also received threats against President Jackson from Mohmand's supporters.

@@@@@

The EIBLAZE Internet network hosts eight different Internet forum discussion groups. They publish articles and interviews about the damage President-elect Mohmand planned to do to the country. In the years since President Obama appointed Hillary to the Supreme Court, the average American has seen their rights steadily eroded. There was a limit to how many guns and ammunition citizens can purchase and own. The progressives couldn't get enough votes to overturn the second amendment, so they passed laws modifying it. If the courts held that citizens could own weapons, there was nothing in the second amendment that said anything about how many weapons a citizen could own. Anti gun messages were taught in schools as early as mandatory preschool. The first amendment was altered so that hate speech was extended to cover any negative Islamic comments. By the year 2050 courts ruled that crossing one's self in public or openly wearing a cross or Star of David was hate speech because it might offend someone of another faith. The Federal Department of Anti Hate Speech spent billions trying to shut down hundreds of Internet forums where people post hate speech against groups they didn't trust or like.

The media and activist courts gave special allowances to Muslims. The percentage of people in America who were Muslim skyrocketed. During the election cycle of 2052 the EIBLAZE network tried to explain that the Green Party wasn't an environmental group, they were green because the flag of Islam was green. The Green Party candidates all spouted phony statements and commitments for cleaner air and water. They said anything in order to get elected so they could transform America. Rush, Glen, and Mark begged their audiences to spread the message not to fall for the Green Party's lies. The media gave the Green Party hundreds of millions of dollars worth of free PR and advertising. Mohmand was invited on every television program while his major challenger from the Tea Party wasn't invited on a single program. The only PR the media gave the Tea Party was negative, most of it was made up lies. The Tea Party's advertising was rejected by the major networks. Mohmand refused to share the stage with an infidel. Hence, for the first time in one hundred years there were no presidential debates.

The crowd waiting for the President-elect Mohmand's inauguration broke all records. Hundreds of thousands of Islamic green flags flew in the crowd. They chanted Allah Akbar (God is Great) to celebrate one of their own becoming President. As the two Presidents walk towards the podium, the crowd screams as one, "ALLAH AKBAR" the air vibrates with the crowd's screaming. President-elect Mohmand lifts his hands over his head smiling, the hundreds of thousands standing in front of the White House goes crazy with excitement. The hundreds of thousands cheer and scream their joy. Tens of thousands cover their eyes in prayer of thanks to Allah for making it possible for Mohmand to be elected.

A sound shocks the millions watching the inauguration, they are frozen in place. The sound was a gun shot. The Secret Service jumps into action when they hear the gunshot, they push both men to the ground, some lay over the two men, trying to protect them with their own bodies. Other agents draw their hidden weapons. They try to scan the crowd in the millions looking for the shooter, President-elect Mohmand pushes the secret service agent off of him. He stands, pushing other secret service agents away from him. He calmly walks to the microphone where he says, "Hello America. I hope that shot was simply someone shooting into the air due to the excitement of my inauguration. If it was, please don't shoot anymore, you scare the secret service. When they get scared they get trigger nervous, they may shoot you by mistake. In addition your bullets are going to come back to earth, where, they may hit one of the faithful who are here today to witness the beginning of America becoming part of the worldwide Caliphate. For the first time in human history, all of mankind will be bound together under Allah."

A second shot rings out from somewhere in the crowd. The secret service agents form a human shield around the President-elect. He places his hand on his personal copy of the Quran, which has been handed down to him from his father's father's father. He says, "I do solemnly swear (or affirm) that I will faithfully execute the Office of President of the United States, and will to the best of my Ability, preserve, protect and defend the Constitution of the United States. I swear this in my faith to Allah."

The crowd goes crazy, they cry, they dance, they cheer. The media talking heads are excited about the countries first openly Muslim President. While it was proven that President Obama was a Muslim, he kept it hidden. The millions watching the swearing scream "Allah Akbar! Allah Akbar!"

"In the Year 2050."
"America's Religious Civil War" will be published the end of June 2015

Other books by the author available on Amazon-Kindle
37 Miles
37 Miles, Book 2, Patty's Journey
My Story
A History Lesson (a short story)
2015 Second American Civil War, Book 1
2015 Second American Civil War, Book 2
2015 Second American Civil War, Book 3
2015 Second American Civil War, Book 4
2015 Second American Civil War, Book 5
By the Light of the Moon, Book 1
By the Light of the Moon, Book 2
By the Light of the Moon, Book 3
Christmas Eve
The Shelter, Book 1, The Beginning
The Shelter, Book 2 (Coming Summer 2015)
In the Year 2050, America's Religious War (Coming June 2015)

Feel free to contact me at itabankin@aol.com

Printed in Great Britain
by Amazon

21485476R00171